TOOTH AND CLAW

Carl Whittley must stay at home and care for his crippled father. But he has distractions. He's just tortured a TV presenter to death and he's planning to blow an anonymous commuter to pieces. Also remaining at home is DCI Mark Lapslie, his rare neurological condition has forced him to leave his family and to avoid the police station. His superiors regard him as a nuisance to be avoided. As the spate of brutal deaths catches the media's attention, the Chief Superintendent brings in Lapslie. He knows this case could break him, then the press will be placated and he will be free of the troublesome DCI. But the deadly game Carl wants to play might be just what Lapslie needs to come out of hiding.

Books by Nigel McCrery
Published by The House of Ulverscroft:

SILENT WITNESS
THE SPIDER'S WEB
STRANGE SCREAMS OF DEATH
FACELESS STRANGERS
STILL WATERS

NIGEL McCRERY

◆

TOOTH AND CLAW

Complete and Unabridged

CHARNWOOD
Leicester

First published in Great Britain in 2009 by
Quercus, London

First Charnwood Edition
published 2010
by arrangement with
Quercus, London

British Library CIP Data

McCrery, Nigel, *1953* –
Tooth and claw.
1. Synesthesia- -Fiction.2. Police- -England- -Essex- -
Fiction. 3. Murderers- -Fiction.
4. Detective and mystery stories. 5. Large type books.
I. Title
823.9'14–dc22

ISBN 978–1–44480–353–2

Published by
F. A. Thorpe (Publishing)
Anstey, Leicestershire

Set by Words & Graphics Ltd.
Anstey, Leicestershire
Printed and bound in Great Britain by
T. J. International Ltd., Padstow, Cornwall

This book is printed on acid-free paper

Ashley McCrery
My brother and my friend

Prologue

'Tip your head back and open your mouth.'

The voice was cultured, smooth, devoid of any obvious emotion. No anger, no hatred, no lust. Just the faintest tinge of academic curiosity; nothing else.

He shook his head. 'Please,' he begged, his voice cracking, 'I don't — '

'I *said*, tip your head back and open your mouth.'

He could smell alcohol on his captor's breath. The blindfold around his eyes meant he couldn't see what was happening, so when fingers entwined themselves in his hair and pulled his head back until his face was pointed up towards the ceiling he gasped in shock at the pain. His hair felt as if it was being pulled out by the roots. While that hand was still entangling his hair another one took his chin and forced his mouth open. It let go, but before he could close his mouth something was pushed past his teeth: something that felt like a dental dam of some kind, a plastic plate with a hole in the centre, too rigid for him to crush between the roof of his mouth and his tongue. It kept his mouth gaping open in a silent, frozen scream. He wanted to fight against it, to push his captor away and rip the thing from his mouth, but his arms were tied to the chair and he couldn't move.

His breath came in ragged gasps past the

1

obstruction in his mouth. He wanted to gag. The insides of his cheeks and tongue were drying out as his saliva evaporated. Tears squeezed their way out of his closed eyelids and prickled their way down past his temples and into his hair. He felt a hot flush of shame across his skin. He wanted to be strong but helplessness made him feel faint.

'I'm going to put something into your mouth,' the voice said, as calm and as measured as if his captor was reading a set of instructions for some new beauty treatment. 'It's important that you don't swallow. Close your throat up and breathe through your nose.'

He tried to shake his head but the grip on his hair intensified. Something smooth and warm touched his lower lip. He tried to pull away but the hand on the back of his head pushed him suddenly forward.

A tube pushed past his teeth and into his mouth through the hole in the dental dam. He nearly gagged on the plastic as it scraped his tongue. Before he could even take a breath, a warm, thick liquid invaded his mouth; trickling around between his teeth and his cheeks, infiltrating its way beneath his tongue, sending questing fingers down his throat until he blocked it. He felt his stomach rising up in protest. He had to breathe through his nose, but he was hyperventilating and his nostrils were closing and his breath wasn't coming fast enough. He began to feel light-headed.

'Don't worry, my dear,' the voice said as a hand stroked his hair. 'It'll all be over soon.'

And then, nothing. Nothing but the solidifying

waxy mass in his mouth, and the increasingly difficult whistle of breath through his nostrils, and the red static that invaded the darkness of his blindfolded eyes, creeping in from the outside until everything was red and he knew, without a shadow of a doubt, that he was going to die . . .

1

Dawn arrived in Mark Lapslie's bedroom an hour before the sun rose.

The increasing blush of light brought him gradually from a dream in which sound, sight and touch were all melded together into a slippery mass of inchoate, abstract sensation, and where he knew, with increasing terror, that some clue, some vital piece of evidence, was slipping away from him, disguising itself as something else, although he had no idea what it was or what case he was investigating.

Eventually, awake, he scrunched himself over in the bed and looked at the display on the alarm clock: 05:00. Time to get up.

The clock was one of the many concessions he'd had to make to the synaesthesia that was increasingly ruling his life. For a while he had switched to a digital alarm clock with an LCD display, but he had found that the repeated *beep* of the alarm caused him to wake tasting crab apples. Eventually, in desperation his wife had bought him a sunrise alarm: a clock with a globe on top that gradually glowed brighter and brighter as it approached the time he set it for. No beeping, no clanging, no audible alarm at all; just a gradually false sunrise that brought his body gently out of sleep.

It had been the most thoughtful present his wife had ever bought him. Shortly after that

— bolstered, perhaps, by the thought that she had done her duty and made sure he was all right despite his health problems — she moved out, taking the children with her.

Things could have been worse. At least they still saw each other, even slept together from time to time.

Lapslie sat up in the bed and ran a hand through his hair. He glanced across at the windows. They were double-glazed to screen out the taste of the foxes that screamed in the night and the dawn chorus of birds that greeted the real sunrise. It was still dark outside, but he wanted to get started on his paperwork before the world outside his cottage began to wake up. After a period of relative stability his synaesthesia had been getting progressively worse over the past year. It had gone from a state where he could just about bear to be in an office environment, as long as he had a quiet room to which he could retreat when things got too much, to the point where the background hum of casual conversation would make him feel as if he was travel-sick, throwing up every half hour or so, despite wearing earplugs. Only his cottage, isolated in the countryside near Saffron Walden, allowed him some respite, and so Chief Superintendent Rouse had grudgingly shifted his responsibilities to allow him to work from home, writing a series of reports on potential restructurings of the Essex Police Constabulary. Rouse wasn't happy about it, demanding a medical report from Lapslie's consultant before he would put anything in writing, but in the end he had to accept that Lapslie could either work at home or resign. The choice was that stark.

If Lapslie was lucky then he could crack a couple more sections of the report before noises from outside intruded too much and he had to retreat to his bedroom and try to sleep through the afternoon before starting work again in the evening. The cottage was isolated from main roads — standing alone in the middle of several acres of trees — but there were still the sounds of tractors and chainsaws and every passing aircraft to contend with. He had even considered switching to a nocturnal cycle, but the mainstream of police activity still took place during the day and there were phone calls to field and emails that needed responding to urgently. Headphones or earplugs blocked out the noise, but stopped him from hearing the phone if it rang, and he found the artificial absolute silence unnerving and oppressive if he was alone in the house and working on something.

The sunrise alarm clock was at full illumination now, casting a bright yellow glow across the room. He threw the duvet off, stood up and padded naked across the bedroom towards the bathroom. He showered quickly, the hiss of the water sending torrents of cauliflower down his throat, and dressed for the office — a light blue, French-cuff cotton shirt, a dark blue tie whose pattern of an interlocking grid of golden rings and chains made senior officers think he might be a Freemason without actually confirming it, and dark suit with a subtle blue pinstripe effect.

If he was going to work while he was at home then he wanted to *feel* like he was working.

But even the solitary refuge of his cottage was turning slowly but inexorably into a prison of noise.

Sometimes, if he turned a tap off too quickly, the pipes would bang and clatter as if someone was hammering them with an iron bar. For an hour or so after the central heating came on the house would creak as the joists expanded slightly. The wind, blowing around the walls, caused the air vent in the bathroom to vibrate if it caught them at the wrong angle. And sometimes there were noises behind the walls or in the ceiling that might have been mice scurrying past, or might just have been fragments of plaster falling down gaps between the bricks. The sounds caused a continual and unpleasant background taste in his mouth when he was in the house; a strange combination of lime juice and walnuts that had been allowed to rot.

His office was at the back of the cottage, but he hesitated before heading there to pick up work on the report where he had left it the night before. He had to brace himself. He had to prepare himself for the task. He hated using a keyboard — the repetitive click of the keys made him taste hot pilchards in tomato sauce — so whenever possible he tried to write longhand using a biro and then drive the pages to a woman in Saffron Walden who would type them up for him and put them on a CD-ROM. It was old fashioned — Victorian, even — but it was the only way he could manage. Even then, however, while writing he had to try not to shift his position in case the chair creaked or the stuffing in the cushions shifted.

He felt sometimes as if he was spending his time standing perfectly still, perfectly quiet, while life slid past him like water past a rock. Other people could enjoy themselves in bars and pubs, restaurants and cinemas, but he was condemned to a monastic life of near-silence and contemplation. There were times when he wished he could just ask a surgeon to slice through the nerves that transmitted sensation from his mouth to his brain, but even then he thought he would probably still experience the unwanted tastes. After all, they weren't real — merely phantoms originating somewhere in his brain. He knew that because, in the early days of the synaesthesia, he had sometimes tried to numb his taste buds, either with an oral anaesthetic gel that he had found in a pharmacy or, in desperation, with the hottest *murgh phall* curry that he could order in the takeaway nearest his cottage. Neither option worked. With the oral anaesthetic he found he could still experience sounds as tastes, although they were unpleasantly muted and distorted, while the *phall* just gave him heartburn for two days.

A soft knock on the cottage door caused smoked herrings to chase themselves around his teeth and tongue. He checked his watch. Five thirty a.m. — far too early for the postman.

It was work. It had to be work.

He opened the door. Detective Sergeant

Emma Bradbury was standing outside. Her car was a hundred yards away, considerately parked so that the noise of her idling engine wouldn't bother him too much. The glow from the headlamps combined with the faint mist in the air silhouetted her, haloing her body in grainy light. She was wearing a grey silk blouse with a black bolero jacket over the top and black jeans.

'Emma?'

She acknowledged Lapslie with a nervous nod of her head. 'Boss — sorry to disturb you.' Her voice held a citrus tang. 'I was going to ring from the car, but I saw your bedroom light was on.'

'I wanted to make an early start. Rouse has got me writing reports for him.'

She nodded. 'Yeah, he said.' She looked towards the side of the doorframe, where the nameplate for the house was attached. 'Thyme Cottage? I'd never noticed that before. Rather twee, isn't it?'

He took a deep breath, feeling the vestiges of sleep still tugging at the corners of his vision, making his head heavy and his eyes gritty. 'My wife's idea. She's a holistic therapist. Look, I take it this isn't a social call? I haven't seen you for months.'

'No, we've — we've got a case. You and me.' She kept raising her fingers to her mouth as though she wanted a cigarette, then rubbing her upper lip nervously when she realised that she wasn't holding anything in her hand.

'I don't do cases any more, Emma,' he said gently. 'They've put me out to pasture. And I

10

thought you were working with someone else now.'

'I am. I *was*. Chief Superintendent Rouse told me specifically to come and get you. He said he needed you. He was very insistent.'

'I don't care.' Lapslie took a deep breath. 'Emma, I just *can't*. It's physically impossible. Rouse knows that.'

'He told me to tell you that he needs you on this one. He called me from home.'

'Tell him I refuse. No, I'll call him and tell him myself.'

Again, that nervous lift of the hand to the mouth. 'He told me to tell you that he's got another report for you to write. It's an analysis of the way police witnesses give evidence in court. He said you'd have to spend the next three months attending hearings and cases at Southend, making sure you had all the evidence you needed.'

Lapslie closed his eyes and shook his head. He could feel his pulse beating fast in the arteries of his neck. 'That's blackmail.'

'Yeah, he said you'd say that. And he told me to tell you that you're right — it is blackmail.'

'Okay. All right. Give it to me in as few words as you can manage.'

Emma paused for a few seconds, marshalling her thoughts. 'A young and beautiful TV newsreader found stark naked and mutilated on her bed, to which she had been secured with plastic builders' ties.'

'Jesus.' Jerked out of the ruts of self-pity that it had been trapped in, Lapslie's mind skittered across the various potentials for trouble a case like that could bring. 'Is she dead?'

'I hope so,' Emma said sombrely. 'I *really* wouldn't like to think that she might still be alive looking like she does now.'

'You've been there already?'

'I was on duty when the call came in. As soon as I found out who the victim was, I informed my superiors. They ran it right up the chain of command, and Chief Superintendent Rouse called me back and told me to get you on the case.'

'Who *was* the victim?' Lapslie asked, remembering with a visceral clench of his stomach muscles the investigation into the shooting of the BBC newsreader Jill Dando ten years before.

'Her name was Catherine Charnaud,' Emma said. 'She read the news on one of the satellite channels.'

Lapslie wasn't really listening. He was remembering, instead, those days, weeks, months of the Jill Dando investigation, and how the microscope of publicity had caused a calamitous build-up of errors and assumptions in the investigation. When a policeman was killed, the police pulled out all the stops to find the killer. It was an immediate, instinctive response. Nobody took leave; everyone did what they had to, no matter how small. When Jill Dando was killed her colleagues reacted in a similar way. The subsequent investigation was probably the most scrutinised, the most discussed, the most journalistically dissected that the police had ever undertaken.

And now it was going to happen again. He could feel it.

No wonder Rouse wanted him on the case. He almost forgave the man. Almost.

'Okay,' he said, 'where do we need to go?'

'Chigwell: Holy Cross Road. The house is called 'Manor Farm', but I can't see much evidence of farmland around there. Right in the Footballers' Wives and Girlfriends' belt.'

'Which is about as far from a chastity belt as it's possible to get.' His mind raced through options and plans that he'd thought were behind him now and receding in the rear-view mirror of his career. 'Get on the phone. Keep sightseers away and make sure whoever's manning the boundary of the crime scene doesn't talk to reporters. And I mean doesn't talk at *all*. Not even a 'No comment'. If I hear anything apart from informed guesswork from the reporters I'll have someone's skin as a seat cover.'

'Understood. You want the Crime Scene Investigators to get to work before you get there?'

'Time is always of the essence in these cases. Make sure they get access as soon as they arrive.'

'Got it.'

'And make a point of reminding the Crime Scene photographer that the pictures taken by police cameras are all digitally watermarked, so if they try and sell them to the *Sun* we'll have them up on a charge before they can even book their one-way ticket to St Lucia.'

'Understood. You want me to drive you down, or are you going to drive yourself?'

13

He thought for a moment. 'You drive. I need to think.'

He followed her towards the car. It was an Audi A4. He was surprised — he seemed to remember that she'd had a Mondeo the last time they had worked together.

'New car?' he asked.

'A present from a friend,' she said, opening the door for him. From the tone of her voice he guessed that she didn't want to discuss it.

Emma handled the car with the skill and the verve that he remembered from the brief time they had worked together on the Madeline Poel case. The drive towards Chigwell took them up through the centre of Saffron Walden before Emma could veer off and head south on the M11. The roads were lightly occupied. Aware of his condition, Emma kept the radio off, but the drone of the engine and the occasional raucous beep of horns or the rasp of an over-torqued engine as a car accelerated past them caused spasms of indescribable flavour across his tongue.

Lapslie gazed blankly at a low ground mist lying on the fields as they drove, concealing the rutted ground beneath. Bushes and hedges emerged from it like islands in a milky sea.

He spent the drive bitterly cursing the chief for riding roughshod over his medical condition and throwing him this case like you would a scrap to a dog. God alone knew that Lapslie hated the place to which his illness had brought him, but at least it was preferable to the constant sensory anguish of an investigation. Now, however, it looked as though he was being forced back into the fray whether he liked it or not, and regardless of the consequences to his mental and physical health.

Or perhaps, he thought darkly, there was more to it than that. Perhaps Rouse had decided it was time to push Lapslie out of the Force, but rather than do it directly and lay the police open to being sued Rouse was trying to put Lapslie into a position where he would have to resign. Either that or suffer a complete mental collapse. Would Rouse do something that devious? Remembering back to their time together as colleagues in Brixton, years before, Lapslie decided that he would, and he'd do it without a trace of angst.

The sun came up as they sped onto the M25: a pale wash of indeterminate colour across the sky, against which the branches of the trees stood out starkly, although they had been invisible against the darkness just moments before. The ground mist burned off rapidly as the temperature began to rise. Emma stayed on the M25 for only a few minutes, enough time to travel from Junction 27 to Junction 26, then she came off onto the A121.

Chigwell arrived like a bad smell: industrial estates, travel hotels and identikit housing replacing the fields of hay and stretches of woods that had been the backdrop to most of the drive. Civilisation, pushing nature to one side.

Emma guided the car through the last few turns and into Holy Cross Road. A small knot of gawkers, undeterred by the cold or by the early hour, had already gathered by the police tape

15

that segregated the house at the end. She let the car coast towards them, waiting until she was within a few seconds of hitting them in the back before beeping her horn. Lapslie braced himself against the sudden stab of salmon and caramel. The small crowd parted for them; Emma let the car roll forward while she lowered the window and held her warrant card out to the constable who, wrapped-up against the weather, approached the car from beside the gateposts that separated the house from the road.

'DS Bradbury and DCI Lapslie,' she said. 'We're expected.'

'Go right in ma'am, sir,' the constable said, lifting the yellow and black striped tape from where it had been looped around a projection on the open gate and ushering Emma's car through.

'Surprised the gate isn't closed,' Lapslie called across Emma. 'A bit of tape's not going to stop a determined rush.'

The constable shrugged. 'We had the gate closed for a while, sir,' he said, 'but there was so much traffic through, what with the investigating officers, the CSIs, the photographer and whatnot, that I decided it wasn't worth it. Tape's a lot faster.'

'Fair point.'

Emma accelerated towards the house; a rectangular pile of red bricks with a cream portico stuck on the front and tall, fake-Edwardian windows. Gravel crunched beneath her tyres. Lapslie could taste something bitter and watery, like lettuce, washing around his tongue.

Several police cars were parked up in front of the portico, along with two vans that presumably had brought the CSIs from their usual lair; all were watched over by a couple of security cameras attached to the front of the house. Emma parked up alongside them and Lapslie headed towards the open front door. Another uniformed constable examined his warrant card before letting him inside.

Emma turned towards him before he could enter the house. The expression on her face was a mixture of embarrassment and pity. She reached into a pocket and pulled something small and green out, which she gave to him. It was cold in his hand.

'Look, I thought you might need these,' she said.

He looked at the object she had handed him. It was a pair of headphones: plastic hemispheres lined with black foam rubber and linked by a metal wire headband. For a moment he wondered what the punchline was going to be — was she proposing giving him an audio tour of the crime scene, like some macabre tourist guide? — and then he realised that there was no flex dangling from the headphones.

'Industrial strength noise suppressors,' she said, avoiding his gaze. 'Tell me if I'm being stupid, but I thought — '

'You're not being stupid,' he said gently. 'You're being considerate. Thank you.'

Lapslie slipped the headphones on, and the world seemed to take a step backwards. It wasn't completely silent — he could still hear the regular thudding of his heart, the occasional wheeze in his chest, the rush of blood through the arteries of his neck and the squeak of shifting mucus in his nose — but it was better. A lot better.

Feeling energised, he stepped into the house.

The first thing that he noticed was the smell. It was an old, familiar smell; one that had greeted him so many times over the years that he'd lost count, and yet still had the power to close up his throat and make him wince; old and musty and coppery, the kind of smell that was sometimes provoked as a taste in his mouth by background conversations in bars and restaurants. But this time it was real. Blood. Lots of blood.

The house was surprisingly well furnished: walls painted in faded pastel greens and blues, natural cotton throws over the furniture, wooden skirting boards and doorframes bleached to look as if they had been left out in the sun, shallow glass bowls of pebbles left scattered around in strategic locations. The overall effect was of something old and comfortable that sat amongst sand dunes, near a beach. Several sculptures were set on bookshelves: driftwood twisted either by accident or design into shapes like dancing figures. Paintings on the wall looked like originals: ripples of light on water, captured in time for ever.

The main focus of activity seemed to be upstairs. Followed by Emma, Lapslie walked up to the first floor. Three uniformed officers were clustered together in a doorway. A sudden actinic

18

flash silhouetted them, black against white. Lapslie blinked, then coughed gently. 'Any chance of a senior officer getting past?' he asked. His voice sounded flat and thunderous in his head.

One of the men turned. 'Sorry, sir.' He moved to one side, letting Lapslie into the room, staring at the headphones in puzzlement.

It was one of those moments when the totality of a crime scene built itself up incrementally in Lapslie's mind, element by element, as if the complete effect was too stark, too terrible for him to absorb in one go.

Firstly, Lapslie took in the room itself, as though his brain were shying away from the horror that lay on the bed and taking refuge in details, fripperies, inconsequentialities.

The room was large and airy, and one side was almost entirely taken up with a window. Outside Lapslie could see the back garden, lit from one side by the rising sun shining through the ash trees that lined the boundary. Each blade of grass seemed distinct from the others, and cast a straight-line shadow. A metal sculpture sat in the centre of the lawn: an orrery of some kind, with a globe on a plinth surrounded by rings; the whole thing suggested by lengths of straight or curved metal wire. It was rusted and pitted, but it looked as though it was meant to be that way. Artfully distressed, rather than disintegrating due to nature.

Two uniformed coppers patrolled the grounds, looking for intruders rather than evidence. Given the celebrity status of the victim, those ash trees

19

would be populated more by photographers than by birds unless the police were careful.

Bringing his attention reluctantly back inside the bedroom, the next thing he saw was a pile of clothes thrown onto a chair: jeans, a hooded blue tracksuit top, woollen socks, and a black bra and pants set on top. A pair of trainers sat beneath the chair. Unlike the clothes, which looked as though they had been abandoned in haste, the trainers were set neatly together, heels and toes, with the laces pushed inside. They were silver, with pink stripes. Nike. Small. There was something about them that struck a chord in Lapslie's mind; they were almost unknowingly erotic in their innocence, their abandonment, their careless statement about the youth and the nakedness of their owner.

His attention was drawn to the group of people clustered around the body, standing on rubber pads that had been scattered around the floor so that traces of evidence were not trampled underfoot. Usually, in cases where someone was found dead, either by natural causes or otherwise, the body quickly became part of the background: a piece of evidence, like a discarded cigarette filter or a used tissue; something to be examined and exploited rather than agonised over. The usual mixed group of police, forensic investigators and photographers went about their normal business without even acknowledging that the victim was once a person like them. Jokes were made, conversations occurred about what they'd done the night before or intended to do over the weekend, and life went on as normal.

Here, however, it was different. Hushed by the silence of the headphones, the attending personnel were moving slowly and deliberately, as though they were in church or under water. Lapslie had never attended a scene quite like it. Standing in the doorway, he was put in mind of a Renaissance painting of relatives and servants gathered around the body of a consumptive patriarch, illuminated by a hundred flickering candles. Here the servants were the uniformed police, standing with their backs against the walls, faces in shadow, while the relatives, closer in, on their knees around the bed and with their heads bent as if in prayer, were the Crime Scene Investigators, each dressed in a papery white coverall. And standing off to one side, offering benison with her camera hanging around her neck was the photographer. She, like a priest, had the look of someone who had seen too much, and could forgive but not forget.

Sean Burrows was leading the CSIs. Lapslie recognised his small frame, almost dwarfed in the folds of his coverall, and the quiff of white hair that stuck up from his forehead.

Next, it was the bed that Lapslie noticed. Huge — king size at least, and probably larger — covered with a duvet whose cover had probably once been blue but now glistened a rusty red. Tassels hung off it all around. Thin threads of congealing liquid linked some of the tassels to the carpet, like glutinous spiders' webs.

Lapslie was perversely grateful for the absence of cuddly toys. In his experience, young women tended to keep reminders of their girlish past around as they grew into adulthood, and some of the memories of previous cases that kept him awake at night were of teddy bears and velvety lions whose plush fur was matted with sticky red blood, whose eyes hung by threads and whose smiling faces were disfigured with slashes and gouges where white stuffing bulged through. But not here. The only things on the bed apart from the body of Catherine Charnaud were a circular pillow and a hardback book, cast cover upwards to one side up by the headboard. It had fallen open, or been placed that way to keep a particular page. Whatever the book was, wherever Catherine Charnaud had paused, it would never be completed. The story had ended too soon.

And then there was the body, posed in the centre of the bed like someone posing for a painting.

Catherine Charnaud had been beautiful, once upon a time. Looking at her now, her eyes wide in terror and pain and dulled by death, her mouth unnaturally wide, Lapslie remembered the times he had seen her on TV and in the gossip pages of newspapers and magazines. She had been one of those minor celebrities more famous for what she did in her private life than on screen. He had a vague memory that she had started out in children's TV programmes before moving onto fronting news updates; one of those incessantly bright and bouncy blondes who tried to show that they were 'down' with the kids even as they went out and got wasted every night.

'Ladettes' — wasn't that how they were referred to? She was thin — perhaps anexorically so, judging by the way her stomach fell away from the sharp edge of her ribcage and the corners of her hips stuck up like mountains rising from the plains of her groin. Her breasts were small, the nipples dark and raised now into tiny berries by rigor mortis; the tissue of the breasts themselves pulled downwards and sideways against her ribs by gravity. Her skin was porcelain-white on top, but what little blood remained in her body had pooled where her skin touched the duvet, looking like a bizarre tidemark all the way up her legs and body. Her arms were outstretched in a parody of crucifixion. They were tied to the bedhead by bands of some kind, like the plastic ties that builders and gardeners used sometimes, where a corrugated plastic tongue loops back through a slit in the top of the tie and is pulled tight, the zigzag corrugations engaging with the sides of the slit to hold the whole thing tight.

And that led his gaze to where it had always been heading, even while he had tried to distract it by looking at the garden, the room, the clothes, the people, the bed and the body. Her arm. The terrible, impossible ruin that was her left arm.

The flesh had been stripped from the radius and ulna from bicep down to wrist. The bones themselves were yellow and waxy; not the matt ivory of skeletons in museums. Pockets of gristle and bubbly fat surrounded the complexity of the elbow joint and the numerous small bones of the wrist where the killer's tools, whatever they were, hadn't been able to gouge all of the surrounding flesh away. It was clear that they had gone to some trouble to remove as much flesh as possible, and clean the bone back to its natural state — if the word 'natural' could be applied to what had been done here. Artfully distressed, rather than disintegrating due to nature.

Looking closer, Lapslie could see that the skin above Catherine's bicep and below her wrist was compressed by plastic ties, similar to those that were securing her limbs. The aim had obviously been to stop blood pumping from the exposed flesh as the murderer worked, but that hadn't stopped blood from the arm itself splashing across the duvet, the headboard and the pillow. And judging by the way the blood was smeared, Catherine Charnaud had been alive when the painstaking work of stripping tissue from underlying bone was started, although only time would tell whether she had been alive when it was finished.

It occurred to Lapslie that there was no sign of the flesh that had been removed from the arm anywhere in the bedroom. Catherine Charnaud was a small girl, but even so there was enough meat on her right arm to fill a decent-sized dinner plate. The murderer had taken the stripped flesh with them, or disposed of it somewhere else in the house.

There was something about the way that Catherine's hand lay, palm upwards, thin fingers curled inwards like the legs of a dead and desiccated spider, that dragged Lapslie's attention away from thoughts of evidence, motive and personality profile and kept it pinned. Terrible in the silence, the hand lay at the gravitational centre of the room, pulling everything towards it. Somehow the hand had avoided any splashes of blood. Perhaps the killer had accidentally shielded it with their own body as they flayed Catherine's flesh away from her bone like a butcher preparing a joint of lamb for a casserole. Perhaps they had deliberately covered it for reasons that made sense only to them. Whatever the reason, it rested like a surreal joke; a perfect and untainted hand, fingernails painted pink, at the end of two lengths of yellow bone. And on the third finger of the hand, the golden band of an engagement ring glittered in the light of the dawn.

Somewhere off in the distance, Lapslie thought he heard something: a pulse, a rhythm, a pounding of drums. For a moment he thought that he was hearing the sound of his own blood, thudding in his ears, but the rhythm was too complicated for that. He pulled the headphones off, thinking for a moment that they were somehow bizarrely picking up a radio station, despite the absence of any electronics inside. The sudden drone of conversation and the whisper of the papery coveralls flooded his mouth with salt and metal, but the drumming noise became neither quieter nor louder. His brain began to split it up, classify it into its constituent parts: four

25

sets of four beats, the accent on the first beat of each quartet for the first three quartets, then the emphasis on the second, third and fourth beats for the last quartet. It was precise, organised, almost primal: like African tribal drumming. He'd heard something like it before: on the radio perhaps. He didn't have any CDs — the music caused too many unplanned sensations — and he didn't watch television for the same reason, but sometimes radios were hard to avoid.

'Has someone got a radio on?' he snapped, breaking the macabre silence.

Faces turned towards him. Emma Bradbury frowned.

'I asked if anyone's got a radio on.'

Several CSIs shook their heads.

'I can't hear anything, boss,' Emma said, detouring around the bed and towards him.

'I can hear music,' he said. 'Like drums. Can't you hear it?'

She tilted her head slightly, listening. 'Nothing.'

'Check downstairs. And see if anyone else can hear it. Might be neighbours.'

'Unlikely,' Emma said. 'It's a detached house, and the nearest neighbour is quite a way away. But I'll check.' She left the room, looking dubious. Everyone else returned to whatever they had been doing before he arrived.

Lapslie found his gaze drawn again to the body on the bed. The flensed arm. The hand.

''Cover her face,'' he quoted softly; ''mine eyes dazzle; she died young'.'

'What was that?' Sean Burrows said from his

26

position bending over the body. His voice still had the blackberry wine taste that Lapslie remembered of old.

'It's a tragedy,' Lapslie replied, but he wasn't sure whether he was talking about the quotation or the scene in front of him.

2

There was a fine suspension of rain in the air. It coated every surface that it touched, leaving a slick and slightly oily residue on leaves, grass, tree trunks and the brickwork of Carl Whittley's house.

He stood in the shelter of the bus stop across the road, gazing over at the house. The rain soaked into his hair and trickled down his cheeks but he didn't react to it. Inside his waterproofs he was uncomfortably warm, sweat prickling his skin despite the coldness outside, but again he hardly even noticed.

He held a package, wrapped in plastic, in his hand. It was the size of two hardback books, and the plastic around it was secured with thick rubber bands. Mud smeared its surface, a remnant of the hole in the ground where he had buried it, months ago. It had lain, undisturbed, from then until he had dug it up, just an hour ago.

His waterproofs were a muddy khaki colour, and years of use had left them faded and blotchy. He had deliberately removed the metal tips that terminated the tie-cords around the waist and neck. Those tips could brush against material, or brick, and the sound, slight though it might have been, could warn birds and animals of his presence and frighten them away when he was trying to catalogue them. The frayed ends of the tie-cords would not give him away.

The sky was a uniform nothingness, a neutral tone that had no depth to it. Somewhere behind the clouds that blanketed everything was a dim, hot sun, but it was impossible to tell where it was located. Its rays refracted through the cloud, making them glow with a sickly, pearlescent light that cast no shadows and made everything appear dimensionless, timeless.

He had been watching the house for nearly fifteen minutes, the package held unfeelingly in his gloved hands, ever since returning from his walk across the Essex salt marshes to the place where he had buried it.

The house was semi-detached; separated from the neighbours on one side but connected on the other, like one larger house split into two. The neighbours on the side that was separated from his home by a narrow alley both worked in financial services in Chelmsford; they were out most of the time, and he hardly ever heard them when they were in. Sometimes, in the summer, they left their windows open while they were in the garden, blasting the noise of their stereo everywhere while they sunbathed, and he had to walk around and ask them to turn it down, but most of the time they were okay.

The ones in the connecting house, how-ever . . .

Kev Dabinett was out of work, his wife Donna was a slut and the kids ran round the estate uncontrolled. The garden had three different cars in it, and Carl had noticed that the makes and models changed every few weeks. He was keeping a list, so that he could inform the council when he was absolutely sure that the husband was illegally running a second-hand car business from what was a residential property. The garden was a mess of churned-up grass and cracked paving slabs, with bits of engines and two car doors scattered along the edges. It was a disgrace, and every time he looked at it Carl could feel his blood boiling. Some people shouldn't be allowed to live in houses; they should be restricted to blocks of flats with others of their kind. With the evidence he was collecting, he could get them evicted. He was sure of it.

He had planted *leylandii* hedges along the perimeter of the garden, just so he didn't have to see the cars and the mess every time he left the house, but he still knew. It still burned at his heart, day after day.

Carl walked every morning and every afternoon, although he chose a different route every time. As well as providing him with the opportunity to catalogue the birds and animals of the salt marshes, it also gave him time to think. Time, but not necessarily the impetus, and he often found his mind blank for the entire walk, fixated entirely on the moment and ignorant of both the memories of the past and the predictions of the future that constituted a stream of consciousness. There were occasions, while he was out, when he imagined walking up next door's path, knocking on the front door and, when it opened, smashing in the face of whoever opened the door with a tyre lever.

Sometimes, in his imagination, it was Kev, sometimes it was Donna. Sometimes it was one of the kids, but it didn't matter. Removing them from his nicely ordered life was the only thing that mattered.

He rarely, if ever, saw anyone else on his wanderings. The salt marshes were anything but picturesque, and those few people who walked their dogs in the area almost always encroached only a mile or so from the border and then turned around again. The centre was practically deserted. Apart from him. Him and the birds and the various animals that lived out there.

'Carl!'

He turned. Kev Dabinett was walking along the road holding a bag of shopping in his hand.

'Kev,' he called back, 'how's things?'

'Yeah, fine. How's your dad?'

'Dad's good. Still finding it difficult to get around.'

Kev nodded in sympathy. 'Let me know if there's anything I can do.'

'Sure. Donna okay?'

'She's got a job. Working in Waitrose in Chelmsford.'

Carl forced a smile across his face. 'That's great. All the tapas and goat's milk you could ever want.'

Kev frowned. 'Sorry?'

'Nothing. Just a joke.'

'Okay.' Kev paused awkwardly. 'Look, sorry about the cars and stuff outside the house. It's only a temporary thing. I can get them moved, if you want.'

Carl could feel the rage boiling within him, hot and volcanic, but he forced it down. Kev apologised half-heartedly like that, as regular as clockwork, every couple of weeks but it didn't change anything. He seemed to think that an apology was a replacement for a change, not a precursor to it. 'It's not a problem. Don't worry about it.'

'Thanks. See you later.' Kev waved vaguely and headed towards his front door, past the litter of engine parts and tools spread across his scrappy lawn.

When Kev had shut the door behind him, Carl moved too, approaching his own front door, alert in case something unexpected happened. Nothing moved behind him, and he cautiously reached into his pocket with his free hand for the key. This was the danger point; this was when anyone would strike — if they were there. While his attention was momentarily distracted, and before he could achieve the safety of his home.

He slid the key into the lock, holding his breath. No sound. Nothing. The key *snicked* into the mechanism and he turned it slowly, head slightly twisted so that his peripheral vision would detect anything that suddenly appeared behind him.

He could feel an itch between his shoulder blades, as if someone was watching him, but it was caution rather than a specific warning. He pushed the door open. Just inside the door he had screwed a full-length mirror to the wall, and he now switched his gaze to the silvered glass, sweeping the area behind him to see whether someone had betrayed themselves.

Nothing. He was safe.

He pushed the door shut behind him and leaned against it for a moment. It sometimes seemed to him that he spent much of his waking life these days wondering if someone was watching him. When had it started? He never used to be like this. There were times he wondered why he was letting paranoia etch his life away, but there were other times when he knew with heavy certainty that one day there would be someone there behind him, and he would have to be ready.

He took a moment to regard himself critically in the mirror. He was young — still under twenty-five — and his body was fit and muscular from the regular walks he took, but his expression was grim and his hairline was receding. He was getting old before his time.

He pushed his way into the house, past the grey metal crutches and the rucksack that sat by the front door, beneath the mirror. Inside, the house was dark, shadowed, smelling of pine, varnish and books. The furniture was sparse and wooden, the pictures that lined the walls landscapes and abstracts rather than portraits. Motes of dust glittered in the shards of light that knifed their way between the closed curtains.

'Eleanor? Is that you?' The voice drifted weakly down the stairs.

'It's me, Dad,' he called back. 'It's Carl. I went out before you woke up.'

'You've been gone for hours.' The unspoken comment hung in the air: *I was worried about you. How am I supposed to do anything without your help?*

'Sorry. Lost track of the time. Saw a couple of badgers out in the marshes. If I'm lucky I can find their sett and then get some really good photographs. Do you want a cup of tea?'

'Tea would be nice. And some food. I didn't have any breakfast.'

'I left a tray by the side of the bed before I went out. Cereal, and a jug of milk.'

A pause. 'Oh. I wondered what that was.'

Carl headed for the kitchen and poured himself a glass of water from the tap. The liquid slaked his thirst and he drank greedily, then poured himself another one. When that too was finished he leaned against the old porcelain sink, letting its solidity support him. He felt dizzy, disconnected.

Pushing himself upright again with some effort, he switched on the kettle and then, while it was boiling, unlocked the kitchen door and walked out into the back garden. The herb garden could do with some pruning — especially the rosemary bush, which was threatening to run wild — but the rest of the plants were looking reasonably healthy.

At the end of the garden was a wooden building that he'd had built a year or so back. He told his father that it was where he kept his bird-and animal-watching stuff — his cameras, his files, his reference books. That was true, but it was more than that. It was his refuge. His burrow. His sett.

Returning to the kitchen he walked across to

where the fridge sat, humming, in one corner and opened the door. Sterile light illuminated the tiled floor. He reached inside and took out a raw chicken breast, pink and naked, wrapped in cling film. For a moment he weighed it in his hand, then he slipped it into another pocket of his anorak. A 'poacher's pocket' it was called; big enough to take a rabbit. Or perhaps even a badger.

He left the kitchen, kettle steaming gently, walked down the garden and, passing the coiled mass of the hosepipe, unlocked the door of the outbuilding with a key from his keyring. The building was connected for electricity and water, and he switched the light on as he entered. There were two rooms, one leading off the other, and the rough pine walls of the first room were lined with glass-fronted cabinets. Each cabinet contained an animal, posed in some naturalistic way: standing on its hind legs and sniffing the air; lying curled in a hollow between some rocks; poised, alert, looking for prey. Foxes, ferrets, voles, mice and rats. Not stuffed, though. That would have been too artificial. No, these animals were natural in all senses — sunken holes where their eyes should be, dull pelts, skin drawn sharply over the underlying bone, they were posed using wire that had been wrapped around their limbs, and the landscapes they were posed in were decaying as well: the grass dry and brown, the branches withered.

A plain pine table was positioned in the centre of the room. On it were six boxes containing mobile phones that he had bought in Ipswich the last time he had visited the town to buy food and other supplies. They were pay-as-you-go phones; the price included ten pounds of free airtime with the provider whose logo was plastered all over the boxes. The limit could be topped up using a credit card or debit card, but Carl had no intention of ever drawing attention to himself by doing that. No, the reason he had chosen the pay-as-you-go phones in the first place was that they didn't require a contract or any kind of standing order or direct debit in order for them to work: they could make calls straight out of the box, once the SIM cards were pushed out of their little holders and inserted inside them. There would be no way to connect the calls made back to the person who had bought them, and that was exactly what he wanted.

Next to the phones was a plastic box with a transparent lid. The inside of the box was subdivided into smaller sections of varying sizes and shapes. Each section had something different inside: nuts; bolts; screws; lengths of wire; capacitors; fuses; wire strippers; a roll of insulating tape and another roll of silvery solder; a soldering iron; and several small screwdrivers of the kind that jewellers and watchmakers used. Usually the tools were for making his animal sculptures. Now he was going to use them for something entirely different.

Placing the plastic-wrapped package that he had been carrying down on the table, Carl pulled out a chair and sat down. Watched by the sunken eye-sockets of the animals around the room, he selected two of the mobile phone boxes from the pile and compared the phone numbers printed on stickers on the outside with each other. He had already made sure that none of the phones had consecutive numbers, but diligence and repeated safety checks paid their own rewards. Having two or three numbers separated by a single digit meant that a simple misdial could have serious consequences.

Having established that the mobiles were safe, he opened the boxes and sorted out the items he would need — the SIM cards and the mobiles themselves — from the rest of the detritus that filled the space: CD-ROMs, manuals, chargers, several leaflets and slips of paper and two faux-leather pouches which could clip to belts with the mobiles protected inside.

He chose one of the phones at random, took the back panel off and unclipped the battery from inside, exposing the tiny clip where the SIM card went. The SIM card was separate, attached to a credit-card sized piece of plastic by two small tabs. He pushed it out of the plastic and slipped it into the clip in the phone, then replaced the battery and the back panel. Retrieving one of the chargers from the pile of stuff on the edge of the table, he got up and plugged the phone in to one of the sockets that were mounted chest-high on the wall on one side of the building.

Somewhere in the back of his mind he was aware that the kettle would have finished boiling in the kitchen by now, and his father would be working himself up into a tizzy about his cup of tea. But that could wait.

Returning to the table and working methodically, he opened up the back of the second mobile, removed the battery and set it safely to one side. Then he slid his fingernails beneath the label that was affixed under the battery and peeled it off. The glue was strong but the label was laminated and gradually came off in one piece. Underneath, set into the baseplate, were two tiny screws. Using one of the jewellers' screwdrivers he carefully undid them, setting them to one side where they would not roll off the table and where he could find them again.

The inside of the second mobile phone was now vulnerable, and he lifted the two halves apart, keeping the side with the keypad on the back and setting the other down next to the two screws. His gaze catalogued the various components in the inner casing: the loudspeaker, the microphone, the tiny offset motor that worked as a vibrating alarm, the circuit board and, crucially, the programmed integrated computer chip that sat in the centre of the board like an electronic spider.

It was the wires that led away from the circuit board and towards the loudspeaker that he wanted. Delicately, he used the wire strippers to sever the wires just before they made their connection to the loudspeaker, and then splayed them in different directions so they wouldn't inadvertently touch each other if he knocked one of them. Selecting two lengths of narrow wire from the plastic box of parts, he plugged the soldering iron in and, when it had heated up enough, gently melted a bead of solder on first one wire coming from the mobile phone and then the other, and then carefully attached the new lengths of wire to them. A few seconds of soft blowing to cool them down, and the connection was made.

The mobile phone sat there on the table with its innards exposed, twin wires trailing out and quivering like the antennae of some bizarre robotic beetle.

Reaching again into the tray, Carl removed a cylindrical object about the size of a cigarette. It was a detonator. With the greatest care, he again used the solder and the soldering iron, but this time to attach the detonator to the pair of wires that emerged from the disassembled mobile phone. Then, using a small file from the tray of components, he etched away two notches in the edge of the phone cover, just large enough to take the wires. Once he had done that, it was the work of a few moments to put the other half of the inner casing back on and fasten it into place with the two small screws, leaving the two wires emerging from the notches he had cut. The battery slotted straight back in to the case, and the rear panel slipped back on, leaving the phone whole again. Carl retrieved the second of the chargers from where he had left the contents of the boxes, plugged it into the phone and then, holding his breath, plugged the whole thing into a second wall socket. The phone was off, but even if something had gone wrong and a spare flicker of charge had got to the detonator, all that would have happened would have been a small explosion, barely enough to scorch the Formica counter. Detonators were just means of charging a larger chunk of explosive. They were pretty harmless by themselves, unless you happened to be holding them at the time.

The device was almost complete. Only a few steps left, and then he could test it out.

Carl turned his attention to the plastic-wrapped package that he had retrieved from the salt marshes and which he had left to one side of the table. He removed the rubber bands, one by one, and set them to one side, then carefully unwrapped the grey plastic wrapping. It crinkled between his fingers. There were two separate layers, and they had been wrapped several times around the contents in order to protect them from rain and ground water; necessary, since the package had spent several months buried beneath a stone out in the salt marshes, far enough from the house that it would not have implicated him immediately if it had been found but close enough that he could retrieve it with no difficulty when he needed it.

Carl unwrapped the first layer and set it to one side, then unwrapped the final layer, pulled it stickily from the object it surrounded and flattened it on the table as a safe base.

There, on the table before him, was a half-kilogram block of explosive, manufactured in Czechoslovakia back in the early 1990s but still just as dangerous as the day it had left the factory. It was grey, slightly moist, and smelled oily and comforting, like linseed.

Carl reached out and placed his finger against it, pushing until his fingernail indented the explosive in a shallow crescent. It was like modelling clay: inert and malleable. He got up from the table and walked back down the garden to the kitchen. The kettle had switched itself off, and he flicked the switch back on to reheat it. There was silence from upstairs.

The phone rang as he was about to leave the kitchen. He quickly picked it up before it could disturb his father.

'I called earlier on,' his mother's voice said. No greetings. No small talk. 'Nobody answered. Is everything all right?'

'I was out, and Dad was asleep,' Carl replied. 'Sorry.'

'Saying 'sorry' does not provide an automatic absolution. Anything could have happened to your father up there. He might have fallen out of bed. He might have had a stroke. You *have* to be there for him.'

Because you're not. Carl thought, then buried the thought. 'I went down to the shed to check something. I lost track of time.'

'You can't lose track of something you never had to begin with. You've always had a tenuous grasp of priority and timing. You got that from him.'

'He's fine. We both are.'

'I suppose it's too much to ask if you were out looking for a job?'

'Make up your mind,' Carl snapped. 'I can either stay at home looking after him every minute of the day or I can go out looking for work. You can't have it both ways.'

He could imagine his mother's lips twisting at

41

his momentary rebellion. 'Don't be argumentative; you haven't got the intellect. If you had a job we could afford to hire a nurse to look after him. As it is, the incapacity benefit, the consultancy work, and the advance on my next book is only just enough to keep paying the mortgages and buy the food.'

Mortgages. Plural. Half their financial problems would be solved if Eleanor Whittley moved back into the family home, but she and Carl had gone through that argument many times before. She needed peace and quiet to do her work, she said. Living in the house, being at Nicholas Whittley's beck and call, she would never get anything done. She and Carl had to split the work between them: she would pay the bills and he would look after his father.

So why did she keep pressing him to get a job? So she could disengage from the family completely, Carl suspected, and that was why he was holding back on applying for jobs and going to interviews. His mother's will was an unstoppable force — he'd known that since childhood — and so he had to be an immoveable object, whether he wanted to or not.

'Dad was asking about you,' he said, twisting the truth slightly. 'When are you going to come over and see us? If you came tonight I could fix us some food. A proper family dinner.'

'Not tonight,' she said quickly. 'I've got a dinner party to go to.' A pause, then a concession. 'I'll come over tomorrow. I can spare an hour or so.'

'Thanks. Dad'll be pleased. See you tomorrow.'

'Goodbye.'

He put the phone down and stood for a moment, not thinking, not moving. Just existing, independently of everything and everyone else. Eventually, without making any sounds that would give him away, he retrieved a steak knife from the kitchen, then walked back down the garden to the outbuilding. Sitting at the table again, he used the knife to separate the explosive into two equal blocks. He wrapped one of the blocks back up in the spare plastic sheeting that he had left on one side, then retrieved the modified mobile phone from over by the fridge and placed it on top of the other block. The first phone — the intact, unmodified one — was still charging, but he didn't need this one to have a full charge: just enough for it to receive a call and send the call tone to where it thought the loudspeaker was. He pushed the 'on' button, and watched as the mobile's screen lit up. A few messages cycled past as it looked for a service provider. Finally it managed to lock onto a signal.

He waited for three minutes, breathing shallowly, for any stray currents, error bleeps or 'welcome' messages to cycle their way through the phone. Then, hesitating only slightly, he pushed the detonator inside the block, meeting some resistance. It was like pushing a skewer into a side of beef. When it was three-quarters of the way in, he stopped.

There was a roll of weatherproof electricians'

tape in the tool tray — 'black nasty' it was called in the building industry — and he quickly pulled a length off, cutting it with the wire strippers. With a deft, well-practised movement he wound the tape around the mobile and explosive, anchoring them together, then wrapped the whole package in the other plastic sheet and made it secure with rubber bands.

And now he had a fully primed and working bomb in front of him. One wrong number and his limbs and internal organs would be spread across the smoking remains of the outbuilding, but only he and the service providers knew the number.

With a cold feeling in his limbs and a dry mouth, he slipped it carefully into a pocket inside his anorak.

Carl crossed over to the power sockets and detached the second mobile phone — the unmodified one — from its charger. This one had more charge in its battery, but this was the one that would need to actually make a call, rather than just receive one. He slipped it into an outside pocket, on the opposite side to where the explosive was located. No point in tempting fate.

He took a last look around the outbuilding. The tools and pieces of wire were still spread out across the table, and he spent a few minutes tidying them away. There was no point in leaving evidence scattered around. The chances of his father making his way painfully downstairs and out into the garden while he was away were vanishingly small, but people bet on the National Lottery with even smaller odds of winning, and sometimes they did win. Unlikely things sometimes came to pass.

Back in the kitchen, with the mobile phones, Semtex and chicken breast secreted in various pockets around his anorak, he set a mug on the counter and slid a tea bag into it from the container by the sink. He poured boiling water into the cup and watched as brown fluid swirled out of the tea bag, gradually darkening the water to the colour of the brackish puddles and rivulets that made the Essex salt marshes into the unique environment they were. When he couldn't see the bottom of the mug any more, he retrieved the tea bag and placed it into the small rubbish bin that he kept beside the sink for that very purpose, then carefully poured some milk into the mug.

Retrieving a cling-film-covered plate of mince and rice from the fridge, Carl set off up the stairs. Each step brought his heart a little lower. He could feel his pace slowing as he got closer to the bedroom.

His father was sitting up in bed. He was wearing his reading glasses low on his nose; the black rims prominent against his pale skin. The newspaper that the paperboy had delivered that morning was still folded on the duvet beside him. The tuft of chest-hair that emerged from the top of the jacket was as grey as the hair on his head.

'I brought you some lunch.' He placed the plate on the bed where his father could reach it.

'Mince.' Nicholas Whittley looked dubiously at the plate. 'How thoughtful.'

45

'Does your . . . colostomy bag need changing?'

His father winced and looked away. 'No. Not yet.'

'And what about your urine bottle? Does it need emptying?'

'No. It's fine.'

'I'll check again after you've finished your cup of tea and your lunch. How are you feeling?'

'I had a dream. I think it was a dream.' His father's gaze fastened on Carl's anorak. 'You're leaving me alone again?'

'You know you get more rest when you can't hear me moving around. I'll be a couple of hours.'

'A couple of . . . ' His father took a deep breath. 'I'll see you later.' He turned his attention to the plate, looking over the top of his reading glasses at it. 'What kind of mince is this? Beef? Turkey?'

Carl hesitated. 'Pork, for a change,' he said eventually. 'What was your dream about?'

'I thought that Eleanor was here. I thought she'd come back.' His face was pathetically hopeful. 'Did she call?'

Carl took a deep breath and closed his eyes for a moment. 'No,' he said. 'She didn't call.' Before his father could respond, Carl turned and went downstairs. Picking up the rucksack that sat by the front door, he left, locking the door behind him.

Outside the house, the rain still loitered as a fine mist in the air as if it wasn't sure whether it was supposed to fall to the ground or not. Carl locked the door behind him and walked off, hands in pockets, feeling the dull edges of the packet of explosive through the thick, waxy material. It banged against his legs as he walked, head down and hood up. Past the other houses, through the alleyway, past the garages on the edge of the Creeksea estate and into the Essex wetlands which spread away into the distance; a plain of grasses and low bushes fading away into the grey mist, broken up by meandering streams whose steep-banked sides dropped away without warning and raised dykes and banks that hid the horizon in most directions. Surreptitiously he looked around, checking for anyone nearby — hikers, perhaps, or someone making a delivery — but he was apparently alone.

Carl struck out across the marshes, letting his legs settle into a steady rhythm as he walked. He knew the area where he wanted to test the device, and it would take him about twenty minutes to get there. He consciously kept his mind from thinking about what he intended to do when he arrived. All the preparations were made; now he had to make sure that the various components worked in the way he intended. And then he could proceed with the next phase of his plan; a plan which, like the landscape around him, went on and on until it faded into the mist.

After some indeterminate time, Carl knew that he had arrived at the right spot. Some minor variation in the grassy mounds, some small difference in the colour of the leaves on the bushes told him that he had reached his goal. He looked around. The rain had thinned out and the mist had lifted, and he could see for probably a

47

mile or more. There was nobody around. He put the rucksack down and reached into his pocket for the block of explosive and the mobile phone that he had attached to it. They felt almost exactly like a brick, weighing down his hand. Walking forward to an area where the ground fell away slightly and the bushes thinned out, he placed the explosive and the mobile phone on the ground. The plastic sheet that it was wrapped in would protect it against the rain; after all, it had protected the explosive from the elements for the many months that it had been hidden, buried out in the marshes.

He took the chicken breast from his anorak and unwrapped the cling film from it. The flesh was warm and tacky beneath his fingertips. He balled the cling film up and put it back into his pocket. No point leaving any traces around if he could help it. He would dispose of it later.

Kneeling down, he brushed the chicken breast over the plastic wrapping of the bomb, leaving smears of watery blood over the slick surface. He draped the breast across the top of the bomb and then backed away to where he had left the rucksack. Kneeling again, he opened the rucksack and pulled out two green canvas camping groundsheets, their edges perforated with metal-edged holes, some cord, a hammer and a handful of metal coils. With swift, economical motions he spread one of the groundsheets out, wove the cord in and out of the holes around the edge and then anchored the groundsheet to the grassy surface using four of the coils which he twisted into the ground in a square, larger than the sheet.

He did the same to the second groundsheet, placing it over the first and attaching it to the ground. Together, the two sheets formed a cocoon, an envelope inside which he could remain dry and unseen. A hide. A sett.

A couple of handfuls of earth and grass thrown over the sheets completed the illusion.

And then, with his rucksack held in one hand, he dropped to the ground and wriggled beneath the top groundsheet, fingers pulling at the rough weave of the canvas.

The smell of wet grass and disturbed earth prickled his nostrils. He felt dissociated, detached from reality. How many times in how many different places had he taken up that position, sandwiched between two sheets of canvas, waiting for an animal to come by?

His hand groped in his pocket for the second mobile phone. He switched it on, and in the meagre light from the display screen he typed, using his thumb, the number of the other phone, the one connected to the bomb. A few button presses and the number was committed to the mobile's memory, able to be recalled with the press of just two buttons.

Outside his hide, in the thin slice of marshland that he could see from between the two sheets, the bomb sat innocently in the centre of its hollow. The chicken breast on top drooped over the block of explosive like a Salvador Dali watch.

Time passed; seconds, minutes, perhaps hours. Carl's mind slipped into a reverie that was not quite a dream and not quite a waking stream of consciousness; a slow progression of memories that slipped over and around each other like the dappled bodies of trout in a stream.

Eventually, there was movement. It might have been a fox, it might conceivably have been a badger, but it was in fact a polecat; a sinuous streak of dirty grey with a pointed head and two beady black eyes set in a mask of fur that made it look as if it was wearing glasses. Reading glasses. It placed its forepaws, almost like tiny human hands, on top of the explosive and looked around suspiciously. Carl held his breath, willing the polecat not to see him. Its black eyes seemed to pass over him and then return, as if it knew there was something, some*one*, out there, watching, but it couldn't quite work out where.

Carl's thumb caressed the button that would route a call to the mobile phone connected to the bomb.

The polecat bent its pointed head to the chicken breast. Its mouth opened, small teeth ready to tear at the flesh.

Carl pressed the button.

The polecat, the chicken breast and the wrapped block of explosive vanished in a flash and an expanding cloud of flesh and blood and dust and burning gas. Disconnected from the flash, a few microseconds later, Carl heard a loud blast. The ground shuddered beneath his prone body.

The smoke drifted away on the breeze. Where the polecat and the bomb had been, there was just a rough circle of churned and bloody earth.

3

When Emma Bradbury re-entered Catherine Charnaud's bedroom, she was looking even more doubtful than when she left. 'Nobody's playing a radio, boss,' she said. 'And there's no noise from the neighbours. Is it possible you heard a car radio going past?'

Lapslie shook his head, fighting against a wave of nausea. With the sound-deadening head-phones off he was subject to the noise of the Crime Scene Investigators in the room talking to one another and the intermittent *click* as the photographer's digital camera captured another image. His salivary glands were spasming with the overload of unexpected, unwelcome tastes, and he kept having to swallow. 'It was louder than that,' he said eventually, 'and there was none of the distortion you get from overloaded speakers.'

'This is Essex, remember? There's kids driving round Southend seafront with speakers in the back more powerful than anything the Ozric Tentacles ever had.'

'The Ozric Tentacles?' he asked, intrigued enough at this sudden, unexpected insight into Emma's musical preferences that he could push the melange of tastes in his mouth to one side for a moment. But just for a moment.

'Er . . . they're a group. They do a lot of festivals. Sort of acid-folk-jazz, if you know what

I mean.' She paused, embarrassed. 'And you obviously don't.'

Lapslie let a smile pull at the corners of his mouth. 'Let's be charitable and assume you were undercover at the time.' He swallowed a mouthful of saliva again. 'But even so — it didn't sound like a car.'

'Is it that thing you get? The synaesthesia?'

He shrugged. 'It usually works the other way around. Sounds cause tastes for me; it's very rare that it goes into reverse and other sensory input causes sounds. Although it's not unheard of.' He thought for a moment. 'And I was wearing the headphones. I wasn't hearing anything apart from my own body, and that's never affected me so badly before.' Gazing back at the ruin of Catherine Charnaud's arm, he said, 'Oh, let's get out of here. I've had about all I can take.'

The two of them headed downstairs. Rather than move into the lounge, which would probably be too personal, too much imprinted with Catherine Charnaud's personality, Lapslie led the way into the kitchen. It was a large, square room with various cupboards, fridges, cookers and dishwashers around the edges, all furnished in a kind of plain Amish style, and a freestanding unit in the centre which could either be used for preparing food or, with a couple of place mats, as a breakfast bar. Lapslie hoisted a couple of stools across to the unit and he and Emma sat.

'What have we got?' he asked simply.

She shrugged. 'Apart from a dead body, very little. No signs that anyone else was here, like

52

two wine glasses; no indications of forced entry, either on the house or the body, as far as I can tell; and no reports from the neighbours that anything was amiss — no prowlers, screams in the night, or anything else.'

'Then why are we here?'

'Sorry?'

'How was the body discovered?'

'Apparently the boyfriend is a professional footballer. He was out last night with friends. Got back about four o'clock this morning, let himself in and . . . '

Lapslie grimaced. 'Not nice. Where is he now?'

'One of the uniforms is taking his statement. Outside, in the fresh air.'

'We'll question him later. What do you make of the state the body's in?'

Emma frowned. 'At the risk of stating the obvious, it's a mess. On the one hand, torture is usually a personal thing: pain and mutilation inflicted in spades in return for some previous slight — some insult or injury that the torturer has blown out of all proportion. But that kind of goes against the meticulous nature of the torture here. Cutting that much flesh away that precisely takes time and care. It's not something you do in the heat of the moment.'

'It looks to me more like a message of some kind,' Lapslie said.

'What kind of message?' she asked, obviously intrigued at the idea.

He shrugged. 'Who knows? It might be the kind of message that only makes sense to someone who's clinically insane, or refers to something that only one or two other people know about.'

'Or perhaps the killer was removing something or obliterating something?'

'What, like a tattoo?'

'Might be.'

'There are easier ways. And besides, women don't usually get tattoos done on their arms. They normally opt for the ankle, the shoulder blade or the small of the back.'

'I've got a — ' Emma stopped abruptly. 'I've got a feeling you're right,' she continued, rubbing the fabric of her left sleeve with her right hand.

Lapslie gazed around the kitchen. 'Nice place. She must be doing well.'

'With a job fronting the TV news and a footballer boyfriend, I guess she's not short of a few bob.'

'Any tensions with the boyfriend? Is he playing away, metaphorically as well as literally?'

'We'll look into his background.'

He remembered the Jill Dando case, and the possibility — strong at the beginning but then progressively replaced by a belief that a stalker was responsible — that she'd been targeted by Serbian hitmen. 'Check her recent broadcasts for anything contentious.'

'Define contentious.'

'You know the kind of thing. Suggestions of illegal activities involving Russian billionaires. Investigations into people-smuggling gangs in Eastern Europe. Hard-hitting exposés of corruption in the building work for the 2012 Olympics.

Anything that might have made her a target in the eyes of someone willing to have her killed and ruthless enough to want to do it in a way that dissuades anyone else from following the same leads.'

'She was a figurehead, boss, not a reporter. Her job was pretty much to read what was on her autocue as naturally as she could and look gorgeous while she did it.'

Lapslie smiled as a stray thought tugged at a corner of his brain: something Sonia had told him, years before, when she was doing an MA in Fine Art. 'You know the difference between naturalism and realism?' he asked.

'No.' Emma's voice was wary.

'Naturalism is showing the world the way it is, and realism is showing it the way it *really* is.'

'Hmm. You need to work on your delivery, boss. Anything else?'

Before he could answer, a uniformed constable entered the kitchen and approached them. 'Excuse me, sir,' he said, 'but the pathologist's people are here. They're asking if you can release the body.'

'Check with the CSIs and the photographer. If they've all got everything they need then I'm happy the body gets taken.'

The constable nodded, turned on his squeaky rubber heels and left.

'Where was I?' he continued.

'Adding to my 'to do' list,' Emma replied sourly.

'Okay. If she was in the media then there's a fair to middling chance that she was doing recreational drugs: probably cocaine. That's the drug of choice in TV and journalism. The post mortem will throw up any traces of the stuff in her system, but it's worth making some preliminary inquiries. Find out if she's ever been in trouble with the local police. It could be that she's fallen foul of some kind of drug deal gone wrong. Perhaps she couldn't pay for her last delivery.'

'I'm on it.'

'Coordinate a search of the house, inside and out, paying particular reference to footprints in the soil outside; get statements from the neighbours; talk to the girl's friends, relatives and co-workers to see whether there was any strain in her relationship with her boyfriend; get someone to check through her fan-mail for evidence of obsessive behaviour or stalking; get details on whatever security system the house has; and then get an incident room set up in the nearest police nick.'

'In other words, all the standard stuff that I was already going to do.'

'Of course. When in doubt, fall back on routine. That's why it's there. Find out if she had a computer in the house and impound it. Check for emails, blogs, anything that might give an insight into any odd relationships she's developed. Do the same for her mobile phone as well. And check to see how many mobiles she has: sometimes celebrities have two; one for work and one for home. I'd hate to find out in a month's time that we'd completely ignored a mobile phone that was almost in our laps.'

'A month's time? Do you really think the case will last that long?'

'The Jill Dando case lasted over a year before they arrested someone, and even then they got it wrong.' He glanced around the kitchen. 'Do you think it'll compromise the evidence chain if I use that percolator over there to make a jug of coffee?'

'Yes,' she said firmly. 'I'll get something sent in from outside.'

Something that tasted very much like a pork pie invaded his mouth. He grimaced involuntarily as saliva pinpricked his cheeks and flooded his tongue. Something out in the hall was making a noise. He stood, and headed for the kitchen door.

Two figures in coveralls were manoeuvring a black body bag down the stairs. Each held one end, and the bag sagged in the middle. The sound he had heard had been the hem of the bag scraping against one of the pictures hanging on the wall. To Lapslie's eyes the whole thing looked grotesquely like the start of a comedy sketch: two men with a piano, on the verge of dropping it or letting it slip, to zany comic effect; that 1960s Bernard Cribbins song 'Right, Said Fred' recast as a black comedy.

'Careful,' he snapped, aware of a dull headache forming behind his eyes. 'That used to be a person.'

One of the men looked sorrowfully at him. 'No need to be like that, mate,' he remonstrated. 'We're doing the best we can.'

Lapslie watched them go, then wandered into

the lounge, relishing the comparative silence. Two of the CSIs were dusting for prints, their gestures causing no more noise than a butterfly landing, and he stood in the centre of the room watching them for a while. There was a slight scent of perfume in the air, evident even above the smell of the fingerprint powder; *Eau Jeune*, he thought. Catherine Charnaud's presence would take a while to fade away.

Emma brought him a coffee after a few minutes, scared up from somewhere outside, and he sipped at it, letting his brain sort out the various impressions it had absorbed over the past hour or so. He had a feeling that this would be a tricky one. A straight crime of passion and he would have put a pony on it being the boyfriend, but torture and mutilation on the scale that he had witnessed up in the bedroom? That took it into a different world entirely.

'Let's follow the body to the mortuary,' he said eventually. 'If nothing else, it's quiet there.'

Emma looked around. 'I should keep an eye on what's happening here,' she said dubiously.

'They know their jobs, and I need you to drive me.'

Emma shrugged. 'And I know *my* job,' she muttered.

The drive took two hours, a good half hour of which was due to a burst water main, and Lapslie spent most of the time with the headphones on, drifting in a world of his own breath and blood. The mortuary was located on one side of Braintree, next to a park; a low, anonymous building that could have been mistaken for a nursery, an accountant's practice or the offices of a rather down-at-heel architect if it hadn't been for the industrial-size air conditioning pipes that plunged in and out of the side walls, and the metal chimney that towered over it from the rear.

While Emma parked near to the door, Lapslie walked over and pressed the button on the intercom. 'DCI Lapslie to see Dr Catherall,' he said crisply. He had to bend down to do it. For a while he had toyed with the idea that the security intercom had either been fitted by midgets or the workmen had misread imperial measurements for metric when they were measuring up. Having met Jane Catherall, he now had an alternative explanation. He strongly suspected that she had browbeaten them into fitting it at a height convenient to her, and bugger anyone else.

The door clicked open, and Lapslie entered, with Emma following. The foyer was as he remembered it: reminiscent of a dentist's surgery, what with the worn floor tiles, the plasterboard ceiling tiles, the chairs that looked like they dated from a decade before and the slight smell of disinfectant. The only thing indicating that the medical procedures that went on behind the closed doors was done to dead bodies, not live ones, was the underlying smell of blood and faecal matter that the disinfectant couldn't quite hide.

Dr Catherall's assistant, Dan, stepped out from a side room. Lapslie had met him before, but still couldn't quite remember his name.

'DCI Lapslie — Dr Catherall said you'd

probably be popping in. Please, come this way.' Dan led him through a set of double doors edged in plastic, to keep the sounds and the smells from drifting too far. 'Dr Catherall? You've got visitors.'

The room was large, and so cold that Lapslie and Emma's breath misted in front of their mouths as they breathed out. Lapslie tried not to breathe in through his nose: the smell was more marked in here.

The stench of the mortuary was worse than he remembered, despite the number of times he'd been there over the years. It was something like the sweet, cloying odour of rancid meat underpinned with a fouler reek, all of it covered but not hidden by the nostril-grating tang of bleach and detergent. Somehow his brain managed to edit out the sheer visceral reaction that it always engendered in him; he could recall that it *was* bad, but not *how* it was bad. It was like Sonia had once told him about having children; if women remembered how painful it was the first time they'd never go through it again. And Sonia had borne two children for him, which probably went to prove her point.

'How do the people who work here stand it?' Emma muttered. 'Surely the smell must get into their clothes, their hair and their skin? What do their families say? It's like people who work in fish-and-chip shops always smell of hot oil, no matter how many showers they take.'

'You're supposed to get used to anything,' Lapslie replied.

'I know, but there are limits.'

When he had first been diagnosed with synaesthesia, some years back, Lapslie had gone along to a support group of similar sufferers. It had been Sonia's idea. She had somehow thought that sharing his experiences with others, and sharing theirs, would help him come to terms with his problem. It hadn't, and he had soon left, dismayed by the whole touchy-feely experience, but one thing did stay with him. One of the men in the group, a taxi driver named Andy, had suffered from a form of synaesthesia where smells were associated in his mind with particular colours. Lapslie sometimes felt as if he understood how that might work. And to him, the smell of the mortuary was khaki: dark brown and dark green mixed together into a deep, unpleasant mess.

Three large post-mortem tables dominated the room, air conditioning vents hovering over each one like big metal snakes about to strike. Either they were switched off or the fans were so quiet that he could neither hear nor taste them. The sides of the tables were lipped to prevent bodily fluids from dripping over the edge and their surfaces slanted to allow the same bodily fluids to trickle down to a drain at the bottom, from where they were presumably whisked away and stored for future disposal. Whatever happened to them, Lapslie didn't want to know. He just hoped they weren't dumped straight into the sewers.

Jane Catherall was standing over the middle table, where a naked body was laid out. She had a minidisc recorder in her hand, and was dictating notes on her first, visual examination of the body.

Standing *over* it? No, standing *beside* it. Jane Catherall was, as she had once told Lapslie, a survivor of poliomyelitis, a disease that attacked the nervous system and could have been cured, or at least treated, if she had been born a few years later when the vaccine was widely available. As it was, she had spent a number of formative years incarcerated in an iron lung, and now, in her middle age, she was just over five feet tall: enough to reach the table, but not to reach over it. Her spine was twisted, her stomach distended — a sign that her internal organs were swollen and misplaced — and her eyes protruded further than normal, giving her a perpetually surprised look. She was also the sweetest person that Lapslie had ever met, although he would never tell her so. Her character was pugnacious enough already.

'Lemons,' she said in her warm brandy voice without looking up.

'Dr Catherall. You startled me.'

'I'm pleased that my elfin ability to surprise has not waned with the passing years.' She smiled up at him.

'Did you say 'lemons'?'

'Yes. Your sergeant was wondering about the smell, and how we get it out of our hair and our skin. The answer is lemons.'

'Sorry,' Emma said, discomfited. 'I didn't mean to offend you.'

'No offence taken. Everyone asks, at some stage. It's usually the first question asked by journalists and by the new lab assistants who start work here. We get through quite a few, as you can probably imagine.'

'So what is it about lemons?' Lapslie asked.

'The citric acid and the essential oils are excellent at dissolving the odour of decay that surrounds us during the course of our work. There are various products on the market that are meant to do the trick, and there is not a week goes past when I do not receive a telephone call or an email from some company who claim to have developed the perfect solution, but the fact remains that half a lemon rubbed all over the body does the trick.'

'You live and learn,' Lapslie said.

'I heard that you had been assigned to this case. It's a pleasure to be working with you again.'

'And you, Jane,' he replied.

'Would you like a coffee?'

'No, thanks.' Emma shook her head too, and Lapslie indicated the body on the table. 'I'm keen to see what you make of it.'

It. Lapslie suddenly wondered when Catherine Charnaud had changed from *her* to *it*. Back at the house, when the body had been only an hour or so from warmth and vitality, back when the blood and the saliva had still been wet, both Lapslie and Emma had regarded her as a person. Now, spread out naked on the metal table, the blood making the back of her torso and legs noticeably darker than the front as it drained downwards under the force of gravity, she was just meat. Just flesh. Despite the fact that she was young, attractive and naked, lying with her breasts and pubic area exposed, Lapslie could feel nothing for her apart from a diffuse sympathy. Whatever had been there, whatever had provided the vital spark, had drained away from her in the same way that her bodily fluids would shortly drain away as Dr Catherall cut her open and scooped out her internal organs for examination.

'Mark?'

'Sorry. Just thinking.'

Dr Catherall smiled gently at him. 'This place is very conducive to deep questions about mortality and the nature of life. Questions, but no answers. I can tell you why people died — that I can do very well. What I can't tell you is why they lived in the first place.'

Lapslie nodded. ''Never to have lived is best, ancient writers say,'' he quoted softly. ''Never to have drawn the breath of life, never to have looked into the eye of day. The second best's a gay goodnight and quickly turn away.''

'Yeats, I do believe. From *Oedipus at Colonus*.' She glanced over at Emma. 'Mark quoted Robert Browning at me when we first met. His erudition is showing.'

'I apologise,' Lapslie said. 'I realise that all policemen are meant to reach for their guns when they hear the word 'culture'. I'll try to control myself in future. Are you ready to carry out the post mortem?'

'As ready as I will ever be,' Dr Catherall replied. '*Lasciate ogne speranza, voi ch'intrate*,' she murmured, turning to the tables.

'Dante,' Emma muttered. At Lapslie and Jane's surprised glances, she flushed. 'GCSE,' she said. 'We did it at school. 'All hope abandon ye who enter here', it means.'

'There's hope for the police force after all,' Jane said quietly, and smiled.

Lapslie and Emma pulled up stools and watched, for the next hour, as Jane deconstructed the body of Catherine Charnaud as expertly and as dispassionately as a chef jointing a chicken. She started by washing it, checking the skin carefully as she did so. Next she made a Y-shaped incision, starting at each shoulder and moving above the nipples to join up between the breasts, above the sternum, and then progressing down the stomach and further, down the pubis. Dan moved in with a pair of shears, similar to those Lapslie had seen used by firemen at car crashes to cut through sections of the car body in order to reach someone inside. 'The jaws of life', they were called. These were the jaws of death, and Dan used them to cut his way up Catherine Charnaud's ribcage so that the entire front of the chest could be removed and set to one side.

Emma was shifting on her stool, edgy at the enforced stillness. She liked to keep moving, Lapslie had noticed. Even when she was sitting still her legs were quivering or her fingers twitching. On the drive over, divorced from the sound, Lapslie had been fascinated by the way her fingers kept tapping out complicated rhythms on the steering wheel.

Now that she had access, Dr Catherall removed each organ from the body cavity and examined it carefully, made verbal notes into her recorder, then handed it to Dan for weighing and sealing in a transparent plastic bag. The heart especially came in for detailed scrutiny, and several photographs. She then made a deep incision across the top of the corpse's head, cutting right down to the bone, and then tugged at the exposed edge of the skin with all her strength, pulling the scalp down like a flap to cover the face from brow to lips with a raw mask of flesh. The crunch of gristle and flesh separating made Lapslie's mouth tingle with sparkling wine; not Champagne, but something sweeter, like Asti Spumante. Stepping back and resting for a while, Jane allowed Dan to use a power saw to make two cuts through the exposed bones of the skull; one across the top, paralleling the first cut she had made, and the second lower down, above the forehead. Lapslie winced as the dentist-whine of the saw biting into bone sent a torrent of savoury meat across his tongue. The two cuts intersected above and forward of the ears, allowing Dr Catherall to delicately remove the wedge of skull, and expose Catherine Charnaud's brain tissue.

Lapslie was surprised at how easily the brain could be lifted out of the cup of the skull. Only a few cuts were necessary, and it came free, small enough to nestle in the palm of Dr Catherall's hand as she talked into the minidisc recorder. Bizarrely, he was reminded of delving inside the engine of his Saab, undoing the bolts on the alternator and lifting it free so he could replace it. No replacements here, however. The brain too was examined, weighed, bagged and placed to one side.

And then, as meticulously as she had taken the body apart, Dr Catherall put it back together again. The segment of skull was replaced, the flap of skin covering the face was eased back into its original location and stitched to stop it coming loose, and the chest cavity was stitched back with thick, heavy strokes, leaving the corpse looking as if it had a Y-shaped zip running up its front. And then, while Dan washed it again, Dr Catherall dictated her final notes.

'So what can you tell me?' Lapslie asked as Dr Catherall wearily pulled her rubber gloves off and dropped them into a bin marked *Waste*.

'I can tell you that she was young and fit, that she smoked occasionally, that she was not a virgin and that she had never had a baby, although she had been through several abortions.'

'We could have got that from the pages of *Hello* magazine. What else?'

Dr Catherall glanced over at the body on the table. 'Was she a celebrity of some kind?' she asked, puzzled.

'Of some kind, yes.'

'Hmm. I do not watch television, or read the more celebrity-obsessed newspapers.'

'Signs of drug abuse?' Emma asked.

'No signs of intravenous introduction of drugs, ruling out heroin, and her nasal cavity is in good condition so I can say with some certainty that she has not been sniffing cocaine either, at least not for any length of time. I will send blood samples off for testing.'

Emma nodded. 'Any sign of rape or other sexual interference?'

'There is no obvious trauma. I will send samples of her vaginal fluids off for testing as well. There may be some traces of semen, or lubricant from a condom.'

'Make sure we get a DNA sample from the boyfriend,' Lapslie said to Emma. 'We'll need to screen him out.' Turning back to Jane, he asked: 'The mutilation that was committed on her arm — was it done while she was still alive or finished after she died?'

'She died while it was being committed,' Jane told him.

Lapslie took a moment to consider the information. 'So what killed her? The shock?'

'Yes. That and the loss of blood. If you want me to be truly accurate then I would say that she died due to a lack of oxygen to the brain, but then almost every death that occurs in the world is ultimately due to a lack of oxygen to the brain. It can either happen quickly, when the heart stops for some reason, or slowly, as when a developing tumour gradually chokes off the blood supply, but it all comes down to oxygen starvation in the end.'

'However . . . '

'However, in layman's terms the sheer agony of the mutilation caused her heart to fibrillate.'

'She had a heart attack?' Emma asked.

'That's what I will be putting on the death certificate.'

Lapslie grimaced. 'And could that have been

predicted by the person who mutilated her?'

Dr Catherall smiled mirthlessly. 'Her death was not unintentional, if that is what you are getting at. Whoever did this to her would have known that if the shock didn't kill her then blood loss would, and if blood loss didn't kill her then whatever infection got into her bloodstream would have. She could not have lived long like that. Nor would she have wanted to.'

Lapslie walked over to the body and stared down at it, trying to make sense of what had been done. Now that the body had been washed and the blood splatter coating the limbs laved away the injuries were starker, more like something from a medical textbook. Dr Catherall had removed the tight bands that had closed off the arm above the elbow and below the wrist, and the flesh had plumped out again to the point that Lapslie could draw, in his mind, two smooth lines to close up the missing skin and muscle and tendon. 'What do you make of this?' he asked. 'You know more about bodies and the way they are constructed than anyone else I know. Why would anybody *do* this?'

Jane took a few small, precise steps across to join him. 'My initial reaction was that someone was practising their anatomy skills,' she said, sighing. 'But there's no mystery about the way the muscles are laid out in the arm, and separating them out is hardly something that requires a great deal of skill. Any competent butcher could do it. If someone had taken the immense risk of immobilising a living specimen, they would surely want more of a challenge

— getting into the chest cavity, for instance, or the skull. And why keep the person alive while you are doing it? The noise and the agonised thrashing around just makes it much more difficult. No, we have to assume that having her aware of what was being done was a necessary part of the process, which just brings us back to the same point — why?'

'Torture, perhaps?'

Dr Catherall pursed her lips dismissively. 'If I wanted to torture someone,' she said, 'then I wouldn't do it this way. Bones don't have any nerves; not on the outside, anyway, although there are nerves within the marrow, along with blood vessels. There are parts of the body that have a much higher concentration of nerve endings than the forearm. I would probably start with the soles of the feet and work my way up. The genitalia would be next, of course, and then the inside of the mouth and nose — '

'Thank you,' Lapslie said rapidly. 'That's very clear. Remind me never to make you angry.'

'My knowledge is entirely theoretical,' she giggled unexpectedly. 'You should have no worries about me becoming a rogue pathologist, stalking my prey through the shadowy streets of the city.'

'That's . . . reassuring.' He paused for a moment, thinking.

'I don't suppose you can tell us anything about the tools that were used or the technique that the killer displayed?' Emma asked from behind them.

Dr Catherall laughed lightly. 'You are hoping

70

that I will say 'The killer used a number five surgical scalpel, and displayed a great deal of medical knowledge', aren't you?'

'A girl can hope.'

'This isn't the Jack the Ripper investigation, Detective Sergeant Bradbury. No, whoever did this could have used any small knife, from a common kitchen knife to the kind a fisherman uses to gut and descale a fish. There are no defined marks on the bones, apart from some indeterminate scratches. I am afraid you will not be able to classify your killer thanks to some unusual weapon. And cutting through skin and muscle tissue until you find the bone and then scraping it away takes no more skill than de-boning a chicken carcass.'

'Make sure Sean Burrows and the CSIs check the knives in the kitchen,' Lapslie said to Emma. 'There's always the chance the murderer used whatever was at the scene to commit the crime with. Same goes for those plastic ties — they might be from the garden or a toolbox. And let's see if we have a budget to call a profiler in. Find out for me who the current favourite is within the department — I think we're going to need an expert view on the psychology of the killer. This murder has all the hallmarks of something very simple and domestic, with the exception of the way it was done, and that worries me.'

'There is one thing that occurs to me,' Dr Catherall said tentatively.

'What's that?'

'The meticulous way that the mutilation was done, associated with the way it has been almost presented to us, makes me think of an artist working on a canvas. Is it possible that whoever did this regarded it as a work of art?'

'But why keep her alive while he was doing it?' Emma asked.

Dr Catherall gazed up at Lapslie, her eyes filled with something dark and sad. 'Because every artist needs an audience,' she said.

4

The darkness outside the house was something oppressive, palpable. It seemed to press against the walls and windows like some rough beast trying to infiltrate its shadowy claws through any cracks. The sounds of the wind gusting against the exposed sides of the house were the sounds of the beast moving, adjusting its position, trying to get a better grip on Carl's home and find a different way in, testing the strength of the walls, wondering if it was strong enough to just tighten its hold and break the house into fragments and let the darkness spill in everywhere, victorious.

Carl Whittley sat hunched up on the sofa of his darkened living room, listening to the beast outside. In his mind the beast was as black as tar, and its skin was rough and covered in warts. In his mind the beast's skin erupted in blisters, and each blister was an eye, the pupil slotted like a goat's. He knew he was being foolish, that he was ascribing sentience and purpose to something as natural as rain and sun, but he couldn't help himself. The beast was out there, and it wanted him.

Sometimes he feared that he was going mad. He worried that the loneliness was gradually etching away at his sanity like rain washing away the mortar between the bricks of his mind, leaving the whole edifice unsteady and ready to topple. It was the darkness that did it; in the daylight he could push the fears to one side but at night they clustered in, crowding him and making him jump at the slightest sound.

In the bedroom above, he could hear his father shifting position. The colostomy bag made sleeping on his side awkward, but when he slept on his back he started snoring and kept waking himself up. As far as Carl could tell, his father hadn't had a good night's sleep for years. That was the trigger that had driven his mother away: first to a separate bedroom, and then to a separate house. And all Carl had to lure her back with was guilt, and the promise of a family dinner.

After testing his bomb in the wilds of the Essex salt marshes, Carl had driven into the nearest town to stock up on food and bottled water. No alcohol and no dairy or wheat products. They all aggravated his father's condition, and it wouldn't be fair of Carl to buy those things and then keep them to himself. No, he had promised himself years ago that whatever his father ate, he would eat. He didn't want his father to feel as if he was being treated as anything special.

Standing in the checkout queue, waiting for the stupid woman ahead of him to separate her shopping into various plastic bags — one for frozen items, another for fruit, a third for cans and dry goods — and then delve around in her handbag for her debit card and then again for her loyalty card, Carl began to feel a prickling on the back of his neck. Someone was watching him. He turned his head, slowly, taking in the people in the queues to either side of him. Nobody was looking in his direction, but they seemed poised, edgy, as if they'd only just turned away as his gaze scanned across them. He tried looking down and then back again quickly, trying to catch them out, but they were too quick for him. He glanced behind him, at the people in his own queue. One or two of them were looking at him and frowning. He glared back and they lowered their gaze, flushing.

He felt like calling them out, asking them why they were watching him, following him, but he knew they would deny everything and pretend they were just there to do their shopping. It wouldn't do any good, and they knew he was on to them now, which meant they would be doubly careful in future. He would just have to make sure he was even more watchful.

There was a travel agent's concession in the supermarket; an area just past the checkouts where a woman sat at a desk surrounded by brochures and posters showing blue skies and white beaches. While waiting for the incompetent checkout girl to find the barcodes on his items, Carl had found himself mesmerised by the posters. What chance did he have to take a holiday with his father the way he was? If he was out of the house for more than an hour his father would complain loudly and bitterly about what might have happened.

And there was the woman at the desk; crisp white blouse and navy blue jacket, blonde hair pulled back into a ponytail. Her fingers were thin, he noticed, the nails lacquered in blue, and she wasn't wearing a ring.

After he had paid, he walked over and pretended to be interested in one of the brochures.

'Thinking of a holiday?' she asked brightly.

He smiled back. 'I could do with one right now,' he said.

'We have some good last-minute deals on at the moment. What kind of thing were you looking for? Complete rest on a Caribbean beach, cultural excursions to historical sites in Europe or all-out adventure holiday in Asia?'

'I'm flattered you think I'm capable of an all-out adventure holiday.' He grinned to take the cheesiness out of the words.

Unconsciously her gaze flickered up and down his body, taking in the flat stomach that he took so much pride in and the way his T-shirt exposed his muscular arms, then frowning slightly when she saw the leather driving gloves he was wearing. He felt himself blush. 'I don't think you'd have any problems surviving,' she said after a moment, smiling slightly and brushing the hair from her forehead. 'Paragliding? Snorkelling perhaps? I think I've got a caving expedition in Borneo in here somewhere, although you'd need extra insurance for that one, and you probably need some previous experience of caving as well.'

'Actually,' he said, 'I was thinking more of a relaxing break. Suitcase full of books, iced coconut milk and lots of sun cream, followed by long dinners and cocktails as the sun goes down.'

She seemed to shiver slightly, and straightened up in her swivel chair. 'I'm sure we can find something like that. Holiday for two, is it? Or are you on your own?' Her gaze was challenging.

He was so caught up in the dream that he almost went along with it, but somewhere in the back of his mind he could hear his father's voice, asking what he thought he was doing. He sighed, and closed his eyes for a long moment. 'Actually, I'm looking after my father. He's . . . unable to do anything for himself. I'd need something that I could take him on as well.'

She retreated abruptly behind a transparent sheet of professionalism. 'Well,' she said primly, 'we don't do many holidays for invalids and their carers. It's not really our core business. I'm sure you could find something on the internet, if you tried.' She wouldn't even meet his gaze. He could feel the disappointment and the contempt she felt for him, bitter and corrosive. He wanted to slap her, but he knew it wouldn't change anything. What was he thinking, anyway? It wasn't as if he could ask her out, take her for dinner, spend evenings and even nights with her, not when he had to go home and make sure that his father was safe, and that his colostomy bag didn't need changing. He was tied to home by invisible chains. Dragged down by the stone.

'Well, thanks,' he said, and left.

In the car, on the way home, Carl had noticed that his arms and cheeks were itching. It got so bad that he pulled the car over and parked in a lay-by, then checked his face carefully in the mirror. His first thought was that he'd been bitten by insects out in the salt marshes, but there were no raised red areas. He slipped his gloves off. The skin from the backs of his hands to his elbows was blotchy, red and hot to the touch. The illness that was affecting his fingers was starting to spread up his arms now. He made a note to go and see his doctor again. The man would lie to him — that's what doctors did — but Carl could force him to prescribe something.

He had started the car and driven back home, wondering all the time what was happening. It hadn't been this bad before. Maybe it was a reaction to the chemicals in the Semtex. Or perhaps this wasn't just a relapse, but a worsening of the symptoms. It could be a chemical reaction to something in the house — washing powder perhaps, or a cleaning product, or the disinfectants he had to use when he was helping to empty his father's colostomy bag.

In the house, Carl pulled himself into a smaller bundle on the sofa, feeling the burn on his arms where the rash was still throbbing. He knew that he should be planning his next move, deciding where to put the bomb that he would build, but he couldn't find the energy. Inertia pressed his back into the sofa. Moving required too much effort.

The bomb led him back to the TV presenter, and before that to the taxi driver, and before that . . . His mind drifted backwards, over the various murders that he had committed, back to the first one at a Countryside Alliance demonstration. He'd not planned it — the murder had been a spur of the moment action, violence created by the energy and aggression of the riot going on around him. Carl had never forgotten that energy. The screaming, the crack of the guns as the police released their plastic bullets into the crowd, the smell of the boy who'd set himself alight with the petrol bomb. The sheer exhilarating sense of unleashing the violence that bubbled within him, of letting himself go, of finding an expression for the anger that gnawed at him, and nobody noticing.

And then there had been the expanding cloud of CS gas that had spread over the rioters. Within moments his nostrils had been prickling and he could feel a catch at the back of his throat. His eyes began to itch violently, and he had blinked several times to try and clear them. But he'd come prepared, and had managed to pull the plastic bag with a dampened handkerchief inside from his pocket and hold it over his mouth. He needed to move, and quickly. CS didn't just get into the body through the mouth and nose — it could be absorbed through the skin, if it was moist enough — and it hurt. It really hurt, to the point where you couldn't do anything else apart from think about how to stop it.

Carl had been swept along with the crowd, wet handkerchief clenched tightly to his mouth. People were choking around him, and he could feel his eyes burning. A teenager in front of him stumbled and fell. Other people kicked him and stepped on him in their panicked attempts to get past. Carl bent down to try and get him back on his feet. His face was covered with a balaclava, and he pulled it off, needing to see whether he was breathing, whether his eyes were open. He was about the same age as Carl. His nose was freckled, his hair blond, and Carl suddenly had an overriding desire to smash something into his young face, disfigure it beyond recognition. It was like a scarlet wave sweeping over him, and like a swimmer too far from shore he found himself buffeted by forces beyond his control. He reached for a half-brick on the ground, fingers closing round the rough, gritty edges. He glanced up. Nobody was looking at them. The rest of the crowd were too busy looking forward at the police or back in the direction they were retreating to pay them any attention, and the sheer press of bodies would shield them from the media cameras ahead.

Anything that happened there, in that little space, was private. Secret. Just between the two of them.

He raised the half-brick and brought it down on the teenager's nose. Skin cracked open revealing red, wet tissue and white bone. The kid's hands came up to protect himself. Carl smashed the brick down again and blood spattered across the kid's face, covering the brown freckles with crimson ones. The hands fluttered weakly. Carl raised the brick again and hammered it down on the kid's forehead. Something seemed to give way; the smooth expanse of flesh buckled, dented, crumpled inwards.

And then Carl dropped the brick and moved off into the crowd, expecting at any moment to feel a hand on his shoulder. But nothing came.

Nothing ever came.

He felt his breathing returning to normal, and his heartbeat gradually slowing. There was no sound from outside — the near-storm appeared to have abated — but it was still dark. Dawn was some time away.

Carl let himself sink back down into the sofa's warm, slightly damp embrace. He knew he should head for bed, or at least check on his father, but the effort of getting up and climbing the stairs seemed far too hard. He closed his eyes and let himself slip backwards into a restless and thankfully dreamless sleep.

Morning came slowly and unwillingly. When Carl finally awoke the sun was casting a hard-edged light through the windows and there was no sound outside save the singing of the birds. He lay for a while, mind blank, and then forced himself to get up. He had things to do. He had people to kill.

His head was muzzy, and he slowly made himself a cup of coffee, having to take each action in turn and think it through carefully — switch kettle on, take top off jar of coffee, put spoon in jar, transfer granules to cup, wait until kettle boiled, pour water into cup. The mechanical movements calmed him down, and the musky smell of the coffee cleared the mists from his head. He needed to focus. He needed to think clearly if he was going to select a place and a victim for his improvised explosive device.

Where to hide it? He wasn't aiming to cause mass panic, and neither was he aiming to cause

81

large numbers of casualties. This wasn't terrorism, after all. No, he just wanted to commit a murder, a single murder. But it didn't particularly matter whose murder it was, except that it had to meet certain criteria of age, size and sex and be done remotely, at a distance. He didn't need to know their name; just see their face before he made the final call.

For a while, as he stood at the kitchen counter, staring blindly out of the window, he considered leaving the device in a supermarket toilet, but they tended to be cleaned on a regular basis and any suspicious package would be spotted and the supermarket evacuated. Perhaps he could bury the device by the side of a road. If he chose his location carefully he could watch from cover and trigger the bomb as a car passed by. The problem was that he would only have a split second to see the driver before he pressed the button, and the vagaries of the various network providers in the UK meant that he wouldn't quite know how long it would take for the call to be connected to the mobile phone attached to the explosive. And there was no guarantee that the explosion would actually kill the driver — it might cause them to swerve or crash, but the sudden deployment of an airbag, or just a lucky combination of circumstances, might save their lives. And that would destroy his careful pattern. He could place the bomb in a lay-by and wait until a driver pulled off the road to make a call, check a map or just relieve themselves, but it could take hours of waiting until the right person turned up — the person who best fitted his criteria. The problem was that he needed to kill someone in the open, but be able to separate them from the crowd, identify them.

What about a car park? He could place the device in a bush, or bury it in the ground in one of the areas that separated the lines of parked cars, then wait in his own car until the right person parked beside the device and stepped out. It might take a while, but he was used to waiting. He could survive a few hours in a warm car with no problems, as long as he had a bottle or something to urinate into. Perhaps he could find a shopping centre or outlet village. There was bound to be a wide selection of potential victims there.

Something was bothering him about the car park idea. He sipped at his coffee, mulling the idea over. Security was likely to be an issue: there would be cameras covering the parking area, looking for car thieves, and there were likely to be security guards on patrol. And someone who sat in their car for several hours without leaving or moving was likely to attract attention, if only because people would think he was ill or suicidal or dead. No, despite the opportunities for selecting the ideal victim, the car park wouldn't work.

Something else was tugging at the edges of his mind: a potential idea that had spun off from thinking about the car park. What about a railway station? It would have to be fairly open, so that he could see the platform from various locations, but the advantage was that people usually stood still, waiting for their train. He wouldn't be catching someone in momentary transition. The device would have to be hidden quite carefully, but there were usually plenty of opportunities at a station: rubbish bins, wheelie bins, flower beds, those folding access ramps for disabled passengers that were usually left upright by a pillar. And cars with people sitting in them were rarely remarked on in station car parks; people waited for spouses, partners or friends all the time. He would have to choose the right time of day, of course — he wanted to target an individual, not a crowd, but as long as he avoided the peaks of rush hour he should be okay.

He lifted his cup to take another sip of coffee, but it was cold. He poured the dregs away into the sink. Where was the best station? Termini and major interchanges were out: he would be spotted placing the device, and there were likely to be too many passengers waiting for trains. He needed somewhere smaller, but somewhere that either had a large car park or was overlooked by another building to which he would be able to gain easy and unnoticed access. There was a particular station he remembered, near Braintree. He had travelled through it a couple of times, huddled anonymously in the corner of a carriage. It had a shopping centre of some kind just across from the station. If he could get up on the roof, he could command a perfect view of the platform.

He needed to conduct a reconnaissance of the area. Carl placed the coffee mug decisively on the counter and headed out of the kitchen, towards the outbuilding where he kept his stuff.

Bypassing the pine table with its wires and tools, Carl went into the second room. In it, on a couple of scavenged school desks, were two computers with 17-inch LCD screens — one Windows-based, one Mac — five printers, a card-encoder, an embossing machine and several piles of paper of various sizes. One of the computers was connected to a high-definition webcam that was aimed at a bare stretch of wall that Carl had painted white, as a conveniently neutral background.

On top of the filing cabinets were more animal dioramas made out of the dried-up corpses of creatures which Carl had found — or killed — out in the salt marshes. Unlike the ones in the outer room, which represented creatures in their natural habitats, Carl thought of these as more like Beatrix Potter fantasies of the ways animals would act if they had human characteristics and were subject to the same inexplicable rages. There was a rather dowdy fox, its pelt faded from red to dull beige, crumpled on the ground; a small replica knife plunged to the hilt between its visible ribs. Next to it, behind glass, was a cat, limbs contorted in the throes of arsenic poisoning. And there were more: two mice, one delicately strangling the other; a badger with its head messily removed; a seagull whose breastbone was marred by a ragged bullet hole.

In pride of place was a box containing Carl's latest creation: a rat lying on a blue silk cushion, back legs wired together and front legs spread wide, the skin of its front left leg stripped back to the bone.

It was his homage to Catherine Charnaud, but soon he would replace it with another one, just as soon as he had planted his bomb and watched to see who was unlucky enough to be passing by when he triggered it . . .

5

'Where were you between eight o'clock last night and three this morning?'

'I told you, I was trainin' with the team. Ask any of 'em. Ask the coach, he'll tell you.'

Mark Lapslie sat in the office at the back of his cottage and listened to the two voices emerging from the speakers of his computer; a Pinteresque dialogue that flickered back and forth between the grapefruit harshness of Emma Bradbury's voice and the cardboard sullenness of Catherine Charnaud's boyfriend.

'When did you start the training?'

'Five o'clock.'

'And when did you finish?'

'Ten o'clock.'

'It was dark at six. How did you manage to train in the dark?'

'The floodlights was on, weren't they?'

'You tell me. Why did the training start so late?'

'They was usin' the ground for some competition game or somethin'. We couldn't get on till it was finished.'

Lapslie could picture him, just based on the Essex accent that made the boy sound like he was speaking through a blocked nose. Or, more likely, a broken one. Face probably good-looking, in a coarse kind of way; hair cut close to his scalp; ears slightly cauliflowered from too

87

many rucks on the pitch and off. Oswald Boateng suit over a Ben Sherman shirt. No tie.

'So what did you do *after* the training finished?'

'We went clubbin'.'

'Which club?'

'China Blue in Romford.'

'Anyone see you there?'

Smugness replaced the sullenness. '*Everyone* saw us there.'

The interview had taken place the afternoon of the day before, after Lapslie and Emma had returned from the mortuary. Lapslie had not sat in on it as he knew from experience that the taste of the two voices building up in that small room would make him feel sick. Instead, Emma had copied the tape onto computer and emailed it through to him. Now, in the stillness of the hours before dawn, he could listen to it without being distracted. Listening for the sweet, tropical taste of lies, and not finding any.

'What time did you leave the club?'

'Dunno. Ask the taxi driver.'

'What's your best guess?'

'What?' He sounded confused; the dialogue slipping off the expected rails.

'Was it still dark? Was the club closing? What did it say the last time you looked at your watch?'

A vague sound as the boyfriend shifted in his seat. 'It was prob'ly around half three in the mornin'.'

'So you got a taxi home. What happened then?'

'Then I found her, didn't I? All cut up
and . . .'

Grief had its own flavour. The boyfriend's
voice hadn't obviously changed in tone, but
suddenly it tasted to Lapslie of tonic water and
bitter lemon. He winced. If he'd still been in the
room at that point, he probably would have
thrown up at the sheer intensity.

'Was there an argument?' Emma's voice asked.
'Did she want to know why you were back so
late?'

'She was dead.' Flat, but flavoured with so
much grief that Lapslie felt his mouth puckering
up. 'She was dead when I got there. And you
know somethin'? When you find out who did it,
they ain't goin' to survive to the end of their
trial. That I can promise you.'

Lapslie reached out and clicked on the screen
button that stopped the playback. He'd heard
enough. Emma had already told him that the
boyfriend had maintained his innocence all the
way through, but Lapslie had needed to hear it
for himself. And grief that intense couldn't be
faked, but it could be redirected. Perhaps the
boyfriend had discovered that Catherine Charnaud was having an affair with someone and
killed her in a fit of anger. The subsequent grief
would be genuine, but didn't prove anything.

All in all, the boyfriend was looking like a
good choice. Statistically, most murders were
carried out by someone known to the victim.
Lapslie made a note to investigate his background further. Any violent incidents, fights,
childhood pets that might have died or gone

missing . . . it was all grist to the mill.

He became aware that his mobile phone was ringing on the desk beside the keyboard: Bruch's 1st violin concerto. Usually, during the day, he set it to vibrate rather than ring, but there was no guarantee at night that it would wake him up if he was asleep. He had tried it once or twice, but had woken up to find the mobile on the floor with a message on the screen saying that he had three missed calls. The vibrations had obviously caused it to jitter across the bedside table before it had fallen off, all without waking him, and in his job Lapslie needed to be on call at all times.

'Lapslie,' he said into the mobile.

'Boss? It's Emma.'

'I was just listening to the interview. I wanted to ask you something — '

'It'll have to wait. I've just had the chief on the phone again. There's been an explosion at a railway station in Braintree, just before rush hour. One confirmed casualty. Police are already on the scene, but Rouse wants you to provide top cover.'

'Top cover?' Lapslie shook his head. 'Why do they need top cover for an explosion?'

Emma paused. 'Not a gas-main explosion. A bomb explosion. Someone planted a bomb at a railway station.'

Lapslie felt his train of thought suddenly and judderingly switch onto a divergent track. 'A bomb?' he repeated stupidly. 'In *Braintree*?'

'Yes,' she said slowly. 'A bomb. In Braintree.'

'A *terrorist* bomb?'

'Too early to tell. Don't you listen to the

radio?' She caught herself. 'No, of course you don't. Stupid. Anyway, nobody's claimed responsibility.'

Lapslie sighed. 'I ought to feel flattered that Rouse keeps calling *you* so that you can give his bad news to *me*. I take it you told him that we were working on another case?'

'I did. He said that this one needs sensitive handling, and he doesn't trust anyone else to do it apart from you. We're going to have to run both cases in parallel — the Charnaud murder and this bombing.'

'And you also reminded him that I'm physically unable to stand too much noise, and a bomb explosion at a train station is just about as noisy as it gets?'

'I did say something along those lines.'

'And?'

'And he mentioned something about getting you seconded to a study into security at football grounds. A hands-on study.'

'He's trying to get me back into harness, isn't he?'

Emma's citrus voice took on a buttery flavour of sympathy. 'It does look that way, boss.'

'Okay. I take it the army's Explosive Ordnance Disposal Team are at the scene?'

'They apparently turned up half an hour ago. Long way to come, they said. They're in the process of checking the station for other devices.'

'How long will that take?'

She made a noncommittal noise. 'They have to go through a set list of things. There's something called a 'soak time', which is the

91

amount of time that they leave an electronic timer for before they can be sure it's got to zero. They estimate another hour or so before they can declare the place clear.'

'Understood. How's the victim?'

'Pronounced dead at the scene by a local doctor who happened to be waiting for a train, but apparently there wasn't much doubt. Waiting for the pathologist to turn up now.'

'Okay. Which station?'

'Braintree Parkway.'

He thought for a second. 'I can be there within the hour,' he said, 'traffic allowing. Is the station closed?'

'Yeah, and one line is powered down, but the fast line is still working. It's not making us popular. They're just ramping up to rush hour. Rush hour there being like Happy Hour: it lasts for two hours or more.'

'It's not our job to be popular. Make sure nobody opens the station up until after we arrive.'

'Yes, boss.'

'I'll see you there.'

The roads were largely clear on the way from Chelmsford to Braintree. Once or twice Lapslie was becalmed behind a lorry trundling along the narrow country roads, but lessons learned during his advanced driving course several years before allowed him to overtake safely. Rather than swing out from behind the lorries on long stretches of road and hope that nothing was coming the other way, he held back and used bends in the road to allow him to look along the inside of the lorries as he followed them round. When the road visible round the bend was straight and clear, he moved out and zoomed past them, feeling the effortless brawn of the Saab's engine.

He spent the time ruminating darkly on Rouse, and his devious scheme for forcing Lapslie to proffer his resignation on medical grounds by giving him cases that required him to engage with noisy and chaotic humanity rather than staying in his own quiet world. One case wasn't enough — or perhaps Lapslie was dealing with it too well — so Rouse had decided to throw another one on the pile. How long would it take before Lapslie wasn't able to function any more? Perhaps Rouse and his senior colleagues were running a book on it.

In all, it took forty-five minutes from the time he left Chelmsford, and he arrived depressed and angry. By the time he pulled into the station car park the sky was a blue canvas decorated with white daubs of cloud. The air smelled fresh and slightly damp.

Lapslie felt an unaccustomed nervousness, a fluttering in his chest. He wasn't used to being outside, in uncontrolled circumstances. Anything could happen here, and he wouldn't be able to manage the noise.

The padded earphones that Emma had got for him were sitting on the passenger seat, and he debated for a moment whether to put them on or not, but while he could probably get away with it in an isolated environment where he didn't have to talk to anyone, like the Charnaud crime scene, he would look like an idiot here, wandering around wearing them. And he was likely to have to talk to people as well, so he'd have to keep on whipping them off and on again, making them as useless as a chocolate teapot. Reluctantly, he decided to leave them where they were. They would come in useful another time.

He wondered morbidly what it was like, being caught in a bomb blast. A sudden flash of light? A deafening thunder in his ears? Intolerable heat washing across his face and chest? And what would a bomb actually *taste* like? Perhaps his last few moments would have been like drowning in Turkish Delight; suffocating in sweet, gooey roses, like the scent of Heaven. Or perhaps he would instead have died choking on stagnant, foul pond water riddled with decaying leaves. Thank God, he would probably never find out.

He took a breath and forced the nervousness down, imagining it as a ball of clay that was being squeezed smaller and smaller in his stomach until it was the size of a marble, safe and manageable. He could leave it there for a while, quiescent, while he got on with the investigation.

There was an obvious official presence. Several police patrol cars were drawn up in a defensive formation near the ticket office, regardless of the strictures of the parking bays, and two army EOD vans, painted in dull khaki, were parked off to one side. Lapslie noticed that the ARMY EXPLOSIVE ORDNANCE DISPOSAL sign on the van was fixed to the side, rather than painted on, and it appeared to be hinged, with the ARMY part above the EXPLOSIVE ORD-NANCE DISPOSAL part. He wondered for a moment what the reason was, then realised with a flash of dark humour that it was probably so the army could close the sign up and drive the van around on public roads without anyone getting panicked about the possibility of a bomb in the vicinity.

Emma was standing with a couple of uniformed policemen who were chatting to some army personnel in camouflage. Ironically, the army camouflage stood out more starkly against the flat colour of the advertising hoardings than the dark blue police uniforms. They all appeared to have cups of coffee and bacon rolls. Nearby, a cluster of travellers in suits and smart clothes were standing rather forlornly in a group, like a welcoming committee who had chosen the wrong day.

A young man in a blue suit that looked more like a uniform than something he had chosen himself was standing alertly outside the station entrance. He had a name badge pinned to his breast pocket. He appeared to be looking for someone to berate, and latched onto Lapslie as soon as he saw the car.

'Euan Murray,' he said, extending his hand. 'Station Manager.' His voice was like ripe Stilton. Lapslie couldn't help wincing. He wasn't sure whether the sound of the man's voice was provoking a cross-firing of his senses or he just had chronic halitosis. The ball of clay in his stomach spasmed momentarily.

Lapslie shook Murray's hand, noticing as he

did so that the man's tie was patterned with small corporate logos of whichever network was running the trains in this part of the world. 'Detective Chief Inspector Mark Lapslie.'

'Are you in charge of this investigation?'

'I am,' Lapslie said.

'I know you're letting trains go through on the fast line without stopping,' Murray said, 'but I've got commuters stacking up here.' He looked as if he was barely out of college. Did they offer degrees in Train Line Management these days? Lapslie wouldn't have been surprised.

'I sympathise,' he said firmly, 'but I have a dead body and an explosion. That trumps your commuters. We're going to be a few more hours, I'm afraid. We'll need to search the line for evidence. There might be fragments of the bomb.'

'Or the victim,' Emma added helpfully.

Murray's face fell. He turned away, talking almost to himself. 'I'll have to arrange buses,' he muttered. 'I need to make some calls.'

'All right,' Lapslie said to Emma, 'I'm going to need coffee and breakfast. I'm guessing that since this is a station, and I can see the local plod standing around stuffing their faces, there's a snack bar around somewhere?'

'There is, according to the local team.' The grapefruit of her voice sluiced across his taste-buds, washing the mouldy cheese away. 'Does a roaring trade of a morning, by all accounts, although it usually closes down once the rush has died away.' She gestured to a nearby constable. While she gave him instructions,

Lapslie looked around. The station looked new, as did the approach roads and the car park. He wouldn't be surprised if it had only been recently added to the line, servicing the growing community as well as the retail centre whose bland, sandy exterior he could see rising above the nearby houses like anonymous, artificial cliffs.

'Okay,' he said eventually. 'Who's been keeping this thing warm for us?'

'Detective Inspector Morritt,' Emma replied. 'A bit of a prat. I've worked with him before. He's with the witnesses now.'

'Is he going to object to me taking over?'

'Big time. He's a process-Nazi, from what I've heard. He's memorised all the books and the lectures on how to deal with crime scenes of this magnitude, and he's keen to put it all into practice. Ambitious.'

'Great,' Lapslie said with feeling. 'Nothing like having a poodle yapping at your heels while you're trying to get some work done. Okay — while he's busy, let's take a look at the body.'

As they crossed the station forecourt Lapslie noticed a van drawn up to one side. A teenage lad who looked like he was half asleep was shuffling tied-up bundles of newspapers onto the kerb. Lapslie guessed that whoever ran the newsagent's concession that was almost certain to be inside would come out and untie them, ready for the commuter flow that they probably weren't going to get that morning.

As they drew closer, Lapslie caught sight of the screaming headline plastered across the front of one of the tabloids: BIG BROTHER HOUSE OF HORROR. In slightly smaller type underneath it added; *Kids' Presenter Tortured to Death*.

'Big Brother?' he asked Emma, picking up the top copy and waving it at her.

'Catherine Charnaud. She got down to the last five in *Celebrity Big Brother* earlier in the year.'

'I know I'm going to regret this, but *Big Brother*?'

She looked at him strangely. 'Sometimes I think you're like something from the nineteenth century. Are you really telling me you haven't heard of *Big Brother*?'

'Not only that: I'm proud of the fact.'

'A group of mismatched and dysfunctional people are put into a specially constructed house and have to live together for six weeks or so.'

'And?'

'And people watch them. The whole house is rigged with cameras. Well, except for the toilets, of course.'

'Of course,' Lapslie said drily. 'That would be intrusive. What happens then?'

'Every week someone gets voted off, based on their behaviour during the previous seven days. Oh, and they're set tasks, as well.'

'And she was on this thing?'

'Yeah. Did pretty well.' Emma caught herself. 'By all accounts.'

'Okay.' Lapslie sighed. 'Get someone out to the TV company — see if there were any stalkers, anything strange during the show's run. I doubt if it's relevant, but we have to be sure.' He waved

98

the newspaper. 'Because we're being watched as well.'

Emma led the way into the station concourse. The ticket barriers had been left open to facilitate the toing and froing of the police, but Lapslie still felt a momentary twinge of guilt as he walked through them and onto the station platform without a ticket.

He could smell coffee and pastry. He hoped he'd be able to get breakfast before he left.

With only a few seconds' warning, a train suddenly *shwooshed* through the station on the fast line, dragging grit and bits of paper along in its wake. Carriage wheels clattered on the rails in syncopated jazz rhythm. Lapslie's mouth suddenly overflowed with tinned peaches covered with sea salt. He could feel the grittiness of the salt in the smoothness of the syrup; the noise was that loud and that unexpected. The sensation overtook him; there was nothing else in the world; no sight, no sound and no feeling, just the overwhelming taste filling his mouth, making him cough, making him gag. He fell to his knees, hand clamped to his face. His salivary glands felt as if someone was sticking needles into them. Sweat broke out across his forehead and down his back; big, greasy droplets that became a torrent down his skin the way the saliva was a torrent down his throat. He spat, but the expectoration turned into a burp and then into vomiting as the contents of his stomach unexpectedly spilled from his mouth and nose in a brown, curdled stream. He leant forward, hands on knees, tears filling his eyes. Somewhere in the lost distance he could feel Emma's hand on his shoulder, but his only reality was the tropical heat of his skin and the burning vomit in the back of his throat still overlaid by the terrible sweetness and saltiness of the train receding in the distance. The combination of those tastes made him vomit again, his stomach twisting and sending thin brown mucus up into his mouth and onto the station platform.

'Boss? What's the matter?' The voice was far away, and the grapefruit in it only added another layer to his torment. He threw up again, bringing up nothing this time but air.

'Got to . . . get out of here,' he coughed, wiping a hand across his lips. He pulled himself upright and staggered out of the station, towards his car. Through the blurriness of the tears he was aware of people watching him go, but he didn't care. He just wanted to get into his car, his quiet car, and safety.

He leaned back in the Saab's driving seat, still feeling the burning in his nasal passages and the cold sweat on his forehead. Gradually his breathing eased.

While he was getting himself under control, Lapslie distracted himself by scanning the lead article in the tabloid newspaper that he had picked up. The piece occupied most of the front page and pages five and six as well. To his immense relief there was nothing more in the article than any diligent journalist could have found out with a couple of phone calls and a bit of doorstepping; there had obviously been a statement from the TV cable company that

100

Catherine Charnaud had worked for, as well as from her agent, and someone had managed to get a quote from a neighbour, but there were no crime scene photographs or anonymous quotes from members of the investigating team. It looked like security was holding — for the moment.

The boyfriend had sold his story to the tabloid. Lapslie hoped he'd got a good rate for it. His story was pretty much the same as the one he'd told Emma during the interview, spiced up with a gratuitous description of the terrible scene in the bedroom. Statistically he was the most likely suspect, but Lapslie was still unsure. Why the mutilation? Why the careful posing of the body?

The article was illustrated with various photographs of Catherine Charnaud. Some were obviously publicity shots, whilst others were paparazzi images of her falling out of various nightclubs or rubbing suntan cream into her shoulders on a beach somewhere. The boyfriend was present in some of the shots; a muscular figure with close-cropped blond hair and a permanent sulky frown.

Lapslie found himself staring at Catherine Charnaud's left arm in a photo that showed her lying on a beach towel, arms stretched out to either side. It was just like the pose her body had been in when he saw her in her bedroom, but his mind insisted on overlaying the image of her bloodied radius and ulna bones, scraped free of flesh.

He felt something clogging up his throat

again, and he had to shut his eyes and put the newspaper away before he could breathe properly. So young. Whatever she had done in her life, whoever she had managed to hurt on the way, she hadn't deserved even a fraction of what had been done to her.

After a while he looked out of the driver's side window; Emma Bradbury was standing outside the car, looking back at him.

He wound the window down. 'Hey — ' he started.

'Synaesthesia,' she said, wincing slightly at his breath. 'I'm sorry — it should have occurred to me that the trains going through would have caused a problem. It was thoughtless of me.'

'Not your fault,' he said, smiling weakly. 'It's never been this bad before. I thought it was stable, but . . . '

She nodded. 'We'll have to think this through. If the chief really wants you to work these cases, and if you don't want to play the sick leave card again, then we'll have to find another way to do this. There must be *something* . . . '

Behind her, four army personnel were steering a large device of some kind back along the platform. It was about the size of an armchair, and moved on six balloon tyres. A huge arm with multiple joints sat on top, next to a mast bearing a set of video cameras. The arm was so large that it seemed in perpetual danger of overbalancing the entire thing.

'What about that?' Lapslie asked.

One of the army personnel, a young, fresh-faced major, caught sight of them looking and broke off what he was doing. He approached the car, glancing from Lapslie to Emma and back, seemingly unsure which one was in charge and whether or not he should salute.

'Major McGhee,' he snapped. 'Eleven EOD Regiment.'

'Detective Chief Inspector Lapslie; Essex Constabulary. What's the story?'

'One improvised explosive device, already detonated before we arrived. Basic explosive, no chemical or biological components. We've checked the area, and we're declaring it safe. No other devices. Our job is finished now — over to you.'

'What can you tell us about the bomb?' Emma asked.

The Major shrugged. 'It was small and it was hidden in a rubbish bin. We found fragments of what appeared to be a mobile phone. That was probably what triggered it. We've left everything as close to the way we found it as we could. Forensics should still be intact.'

Emma was watching the device trundling along the platform. 'What's that?' she asked bluntly. 'Some kind of robot?'

'It's called a CUTLASS,' Major McGhee replied. 'It's a remote control manipulator, rather than a robot. No inherent intelligence, you see? It allows us to get close to a suspected device, look at it and potentially do something about it with the manipulator arm without risking a man's life. Replaced the old tracked Wheelbarrow systems that we used to have.'

'CUTLASS?' Emma frowned. 'Is that meant

to stand for something?'

The Major smiled condescendingly. 'It's a codename,' he said. 'All military projects have a codename of some kind. Okay if we peel away now? You have OpCon.'

'OpCon?' Lapslie asked blankly.

'Operational Control,' the Major smiled. 'Sorry — army slang.'

'Actually,' Lapslie said, 'hang around for a while. I want to borrow your robot.'

It only took a few minutes before he was alone inside one of the army vans, seated in front of a bank of monitors and holding a joystick in his hands. The van was air conditioned and sound-proofed, which was just what Lapslie needed. The Major had explained the principles of guiding the robot around — although he kept insisting that it wasn't a robot, it was a remote control device. As long as Lapslie didn't want to move the arm, or deploy a device for a controlled explosion, it was just like a Nintendo Wii game.

The Major had offered to have one of his corporals help Lapslie out, but Lapslie had refused. He didn't want anyone else near him at the moment. He could still taste the bitter vomit in his mouth.

On the monitors, relaying colour pictures from the remote control device, the station platform was long, and mostly deserted. To Lapslie's left a footbridge led across the tracks to the north bound platform, which was also empty. A swing door leading to what Lapslie assumed was the coffee bar was located a few feet away.

About two thirds of the way along a body lay

sprawled face up on the tarmac surface. 'Face up' was a bit of a misnomer. The front of the head was, as far as he could judge through the device's cameras, a raw mask of burned and bloody flesh draped across an expanse of singed bone. What had once been a suit was now a mass of shredded cloth.

Lapslie trundled the device along the platform towards the body. It was lying in front of a pillar which had previously been providing support to the platform roof, but was now twisted and blistered. The remains of what had probably been a waste bin looked like a large metal sunflower, the metal of its construction frozen into crystallised, razor-edged petals. An attempt had been made to separate the scene off with yellow bollards and yellow-and-black striped tape. They lent a curiously carnival air to the situation, set against the pedestrian mundanity of the station itself and the burned and tattered body.

A flicker in the corner of one screen caught Lapslie's eye. He adjusted the angle of the camera to cover the area. In the distance a train was rushing through the station; just a blur of motion on the monitor. No sound, no taste. No problem.

Lapslie stopped the device at the yellow-and-black tape, reluctant to violate the area that it enclosed, as if it was a separate world, a discrete space in which the normal rules of commuter life didn't apply. This kind of thing was not meant to happen to people, he reflected; not on a routine work day.

Close up, the body was a faceless wreck, hardly human any more. For a disconcerting moment Lapslie was thrown back to Catherine Charnaud's bedroom, where her body had been pristine, untouched except for the scouring of her arm. Here the damage was everywhere. The nameless commuter had obviously been facing the rubbish bin when the bomb inside exploded. Everything from the knees up was burned, blasted and blistered. The skin was crisped in places, and some of the body fat on the chest and arms had melted, slowed and then solidified again in yellow rivulets, like candle wax.

The man's shoes were, bizarrely, untouched. He had polished them recently, and they gleamed in the early morning light. His throat had been ripped from front to back by a sharp piece of metal debris. Inside, Lapslie could see the bruised wetness of the tissue, saliva still glistening against bubbles of blood.

His hair was still wet from the shower.

Lapslie used the controls to move the device round in a circle, angling the cameras up and down so that he could see the vicinity. He moved it closer to the platform edge and used the cameras to look over on to the track. The stones were black with diesel and dirt. Wads of greying tissue paper splattered across them showed where passengers had failed to heed the notice to wait until the train had left the station before flushing the toilet. Cigarette filters were scattered everywhere. It wouldn't be long before they outnumbered the stones. Lapslie had a feeling they might last almost as long.

He pulled back and looked around again: not at the station, but at the surrounding locality. From the place where the victim had stood there was no line of sight to anything except the tops of houses and the distant retail centre. 'There are three possibilities,' he murmured to himself, using the monologue to structure his thinking. 'Either the bomb was on a timer, or it was triggered by a sensor of some kind, or the bomber triggered it remotely, using a control. If it was remote controlled then the bomber needed to be watching from somewhere that provided a good view. Even if it wasn't remotely controlled then the bomber might well have wanted to watch what happened. And if I were them, I'd have watched from — ' he zoomed the camera in on the corner of a distant building until it filled the monitor ' — the roof of that shopping centre . . . '

He left the remote control device where it was and got out of the van. Emma was waiting outside for him. As the two of them moved off towards Lapslie's car, the army moved in to recover their device and close the equipment down.

'According to witnesses who knew him, his name is Alec Wildish,' Emma said. 'He lives about fifteen minutes' walk away. I've dispatched a constable to the house.'

'Witnesses?'

Emma gestured towards the coffee bar. 'Taking statements now, but so far nobody has told us anything useful. Apparently he was a regular commuter: used to smile and say 'Good

107

morning' to a few of the others, but nothing more social than that. He'd arrived a few moments before, and he was standing by himself near the edge of the platform. There was a sudden blast and a ball of flame, and he was thrown backwards. People thought it was a firework at first: apparently the kids around here sometimes throw bangers at the houses. He hit the ground hard. Some of the witnesses tried to help him, but he died within a few moments. Not a nice way to go.'

'Did he say anything?'

'Nothing anybody could understand. Apparently every time he opened his mouth he sprayed blood everywhere. I wouldn't mind having shares in the dry-cleaning business around here: I'd clean up. As it were.' Emma suddenly looked shocked. 'Listen to us,' she said. 'Are we really talking about someone setting off bombs on a station platform? This isn't Basra or Islamabad, this is Braintree!'

'Until we've got a better explanation, that's the one we work on.' He paused. 'The question we have to answer, of course, is: was he a specific target, or was he chosen randomly?' He was partly talking to Emma, but partly also talking to himself. 'A search of his house will help establish that. Evidence of a stalker, connections to organised crime, anything to do with animal research that may have attracted the attention of the Animal Liberation Front . . . We need to check with SOCA that he's not on their radar as well. Check his bank account for suspicious payments going out or coming in . . . Need to find out where he worked, as well, just in case there's a connection. If he was in a position of financial responsibility in a bank or a financial organisation of some kind then there might be some connection to extortion or a theft of some kind. Perhaps he was facilitating some kind of white-collar crime and fell foul of the gang he was working with . . . '

'Grasping at straws, aren't we, boss?'

He smiled. 'Well it's not going to be a fight over a parking space at the local sports centre, is it?'

'According to the stuff in his rucksack, he was apparently the manager at an electronics retailer in Oxford Street. I can't see a connection coming out of that.'

'Neither can I. That probably puts paid to the Animal Liberation Front theory.'

A disturbance near the entrance made him glance in that direction. A small group of people dressed in papery white coveralls was approaching. They all held bags or toolkits of various kinds. The man in the lead was small, in his fifties, with a quiff of hair that stuck straight up above his head.

'DCI Lapslie,' he called, his voice like some musty fruit wine in Lapslie's mouth. 'A pleasure to see you again. Busy few days, isn't it? Got an interesting one here, I understand. It'll make a change from the late night bottle fights outside nightclubs.'

'Mr Burrows.' Lapslie gestured to the station. 'Not quite up to the peculiar standards set by the Catherine Charnaud murder, but you might find some elements of interest. There's a potential crime scene elsewhere as well, but we're trying to pin it down now. I'd offer breakfast, but there's a coffee bar just over there. Get whatever you need to keep yourselves going and submit an invoice later.'

Burrows nodded. 'Talking of the Charnaud murder,' he said, 'the knife that was used came from the kitchen. It's an *Usuba bocho*: a Japanese vegetable knife — carbon steel blade. And the ties that were used to secure her and cut off the blood supply to her arm were taken from the kitchen as well. There was a pile of them in a drawer. The report's on your desk.'

'Thanks,' Lapslie said. While Burrow's people knelt around the taped-off area and started to unpack their kit, the lead CSI himself stood back and took in the whole scene.

'You want breakfast?' Emma asked Lapslie. 'They were running short of bacon the last time I looked. Surprising how much a group of coppers can get through, given half a chance.'

'Why do you think they call us Pigs? No, I don't think I fancy it now. Thanks anyway. I think I'll head off. This place — I don't think I can stand it much longer. I'm not sure I can stand anything much longer.'

As Sean Burrows and his team were entering the station, a tall man with dark hair brushed straight back off his forehead appeared. He was wearing a suit that looked better than Lapslie's. Seeing Lapslie, he crossed the forecourt towards him.

'DI Morritt,' he said. His voice, strangely, had

no taste to it. None at all. 'And you are?'

'DCI Lapslie,' Lapslie said quietly.

'Ah. I heard you were taken ill. Not used to seeing dead bodies at your rank?'

Lapslie refused to rise to the bait. 'You've met my sergeant?'

Morritt nodded. 'She apprised me of the situation earlier. I've got to say that I don't think we need any help on this one.'

Lapslie shrugged. 'We can dance around like this all night. It doesn't get us anywhere. Chief Superintendent Rouse assigned me to this case. You can get on with the process; I'll get on with the investigation. That way we'll both be happy.'

Dismissing an indignant Morritt from his thoughts, Lapslie gazed along the side of the station to where the platform projected out, protected by a wire. Some of Burrows's Crime Scene Investigators were still clustered around the body, but two of them had crossed to the other platform via the footbridge and were crouched on the blackened stones, examining the area between the platform and the tracks, beneath where travellers would normally stand. One of them turned, waving to Burrows.

'We've got fragments,' he shouted.

'Bag 'em and tag 'em,' Burrows called back. 'We'll identify them later. And keep looking. I want to be able to recreate that bin and everything in and around it.'

Everything save Alec Wildish, Lapslie mused.

He turned back to Emma. 'If Burrows is right, and all the equipment used to torture and murder Catherine Charnaud was present at the scene, that tells us something about the killer. It implies that they came unprepared, that they just made use of whatever was at hand. I need that criminal profiler on board as soon as possible. Any joy on that?'

Emma nodded. 'I spoke to the preferred profiler in this area yesterday evening. She's happy to help. Former lecturer in criminology at Essex University, and she's written a handful of books on the subject. Very competent, apparently, although a bit prickly to work with. I'm trying to set up a meeting with her.'

'What's her name?' Lapslie asked, half his attention on Sean Burrows's team.

Emma consulted her notebook. 'Whittley,' she said. 'Eleanor Whittley.'

6

There was someone following him.

Carl Whittley was driving along a dual carriageway on the way back from Braintree and his successful explosion. Everything had gone perfectly, and he had felt warm and proud and aroused. He had deliberately chosen a route that took him in a wide curve, via several small towns and villages, in order to avoid being too direct about his final destination.

But now someone was following him. He knew it, for sure. It wasn't as if he could see anyone who was taking more than a cursory amount of interest in him, but someone was out there. He was certain.

The police? He supposed it could be, but surely if they suspected what he had done then they would pull him over straight away and arrest him. They wouldn't let him keep on going, would they? Perhaps it was someone else, but who?

His hands tightened on the wheel of his car, but he was careful not to let his foot press too heavily on the accelerator pedal. He didn't want an unexpected change in speed to give away to his pursuer that they had been spotted.

He checked in his rear-view mirror, cautious not to move his head while he did so, just flicking his gaze upwards for a few seconds, scanning the road behind him.

There were five cars visible in his mirror. Quickly he memorised their key features; one was a black cab with its radiator grille partially blocked by a piece of white card, another had a squarish bumper and an emblem that stuck up above the bonnet; a third had one wing mirror missing. It was unlikely that any pursuer would drive anything so noticeable, but at least he could factor those vehicles out of his calculations and concentrate on the remaining two, which had no distinguishing features and were new enough and painted that anonymous silver that usually meant they were hire cars.

Paradoxically, it would be easier at night to spot being followed. He'd noticed that many cars had headlights that were slightly offset or operated at different levels of brilliance. Taking away all the confusing factors of size, shape and colour, and just concentrating on the distinctive way the lights varied, it should be possible to pin down whether a particular car was spending too long behind you.

Carl's hands were damp inside the gloves, the skin hot and itchy. He could feel a fluttering sensation in his stomach, and a flat, bitter taste in his mouth. The fight or flight response was kicking in; adrenalin was pumping around his system, making him jumpy.

He jerked his attention back to the road. There was a town coming up and he decided to take some evasive action, just to see whether anyone followed, or even gave themselves away by a momentary jerk of the wheel before they caught themselves and continued on their way. The road was heading for a roundabout, and the two lanes of the dual carriageway were marked separately; one for turning left only, one for continuing straight on or turning right.

There were no other cars near him; just the five that occupied his rear-view mirror. Gradually, Carl let his car drift so that it was straddling the white line marking the boundary between the lanes. The roundabout was getting closer and he looked in his mirror again. Two of the cars — the taxi and the one with the square bumper — were moving into the outside lane. The car with the wing mirror missing and one of the two anonymous silver ones were drifting left, into the inside lane.

The fifth car, the other silver one, couldn't make its mind up. Like Carl, it was straddling the white line. Perhaps its driver didn't know which way to go at the roundabout. Or perhaps they were leaving their options open, waiting to see what he did.

As the roundabout loomed ahead, filling his windscreen, he turned the steering wheel left, letting his car slide across the road into the inside lane just as he hit the parallel yellow lines that marked the last few metres. He didn't signal. Let them think he might still be going straight ahead, just from the wrong lane.

Behind him, the silver car did the same.

There was a red car entering the roundabout from his right, signalling to go right. He turned the wheel hard left, hearing his tyres screech as his car shot onto the roundabout in front of the approaching car. A horn blared behind him but he was concentrating on making sure that his own car came out straight on the left hand exit from the roundabout.

He risked a glance at his rear-view mirror. The driver of the red car was making a gesture at him. More importantly, the silver car had slotted in behind it and was signalling left.

The left hand exit from the roundabout led onto a single carriageway road. A hundred yards further on, a side road was signposted for a superstore. He turned late, without signalling, into the superstore's car park, aware that the silver car was behind him again. It signalled late to peel off into the car park, after him.

The car park was about two thirds full. Carl drove slowly but steadily past rows of cars, past the wider parking slots for families with toddlers and for disabled drivers, right up to the pick-up point in front of the store, and then past it, turning right to head out of the car park again, past the inevitable petrol station, dividing his gaze equally between the view through the windscreen and the reflection in his rear-view mirror. If the silver car followed him all the way out of the car park then he would know that it was following him.

It slowed, and darted in to the pick-up point. A woman standing in front of the store with a trolley full of shopping started forward, signalling to the driver.

Carl felt the itch on the back of his neck fade away to a tickle, and then to just a memory. Perhaps the car had been following him and its driver had quickly arranged a fall-back story to reassure him when they realised that he had seen them. Or, more likely, it had all just been a misapprehension on his part.

He was getting jumpier and jumpier recently. Little things were setting him off — people looking away when he glanced towards them, curtains that twitched as he walked past houses, conversations that suddenly went quiet or obviously switched topic when he walked into shops. Part of his mind knew that he was being spooked by nothing, that he was building innocent events into an edifice of fantasy, but another part, an older, more primal part, kept jumping at every shadow and flickering flame.

He drove cautiously out of the superstore car park, still peripherally aware of the cars around him. He headed back to the dual carriageway. Time to go back to the house. He felt safer there than he did anywhere else. And once there, he could start planning the next operation; the next death. Not an explosion this time, but something else. Something different.

The drive back to Creeksea took him along increasingly isolated roads and through scattered villages consisting of a few houses and the occasional shop. The roads were raised on banks a foot or so above the level of the surrounding fields, and every so often they turned in the middle of nowhere where the car diverted around the corner of something that had existed, years before, but had been lost to nature. Some of the fields lining the roads were overgrown, some were barren, and some had big, rectangular bales of hay piled up at their edges in blocks the size of houses. And always, as he drove, there was a quality of light in the sky indicating that somewhere just out of sight was the relentless expanse of the North Sea.

He knew he was getting close to Creeksea when the road began to parallel the single rail track that led from Colchester towards the coast and the ferry port. Just before the slip road leading off to the estate was a side road that led to a chainlink fence. Behind the fence was an area of ground that had been bought for a planned expansion by the company who built the estate, but never used. Carl parked out of sight of the road, just in front of the chain-link fence. Retrieving his own licence plates from where he had left them, wrapped in plastic bags beneath a pile of bricks, he took a screwdriver from the boot of his car, removed the fake number plates that he had been using and substituted his own. Rumour had it that there were digital number-plate recognition systems being installed on all major roads that could identify passing cars, checking them against a database of suspect vehicles, and could count the number of times a particular car passed the same point in a short period of time and send a warning out that someone might be conducting a reconnaissance for a planned terrorist atrocity. With a bomb planted in a Braintree station the police would probably consult all the records they could get to, looking for cars acting suspiciously. If they found his car on a frame of video, Carl didn't want them tracing it back to him.

Just because he was paranoid it didn't mean

118

that they *weren't* out to get him, after all. And they did have good reason. At least ten good reasons.

The fake plates he rewrapped in the plastic bags and placed beneath the bricks, just in case he might need them again. Then he removed the tax disc from the holder on the windscreen and replaced it with one that was identical apart from the fact that the licence number matched his own, not the fake one. That one was registered to Chris Ashwell — a fake identity that he had created for himself some years before, and still periodically updated.

His father called down the stairs immediately the front door closed.

'Carl? At last! I need to talk to you.'

He quickly checked himself over. Nothing that would give away what he'd been doing.

He took the stairs two at a time. His father was sitting up in bed, yesterday's newspaper beside him on the bed.

'Dad, are you okay?'

His father looked at him quizzically. 'I was dozing. Before that I was reading the paper. There's nothing happening in the world. It's all old news.'

'Can I get you anything? A cup of tea?'

Nicholas thought for a moment. 'I'd like to come downstairs later, if that's all right. I feel like watching TV for a while.'

'Okay, I'll help you. Can I have a bath first?'

'Of course.'

'And I'll prepare dinner while you're watching TV.'

A hesitant expression crossed Nicholas's face. 'Is your mother still coming to dinner? That is tonight, isn't it?'

'It is, and she is. In fact, I'll give her a quick ring while the kettle's boiling to check what time she's planning on coming over.'

Downstairs, Carl picked up the handset and pressed the memory button for his mother's number.

'Eleanor Whittley, hello?'

'Mum, it's Carl. I wanted to check what time you were coming round.'

A pause. 'Coming round?'

Carl began to get a cold feeling around his stomach. She was going to cancel. Again. 'Coming round for dinner. You said you were going to. Dad's been looking forward to it.'

'Sorry, I meant to let you know. I had a call earlier from the police.'

Carl took a deep breath. 'You've got a job?'

'With Essex Constabulary. They want me to consult on a murder case. You may have heard about it on the news: a girl, a newsreader of some kind. There are details about the case that mean they need an expert in abnormal psychology.'

Carl felt light-headed. Finally, after all this time, it had happened. His mother would be examining one of the murders that he had committed! He felt as if he had been wrapped in cotton wool, as if he were detached from the world and everything around him was slowly tilting to one side.

'Carl?'

He snapped back. 'Sorry. I was just . . . just thinking how good it is that you've got something to interest you.'

'It's not just interest; it's a great deal of money. Money we need.'

'Yeah, sorry. When are you seeing them?'

'I will be meeting the investigating officer at the crime scene this afternoon. After that I'm going to have to spend several hours going over my notes and my first impressions, transforming them into a potential psychological profile of the killer. It's going to take some time, and I can't afford any distractions. I'm sure you understand how important this is to me.'

'Of course I do.' He paused. 'You could pop round later. For supper.'

'I need to make my notes as soon as possible after seeing the crime scene, otherwise I might lose those precious vital first impressions. I'll ring tomorrow. We'll reschedule.'

'Okay.' He paused, wanting to find out more but uncertain how to proceed without raising her suspicions. Then it struck him. 'Hey — why don't I drive over and pick you up this afternoon, then drive you down to Chigwell? It's a longish drive, and it'll give you a chance to catch up on the details of the case and think it through, rather than tire yourself out driving. You know how you hate wasting time behind the wheel.'

He wanted to go on, reinforcing the point, but he held himself back. His mother hated to feel as if she was being pushed into anything.

Her voice was cautious. 'Are you sure you can spare the time?'

'Of course. I haven't seen you for weeks, and I was expecting to see you tonight anyway.'

'What about your father?'

Your father. Not *Nicholas.* Not *my husband.* 'I'll make sure he's got food and water. He'll be fine watching TV.'

A pause. 'Well, it would give me a chance to review the facts. And I wasn't looking forward to driving.'

'Okay, it's a date,' he said, not giving her a chance to talk herself out of it. 'Pick you up about three o'clock?'

'Okay. Thank you, Carl.'

With a bath run, his father's tea and the news about his mother delivered and a mug of coffee perched on the edge of the tub, he stripped off and stepped into the steaming water. Warmth spread like a slow death through his body, and he sank deeper in the water until just his face and his knees were exposed to the cold air.

The skin on his arms was still red and prickly, and the heat of the bath was uncomfortable against it. There were patches of redness across his chest as well, and he could feel it on his back. What the hell was happening? He *really* needed to see a doctor.

He tried to put the skin rash from his mind. The bath might ease it, and if not he had some E45 cream that he usually used on the skin around his father's colostomy stoma — the opening that had been created when his resectioned large intestine had been attached to his stomach wall. The opening through which all of his food now emerged into a plastic bag which Carl had to empty out and clean every day.

No. Don't think about that. Think instead about Catherine Charnaud, and what you did to her, because you're going to be able to relive it all through your mother's investigation, even if she isn't aware of it.

Relaxing in the placental caress of the bath, Carl let himself drift back, recreating from his memories the architecture of that long and bloody evening . . .

★ ★ ★

The night air was crisply cold, and a light frost was blanching the grass borders outside the walled fronts of the houses. Carl let his left foot relax on the clutch pedal as his car drifted along the road. The engine choked a couple of times, then stalled and died. He let the car drift under its own momentum, turning the wheel until the vehicle ran to a halt against the kerb. He twisted the key a couple of times in the ignition but left the clutch in first gear. The engine failed to catch.

He got out of the car and looked around, letting an expression of mild worry tighten his face, scrunching his eyes and mouth up. It was just past midnight. The sky was wisped with cloud and decorated with stars. There were no other cars on the road, and no lights on in the houses behind their high walls.

Carl's breath clouded in front of his face. He

leaned back into the car and released the bonnet catch, then walked around to the front and pulled the bonnet up, propping it in place with a hinged rod inside. The massive block of the engine steamed slightly in the cold, and clicked like a metal insect as it cooled. Warmth radiated off it. He stood back, hands on hips, staring at the engine as if he had no idea what it was.

He stood there for a few minutes, leaning forward every now and then as though he was fiddling with something inside, although he didn't actually touch anything — acting for an audience that almost certainly didn't exist. Eventually he stepped back and reached into his pocket for a small silvery object that looked for all the world like a mobile phone. He tapped the 'on' button, taking care not to over-dramatise the gesture, then tapped it again and shook his head. It wasn't a mobile phone at all, but nobody watching — in the unlikely event that anyone *was* watching — would know that.

He heard a car engine in the distance. It got louder. He knew the sound — it was Catherine Charnaud's Vauxhall Tigra, and it was right on time.

Every weekday night Catherine finished the Ten O'Clock News broadcast, and then got changed, had her make-up removed and left the offices of the cable TV channel where she worked. She went to a nearby bar with a handful of colleagues — a small core of regulars and a wider corona of hangers on, and had a few cocktails. A smaller group then went on to a nightclub for an hour or so while Catherine left at half past eleven. She was invariably alone. The drive from the nightclub to her home in Chigwell took thirty minutes at that time in the morning. Carl had been watching her every night for two weeks. Some nights her footballer boyfriend was home, but on Tuesday nights he trained late and then went for a Chinese with his teammates and then on to a nightclub. She would be alone until about five a.m.

As the Vauxhall Tigra got closer, Carl stepped back from the car. He didn't try and flag the Tigra down, didn't even try and make eye contact with the driver. He just tried to keep the worried look on his face. People in Catherine Charnaud's position were wary of approaches and entreaties. The newsreader had to think this was her idea.

The Tigra's revs dropped, then rose again as the car swept past Carl and turned towards the gates of the house. If Carl heard the gate mechanism *whirr* into life then he knew that the two weeks of surveillance had been wasted, but the car just sat there, motor still running, as the newsreader debated what to do. Carl raised his mobile again and pressed the 'on' button, then shook his head.

He heard the Tigra's door open. The engine was still running.

'Are you okay?' Catherine Charnaud's voice was familiar from the television but, despite two weeks of surveillance, not something that Carl had heard for real before. It was lighter and slightly more breathless than on television.

Carl turned, making sure that his expression

was a mixture of embarrassment and eagerness, trying to make himself as small and unthreatening as possible. He'd deliberately dressed in clothes that made him look more like a teenager, emphasising his slight stature. 'My engine just . . . died,' he said. 'It can't be the petrol — I filled it up yesterday. I don't know much about cars. I've only been driving a few months.'

Catherine was wrapped up in a bulky suede jacket. Her face was blotchier than it appeared on TV, when it was covered in make-up. 'You probably need to call a mechanic,' she said, maintaining her distance. Her face was fixed, professional.

Carl winced. 'Battery's flat on my mobile,' he said, holding the object in his hand up as if Catherine could spot a discharged battery from ten feet away. 'I meant to charge it up this morning, but I had to help my dad get up and time just got away from me. He's an invalid.' He paused, letting a worried expression cross his face. 'He'll be worried sick about me.'

Catherine was obviously dubious. She probably had too much experience of paparazzi and gutter journalists trying to fool their way into the house she shared with her footballing boyfriend, but Carl was counting on his own youth and innocence and her natural, instinctive helpfulness not having been completely obliterated by the protective armour of celebrity.

'You're out very late,' Catherine said: more of a holding gambit than anything else while she evaluated Carl.

'I'm a nurse,' Carl said, the explanation

pre-prepared as one of the more reassuring ones he could use. 'I was on the late shift.'

'This is a cul de sac, you know? Did you get lost?'

Carl grimaced, and looked around. 'When the engine cut out, I managed to get it to coast around the corner,' he said. 'I felt too vulnerable out on the main road at this time of night. I thought I could wait here until the mechanic arrived.' He waved the thing in his hand. 'And then this failed. It's just not my evening.'

Catherine's expression softened noticeably. She was going to fall for it. 'Do you want to use my mobile?' she said.

'Oh, I couldn't possibly . . . ' Carl said, then, ' . . . well, if you don't mind.' He took the proffered phone and made a big play of consulting a card in his wallet before tapping out a number. In fact, the number he was using was that of a firm of mechanics that he had memorised earlier that day, one he knew closed at five o'clock.

'McGilivray Recovery is now closed,' a tinny voice said.

'Hello?' He pressed the mobile closer to his ear so that Catherine couldn't hear.

'Our hours of business are eight a.m. until six p.m. Please phone back between those times.'

'My name is Dominic Hawely. My car has died. Could someone come and take a look at it?'

'Your custom is important to us,' the voice said reassuringly.

'I'm afraid I don't know my membership

number,' Carl continued, ignoring what the recorded message was saying. 'My dad usually handles that kind of thing.' He paused while the dial tone cut in, listening, then gave the fake licence number of his car and a fake address fifteen miles away in East London. 'Can't you get someone out faster than that? No, I understand. I'm in Holy Cross Road, Chingford. I don't know the postcode. Okay, thank you.' He cut the call and handed the mobile back to Catherine. 'All of their vans are out at the moment,' he said apologetically. 'Apparently they can't even guarantee they'll be here within an hour. I suppose I'll just have to wait in the car. They'll phone when they're nearby.'

Catherine's face was a picture of indecision. 'Why not come in and have a coffee?' she said eventually and slowly. 'I'd hate to think of you out here by yourself. I mean, the area's safe and everything, but it's late, and you never know.'

Carl smiled hesitantly. 'Thanks for the offer,' he said, 'but you probably want to get to bed. I'll be fine.' He glanced around with just the right degree of uncertainty. 'Really, I will.'

'I wouldn't hear of it,' Catherine said. 'Come on in. I work late myself, so I can afford to sleep in. Look, I'll drive the car in and you follow. It's only a short walk to the house. I'll meet you by the front door.'

She smiled at Carl, and Carl smiled back. Catherine headed for her car, pressing a small remote control as she did so. The gates to the house swung open. Catherine climbed into her car, engine still idling, and put it in gear, then

128

glanced over to see whether Carl was following. Carl waved encouragingly, and Catherine drove through the gates. Carl followed. The difficult part of the job was done. All he had to do now was kill the girl.

The house was close to the gate, separated only by a few yards of pebbled driveway. It was large, square, new, and probably had five or six bedrooms. Security lights illuminated the red-brick construction. Carl immediately noticed the security cameras. He would have to find out where their signals were recorded to and delete them, or trash the system.

Catherine parked in front of the house, and climbed out of the car. Carl joined her as the gates were closing, cutting them off from the commonplace world outside. People like Catherine and her footballer boyfriend wanted all the advantages of living in a city without the disadvantages of neighbours. The problem was, as Catherine was about to find out, that isolation in the heart of civilisation had its downside.

Based on his previous surveillance, Carl knew he had at least four hours before the boyfriend came home. That should be enough time, but it was worth checking. 'What about your husband?' he said hesitantly. 'We won't be disturbing him, will we?'

'It's my boyfriend, and he called me earlier,' Catherine said as she slid a key into the door. 'He won't be back until sunrise. We keep strange hours around here.' She opened the massive front door. An electronic whistle started up, slicing through the cold night air, and she typed a set of numbers into a keypad just inside the lobby. The whistle cut out. 'Security,' Catherine muttered. 'Bane of my life.'

'But so necessary,' Carl murmured. He still had the object that resembled a mobile phone, even down to the bright LCD screen, in his hand. He pressed a button on the side and two prongs sprang out from just above the screen. Jabbing the prongs into Catherine's exposed neck he pressed the large red 'call' button.

Eight hundred thousand volts shot from the stun gun batteries into Catherine Charnaud's nervous system. She jerked as every muscle in her body contracted, then dropped gracelessly to the floor. Carl pushed her further inside the lobby with his foot, then shut the door behind him. It closed with a definitive *thunk*.

The hall was carpeted in a deep-pile wool in a pastel blue. The stairs were bare wood, probably oak. Carl needed somewhere he could immobilise the girl and get to work on her. The bedroom would probably be best — he could tie the girl's hands to the headboard, assuming there was a headboard, and the placing of the body would have a neat kind of erotic symbolism about it that would send the police off in entirely the wrong direction.

Carl gazed down at the vaguely twitching body. Perhaps he should have waited until Catherine was upstairs, but coming up with an excuse to get both of them up there without it looking like he was trying to seduce the girl might have been tricky. Perhaps the seduction line might have worked, but there was no guarantee. Not with only four hours until the boyfriend came home, unless Catherine liked living dangerously or the boyfriend liked threesomes.

He bent down and, taking one of Catherine's arms, turned her over then pulled her to a sitting position. Crouching, Carl pulled the girl's arm over his shoulder and then straightened up, bringing her with him in the standard 'fireman's lift'. She was light — verging on the anorexic — and Carl could carry her up the stairs with relative ease.

The main bedroom was easy to find. It was obviously Catherine's house, judging by the way the room was decorated. Carl couldn't imagine a footballer choosing it of his own accord. Fortunately, the bed did have a headboard. He bent over and allowed Catherine to slump onto the duvet. The girl's eyelids were flickering and she was still twitching. The marks where Carl had jabbed the prongs into Catherine's neck were blistered slightly, and red, but there was no blood. A few more minutes and she would be able to move properly. Carl had to work fast.

He went rapidly down the stairs and into the kitchen. Quickly he checked the various drawers, looking for string, electrical wires, anything he could use to restrain the girl. He located a couple of mobile phone chargers that might suffice and was about to pull them out when he discovered, at the back of the drawer, a handful of plastic ties — the ones that plumbers used to attach lagging to pipework. Next to them were a couple of squash balls which he scooped up as well. He took them upstairs. The girl was stirring. Taking her wrists in turn, he bound them to the headboard, making sure that they were attached firmly and that no amount of pulling would loosen them.

He anticipated quite a lot of pulling before he was through.

The girl's ankles he bound to the bed frame using more ties. There was always a chance that Catherine might manage to kick him, either deliberately or accidentally, in her agonised thrashing around, and he wanted to avoid that if at all possible.

Catherine's eyes were clearing now. She gazed up at Carl in disbelief.

Carl leaned forward and, taking a squash ball from his pocket, shoved it hard into Catherine's mouth, pushing it firmly past her small white teeth. Catherine gagged, bucking against the restraints.

Carl stood back and critically examined his handiwork. A couple more touches, and he would be ready to proceed.

He headed downstairs again. In the kitchen — stark pine and tiles he now had time to notice — he found a pair of scissors obviously designed for shearing through meat. He also found a set of what looked like Japanese carbon-steel kitchen knives in a wooden block. He chose one which was small, fitting neatly in his hand, and viciously sharp. That would do nicely, he decided.

He headed back up the stairs, aware suddenly that his bladder was full. Instead of heading into the bedroom, he diverted into the bathroom.

Dropping his chinos he quickly emptied his bladder, noticing with dismay that the urine was dark purple in colour. There was no doubt about it. The illness was back again. He flushed the toilet, making sure he used a piece of toilet paper to hold the handle so as not to leave any fingerprints. The toilet paper was thrown into the bowl before the water had finished sluicing around the porcelain.

Back in the bedroom, Catherine was fully aware now, pupils dilated in shock. Her wrists and ankles were red where she had been trying to pull herself free.

Without saying anything, Carl leaned over the girl with the shearing scissors in his hand. Catherine froze, then shook her head violently. Carl smiled reassuringly. 'Don't worry,' he said. 'These scissors aren't for hurting you.'

Catherine looked confused. A flash of hope crossed her face.

'No,' Carl said, 'they're just so I can remove your clothes.' He held up the Japanese kitchen knife which he was holding in his other hand. 'This is the one that's going to hurt you,' he said.

7

The car park of the retail centre was eerily deserted as Mark Lapslie and Emma Bradbury drove in. A few cars — cleaners probably, or security staff — were clustered close to the main doors. One car, further away, looked as if it had been abandoned by joy-riders; the tyres were under-inflated, and the paintwork had a layer of dust over it that suggested it had been sitting there for a few days. Lapslie thought he could just make out a yellow *Police Aware* sign stuck on the windscreen. Not that it meant anything; he remembered a case some years before where a police patrol had been called out to an abandoned car and dutifully stuck a *Police Aware* sign on the windscreen before driving off, blissfully unaware that the car's owner was sitting, dead, in the driver's seat, victim of a sudden heart attack.

A large sign by the entrance to the car park welcomed shoppers, and provided the information that the outlet would be open daily from 10:00 to 20:00 (16:00 on Sundays). Lapslie checked his watch as Emma drove her Audi diagonally across the empty bays. 09:00; still an hour to go before the shops opened: time enough to get a look up on the roof for evidence of an observer, possibly a bomber, before the crowds descended in search of a bargain; before their incessant chatter caused the taste of dried blood to settle like sediment in Lapslie's mouth for the rest of the day.

He was still feeling nauseous from his reaction to the passing train earlier on. His joints were aching, and he could feel a strange pulsing pain that seemed to radiate up his neck from his chest along the line of his carotid arteries. He'd never felt this bad before. He wasn't even sure if this was the synaesthesia or some other problem — a virus, perhaps. Whatever it was, it was progressively stopping him from carrying on the investigation. Investigations, plural, he reminded himself.

Emma pulled up in a disabled bay by the doors. Lapslie raised an eyebrow at her.

'All those empty slots, and you have to choose the one that's actually illegal to park in.'

'You're synaesthetic. That must count as a disability.'

He thought for a moment. 'I might be missing a trick there.'

Together they walked to the entrance of the shopping centre. The automatic doors weren't working, but Emma found that one of the ordinary doors to the side was unlocked. She opened it, and they walked in.

The interior of the centre was cavernous, echoing. The main thoroughfare stretched ahead of them like the nave of some modernistic cathedral, lined with shops and with other thoroughfares crossing it every hundred yards or so. Skylights in the roof let in a general glow of illumination that seemed to eradicate any shadows. Lapslie breathed in, wondering if there

135

would be any trace of the crowds who had presumably thronged there for ten hours the day before, but he could detect nothing apart from an antiseptic pine scent, left over presumably by the cleaners who had scoured the place of chewing gum, sweet wrappers and shoe-scuffs on the polished tiles overnight. There was a sense of expectancy in the air, of waiting, of a place that had no meaning, no definition unless it was full of people milling around.

'Look,' Emma said, turning to face him, 'do you want me to go and do this? You can wait in the car. Keep in touch via your mobile, if you need to. If there's anything I think you need to see I can take a photo on my BlackBerry and send it through to you.'

Her voice reverberated in the empty halls, the grapefruit essence of it doubling and redoubling until Lapslie's entire world seemed tainted by it and his mouth screwed up against the bitterness. He was tempted to accept her offer. Tiredness was hampering his movements, and a headache was settling just behind his eyes and looked like it was there to stay for a while. He thought longingly of the headphones back in his car.

'Thanks,' he said eventually, 'but I'm not completely disabled yet. I can still climb stairs and look around. If things get too bad I'll just come back and let you get on with it.'

A security guard turned a corner ahead of them. 'Sorry!' he called, 'but we're not open for another hour.' His voice was dry ash and candy-floss.

'You are for us,' Emma said loudly. 'Police.'

The guard came closer, frowning. He had the look of someone who loved being in uniform but wasn't fit enough or disciplined enough to join the army or the police. 'I didn't hear no alarms go off. Has one of the shops been broken into? Or is it that car outside? We keep reporting it, but nothing happens.'

'It's not the shops and it's not the car. We need access to your roof.'

He shook his head automatically. 'No access to the roof.'

'Let me repeat myself,' Emma said patiently. 'Police. We need access to the roof. Which part of that wasn't clear?'

'I don't have no keys,' the guard said, surly and obviously uncomfortable that the conversation had deviated from the set patterns of his usual interchanges with the public.

'Then find out who does, and get them here.' Emma looked at her watch. 'Twenty minutes, then I'm going to find the door to the roof myself and break it down with a crowbar if I have to.'

In the end it took five minutes and a furtive radio conversation between the guard and his supervisor to locate the keys in a cupboard in the grandly named 'security suite' — actually a whitewashed room with a coffee-stained carpet, a kettle and a bank of TV monitors showing different black-and-white views of the empty thoroughfares. The cameras had been fixed in place for so long that the straight lines of the shop fronts — their windows, their doors and the edges where they butted up against the floor tiles

— had become etched by cathode rays into the phosphor of the monitors, and the occasional passing security guard or cleaner looked like a ghost drifting past. It occurred to Lapslie that when the thoroughfares were full of shoppers it must look like a river flowing between ancient and immovable banks.

His nose tickled with the smell of coffee. For a moment Lapslie thought it was drifting across from a cafeteria somewhere inside the shopping complex, but when he heard the violin solo from Bruch's 1st Violin Concerto echoing tinnily through the empty halls he realised that his mobile was ringing.

'Lapslie,' he said, flipping it open.

'Inspector Lapslie, this is Sancha Starkey from the BBC.' Her voice was honey and cigarette smoke combined. 'Do you have any leads in the Catherine Charnaud murder?'

Lapslie felt his fists clenching. 'How the *hell* did you get this number?'

'But you *can* confirm that Catherine Charnaud was murdered — '

'Investigations are ongoing,' he said, wanting to swear down the phone but aware that would do him no good at all. He might need the media on his side, if he wanted to make an appeal for information later, or if the case dragged on with no resolution and people began to demand that he be replaced. 'That is all I can confirm at the moment.'

'Do you have any suspects?'

Bizarrely, he wanted to quote Peter Sellers playing Inspector Clouseau in *The Pink Panther*

Strikes Again — 'I suspect everyone, and no one,' but he stopped himself just in time. There was a time and a place for humour, and he knew how easily a throw-away statement could be used against him. 'A press conference will be arranged in due course,' he said instead. 'Until then, I cannot confirm or deny any matters pertaining to this investigation. I'm sure you understand.'

'Is it true that you've arrested Catherine Charnaud's boyfriend?'

'I can neither confirm nor deny that. I'm sorry.'

He clicked the phone off as she was halfway through her next question, bitterly aware that the next BBC news report on the Charnaud case would probably contain the words 'Essex Police refused to comment on the case', turning what was his simple unwillingness to speculate in the absence of evidence into something conspiratorial and suspicious. And so it began.

Seconds later, the mobile began to ring again. He switched it off entirely, cursing.

'Problem, boss?' Emma was standing beside him. The grapefruit of her voice sluiced the mixed coffee, honey and nicotine of the phone call from his mouth.

'Bloody journalists. Somehow they've got hold of my mobile number. They're asking about the Charnaud case.'

'Amazing what you can get with a few minutes' research these days,' she sympathised. 'Someone probably took your business card somewhere along the line and put the number up on the internet for some reason, or you were at a conference and your details got amalgam-ated into an address list with everyone else's. Or someone's got a friend working for your service provider who passed the info on. There's no privacy any more.'

'Yeah, everything is available except the stuff that we need to crack the case, like the name of the killer. Even their motive would do.' He sighed heavily. This was just the start. It was all going to snowball from here — the press would soon be crawling like cockroaches over every aspect of the investigation. 'Come on,' he muttered. 'Let's crack on.'

The door to the roof was hidden down a service alley where Filipino cleaners went about their business without looking at Lapslie, Emma or the guard, as if they were in a separate but intersecting world. It was fitted with an alarm which the guard disabled by typing a code into a keypad set on the wall to one side. Stairs led up to another locked door at the top. He opened the door and gestured them through.

Out on the tarmac roof, punctuated by long, greenhouse-like stretches of skylights, the wind was fresh and strong. Lapslie walked across to the nearest edge, bounded by a low wall. He felt like he was standing on the edge of a cliff. Somewhere in the back of his mind he expected to hear the crying of seagulls. The car park stretched away from him like an impossibly flat ocean: the geometric lines of the bays receding like strangely straight wave tops. Off in the distance he could see the red tiled roofs of houses on the nearby estate, each looking the same but artfully curved along their roads so that no house had quite the same view and each could claim some morsel of individuality. He orientated himself. If the houses were over *there*, and the car park was *there* . . .

'The station is on that side,' he said, gesturing to Emma. 'Let's go.'

Leaving the guard standing uncertainly by the door, they walked together around one of the raised skylights. Through it, Lapslie could pick out lit signs for the shops beneath: Superdrug, Game, HMV. Stones loosely embedded in the tarmac of the roof crunched and skittered like ginger underfoot. Lapslie stopped, ten feet or so away from the edge; close enough that he could see the loading and unloading area beneath them, the station platforms in the distance and the railway lines that led away to either side — not visible themselves, but marked by unnaturally straight hedgerows — far enough away that neither he nor Emma would disturb any evidence.

He quickly scanned the tarmac near to the edge. 'If our bomber was up on this roof,' he said, 'they must have been somewhere along here. It provides the best vantage point for the station.'

'How would they get up here?' Emma asked.

'They could get through the doors with lock-picking equipment, if they knew what they were doing. Or they could have stolen the keys and made copies. I wasn't too impressed with the security inside the shopping centre.'

'What about the code on the alarm?'

'It's always possible they could have watched someone type the number in and memorised it. I don't know how often anyone comes up to the roof. Get someone to look into the guards and the cleaners, just in case it's an inside job. I don't think it is — something smacks of careful planning and cautiousness here — but it's worth checking, just in case.'

A mournful train horn sent tendrils of yeast worming their way through his mouth. Lapslie braced himself and raised his hands to cover his ears. Too late. The rush of the train pushing the air away in front of it, and the metallic clattering of wheels on rails caused his mouth to fill up with the improbable taste of syrupy peaches and salt again. He felt his stomach rise, and he clenched the muscles of his throat and chest against it. Bile burned at the back of his throat. He leaned forward, dropping his hands to steady himself on the wall running along the edge of the roof. If he threw up here he might be compromising evidence. He couldn't afford to do that.

The roof and the wall were fading away from him. Only the tastes were real. He could hardly feel the rough edges of the stone wall biting into the tender undersides of his fingers. His body appeared to be toppling, falling from the high roof to plummet into the car park, but he couldn't stop himself.

'Are you okay, boss?' Grapefruit scented with an unnameable flavour of concern, like smoke and spice together.

The train was receding now, along with its

noise. The horn sounded again; fresh bread soaking up the peach and the salt. The world came back into existence.

'Yeah,' he muttered. 'I'm okay.'

Emma looked along the surface of the roof. 'There's a couple of areas where the stones have been disturbed on the tarmac. Might indicate that someone was crouched down there. And I can see a couple of places on the wall where there are some fresh scratches, or the moss has been disturbed. Nothing left behind, though.'

'Again,' said Lapslie, straightening up, 'that indicates caution on the part of the bomber. If they did trigger the device, or at least watch it explode, from here, and I believe they did, then they cleaned up after themselves. They collected whatever traces they had left, and made sure there was no obvious sign of their presence.'

'You're beginning to profile them,' Emma said. 'I thought you wanted to hire in this Eleanor Whittley to do that?'

'Only on the Charnaud case,' Lapslie replied, 'We probably couldn't afford to have her working on two cases simultaneously. And doing a bit of your own profiling is okay, as long as you don't let the profile blind you to any evidence that doesn't agree with your theories.'

He moved cautiously over to the wall and knelt down; trying to ensure that there was nothing of an evidential nature near him. He gazed again out at the distant station, trying to trace in his mind the killer's point of view. What would have been going through their head. Did they know who Alec Wildish was: were they

143

deliberately waiting, scanning the faces of the commuters until he arrived, then waiting until the right moment to press the button, or would anyone have done? Had they been scanning the faces of the commuters, but not so much looking for a familiar face as someone that fitted some insane criteria: a certain age, a certain weight, a certain hair colour, a certain brand of jacket?

Somewhere in the distance he could hear a drumming sound. For a few moments he thought it was just the thrum of the blood in his veins, the beat of his heart echoing through his chest, but gradually he realised that it was more complicated than a natural rhythm: a ritualistic beat in 4/4 time; three groups of four semi-quavers with a stress on the first, then four semiquavers again with the stress on the first but with the following three beats deeper in tone and heavier.

It was the same sound he'd heard when he was in Catherine Charnaud's bedroom, looking down on her dead, flensed body.

'Can you hear that?' he asked.

'Hear what?'

'That drumming sound?'

Emma looked around. 'I can't hear anything apart from traffic, and the sound of a station manager having a coronary nearby.'

'Is someone playing a radio?'

She shrugged. 'Not that I can tell.'

'Wind in the power cables, perhaps?'

'Not that I can hear.'

Lapslie straightened up and brushed his hands down his trousers to remove the moss and the dust. What the hell was happening to him? As if the overreaction to noise wasn't enough, was he hallucinating now? Was his mind, unable to cope with the bizarre input it was getting, beginning to snap under the strain of the cross-wiring of his senses?

He had to talk to someone. Perhaps he could get an urgent appointment with his consultant. There had to be *something* he could do, some drug he could take, that would allow him to function properly as a police officer. If he had to retire early on medical grounds, or was even forced out, then all that remained for him was a barren expanse of future time in which he would be condemned to stand quietly in the centre of his cottage, not moving, not doing anything, until he went mad.

He would rather die.

'Never mind,' he said finally. 'Let Burrows know to get his team up here. I need a full forensic sweep.'

'No chance of getting fingerprints,' Emma said dubiously, looking at the wall.

'Unlikely, but there might be traces of something else. Tobacco, maybe, or saliva if they spat something out. Worth a go.'

After a few minutes, during which Emma used her BlackBerry to call the CSI team, Lapslie led the way back to the door where the security guard waited for them. As he moved away from the edge of the roof, the drumming sound seemed to fade away, until it was lost in the whistling of the wind and the distant sound of cars on the main road.

'Are there any other doors leading up here?' he asked the guard.

'This is the only one I know of,' the guard said.

Lapslie looked out across the car park. Poles with lamps on top were spaced around on a regular basis, but every fourth one appeared to have a security camera attached to it. 'Get copies of the security tapes,' he said to Emma. 'The angles are probably wrong — they're looking down rather than up — but we might get lucky and catch the bomber silhouetted against the sky. Or even parking a car and walking across, although I suspect they're too careful for that. They would have parked some distance away, and probably avoided the security cameras as they walked across.'

Back at the station, Lapslie noticed that the body had been removed.

'Has the pathologist taken the body back to the mortuary?' he called to Sean Burrows, who was examining something in the area between the platforms.

'Yes.'

'Which one?'

'Small lady. Looks like there's something wrong with her spine. Dr Catherall.'

He opened his mouth to say something, but his phone *beeped* chocolate at him. He glanced at the screen. There was a text message waiting for him. He accessed it, and noticed that it was coincidentally from Jane Catherall.

I would be grateful if you could come to the mortuary, it said. *I have more information on the Catherine Charnaud case.*

'We're going to the mortuary,' he said to Emma. 'Something's come up. Follow me.'

Walking over to his car, Lapslie noticed that a double-decker bus had pulled up, engine still running and pumping out a mixture of diesel fumes and delicate lavender flavour, next to the station. Harassed commuters were climbing on board. The Station Manager was standing nearby, fielding angry comments. He didn't look happy. Lapslie didn't know what he was worried about. The task of looking after a station when everything was running fine must have been tedious in the extreme; he should have been pleased that he had a crisis to deal with.

Lapslie got into his car and pulled out of the station car park, priming the satnav with the postcode of the mortuary located on the outskirts of Braintree. The crunch of his tyres on gravel as he pulled away sent a cinnamon wave crashing across his tongue — complex, bitter and yet dry at the same time. Not for the first time he wondered, as he guided the car out towards the motorway, how tastes worked. Was it like colours, where any shade of paint could be made by combining red, blue and yellow? He had read somewhere that the taste buds on the tongue could only recognise five flavours — salt, sweet, bitter, sour and the mysterious *umami*, which normally got translated from the original Japanese as 'savoury'. Could you really create any taste, from cinnamon through petrol to blue cheese, using just those five flavours? And did that explain how his synaesthesia worked

— particular frequencies mapping onto particular building blocks of flavour so that any combination of sounds would create a matching mixture of tastes? Surely there must be more to it than that? But it did indicate that simple sounds — a single vibrating string perhaps, like a violin playing middle C — should relate directly to a simple taste, like pure salt, or pure sugar, while a multilayered sound — tyres crunching on gravel — would be a more complex combination. He couldn't say that he'd noticed the connection, but it was a theory. He made a mental note to mention it to the consultant at the hospital the next time he had an appointment. Perhaps they could conduct some experiments. It wasn't as if they were going to come up with a cure any time soon.

He reached Chelmsford with Emma only seconds behind in her Audi. He had sensed her holding back all the way on the drive over, reluctant to overtake her boss.

He pressed the buzzer on the front door and waited for Dr Catherall's assistant to let them in. The smell that wafted out of the building was the familiar combination of industrial strength cleaners and rotting flesh. He tried to tell himself that it was just salt, sweet, sour, bitter and savoury mixed together, nothing that should affect him, but he still found himself breathing through his mouth and imagining the foetid vapours coating his throat and his lungs like a thick scum.

He pushed through the swing doors that led into the post mortem room, feeling as if he was actively pushing them against the smell, Emma right behind him. Dr Catherall was bent over the corpse of Alec Wildish, examining the burned front of his skull with a magnifying glass. There was a smell of cooked meat in the air.

'Dr Catherall,' he said, his mouth watering in a way that made him feel sick.

She glanced sideways at him. 'Detective Chief Inspector Lapslie, and so soon after the last time we met.'

He indicated the body on the table. 'So, what can you tell me?'

'I was just making my preliminary inspection when you arrived. As you will remember, I try never to speculate about the cause of death before I have solid evidence; however, in this case I would be surprised if it was anything but exsanguination and vascular shock due to a series of penetrating wounds, made almost certainly by fragments from the device and from the waste bin in which it was hidden entering the body.'

'Make sure all the fragments go to the CSIs. Sean Burrows might be able to reconstruct the bomb. But that wasn't why you texted me, was it?'

'Actually,' Dr Catherall said, 'there is something else I wanted to show you. Please — follow me.'

She led Lapslie and Emma out of the post mortem room through a rear door, and along a corridor that he had never been in before. The room at the end was cold enough for Lapslie's breath to gust in front of his face, and the far wall was occupied by row upon row of metal-fronted drawers about a metre square, their faces battered and scratched through years of use.

'This is the long-term storage area,' Jane said. 'It's refrigerated to a lower temperature than the transient holding area — about four degrees centigrade. We can keep bodies here for months, if necessary.' She indicated a drawer on the second level up, at about eye-height. Lapslie's eye-height. 'Would you be so kind as to pull that open for me?' she asked. 'I am afraid my upper body strength is barely enough to open my front door in the morning.'

Lapslie reached out and took hold of the handle. The metal was cold against his skin. He pulled, and the drawer slid out on metal runners. He had been bracing himself for some kind of squealing or squeaking of metal against metal, provoking who knew what reaction in his taste buds, but the slides had been oiled and were noiseless. As quiet as the grave.

Inside, lying on bare metal, was the body of Catherine Charnaud.

Her skin was mottled with a blue-green discoloration, and her muscles had slackened to the point where her skin looked as if it was gradually sliding off her bones. Lapslie could see the sharp angles and hard curves of her skull beneath her flaccid face.

'What have you found?' he asked, trying not to look at the wreck of her forearm in the shadows within the drawer.

'Look here,' Jane said, leaning over the body

150

and indicating the right shoulder with a thin, elegant hand. 'I found it when I was re-examining the body this morning.'

Lapslie followed the line of her finger. There, in the skin of the shoulder, just in the curve of the neck, were two small pinholes.

'Do you always re-examine your bodies?' Emma asked, curious.

'I do. There are certain signs that only appear several days after death, such as deep internal bruises caused shortly before the time of death, and minor marks that need some shrinkage of the skin and some relaxation of the musculature before they become evident.'

'So what am I looking at here?' Lapslie inquired. 'The bite of a midget vampire?'

'Nothing so abstruse. No, I believe these marks were caused by a stun gun. There are indications of small subcutaneous burns in the area, consistent with an electrical current having been applied.'

'A stun gun? Like a police taser?' Emma was frowning. 'There was no record of her having been subdued by police at any time in her life, let alone recently.'

'Indeed, but it was not a police taser. As you know, they fire small needles attached to wires. The needles penetrate the skin, through the clothing, and an electrical current flows down them, resulting in a tetanising effect on the victim. Their muscles immediately clench tight and they fall to the ground, paralysed. Judging by the size of the marks here, and the spacing between them, I would estimate that she came in contact with a small, hand-held stun gun. A self-defence weapon. They are freely available in America, I believe. Apparently you can even buy them in larger supermarkets.'

Lapslie rubbed a hand across his chin. 'That would explain how she came to be immobilised,' he said thoughtfully. 'There were no marks of violence on her body, other than the obvious mutilation of the arm. I'd wondered how her assailant managed to subdue her and tie her to the bed.'

'Does it help find her killer?' Jane asked.

'It's a new lead,' Lapslie replied. 'And we're very short of new leads.' He glanced at Emma. 'What do you think?'

'We were thinking that someone strong and well-built, almost certainly a man, was responsible for her torture and death,' she replied. 'The use of a stun gun suggests someone smaller, someone who couldn't rely on their own muscles to subdue her. On the other hand, if stun guns are that easily available then we might have problems in tracking down an individual sale.'

'If it helps, I can measure the distance between the barbs. That might help narrow down the make and model that was used.'

'At this point in the investigation,' Lapslie said, 'I'll take anything I can get. Thanks, Jane.'

'Make sure you tidy up after yourselves,' Jane said over her shoulder as she walked off. 'Don't forget — perishable goods!'

Lapslie turned to Emma. 'How are we doing with the investigation?'

Emma shrugged. 'It's currently stalled like an

old Austin Metro in a puddle,' she admitted. 'You heard the interview with the boyfriend?'

'Yeah — I was listening to it when you came to pick me up.'

'His alibi checks out, and I didn't pick up anything in his attitude that made me wonder. He's obviously as thick as pig shit, but equally obviously he felt something for her as close to love as his Neanderthal mind could manage. Oh, and he did confirm that she'd not got any tattoos, which means we still have no real explanation for the flesh being removed from the arm.'

'Okay. Check on his alibi in more detail. I want to know if his friends might have any reason to lie for him. Maybe he's supporting them financially or something. I'm not convinced he's innocent. What about the security cameras around the house?'

'They were connected up to a home computer system with a humungous hard disc. They must have got someone in to set it up; I can't see either the victim or loverboy having the technical nous to do it. Sean Burrows took the hard disc away for analysis, but the video for the past two days has been wiped and he can't get it back.'

Lapslie considered for a moment. 'Would it take a lot of expertise to wipe the files?'

'Nah.' Emma shook her head. 'Just click on a few files and say 'OK' when it asks if you're sure. One day, the world is going to end like that.'

Lapslie let his mind wander across the other parallel aspects of the investigation. 'Fingerprints?'

'Hers, loverboy's, the cleaner's, and that was it. The last time the cleaner did a thorough scrub was Monday, and it looks like nobody unexpected has been in the house since then.'

'We've ruled the cleaner out, have we? Please tell me we've ruled the cleaner out.'

Emma laughed. 'Next best thing to the butler doing it, you mean? Yeah, she was at home with her husband and her unfeasibly large family. Eight kids. And all she can do for a living is go out and clean someone *else*'s house. Weird.'

The skin on Emma's arms was turning to goose-flesh, and Lapslie could feel the chill seeping into his bones too. 'Okay,' he said with finality. 'It looks like we're stymied unless this stun gun lead takes us further forward. Are there any other lines of enquiry we're following?'

'The usual,' Emma replied, crossing her arms in front of her chest to ward off the cold. 'I've got guys going through her fan mail and her emails, but there's nothing there obviously weirder than celebrities normally get. No death threats. People seemed to genuinely like her. And we did check on whether she'd been involved in any contentious reports or investigations, but the riskiest one we could find was a voice-over she did for a documentary on growth hormone abuse by athletes in the run-up to the Olympics. And if someone was going to take exception to that, they'd have gone for the reporter or the director first, not the voice-over artist.'

'Mobile phone?'

'All of the calls have explanations.' She frowned. 'Apart from one. She called a garage in

154

Chingford shortly after she got home. They were closed, but the call seemed to go on for a minute or so.'

'Get her car checked over for problems. And make sure there was nobody working late at the garage — maybe she's got a bit of rough on the side, and she was arranging an assignation when her boyfriend arrived home unexpectedly and overheard.'

She frowned. 'It's a stretch, boss.'

'Yeah, but it's the only theory we have at the moment. You've checked her bank records?'

'Yes. Apart from the fact that she was being paid an obscene amount of money for having make-up slapped all over her and reading off an autocue every night, nothing. No strange payments to drug dealers or blackmailers. She did have a direct debit to Save The Children every month, which made me feel slightly better towards her. Then again, she could afford it.'

'Okay.' Lapslie sighed. 'Keep the team working on it, but it looks like we're going to need a miracle to progress this case along.' He exerted himself, and slid the metal tray containing Catherine Charnaud's body back into the wall. 'You and I might as well apply ourselves to this bombing for a while, if that's what Rouse wants. You head back to Chelmsford; I'm going to hang around here for a while.'

Emma eyed him curiously. 'Some other lead you're not telling me about?'

'No,' he said. 'It's just quiet here. Very, very quiet.'

'That's because they're all dead, apart from

155

Dr Catherall and Dan.'

'I don't care what the reason is — I just appreciate the peace.'

Once Emma had gone, Lapslie wandered back to where Jane Catherall was working on Alex Wildish's blasted body.

'This may seem like a stupid question,' he said, 'but do you have any spare office space around here?'

Jane looked over at him, head on one side like a sparrow. 'We have a couple of empty rooms with desks,' she said. 'Why?'

Lapslie sighed. He always felt awkward, having to explain his neurological condition to people, although he suspected that Jane would be more understanding than most. 'I'm having some . . . problems . . . that mean I need somewhere quiet to work,' he said. 'This mortuary is one of the most peaceful places I've found. I'd like to use it as a refuge, if I may.'

'Problems as in medical problems?'

He sighed. 'It's called synaesthesia — ' he began.

'Ah, the rare case where cross-wiring in the brain means that inputs from one sense can trigger responses in another sense,' she said, straightening up from the corpse.

Lapslie was taken aback. 'You've heard of it?'

'It's a fascinating illustration of how the brain works,' she replied. 'I have read several articles in neurology magazines concerning the things synaesthesia can teach us about the way we interpret the vast flood of data that enters the brain every moment. Tell me, Mark — what

156

form does your synaesthesia take? The most common, I believe, is where sounds give rise to the sensation of colour, although one of the more interesting ones I have come across is the man who can actually feel tastes on his skin. Chicken, apparently, is spiky, while wine is spherical and cold.'

'With me,' he said, taking a deep breath, 'things that I hear get translated into tastes in my mouth. It's not everything, but most things I come across in everyday life cause me to have a reaction of some kind. Lorries are flavoured like asparagus. A fountain or a shower taste of cauliflower.'

'Both of them vegetables,' Jane observed.

'Badly chosen examples. My mobile phone makes me taste coffee when it rings. And, before you ask, your voice tastes of brandy and soda.'

'There are worse things,' she said, smiling. 'You must have been asked that question so many times before.'

'I have, but don't let that stop you asking anything you want. I realise it's an interesting subject for anyone who doesn't suffer from it.'

'What does your voice taste of?' she asked.

Lapslie found himself frowning. Nobody had ever asked him that before. In fact, he'd never even thought about it before. 'I don't think it tastes of anything,' he said slowly, savouring the words as they came out and finding them lacking any flavour.

'That's instructive. What about your parents?'

'I don't remember. They died when I was quite young.'

'Have you always been synaesthetic?'

'No — it seemed to develop when I was a teenager, in a mild form, and it suddenly deteriorated about seven years ago. It's been stable since then, but over the past few days it's suddenly got a lot worse, to the point where it's stopping me from carrying out my investigations properly.' Now that he had started speaking, he couldn't seem to stop. The words came spilling out of him. 'And I think I'm beginning to hallucinate. I keep hearing drums. Loud drums.'

She frowned. 'But this is happening in reverse, surely? You are hearing a noise which is not there, implying that it is being triggered by something else. Does that happen?'

'Occasionally,' he admitted. 'There are one or two tastes or smells that cause the synaesthesia to go into reverse. Seafood that's going off makes me hear high-pitched violins, for some reason. And when I first entered this mortuary, a year or so ago, the smell of the bodies and the bleach made me hear church bells.'

Jane nodded. 'And is that what's happening now? You're smelling something, and it's causing you to hear the sound of drums?'

'It's possible, I suppose, but what is it?'

'You said you had heard the sound before. When was that?'

Lapslie considered for a moment. 'The first time was in Catherine Charnaud's house in Chigwell; the second time was on a roof used by the bomber in Braintree.'

'And the cases are not connected?'

'We have no evidence that they are.'

158

'If you ask me,' Jane said, 'and you usually do, I would suggest that there is a connection between the murders. They each have a certain smell about them that only you can pick up, and I don't mean the smell of death. Somehow, I believe you are smelling the murderer.'

8

Water trickled down the inside of Carl Whittley's collar, cold and irritating against the skin of his neck but growing into a warmer tickle as it made its way round his collar bone and across his chest. He ignored it as best he could. Intermittent rain was hitting the waterproof groundsheet above his head like fingers impatiently tapping a table, and despite his best attempts to string the sheet between two bushes so that it kept him dry, whilst allowing folds and channels for the water to drain away safely, some of it was collecting underneath and hanging in bulbous, quivering drops before falling onto him.

The only good thing about the fact that the sun wasn't shining was that the rash on his arms and hands had subsided. The itching was barely noticeable now, and he was grateful. He'd been slathering it with his father's chlorhexidine antiseptic talc, just in case it was an infection of some kind, but it hadn't helped. He really needed to make another appointment at his local surgery. He'd been putting it off for weeks, if not months, but things were starting to slide out of control.

Time passed slowly when you were watching a fixed spot and waiting for a bird to fly back to its nest or an animal to emerge from its burrow, the seconds trickling past like drops of water and puddling into minutes, hours, days. Lying there between the groundsheets, feeling the dampness beneath his stomach and the trickles of water investigating his body like fingers, Carl shifted position slightly and reached out his hand to pat the rifle beside him reassuringly. It was an old Lee Enfield; light and still fully functional despite the number of years since it had been made. He had stripped it down, oiled all the components and put it back together again that morning, gaining immense satisfaction from the way that each part fitted perfectly against the others. He'd bought it from a man he'd met through the Essex Hunt, when he was younger and used to attend the meets.

The rifle had been buried near the estate, like the Semtex and the detonators, but not with them. There were caches of equipment all around the salt marshes, and Carl carried with him a mental map of where everything was, just in case he needed it.

The rain shouldn't affect the rifle; the film of oil that covered it should protect it against damp, and as long as he kept the barrel pointed slightly downwards then water wouldn't trickle inside. He would strip it down and clean it again when he had finished with it, but for the moment he trusted it.

A movement out in the salt marshes attracted his attention. It was midday, and the weak sunlight filtering through the clouds cast no discernible shadows, making everything appear flat and slightly unreal. A bush moved slightly, although there was little breeze, and a head poked out. Short, reddish muzzle with white patches, little eyes that looked black from that distance and pointed ears that twitched from side to side, targeting slight disturbances. A fox; barely more than a cub. Probably female, judging from the shape of the muzzle. It was alert, hesitant, aware that something was amiss but unsure what it was.

Carl slid the rifle closer to his body and used his right arm to bring it up in front of him. The stock fitted perfectly into the curve of his shoulder. He slid his forefinger around the trigger and moved his head slightly to one side so he could see through the sights on top.

The fox trotted a few more steps out into the open. Its fur was a rich reddish-brown. It raised its head, scenting the air, and something seemed to spook it. Carl had taken pains to make sure he was downwind, but the fox could sense that he was there, somewhere.

He centred the sights on the fox's neck, just below the ears and on a level with the eyes. A shot there would sever the fox's spinal cord, killing it instantly. If it had been a stag he would probably have gone for a chest shot — larger animals like stags moved their heads more than they moved their bodies, and there was always the chance that a shot might miss because the target shifted position suddenly — but the fox was standing stock still and Carl was at the wrong angle to get the heart.

He squeezed the trigger. The rifle jerked against his shoulder, pulling smoothly backwards rather than kicking up. He absorbed the impact, hearing the deafening *crack* of the bullet as it broke the sound barrier. Smoke momentarily drifted across the sight, obscuring the fox, but when it cleared he saw the fox's body collapse gracelessly to the wet earth, its neck gashed open and head lolling forward. A spray of blood was caught in the air, drifting like smoke.

The fox lay still. Beads of blood caught on the blades of grass around it, carmine on green.

Silence rolled across the salt marshes like the antithesis of thunder. Birds fell silent. Even the rain seemed to cease, waiting. Then, after a few moments, the birds started to sing again; first one and then, gradually, more and more.

Carl waited for twenty minutes before emerging from his hide.

While he lay there, he replayed the details of the fox's death in his head. The bullet had struck exactly where he had been aiming. The sight appeared to be perfectly aligned with the barrel of the rifle. He had zeroed it years before, when he used to dream about hunting and rehearse all the actions, but he had been worried that the time in the ground had caused it to drift as the metal expanded in summer and contracted in winter. Fortunately, the soil had acted as an insulating blanket. He would fire a few more shots at different ranges, just to check, but it looked as if the bullets would still go where he wanted them to.

Eventually, when he was sure that nobody was coming to investigate, he slid out from between the groundsheets. Water that had pooled in the hollow of his spine suddenly spilled down his buttocks; warm, like blood. He stood, muscles and joints complaining at the sudden movement, and stretched, easing the kinks in his body. The gentle breeze was beautifully cool on his forehead and on his damp scalp. He looked around, checking that there was nobody else within sight. Shots were not uncommon on the Essex marshes — farmers hunting rabbits or shooting at birds — but a man with a rifle was unusual.

The cold and the wet meant that there were no insects around, and the fox's body was lying undisturbed. Crows would eventually pick at it, badgers and foxes and polecats would tear at it, but the cold would hold back the decay. It was too wrecked for him to take home and use in one of his dioramas. Too mutilated.

After torture and mutilation, and then a bomb, not to mention all the ones that had gone before, Carl had decided to try something more traditional for his next victim. The thought had come to him the night before, lying in bed, wide awake, gently masturbating, excited by the fact that his mother would finally be investigating one of his crimes. He was going to shoot someone. He was going to do it at long range, using the rifle, but to distinguish it from the bomb on the station platform, which was arguably a similar form of long-range murder, he had decided that he was going to shoot someone in their own living room. He would probably choose a block of flats rather than a house, and fire from an unoccupied flat in another, nearby block. Finding the location to shoot from was going to be protracted, if not actually difficult — he would have to conduct surveillance of a likely block of flats that was one of a pair, or a group, and look for windows that were not lit up for several nights on end, then compare their addresses with the register of voters to ensure that they were actually unoccupied rather than just the homes of people who were on holiday — but once he had located a good candidate, facing another block, he would be able to break in easily as long as the doors were not actually boarded up. Then he could take his time, scanning the windows opposite with his sniper scope until he found someone to kill. Someone old, he had decided. Or very young. Most of his victims so far had been between twenty and fifty, although he had done the best he could to ring the changes on social standing, sex and appearance. The rule was that no two murders could share any characteristic in common, save for the fact that someone was dead who had been alive, and that death had been violent and unexpected. So — perhaps a child, shot in their bedroom by the glow of a nightlight as they stared in wonder out at the world below. Hit in the throat so that they choked on their own blood as they died, parents running into the room and trying to make sense of the carnage; the broken glass, the gore and the thrashing limbs. And Carl could watch it all from the safety of his firing position, secure in the knowledge that he was safe until the police arrived, and even then it would take them hours to work out where the shot had come from.

It would be like looking into a glass-fronted

display case, where stuffed animals acted out a private tragedy for his sole benefit.

Something moved in his peripheral vision. He turned his head gradually, trying not to make any sudden movements that might alert someone to his presence, always assuming they hadn't already seen him.

A hiker was making their way across the open ground of the salt marshes. Carl couldn't tell whether it was male or female — the figure was too far away — but it was wearing a bulky water-proof parka in a violent lime green, jeans, a black rucksack and a thermal hat. The boots that the figure was wearing were good, ankle-protecting hiking boots rather than the trainers that he saw some people walking across the salt marshes in. The figure was heading at an angle to where Carl stood, and wasn't looking in his direction. If they had heard the shot, they had just put it down to farmers.

Without thinking, Carl cocked the rifle and brought it up to his shoulder, settling the butt comfortably into the curve of his collarbone. His left hand supported the stock, the cross-hatching rough under his fingers. His right hand curled around the grip, his right forefinger sliding naturally inside the trigger guard and around the cold metal of the trigger. He gazed through the sights at the hiker, brought so close by the magnification that he could see the North Face logo on the jacket and the Kangol logo on the thermal hat.

The hiker was a man in his early thirties, Carl judged. He had fair hair, and he hadn't shaved for a few days. His eyes were green. Unaware that he was being watched, he reached up and picked at his nose as he walked. He gazed around at the landscape of the Essex salt marshes and smiled in simple pleasure. Carl could see the glistening of a light sweat on his forehead.

The notch of the sights was centred on the bridge of his nose. As he walked, Carl moved the rifle to track him.

He had no idea that Carl was watching him. He had no idea that Carl could just move his right forefinger a few millimetres and send a bullet spinning towards him at 1500 metres per second. He wouldn't even hear the shot before the bullet entered his skull and tumbled end over end through his brain tissue, scrambling everything in its path in an expanding cone of destruction before exiting through the back of his head in a fist-sized hole and a cloud of vaporised blood and bone.

He could do it. He could kill him now, add another body to his growing list, another case for his mother to potentially get called in to investigate. He felt his finger twitch as contradictory messages were sent to it — shoot, don't shoot. Shoot, don't shoot.

Carl abruptly relaxed the pressure on the trigger. He was the wrong age, and his eyes were the wrong colour. Carl had already killed a man in his early thirties with green eyes. It had been a few years ago, but he distinctly remembered. Carl had been sitting behind him in a cinema in Ilford, watching *Pirates of the Caribbean: Dead*

Man's Chest, and while the man had been concentrating on the scene where the sea monster was pulling the pirate ship beneath the waves Carl had slid a thin knife into the junction of his spine and his skull. He had died instantly, jerking in his seat and fouling himself as his body shut down. Carl had left the cinema quickly, before the smell of faeces drifted too far and people complained.

He couldn't kill another thirty-year-old with green eyes. It would break the rules, and the rules were the only thing keeping him going. Blue eyes he could have accepted. The same for brown, as long as their owner wasn't Asian, because he had once strangled an Asian man with brown eyes. Green, however, was out of bounds now.

Reluctantly he let the rifle drop. In the distance the hiker carried on, oblivious to the fact that his life had been spared thanks to a genetic quirk.

The blood on the fox was congealing in the cold. He debated briefly whether he should dispose of it himself, but decided in the end that the local wildlife would do it for him. He rewrapped the rifle and then detached the elasticated cords from the bushes and rolled up the groundsheets. Within ten minutes there was no sign that he had been there at all; no sign except, of course, for the rapidly stiffening corpse of a fox and the shell casing lying in the mud.

As he trudged back to the house, his mind ranged over the people that he had killed. He had notched up quite a tally, to the extent that he was running out of variations. The thought depressed him and filled him with a vague sense of panic. He couldn't stop now — the game wasn't over yet. His mother had only just started playing the game, and was a long way from admitting defeat. The long range rifle shot he had been saving up, but by now he had knifed, strangled, blown up, drowned, bludgeoned and tortured ten people. Ten people that he had never even met, and had no knowledge of apart from what little he had been able to glean from watching them for a few hours or a few days. Ten people who had not caused him any pain or inconvenienced him in any way. Ten people who differed from each other in almost every way — height, weight, sex, age, social class and sexual preference.

His route took him away from the direction of the Creeksea estate and towards where he had buried the rifle previously. Part of him, the lazy part, wanted to keep it in the house until he needed it, but the other part of him, the part that would go to almost infinite pains to assure his own safety, told him that having a rifle in the house was inviting trouble. Best to bury it again, even if he dug it up two days later.

As he placed the rifle back in its hole and scooped the disturbed earth back over it, then covered the earth with moss and bracken, he considered when he should kill his next victim. Serial killers, if you believed the television programmes and films, either killed at fixed intervals — every twenty-third of November, for instance, or on a full moon — or with increasing frequency as their obsessions got a tighter and tighter grip of them. That seemed to be mostly how they got caught — they were predictable. From the start, Carl had striven to be unpredictable, not only in his choice of victim but also in when he killed them. The longest he had gone between murders was almost a year; the shortest — between the torture of the TV presenter and the blowing up of the commuter — was two days. In between were gaps of weeks and months. No pattern, therefore no predictability. The trouble was that the more people he killed, the more there was that he couldn't repeat. He might, at some stage, even be forced to go for two or three years between killings.

It would be just like lying still in a hide and watching some animal. He would cope.

After the next murder, he decided, he was going to have to be more creative. Poison was still an option. Perhaps he could run somebody down with a car — not his own car, obviously, but one that he would have to steal. Maybe he could push a victim under a train, or from the top of a building. After that he might have to relax the rules a little bit — rather than just killing one person in their thirties and then moving on, he could actually narrow it down to years and assume that a 32-year-old who was knifed counted separately from a 33-year-old. The thought made him uneasy, as if he was nearing a line that should not be crossed, but he couldn't see any other way around it. Not if he wanted to keep going, and he did. He really did.

After all, what else was he going to do with his time?

He felt a weight lift from his shoulders as the door of the house closed behind him. The house was his refuge, the hide from which he watched the world going by. He felt safe there.

His father was watching TV in the living room when Carl entered. He was even dressed, although his feet were still bare.

'Dad? Are you all right?'

'I felt like getting up. I don't want to end up a complete invalid.' His eyes were watery, defensive.

'That's fine. What about . . . your colostomy bag?'

'I changed it myself. And cleaned everything.'

'With antiseptic powder?'

Nicholas nodded. 'With antiseptic powder. I'm not stupid.'

'I know,' Carl said gently. Reassuringly. 'I know. Would you like some food? I'm going out later for a while, but we can have lunch together.'

Nicholas smiled. 'I'd enjoy that. Where are you going?'

Carl hesitated. He didn't want to tell his father that he was going to be driving his mother around. Nicholas still clung to the increasingly unlikely belief that Eleanor was going to come back to them, once she had got her work life into balance. Carl didn't have the heart to tell him that it wasn't going to happen. Not unless Carl's plans worked out, and that could take a while.

'Just to see some friends,' he said finally. 'I'll have my mobile on. You can call me if there's a problem. I'll be back for dinner.'

'Is it a girl?' his father asked, eyes twinkling. 'You could stay out later. Take her out for a meal.'

Carl felt his stomach clench. When would he ever get a chance to meet a girl, let alone go out with one? 'It's just some friends,' he repeated, controlling the sudden flush of anger. 'From the Hunt. We're having a coffee. Nothing special.'

He prepared soup and some sandwiches, then left his father watching TV and got changed into something at least reasonably smart. Then he drove across to his mother's house, in Maldon. It was an old house, probably dating back to Victorian times, if not earlier. Carl had never been inside. Eleanor had never invited him or Nicholas in. He wasn't even sure if she shared it or lived alone. She kept her life shrouded.

She was waiting in the doorway as he pulled up in her driveway: a tall woman with a shock of grey hair, kept long and styled but never dyed. She had always hated pretence of any kind. She was wearing a loose jacket over a long, rather formal dress. No necklace, no earrings. No rings of any sort. The afternoon sun cast a roseate glow over her papery skin.

'I expected you to be late,' she said, opening the rear passenger door and sliding a large briefcase in, then following it. Anger sparked in Carl's chest at the automatic assumption that he was a chauffeur and she was a passenger, rather than he her son and she his mother and both of them in the front seats, but he snuffed it out. He couldn't alienate or irritate her tonight. He had to be there with her, at the scene.

'I said I'd be here at three o'clock, and I am,' he replied quietly. 'Where are we going?'

'Drive to Chigwell. I will direct you when we get there.'

Chigwell. A small, dark bud of pleasure began to unfold in Carl's chest. Chigwell, where he had tortured and murdered Catherine Charnaud. Back to the scene of the crime!

The thought kept him warm all the way through the journey, just about compensating for the fact that his mother didn't exchange another word with him. Instead, she pulled a set of folders out of her case and sat reading them while he drove.

Although Carl knew the way, he made sure that he waited until his mother indicated right or left without saying anything as they entered Chigwell. Soon they were pulling into the road where he remembered parking his car. *This* car. A momentary chill ran up his back, and he shivered. Would anyone remember it? The licence plates were different, but the colour and the shape were the same. Had anyone been looking out of their window that night?

Goose-pimples rose up on his forearms, and he could feel sweat trickling down his ribs from the warmth of his armpits. This was the moment he'd been dreaming of for years, and now it was here he didn't know what to do, how to react.

'Just keep quiet,' his mother said suddenly. 'Leave all the talking to me.'

Quelling his sudden panic, Carl pulled the car up to the gate of the house. A crowd of journalists jostled forward to see who was in the car, then subsided when they saw that it was nobody special.

'Eleanor Whittley,' Carl's mother said to the policeman on duty. 'I am expected.'

The constable consulted a clipboard, then nodded. 'DCI Lapslie is waiting for you,' he said wearily. 'Park in front of the house. I'll notify him you're here.'

Gravel crunched beneath the tyres of the car as the gate closed behind them. The house looked less imposing by daylight; the cornices and the portico obviously mass-produced plaster.

'Stay here until I come back, Carl.'

'But — ' Carl hesitated. He wanted to see the bedroom again. He wanted to see the blood. 'You might need someone to carry your case. Or take notes.'

'I'll manage.' Eleanor pushed the car door open and got out.

The front door opened and a man emerged.

'DCI Lapslie,' the man said, walking towards the car. His voice was attenuated by the car window. He was tall, and thinner than Carl would have expected. The skin around his eyes looked creased, as though he spent a lot of time wincing.

Eleanor and Lapslie moved out of earshot, closer to the house. Carl strained to hear them, but in vain. Lapslie seemed to be growing irritated, and after a few minutes he led the way back into the house.

Carl sat there for just under an hour, watching

174

the house and remembering what had happened inside. Eventually Eleanor emerged from the porticoed door and crossed to the car.

'DCI Lapslie has offered to drive me into Chelmsford to see the crime scene photographs,' she said. 'He's going to arrange a car for me later to get me home.' She opened the rear passenger door and retrieved her case. 'You can go now.'

'Okay,' he said meekly. He started the car and drove out of the gateway, then around the corner, where he parked. He wasn't willing to go home just yet.

Ten minutes later, a black Saab and a red Audi left, one after the other. Catching sight of his mother's face in the front seat of the Audi — the *front* seat, he noted with a twinge of boiling anger — he pulled out behind them and followed them out of Chingford at a discreet distance.

Knowing they were heading for Chelmsford, Carl overtook the cars once he knew which route they were taking, being careful not to exceed the speed limit by enough to make them pull him over, or report him to someone who would. He then waited in a lay-by on the outskirts of Chelmsford until they came by and followed them to an anonymous seventies building near the centre of town that he guessed must be the police station. He parked across the road and watched as they drove in the back, through an automatic barrier operated by a code that Lapslie typed in to a keypad on a pole.

Leaving his car, Carl crossed the road to the front of the police station. A gaggle of cameramen and reporters were standing in the

175

car park outside the building, huddled together against the cold, chatting and drinking coffee from paper cups. They didn't seem so much to be waiting for some breaking news story as just hanging around because nobody in the news room had told them where to go next. For a moment Carl considered joining them, pretending to be a reporter from a local radio station, but he quickly dismissed the idea. The chances were that most of the reporters knew one another — they probably turned up to the same press conferences and roped-off crime scenes — and he would stand out as a newcomer. And he didn't know enough about the particular language that the reporters used — the slang, the specialised technical vocabulary — to carry it off. Instead he just tried to look like a bored onlooker, the kind of person who would join the edges of any crowd just to find out what was going on.

He was hoping to pick up some fragment of conversation about the two cases, about the progress the police might or might not have been making, but the cases were the last thing that any of the journalists seemed inclined to talk about. Football, girlfriends, gossip, politics . . . anything except what Carl wanted to hear.

He was just about to go home when a ripple of excitement ran through the crowd.

'What's happening?' he asked a cameraman in a leather jacket standing in front of him.

'Press conference,' the man replied, hefting his camera onto his shoulder like a rocket launcher. ''Bout bloody time too. I've been freezing my bollocks off here all day.'

A few minutes later, DCI Lapslie appeared through the doors of the police station. He stopped on top of the steps. Behind him was a woman. Carl looked anxiously for his mother, but she was absent. Perhaps Lapslie had already arranged for a car to take her home.

'Ladies and gentlemen, thank you all for coming,' Lapslie said in a loud, commanding voice that brooked no interruption. 'I will read out a short statement, and then there will be time for questions afterwards. Please appreciate that we have an ongoing investigation, and every minute I spend briefing you is a minute I am not spending with my team of officers sifting through the evidence.' He paused momentarily, then continued against a background of clicking cameras: 'As you will know, a commuter was murdered on his way to work this morning. He died as a result of a deliberate explosion at Braintree Parkway station at approximately five-thirty a.m. The victim's name . . . the victim's name was Alec Wildish, and I can inform you that his family have been notified.'

Carl felt warmth spread through his body. It wasn't the Charnaud murder, which his mother was now working on, but it was almost as good. It was the more recent killing, the one in Braintree.

Alec Wildish. At least he now had a name for his victim. He'd never killed an Alec before.

'This is a traumatic time for them, of course,' Lapslie continued, 'and we ask you to leave them in peace whilst they come to terms with their loss.'

Carl craned his neck for a better look at the girl. She was watching Lapslie with a concerned expression on her face.

'We have conducted a full forensic examination of the area,' Lapslie went on, 'and taken comprehensive statements from everyone who was present. We are pursuing several critical lines of enquiry, and we expect to have results in the near future. I have been asked to stress to you that we do not, at the moment, have any reason to believe that this tragic incident is related to either gang activity or terrorism.' He seemed to Carl to be sweating more than he should. Perhaps he got nervous talking to the press. 'Please understand that, were I to say any more, I might prejudice the progress of the ongoing inquiry. I ask you to respect that, and to phrase your questions accordingly.'

Another girl — an Asian girl with a clipboard — stepped forward from where she had been hidden behind Lapslie, but one of the journalists at the front of the pack called out: 'Do you have any suspects?'

'We are pursuing multiple lines of inquiry, and it would be inappropriate of me to go into details at the moment,' Lapslie said.

'Did the victim die at the scene, or at hospital?' This from someone unshaven, in jeans and a checked shirt, beside Carl. He tried to shrink down so that he wouldn't be noticed.

'The victim died at the scene,' Lapslie said firmly.

'Are you warning the public to stay away from public transport?' Another voice, more cultivated this time.

'We are treating this explosion as an isolated incident. The rail networks have been asked to increase their security measures, but I would stress that we are not expecting this to be the first in a campaign of bombings directed against railway stations, or anywhere else.'

'Does the fact that you've been assigned to this case mean that the Catherine Charnaud investigation is stalled?'

Carl tried to work out what the expression was on Lapslie's face, to see whether there was any evidence, anything his mother could work with, but Lapslie was just looking as if he could hear something far off that nobody else could hear. His head was cocked to one side and he was frowning.

And then, without any warning, DCI Lapslie collapsed to his knees and pitched forward, onto his face, sprawled on the steps of Chelmsford police HQ.

9

When he had been first assigned to Essex Constabulary, Lapslie had done some quick research on the Internet to see what he was getting into. Although he could have checked a lot of the details within either his local library or the specialist information resource where he was then assigned, both courses of action would have meant he would have been sitting in a room for some time with other people, and no matter how quiet a library or an information resource is meant to be, there's always something disturbing the peace — the turning of pages, the clicking of keys, the gentle snoring of someone who has fallen asleep while reading the newspaper — and that translated for Lapslie into an unwelcome taste in his mouth: a metallic tang that tainted every glass of water or can of Coca Cola that he tried to flush it away with. So he chose to do most of his research at home or in an empty office somewhere. Having first found out whatever he could about the constabulary at the top level (it covered about 3600 square kilometres of ground and around one and a half million people with fewer than three thousand officers from its base in Chelmsford), he then delved into the ten territorial divisions for which the Chief Constable was responsible. Braintree was one of them, but having typed 'Braintree Police Station' into the search engine he was surprised to see a photograph of an imposing, square building tiled in beautiful iridescent blue. The sign above the wide doors said 'Braintree Police Department', which was a little strange, but it took him a few minutes to work out that he was looking at the Police Department for the Town of Braintree in Massachusetts, USA, not Braintree in Essex. Needless to say, when he finally discovered a picture of the Braintree Police Station that he was looking for, and then finally saw it in the flesh, it left something to be desired compared with its American counterpart. Built in that peculiar 1970s style of architecture that seemed to major on layers, horizontal lines and terraces, it stuck out like a sore thumb in its location in the centre of town.

And now he was sitting again at a computer screen watching Braintree Police Station at work, although this time he was based in an otherwise bare office in Jane Catherall's mortuary and he was watching the inside, not the outside, of the building.

Emma Bradbury had set up a temporary incident room to investigate the bombing at Braintree Parkway station where the various police officers and civilian support staff assigned to the case could work. Half the room was set up with desks, phones and computers, while the other half was kept clear for team briefings and for the various whiteboards, map boards and pinboards that would proliferate as the investigation widened. She had also managed to set up a videoconference facility, with a webcam sitting on one side of the incident room relaying

181

everything it saw back to Lapslie in the mortuary, and a similar webcam sitting on top of the computer screen in front of him relaying his picture back to a screen in the incident room. Microphones at both ends relayed sounds back and forth, but, unlike real life, they came with mute buttons and volume controls.

Lapslie felt awkward, trying to run an investigation at one step removed, but he had no choice. If the background noise in a library caused him to experience a faint metallic tang then the sound of several officers making phone calls and talking to each other was like a continuous nose bleed. And that was before the recent and sudden escalation in his condition. Incident rooms tended to be noisy places at the best of times. It would do him and the investigation no good at all if he kept having to rush out of meetings to throw up. He could have worn the earphones that Emma had considerately provided, but what kind of message would that send? Leaders had to be engaged with the team; and if he sat there, isolated from them all, they would begin to talk. Rumours about his condition would grow. No, best to let Emma be the visible head of the team while he sat back in the shadows.

A still, small voice in the back of Lapslie's mind kept telling him that he was overreacting, but the racing of his heart and the trembling of his hands told him that he was just being sensible. He could feel a sheen of sweat cold against his forehead. He had to get this sorted. He couldn't live the rest of his life like this, holding the world at arm's length, spectating at his own job.

Over to one side of the incident room, Lapslie saw Emma in deep conversation with a uniformed constable. He pressed a button on his keyboard that caused a light to come on next to the computer screen in the incident room. Emma saw it, and he could tell from her body language that she was disengaging herself from the conversation.

'Boss?' she said, sitting down in front of her screen and camera. 'Is this thing working okay?' Stripped of many of its frequencies, her voice was still tinged with citrus but it was like a memory of a taste, rather than the real thing.

'Seems to be. First thing: well done on securing the space there. It can't have been easy.'

'It wasn't. I think DI Morritt had an eye on this office for himself. He's squeezed into a corner next to the coffee machine at the moment. Every time I see him, he tells me to sort out something where he can shut the door and be alone. I'm thinking of having his desk moved into the goods lift.'

Lapslie laughed. 'And I'd testify on your behalf at the subsequent complaints tribunal. Okay, where are we with the case?'

Emma looked down and to her left for a moment, frowning. Lapslie had read somewhere that the direction a person looked when they were thinking was an indication of which part of their brain they were using. Looking down and to the left suggested they were recalling memories.

'We've collated all the witness statements from the station,' she said after a few seconds, 'and we're combing through them now looking for anything out of the ordinary: people on rooftops, strange behaviours and so on. Separately, we're checking back through Alec Wildish's life. He lived alone, but there's an ex-wife who's based near Maldon. She has an alibi, which we're checking out at the moment.'

'Okay, sounds like we're covering all the bases. Have the next of kin been informed, by the way?'

'DI Morritt did that. I think it was a way of clawing back some measure of control over the case.'

'And I'm happy for him. Anything in the victim's background — family life, work, social — that might indicate a motive?'

'Nothing yet. He lived a quiet life: no big passions, no strong emotions as far as we can tell. He wasn't on the horizon of the local police for any reason.'

'And the locality? Tell me there was a crack-house down the street that he was petitioning against so hard that they decided to do something about him.'

'There's a tea shop. Does that count?'

'The way this country's going, it might do in the future. But not now.' He sighed. 'We're heading for a dead end.'

'Anything come out of the post mortem?'

'Nothing. I don't suppose either the ex-wife or her new boyfriend is in the army? That would explain the bomb.'

'She works at Kwik-Fit. They get a uniform.'

'Not the same.' Lapslie thought for a moment. 'Forensics?'

Emma brightened. 'Sean Burrows sent an email through wondering if we wanted an update on his tests. You want me to head over?'

Lapslie thought for a moment. 'As I recall, the forensics lab is a haven of peace and quiet compared with a police incident room. I think I can stand it for a while. If not, I'll leave and let you get on with it. See you there in an hour?'

She glanced at the corner of her computer screen. It looked for a moment as if she was staring at Lapslie's left knee, but he realised that she was checking the system time on the Windows status bar. 'No problem; I'll be there. Oh, I meant to say: the chief wants you to arrange a press conference. There's a lot of interest in this case — man gets blown up while waiting for a train, no apparent motive. You can imagine what the papers'll make of it.'

'I imagine the *Daily Mail* is already putting together a headline worrying about the state of the country.'

'And they'll probably try and blame it on illegal immigrants.'

The thought of holding a press conference appalled him. Sweat prickled his palms, his scalp and between his shoulder blades at the very thought. The noise, the sheer uncontrolled noise would be enough to send him over the edge as flavour after flavour, some of which had no real counterpart in the world, jostled for attention on his tongue.

He shook his head convulsively. 'Not my cup

185

of tea. Too many people; too much noise. Let DI Morritt deal with it.'

'I asked him. He said it was the responsibility of the person leading the investigation to conduct the press conference.'

Lapslie felt the corners of his mouth turning down, the muscles twitching. He felt like a petulant child. 'Great. When it comes to desks he wants to be in charge; when it comes to dealing with the press then he's happy to step back and leave me in the firing line. He'll go far. Look, Emma, I just can't do this. I really can't.'

She nodded sympathetically. 'I'll get in touch with the chief. See if I can get it put off, or get someone from Public Relations to cover it.'

'Thanks. I appreciate it. Oh, and arrange a higher police profile within the Braintree area, centred on Parkway, if you can. More uniforms on the ground; more patrols. Tell them to look out for any suspicious activity on rooftops. At least it'll be something we can announce at the press conference.'

'No problem.' She left the chair, revealing the incident room behind her in all its glory. One or two of the officers manning the phones glanced warily across at the camera, aware that the boss was watching them, but they soon got swept back into the rhythm of the investigation and forgot all about him.

Lapslie leant back in his chair in the spare mortuary office and let his mind wander across the details of the case, such as they were. He was beginning to suspect that there was no motive at all, that Alec Wildish had been singled out at

186

random by a bomber who might just as easily have killed the person beside him, the person behind him or the Station Manager. An Act of God, albeit a particularly capricious and dark God. And presumably, if the killing was just a random act, they could expect more. But where?

He still couldn't get the image of Alec Wildish out of his mind; opened up on Dr Catherall's post-mortem table. Who could possibly get out of bed in the morning knowing that there was a chance, even a faint chance, they could end up like that? People blinded themselves to all kinds of possibilities in their normal lives.

His mobile began to ring: Bruch's 1st violin concerto. At the same time, he tasted coffee. He picked it up and accepted the call quickly, before the taste became too overriding.

'Lapslie.'

'DCI Lapslie? I have Chief Superintendent Rouse for you.'

Unconsciously, Lapslie straightened up in his chair.

'Mark?'

'Sir. I presume you want an update on the Braintree bomb. Or is it the Catherine Charnaud murder?' He left the obvious implication — that he was handling two high-profile cases at the same time — hanging.

There was a tinge of something tropical about Rouse's voice when he answered that indicated not that he was lying but that he was being careful with his words. 'There's increasing pressure in HQ over both cases. Apparently BBC2 are going to be running an extended

Newsnight piece on the Charnaud killing tonight, and the Home Office have already been on the phone about the bombing. Can you come over at 0900 tomorrow to brief me?'

Driving into Chelmsford. The traffic. The noise. And then the walk up to Rouse's office, and the sitting listening to the man talk. Lapslie felt the tremor in his hands increase, and balled them into fists. Jesus, what was happening to him? Was he going to be frightened of *everything* from now on?

'Sir, could we do this by videoconference? Only — '

'I do videoconferences with the Home Secretary and the Chief Constable,' Rouse said firmly. 'Not with subordinates. My office. Nine a.m.'

'Just me, sir?' Lapslie asked, suspecting what the answer would be.

Rouse paused judiciously. 'DI Morritt will be coming across as well.'

'You've already talked to him?'

'He's already talked to me.'

Lapslie nodded, although Rouse couldn't see him. 'I understand. His nose is out of joint.'

'He feels . . . aggrieved that he has been sidelined, yes. We'll discuss it later. He's a good man, by the way.'

'I'm sure he is.' Lapslie wondered whether to raise the matter of the press conference with Rouse, but he felt like he'd been knocked back enough for one phone call. Let Emma handle it.

Rouse hung up without any of the formalities of ending a phone conversation. Lapslie gazed at his mobile for a few moments, considering his options. Not turn up? Resign? Probably came to the same thing.

If he wore earplugs and took some tranquillisers before setting off, maybe he could just about get through it. Maybe.

On the screen, in the incident room, Morritt was where Emma had said he would be: squeezed in beside the coffee machine. He was talking on the phone while writing notes: in the old days he would have had the handset jammed between his shoulder and his chin while he wrote, but nowadays the police telephone exchanges were computer controlled, and you could wear a headset with a built-in microphone arm to make your calls with while doing something else with your hands. Or just listen to music on your computer while you were working.

On the way out of the mortuary to his car, Lapslie's mobile rang again. He checked the display. *Sonia*, it said.

He stopped dead. His mouth was suddenly dry. He ran his tongue over his teeth, feeling the grittiness of the normally moist enamel. His hand trembled slightly, holding the ringing phone, then pressed the *accept* button.

'Sonia?'

'Mark. I'm not calling at a bad time, am I?' As always, her voice was a blend of Madagascan vanilla and orange blossom honey.

He bit back the first five or six replies that came to mind. No matter the intention behind what he said, Sonia would find a way to misunderstand, just as he always read unintended meanings into whatever she said. That was the state of their relationship: each of them sensitive to sniping and reacting accordingly, whether or not the attack was actually real. They were both emotionally raw.

'It's good to hear your voice,' he said, ducking the question entirely. *I'm always busy* would sound like he was trying to score points, and maybe to indicate that he hadn't got anything else to do with his life now that she and the kids had gone. *It doesn't matter how busy I am, I can always make time to talk to you* sounded too earnest, as if he was going to break down and beg her to come back.

'It's been a while,' she said, and he could almost hear her biting the words back again, knowing that she'd given him an opening to make some kind of point about the fact that she only ever called when she wanted something, never just to chat.

Instead, he ducked that one as well, holding fire until he knew why she had called. 'How are the kids?'

'Jamie's got a commendation at school. I'll scan it in and email it to you. Robbie's got a cold, but he's still insisting on going swimming whenever he can.'

'Can you email some photos as well? I feel like I haven't seen them for ages.' Too begging, too needy. And it gave her an opening to say something about how little time he was spending with them.

'I will,' she said, avoiding the obvious

response. A concession. 'Mark, can we get together for a coffee some time? I need to ask you something.'

'Tomorrow?' he said, surprised. Sonia rarely suggested getting together without the kids being there.

'Early?'

'Apparently I've got a meeting with Alan Rouse in Chelmsford,' he said with a trace of bitterness. 'He's a Chief Superintendent now. How about lunch?'

She paused, reluctant. 'Okay,' she said eventually, 'but it'll have to be a light snack. I have some appointments in the afternoon.'

'Shall I pick you up?' He knew she would refuse, but he got some small pleasure in putting her on the defensive for a moment.

'No,' she said quickly. 'I'll meet you there. Café Rouge in Chelmsford town centre? Twelve thirty?'

'Okay. Twelve thirty it is. I'll see you tomorrow.'

'Tomorrow. Bye.' She rang off so quickly she must have had her finger on the button already. Usually, when people cancelled a call, there was a delay of a second or so while they took the phone away from their mouth, held it away from them and pressed the button. Or was he reading too much into every little thing?

Reluctantly, he headed out of the mortuary and into the car park.

The forensics laboratory was based out in the wilds of Essex; a fenced-off, guarded compound

191

isolated from everywhere else. Only the cherry-flavoured birdsong could be heard. Emma was already waiting for him. They both had to book in at a reception area. Showing a warrant card was no longer enough: in the wake of terrorist attacks around the UK, security around any forensics area had been increased. One of Burrows's people — a thin lad with ginger hair — came to fetch them. He led them through Formica-tiled corridors in which the only sound was the echoing *click* of their heels and the *swish* as fire doors closed behind them. The noises caused a background taste of aniseed in Lapslie's mouth, but he swallowed it back and kept going. So far, he was okay. So far.

Burrows's laboratory was gleaming white and tiled: fume cupboards against the wall and benches lined up in the centre of the room; some with microscopes, some with high-tech equipment that Lapslie was hard-pressed to identify, and some with basics like light boxes and cameras on stands. Burrows came to meet them at the door. Lapslie had forgotten how small he was: barely taller than Jane Catherall, he estimated, although the quiff of white hair that sprung straight up from his scalp gave him another few inches.

'DCI Lapslie, DS Bradbury.' His voice made Lapslie think of blackberries, raspberries, vodka. 'Welcome to my domain.'

'Mr Burrows — you wanted to see us? I presume it wasn't just social?'

Burrows shook his head. 'Lovely though it is to see you, I do have something to tell you. Can

192

I get you a coffee, by the way?'

Lapslie shook his head before Emma could answer. He wanted to get out of there as quickly as possible, and the way his mouth was feeling the last thing he wanted to do was to put another strong flavour in there. 'No thanks. What's come out of the investigation into the Braintree bomb?'

'There's a lot of samples to examine, but so far there's nothing out of the ordinary. We'll analyse all the fragments, of course, check the chemical composition of the explosive and try to track it back to a manufacturer, but that's about the best we can do.'

'Do you know what the explosive was?'

Burrows smiled. 'Ah, you can't beat the old favourites. It was Semtex H — which is technically a fifty-fifty mixture of pentaerythritol tetranitrate and cyclotrimethylene trinitramine with the addition of N-phenyl-2-naphthylamine as an antioxidant and di-n-octyl phthalate and tri-n-butyl citrate as plasticisers.'

'If you're ever on *Mastermind*,' Emma said, 'make sure you choose 'Explosives' as your specialist subject.'

'Funny you should mention that,' Burrows continued, unfazed. 'I do know quite a lot about Semtex. The stuff manufactured since 2002 has been deliberately adulterated with ethylene glycol dinitrate, making it easier to detect by security agencies. It's also been coloured with a reddish-orange food dye named Sudan 1 to make it easier to spot. Chemical analysis confirms that the explosive used at Braintree is the original stuff, not the new adulterated version.'

'No point checking manufacturers or suppliers, then,' Lapslie said. 'What about the potential triggering point up on the roof of the retail centre? Anything there?'

'Nothing useful,' Burrows said sorrowfully. 'There was evidence of someone having been there. We discovered a small pool of urine a little way away: looks like whoever it was got caught short and had to take a piss. I'm assuming it wasn't a dog; not up on the roof. Probably did it into an empty bottle — it's the kind of thing these survivalist types love doing — but a little spilled.'

'Survivalist types?' Emma questioned.

'It's a particular mindset,' Burrows said. 'I've been reading up on it. Military wannabes, ex-army blowhards. All wanting to prove themselves. That's the appeal of a bomb: they can convince themselves that they're hunters tracking their prey, not just common or garden murderers.'

'Duly noted,' Lapslie said. 'Can you get anything from the urine?'

'There's little or no DNA in urine,' Burrows answered, 'and even if we isolated some it wouldn't be much use unless you had something to compare it with. We're running a check of the hormone levels now: should be able to tell you whether it was a man or a woman, at least, but chances are it's a man. Most bombers are.'

'That's the mindset thing again, isn't it?'

'I'm just a frustrated profiler,' Burrows

admitted. 'You get that way, poring over samples of hair and semen every day. You wonder: whose hair is this? Why did they dye it blond and then red a few days later? Are they unhappy with the way they look, or are they disguising themselves? And this semen: does the donor know he's deficient in the sperm department? Is that why he raped so many women so brutally — just a repressed inferiority complex?' He shook himself. 'Evidence without context is just data; that's what I say.'

'Okay,' Lapslie said, taken aback by Burrow's sudden flash of . . . of what? Was it a deep-seated dissatisfaction with his job? Or was it just his underlying humanity shining through the scientific veneer? 'Thanks. Let me know if anything else turns up.'

Burrows paused thoughtfully. 'There is something unusual about the urine, though, and that's why I thought you ought to come over. It had a marked purple colour. Might be a result of something the bomber ate or drank, but it might also indicate some kind of metabolic problem. I'm doing some background research on that.'

'Okay — let me know what you find.'

Leaving the forensics laboratory, Lapslie said to Emma, 'Did you manage to get me out of that press conference?'

She shook her head. 'No joy, boss. Rouse's office were insistent. It goes ahead, and you do it. We've got two hours to get back and prepare.'

'Fuck,' he said bleakly. There was no way out.

'On the bright side, I arranged to see the profiler this afternoon at Catherine Charnaud's

195

house. There's just enough time to fit it in before the press conference. I assume you want to come along?'

'You assume right,' he growled.

The drive back to Catherine Charnaud's place in Chigwell was familiar now, and Lapslie found his mind wandering while he drove, wondering about the drumming sound that he kept on hearing, and whether Jane Catherall was right about it signifying a connection to the murderer. And if so, was it something that only he could smell, or was there some distinct odour that the killer was giving off that anyone could detect, if they got close enough?

The profiler wasn't there when they arrived, so Lapslie and Emma went straight into the house.

'I take it the boyfriend's not living here?' Lapslie asked.

Emma shook her head. 'It's apparently in her name, and we're still processing the crime scene. He's living with a friend at the moment.'

Lapslie grimaced. 'I still reckon him for this. If your profiler tells us that the killer is likely to be a young, muscular sportsman of low intelligence then I reckon we've wasted our money.'

'You can find out for yourself,' Emma rejoined, looking out of the door. 'I think she's arrived. I'll go and make sure the room is clear.'

Lapslie exited the house just as Eleanor Whittley was walking up to the porch. She was tall and elegant, in her mid-fifties, he estimated. Her grey hair was worn long, and her eyes were bright and clear.

'I am Eleanor Whittley,' she said before he

could say anything. He tasted celery and pepper in her voice, and a tinge of juniper berries.

'Pleased to meet you.' Lapslie extended his hand. 'I'm DCI Lapslie.'

Eleanor Whittley looked at Lapslie's hand as if it was a previously unknown species of fish. 'I never shake hands,' she said. 'I'm not being rude, just practical. It's a fetishised custom dating back to the days when warriors extended their right hands to prove they were not holding weapons. It has no meaning these days.' She frowned, as if remembering something. 'You were responsible for the Madeline Poel case, weren't you?'

The name caught Lapslie by surprise. He'd not thought about Madeline Poel for a while. 'Insofar as we didn't know we had a case for some time, yes, I was.'

'An interesting character, as far as I can tell from the reports I have read. A shame you let her die. I would have enjoyed finding out more about her and what caused the aberrant personality that you and others observed.'

A spike of anger flashed across his mind. 'I didn't 'let' her die.'

'You failed to stop her, despite the fact that you knew she had a preparation of cyanide nearby.' Eleanor gazed up at him with the kind of expression Lapslie had seen Jane Catherall use when looking at a particularly problematic corpse. 'Did you *want* her to die? She had, after all, attempted to poison you, and had been responsible for at least eight deaths beforehand and probably more.'

The flash of anger threatened to explode into a

full-scale thunderstorm. 'Nevertheless, it was my responsibility to arrest her, not kill her.'

'The psychologist whose report was attached to the file wrote that she was a classic example of someone suffering from Multiple Personality Disorder, but I disagree.' Eleanor looked away, back towards her car. 'It seems to me that the various personalities she exhibited were not alternative to one another, but sequential. She was not switching from identity to identity, but moving from one to the next, as if she was mentally fleeing from some traumatic event buried far in her past.'

'I tend to agree,' Lapslie said. He was beginning to feel some respect for Eleanor. She seemed to have nailed Madeline Poel's complex psychology in a way that the police psychologists had failed to do. 'From what little I could tell when I talked to her, and what evidence of her past activities I could dig up, she could still access memories from her previous identities. She not only knew who she was, but who she had been.'

'Instructive. We will talk further about that.' It was less of a request and more of an instruction. 'Now I will need to start at the scene of the crime.'

'What exactly are you looking *for*?' Lapslie asked, trying to regain at least some control over the conversation.

'My field of expertise is personality disorders.' At Lapslie's raised eyebrow she explained: 'The phrase 'personality disorders' is generally taken to mean psychological problems arising from personal dispositions, rather than a breakdown or discontinuity in psychological functioning.'

Lapslie knew what she meant, but decided to push her a bit. 'Can you develop that for me?' he asked, using a phrase that a particular chief constable, now retired, had been well known for using when he wanted something explained.

'I mean an underlying problem that has been present for some time, rather than a problem that has suddenly occurred.'

'What kind of problems? Can you give me some examples that I might recognise?'

'The *Diagnostic and Statistical Manual of Mental Disorders* entry on personality disorders — which I helped draft for the American Psychiatric Association, lists a number of different categories such as paranoid, schizoid, schizotypal, antisocial, histrionic, narcissistic, avoidant, dependent, obsessive compulsive, passive-aggressive, sadistic and self-defeating. These are all enduring patterns of perceiving, and relating to, the environment. Criminals falling into one of these categories will commit crimes with distinct 'signatures', and it is my job to recognise these signatures and tell you what kind of criminal you are looking for.'

Eleanor seemed weighed down with the theory and rather light on putting it into practice. 'Not sure how this is going to help,' Lapslie murmured.

'Let me try and make it more clear. The process of 'profiling' draws on both physical and non-physical information. This includes the layout of the crime scene, the disposition of the victim, the presence or absence of significant items and evidence not just of what was done to the victim but also what the perpetrator did before and after the crime. The goal is for me to narrow your field of investigation down, the basic assumption being that the perpetrator's behaviour at the crime scene reflects a consistency of personality which might enable them to be identified.'

'Okay,' Lapslie said. He'd tweaked her enough. 'Let's get up there and see what we can see.'

Emma Bradbury was just emerging from the kitchen when Lapslie led Eleanor into the house. He introduced them. Emma, picking up perhaps on some subtle signal, didn't try to shake hands.

The bedroom was more or less the way Lapslie remembered it, minus Catherine Charnaud's corpse, of course, which was still in storage at the mortuary and would remain so until the case was either complete or closed. Her blood had dried to a dark maroon colour, with a void of unstained material on the blue bedspread the exact width of her body. It looked to Lapslie strangely like an ancient map, with two continents bisected by an ocean. The smell in the room was mustier now than it had been, less metallic and more unpleasant, but the wall-wide window and the pillows and even the trainers under the chair were exactly the same.

They all stood just inside the doorway; stationary and expectant, attention focused on the bed as though they were all waiting for a show to begin. Eleanor leaned forward slightly, head cocked to one side.

'This is — ' Emma began.

'Please!' Eleanor held up a hand. 'I prefer to start with no preconceptions.' Closer to her now, Lapslie thought for a moment that her voice was tasting more and more of juniper berries, but he suddenly realised that she actually did smell of gin. She'd been drinking.

She moved forward slowly, sweeping her head from side to side, taking in everything in the room.

As she worked, Lapslie closed his eyes and listened. He could hear the rustling of Emma's clothes as she moved. He could hear the distant snarl of traffic on the main road. He could hear birds chirping and singing to one another.

And he could hear drums, very faintly, almost as if he was several miles away from a rock concert — the same drums he'd heard the last time he was there, when Catherine Charnaud's body had been splayed across the bed. The kind of rock concert that Emma apparently went to, he thought, smiling.

'You have comprehensive photographs of the scene as you found it?' Eleanor asked, interrupting.

'Of course,' Lapslie replied, opening his eyes. 'They're all back at the incident room in Chelmsford.'

'Why Chelmsford? Surely the investigation should have been run from Chigwell?'

Lapslie shrugged. 'Our Chief Superintendent wanted direct control over the case, given the high profile of the victim. And I think he also wanted to send a message to the media that he was taking this seriously, not just letting the local coppers run with it.'

'I'll need to see the photographs. And the body, of course.'

'I'll arrange all that. Does anything strike you immediately?'

Eleanor shook her head. 'It's too early to make a snap judgement. I take it the girl was restrained in some way?'

'Plastic builders' ties.'

'And did the perpetrator bring these ties with them, or find them here?'

'Here. They were in a kitchen drawer.'

'And the weapon that was used to torture and kill her?'

Emma frowned. 'Torture? You're sure it was torture? Isn't that a . . . preconception?'

Eleanor glanced at her superciliously. 'It doesn't take a forensic clinical psychologist to know that slicing a victim's flesh off while they are still alive takes a lot more effort then when they are dead. There has to be a balancing gain to set against the loss of time and energy; the perpetrator has to be getting something from it, something psychological. This implies that they are enjoying themselves; gaining pleasure from the suffering they are inflicting. Torture, in short.' She glanced back at the bed. 'And the flesh from the arm — did you ever find it?'

Lapslie shook his head. 'No. The murderer . . . the *perpetrator* . . . must have taken it with them and either disposed of it or kept it as some kind of grisly trophy.'

'Or eaten it,' Eleanor murmured.

'*Eaten* it?'

'Anthropophagy is a reasonably common obsession with serial killers. In Kazakhstan they had Nikolai Dzhumagaliev; in America Jeffrey Dahmer; in France Issei Sagawa; in Germany Karl Denke . . . The list goes on.'

'And Dennis Nilsen here in the UK,' Emma murmured.

'Not so,' Eleanor disagreed. 'Although Dennis Nilsen cut up and boiled his victims, he was doing so to dispose of the remains, not to eat. You see the difference? By the way, I presume your forensics experts checked the kitchen for signs of activity?'

Lapslie looked questioningly at Emma. She nodded. 'No dirty plates or cooking utensils, and no signs that anything had been washed up that night.'

'The perpetrator might have eaten her raw, of course,' Eleanor mused. 'Like sushi. But why the arm? Cannibals usually start either on the buttocks if the victim is female or, if the victim is male, on the genitalia. There's a marked sexual element to anthropophagy, and also a kind of trophy-taking. It's a way of truly possessing your victim, of owning them for ever, in the most personal way possible.' She frowned. 'I believe I asked about the weapon that was used.'

'A knife,' Lapslie paused, feeling faintly sick. 'A *kitchen* knife. It was never recovered.'

'But it came from the kitchen,' Eleanor said, her tone more one of explanation than question.

'How did you know?' Lapslie asked.

'Because of the builders' ties,' Eleanor

explained. 'The perpetrator found everything they needed here, in the house. That strongly implies that the murder was not premeditated, otherwise they would have prepared, brought their tools with them. A favourite knife, perhaps, or some rope that they had already purchased. With premeditated murders, the preparation is almost as important to the perpetrator as the actual event. They get sexual satisfaction from a ritualistic anticipation of what is to come. With unpremeditated murders the event occurs almost by accident, perhaps as an escalation of an argument, or an experimental sexual session gone wrong. Something unexpected happens and they suddenly find themselves carrying out a murder using whatever comes to hand, almost acting as voyeurs of themselves. They typically say afterwards that they don't know what made them do it, although looking back at their lives and what they had done in the days and weeks prior to the event it is often possible to discern a pattern, pointing to what is to come; a pattern which they cannot themselves see.'

'Unpremeditated,' Emma said. 'The escalation of an argument or an experimental sexual session gone wrong. Using whatever comes to hand.'

'I know what you're thinking,' Lapslie said. 'The boyfriend. He comes home, he's drunk, they get into a fight, and before he knows it he's — ' He stopped, suddenly wordless. 'Torturing her? Stripping the flesh from her arm?

I still don't buy it. Why the flesh? Why the arm?'

'He's the only suspect we have,' Emma pointed out.

'But that doesn't mean he's guilty,' Lapslie rejoined. He turned to Eleanor. 'What else can we do to help?'

'There's only so much I can do here,' she said. 'The next step would be to see the body and the crime scene photographs. Would it be possible to do that now?'

Lapslie looked at his watch. 'I've got a press conference on another case in an hour,' he said. 'That's in Chelmsford as well. Did you want to follow me there?'

'My . . . driver . . . is waiting outside in his own car. I wouldn't want to hold him up for too long. He needs to get back for . . . well, for other reasons. Could you give me a lift?'

'Of course, and then I could get a police driver to drop you off at home afterwards. If that's okay.'

'That will be acceptable,' she said, nodding. 'I'll tell him to go.'

Lapslie turned to Emma Bradbury. 'You take her,' he said as Eleanor walked over to her car which, Lapslie noticed for the first time, had a driver inside. 'I want her to know that she works for me, not the other way around.'

On the drive to Chelmsford, Lapslie spent the time mulling over what he knew of the investigation so far, and of what he could say. Neither amounted to much. A man was dead, blown up at long range, and his killer was still at large. Various leads were being pursued. That was about as far as it went. The key, of course, was to sound positive and to try not to give the media anything they could use as the basis for panicky headlines or to lead with on the *Ten O'Clock News*. He'd held press conferences before, of course — it was almost impossible to rise to his rank without having some experience of dealing with the press or TV crews — but he never enjoyed the process the way that some of his contemporaries obviously did. Following a deliberately anodyne statement he always seemed to end up replying to every question with one of three standard phrases: 'I'm afraid I can't reveal that at the moment', 'We are pursuing all lines of enquiry', and 'We urge the public to come forward with any information'.

As he drove past the front of the Chelmsford police station and round to the gated back entrance, Lapslie could see a crowd of journalists milling around the steps. A couple of TV cameras were in evidence: probably local news, although that would change as time went on and the focus of the country turned on Braintree — assuming he hadn't caught the bomber by then. When he brought the car to a halt he stepped out, and was immediately accosted by an Asian woman in a nicely cut dark suit. From the corner of his eye he noticed Emma escorting Eleanor Whittley inside the building.

'DCI Lapslie? I'm Seiju.' Her voice sent slivers of butterscotch and beetroot sliding down Lapslie's throat. He could feel his stomach beginning to rebel already. He started walking towards the back entrance to the station. The woman kept pace, step for step. 'I'm the PR rep for this area.' She handed him a thin folder. 'Here's the statement we've come up with for today. Please read through it a few times: it'll make it sound more natural when you come to read it out. Make sure you make eye contact as much as you can. When you've finished reading the statement I'll ask for questions. We've allowed enough time for four or five, then we'll call a halt and say you have to get back to the investigation.'

'Which I do,' he said. No point getting annoyed. This was how policing was done these days, and, who knew, perhaps someone watching might actually come forward with some usable information. Miracles did happen.

Emma came up beside them, having parked her car. 'I've arranged to have an interview room freed up,' she said, making meaningful eye contact with Lapslie. 'So you can read the statement in . . . peace and quiet.'

He nodded at her, not able to bring himself to smile. 'Thanks. I appreciate it.'

'Room eight, ground floor.'

'Do you have another suit?' Seiju demanded. 'No. Hmm. With make-up — '

'No make-up,' he snapped. 'I'm a policeman, not a sodding newsreader.'

He flicked through the folder's contents as he walked through the station to the interview room, shedding Seiju and Emma as he went, trying to move at such a pace that he didn't have time to register any noises. There was nothing that surprised him in the statement, and nothing that gave anything away. The position of the bomber was the only thing he was trying to keep within the investigation team at the moment, and it wasn't referred to in the brief.

In the interview room he sat quietly for a moment, door closed, thinking. Thinking about the way his synaesthesia had suddenly become a problem, rather than just an obstacle. And thinking of Sonia.

They had been married for, what, twenty years, and separated now for three. There was still love there, he was sure of that, but they just couldn't live together. His synaesthesia meant that he needed quiet, especially when he was at home. No radio, no TV, no CDs and no loud noises. The silence had almost driven Sonia to a nervous collapse, but the alternative was that the flood of cross-switched sensory impressions would have driven Lapslie the same way. And the arrival of the kids had just made things worse. Sonia had suggested that he wear earplugs around the house, and that had worked for a while, except that it cut him off from all the normal family activities. If anybody talked to him, he couldn't hear them to answer, and if he asked anybody a question they told him to keep his voice down. He felt like an observer in his own life.

In the end, the only thing worse than living without his family was living with them.

''Now that my ladder's gone, I must lie down where all the ladders start,'' he quoted softly to himself. ''In the foul rag-and-bone shop of the heart.''

A knock on the door heralded the arrival of Seiju, the PR girl.

'Time to go,' she said brightly. 'Ready?'

'No,' he replied quietly. 'Does it matter?'

He strode out and down the corridor, psyching himself up for the confrontation with the press. On the way through the lobby he could see through the glass of the front doors to where they were silently congregating. They were already jostling for position, growling like a pack of dogs trying to get to a single bowl of food.

He pushed the door open at a fast trot. It was like emerging from the hermetically sealed calm of an airport terminal into a howling gale. Everyone seemed to be talking at once. He felt as if he was choking on a torrent of blood. The coppery warmth filled his mouth, his throat, his sinuses. He wanted to gag, but dared not. Not in front of everyone.

'Ladies and gentlemen, thank you all for coming,' he said as he moved to the top of the steps. Journalists opened their mouths all around the crowd, ignoring what he said, ready to ask the first question that popped into their heads, but Lapslie pushed on, not giving them time to get anything out, overriding the nausea that wrenched at his stomach. He placed his hands behind his back, holding the statement folder, so that nobody would see the paper shaking. Sweat broke out across his forehead, but he couldn't wipe it away. That would just draw attention to it. 'I will read out a short statement, and then there will be time for questions afterwards. Please appreciate that we have an ongoing investigation, and every minute I spend briefing you is a minute I am not spending with my team of officers sifting through the evidence.'

He took a quick breath while he was bringing the folder up and opening it, doubling the cover back so that he could hold it easily in one hand. Seiju had printed the words in a large, clear font so that he could read it without squinting. The words came automatically, passing straight from his eyes to his mouth without engaging his brain. He tried to make them sound at least partially spontaneous as he spoke.

He paused fractionally after a few sentences, eyes scanning the text, before continuing with the next paragraph. His shirt was sticky against his armpits, and he hoped to God that the sweat stains weren't blooming through the material of his suit. He swallowed back on the blood that he could taste and yet not feel in his mouth.

As he finished the written statement Lapslie looked around, trying to hold his hands steady. Although most of the journalists present were recording what he said by various means, some of them were still taking written notes.

Seiju stepped forward, ready to act as Master of Ceremonies for the question session, but one of the journalists at the front of the pack got in first, asking a question about suspects.

Lapslie replied with something anodyne and non-committal. He could hear the waver in his voice. Was it obvious? Could anyone else hear it?

Another voice called out from the back asking where the victim died. As if that was important. Lapslie gave a short, factual answer, trying to keep the anger and the pain out of his voice. Jesus, he couldn't take too much more of this.

A man in the front of the pack asked a semi-intelligent question about threat levels and the public. From his suit, and the way he had managed to maintain his position, Lapslie guessed he was from the BBC. Lapslie told him that the explosion was being treated as an isolated incident, trying to keep to short sentences so that his voice wouldn't trail off. His stomach kept rebelling against the tight control he was exerting. He desperately wanted a glass of water.

Someone towards the back — possibly the person who had yelled the question about where the victim had died — called out another question, but Lapslie's attention was distracted by a sound. It had been going on for some time, just below the level of his conscious attention, but something about it was clamouring for him to notice it; a drumming, like a rapid heartbeat, or someone slapping their hands against the metal of a car roof. There was something primal about it, something that shook Lapslie to his very core. It was so loud that he expected the ground to be shaking. Why wasn't anyone turning to see where it was coming from? They were asking questions, mouths flapping like fish, but he couldn't hear what they were saying. All he could hear were the drums.

And then he couldn't even hear the drums, as he mercifully slipped into unconsciousness and crumpled onto the steps of Chelmsford police station.

10

Carl woke up stifling a scream, the back of his hand pressed against his mouth. Light from the streetlamps outside reflected off pools of rainwater on the pavements and in the gutters, stippling his ceiling with inconstant light.

In the bedroom next door his father snorted, then turned over in bed and started snoring.

He only remembered flashes of the dream. Animals, all dry and dusty, their eye sockets empty black voids, scurrying towards him over the bedspread; pinning his arms and legs, winding wire around them and twisting him into a painful pose, then watching from the edges of the room as he struggled against the wire and the blood trickled from the wounds where its sharp ends cut into his flesh.

Eventually he got up and made himself some breakfast: two slices of toast with a thin scraping of margarine and some peanut butter. It was still early, but he poured out a bowl of cereal for his father and put the kettle on, ready for a cup of tea.

He hadn't got much of an appetite any more. He ate to keep his strength up, but he didn't enjoy eating, and he could hardly taste the food. It was fuel, nothing more. He knew why. Back when his mother and father had been together, before the accident, he had sometimes sneaked a look at his mother's textbooks and the forensic reports she had brought home to read, and the things he had seen there had put him off food for days at a time. They still made his stomach churn when they unexpectedly surfaced in his mind like a rotten log in a stagnant pond. He still remembered the photographs of a man who had committed suicide by sticking a gun in his mouth and pulling the trigger. His head looked like it had split open at the top and the sides pushed apart like a smashed melon. His eyes had burst under the pressure of the shot and deflated, leaking fluid onto his cheeks. That image had haunted him through a whole year of school. There had been times at parties, when he was tanked up on alcohol and slow-dancing with a girl, that his mind suddenly flashed to those photographs and he had to run outside and throw up. And there were the photos of various Iraqi suicide bombers. His mother had consulted for the Ministry of Defence on profiling them, and some of the images she had been sent had showed what had happened to them during the explosions. One, he remembered, had been of a man's head and shoulders, blackened skin split like a jigsaw puzzle to reveal raw red flesh beneath, detached from the rest of his body, one arm hanging loose, the other ripped at the joint. That one had haunted him for months.

Or perhaps it was the disease that was causing his lack of hunger, the blisters on his hands and the frequent desire to empty his bladder. He needed to make an appointment with the doctor's surgery. They opened at eight o'clock; he could ring them in less than an hour.

To waste some time until his father was awake or he could make the phone call, Carl turned the TV on. Unless his father was downstairs, the Freeview box was permanently set to BBC News 24. Carl had little time for the endless round of medical dramas, vacuous celebrity interviews and programmes in which ordinary people either found some expensive antique in their attics or at a boot sale and then had to pretend not to care about how much it was valued at. The only thing Carl was interested in was fact, and he was hoping that the broadcasts today would have something to say about the bomb at the railway station, as well as the continuing coverage of the stalled investigation into the murder of Catherine Charnaud.

It gave Carl a sense of power to know that he, and only he, knew that those two events were linked.

After the inevitable pieces about the Prime Minister dealing with terrorism, which just seemed to cycle around, day after day, the newsreader mentioned the bomb explosion. Carl's ears pricked up.

'Adam Till is at the Essex Police Headquarters in Chelmsford now. Adam, what's happening?'

The picture changed to a young man wearing a suit with a padded coat over the top. He was standing in front of a 1970s-style building that continued up out of the frame. People with cameras were milling around between him and the building. He was holding a microphone and staring out of the screen. There was a momentary pause before he responded.

'Dominic, I'm here in Chelmsford, where the officer in charge of the investigation, Detective Chief Inspector, Mark Lapslie, yesterday gave a press conference about the explosion. The police are not giving much away at the moment, but the strong message is that they do *not* think that this is part of a terrorist campaign. Instead, they are working on the theory that this is an isolated incident. DCI Lapslie was unexpectedly taken ill during the press conference, which had to be cut short. Police sources say that he has been admitted to hospital for tests. Nobody has yet said who is heading up the investigation in his absence.'

The reporter was replaced by a recorded shot of the policeman answering questions yesterday. The camera had been off to one side of where Carl had been standing, and had captured perfectly the moment when Lapslie had collapsed to the ground, but as he did so Carl found himself watching the woman standing behind him. Her hair was dark and cut close to her scalp; she wore a silk blouse in a golden orange colour and a black tailored jacket. She had a small golden stud in one ear.

Carl found himself increasingly fixated by the policewoman. Her eyes, her hair, the way she carried herself . . . A thought suddenly struck him, and it was as if there was electricity suddenly playing across his skin from the nape of his neck to the tips of his fingers.

What if he killed *her*? What if he actually killed one of the police team investigating the crime he had previously committed?

215

That would be different, he thought, his heart racing and sweat breaking out across his forehead. That would be very different.

There had to be something new, something different about the murder he wanted to commit next, and having the victim linked to a previous crime would be perfect. The police would be frantically assuming that the policewoman had been shot because she was involved with this investigation, whereas it would in fact be a complete coincidence. Carl wouldn't just be deliberately not setting a pattern; he would be setting a *fake* pattern.

Carl leaned back in the sofa, studying his prey with concentrated intensity. He would still go for a long-range head shot using the rifle, but now he had a target he could start to reconnoitre the best locations. He could shoot the woman through a window of her house or flat, for instance, assuming that there was a clear few hundred yards and a place from where he could take the shot without being disturbed. Or even better, could he shoot the woman through the window of her office, wherever that was, or as she left the police headquarters?

And what about the policeman — Mark Lapslie? Did Carl want him to be there when his assistant was gunned down? Did Carl want to watch him cradle her lifeless body in his arms?

He shivered. How perfect would that be?

The first thing to do would be to find out the woman's name, where she lived and what her habits were. That would then lead to a location and a plan. And then there was the question of *when*. Carl always varied the time between killings so that there was no discernible pattern, and the last two had been very close together. Should he leave a decent amount of time before he shot the policewoman, or would that actually be setting a pattern in itself?

He decided to leave it up to chance. The next number he saw, that would be the number of days before he killed the policewoman.

Turning off the TV, he called the doctor's surgery and was lucky enough to get an appointment later that morning. He took his father's breakfast up and, before he would let his father eat, he checked the colostomy bag. Rather than a strap-on type, it was attached to his father's skin with a small circle of wax and a sticky paste. The bag was less than half full; Carl had changed it the night before, and it looked as if he could wait a few hours before changing it again. It wasn't something he looked forward to.

'Dad,' he said, after checking the bag, 'I've got an appointment at the doctor's. I'll be gone for an hour or so. When I come back, I'll make your lunch. Are you okay for books? Do you want me to pick something else up from the library for you?'

Nicholas Whittley shook his head. 'I think I'll watch TV for a while,' he said in his thin, reedy voice. 'Could you pick up a newspaper for me?'

'No problem.'

After washing up the breakfast bowls and cutlery, he set off for the surgery. He only had to wait a few minutes before his name appeared on the LED sign. *Carl Whittley — please see Dr*

Scotter in Room 5.

Room 5. He suddenly remembered that he was looking for a number. He'd probably seen all kinds of numbers on road signs and car number plates on the way to the surgery, but this was the first one he'd actually noticed.

Five. Five days until he killed the policewoman. So be it.

Dr Scotter was a blonde woman in her twenties. Carl had never seen her before.

'So, Mr Whittley — what can I do for you?' she asked. Her face was receptive, but detached. Politely professional.

He pulled the gloves off his right hand, then off his left. The doctor leaned forward, eyebrows raised at the sight of the blistered flesh. 'Do you know how this happened?' she asked.

'It's happened before,' he replied simply.

She turned her attention to the computer screen on her desk, scrolling through the text of his medical records. 'Ah, yes. You've got quite a history with us. Porphyria is a pretty uncommon disease. I remember covering it at medical school, but I've never actually seen a patient present with it. And you think you're having another attack?'

He shrugged. 'It usually starts like this.'

'Any other symptoms? Abdominal pain, for instance?'

He winced. 'Not yet. I remember how bad it got last time.'

'Any problems going to the toilet?'

'You mean like constipation or diarrhoea? Nothing like that. I seem to need to urinate quite a bit, and it's a different colour. Darker. That's the first thing that made me realise there was a problem.'

'Have you noticed any . . . mood changes?'

He shrugged. 'Difficult to tell. I think I'm getting twitchier.'

'Okay.' She paused for a moment, thinking. 'I'll need you to leave a urine sample for testing, just so we can be sure. As you probably know, acute attacks of porphyria can be dangerous. If possible, I'd like to get you into hospital for a few days for monitoring. Just in case.'

He shook his head. 'It's my dad,' he explained. 'He's got a long-term bowel condition. He's been fitted with a colostomy bag. He really needs someone to look after him full time. I can't spend more than a few hours away from home. Is there anything you can do that means I can stay at home?'

'Is it just the two of you?'

He paused. Swallowed. 'Mum moved out. She couldn't cope.'

'Hmm.' Disapproval. Carl found himself bristling on his mother's behalf, and forced himself to stay calm. 'I could probably arrange for a carer to visit,' Dr Scotter said. 'I could even get a nurse to check on him once a day.'

Carl shook his head. 'I don't think that's going to work,' he said. 'Dad's quite . . . needy. He gets nervous when there are people he doesn't know looking after him. The colostomy bag is bad enough for family. Having strangers fiddling about with it . . . he'd do his nut. He really would.'

'Is there no chance your mother might move back in for a while? Even just temporarily.'

He glanced away. 'I'm working on it,' he said quietly. 'But it'll take a while.'

'Okay. In that case,' she said, typing notes as she spoke, 'we need to start treatment straight away. 'I want you to change your diet to begin with. Increase the amount of carbohydrates that you eat — rice, potatoes, pasta . . . that kind of thing. If the symptoms keep presenting then try glucose drinks — anything carbonated, but obviously avoid the diet ones. I can give you a topical cream for the skin irritation, and I'll prescribe a course of haematin. It's not a complete cure, obviously, but it's an iron-carrying molecule that can help reduce the severity of the symptoms and the length of the attack. Sometimes it can be affected by an individual's metabolism, so if there's no reduction in symptoms within a few days make another appointment with me and I'll prescribe haem instead of haematin. If the one doesn't work then the other often does. Okay so far?'

'I'm still with you.'

'Good. There's a chance that you might experience nausea, vomiting, anxiety, and rest-lessness, in which case I can prescribe phenothiazine for a short time. If you start suffering from insomnia then I can prescribe chloral hydrate or low doses of benzodiazepine, but not a barbiturate. That'll just make things worse. Are you experiencing any of those symptoms yet?'

'Not yet. Bad dreams, but that's about all.'

'Most people with porphyria never develop symptoms. In some people, however, certain factors such as drugs, hormones, or diet can precipitate symptoms, producing an attack.'

'Drugs?' he repeated. 'I don't . . . I mean, I've never . . . '

She smiled, and half raised a placating hand. 'I don't mean cannabis or cocaine or heroin,' she said, 'although they won't help. I mean drugs in the wider sense: barbiturates I've mentioned already, anticonvulsants, and sulfonamide antibiotics for instance. Steroids can have the same effect, as can low-calorie and low-carbohydrate diets, large amounts of alcohol, or smoking. Stress is also a strong provoking factor, and with your father ill and your mother absent I imagine there's a lot of stress in your life. Usually a combination of factors is involved. Sometimes we just don't know what the causative factor is. There's a lot we don't know about porphyria.' She glanced at his hands again, and frowned. 'The odd thing is that skin sensitivity is usually a symptom of a different kind of porphyria than the one you have been diagnosed with. It's unusual to have two different types of porphyria occurring at the same time, although it's not impossible. Just very unlucky.'

'Story of my life,' Carl said quietly.

She typed more notes into the computer, and the printer by her side suddenly disgorged a sheet of paper. She passed it across. 'Here's the prescription for the haematin. If you've had it before you probably had injections, but there's a new tablet form. It's absorbed quickly through

221

the gut and into the bloodstream. Take one in the morning and one in the evening.'

'Can I ask a question?' he said.

'Of course. What is it?'

'Porphyria. Is it likely to make me any more . . . aggressive? Violent?'

She looked at him cautiously. 'Are you feeling any of those symptoms?'

'I mentioned I was feeling twitchy, earlier. I just wanted to check whether I could expect it to get worse.'

'Okay.' She seemed to relax slightly in her chair. 'There can be neurological effects. Paranoia is one of them, and that can lead to the feeling that you're being watched, or followed, or that people are talking about you. In some cases that can cause possible anxiety or argumentative behaviour. If you think you might be feeling like that, I can prescribe something: a sedative like benzodiazepine, or a beta-blocker like propranolol. If you're feeling like that . . . '

He shuddered, and tried to suppress the movement. Take sedatives? That was what she wanted him to do, obviously, but where would that leave him? Doped up to the eyebrows and unable to function. 'Thanks, anyway,' he said, 'but I'm okay at the moment. If I start feeling strange then I'll come back.'

'Make another appointment a week from now,' she said. 'I want to check on how you're doing.'

After leaving his urine sample with the nurse, he stopped off at the receptionist's hatch on the way out to make an appointment for the next week, and again at the pharmacy hatch to get his tablets. They were a rust-red colour, and there were thirty of them in the bottle. He swallowed one straight away, using saliva to wash it down.

Back at the house he made lunch for his father, but he could feel the edginess bubbling away within him. He needed to get out, do something, start planning.

He gave his father the newspaper and lunch, and checked the colostomy bag again. It was fuller than it had been that morning, but he could tell from the pressure that at least some of that was abdominal gas. He could afford to leave it for a few hours before emptying it.

Half an hour later Carl was on his way to Chelmsford in his car, dressed in tracksuit bottoms, a hooded top and a light jacket, with the earbuds of an iPod in his ears. His mind was humming with possibilities as he drove. The thrill of the chase sent adrenalin pulsing along his blood vessels and made his scalp tingle.

He parked in a side street in Chelmsford, just around the corner from the police HQ, the same one he'd been at the day before, and walked past the building to get a sense of it. There was still a gaggle of cameramen and reporters standing in the car park outside the building. Some of them might remember him from the day before, so he needed to find somewhere to observe from. Catching sight of a café across the road he went inside, found a table and ordered a cup of coffee and a slice of carrot cake. He could spin them out for half an hour or so before moving on and finding another location.

After the café, Carl moved to a bench in a

223

park within sight of the building, slumping himself down like a drunk or drug addict and pulling the hood of his top up to conceal his face. He watched as the gaggle of reporters waxed and waned as some of them left to follow up other leads and new ones joined. From the park he relocated to the second floor balcony of a block of flats that overlooked the police HQ — a possible vantage point for him to fire from, *if* he could break into an unoccupied flat and *if* the policewoman's office was on this side of the HQ. He didn't spend too long on the balcony; a stranger would quickly be spotted by the locals, and he would probably be tagged either as an undercover policeman — ironically — a dealer or a junkie looking for a fix. He just hung around for long enough that when he went back to the café it would look as if he had been off somewhere shopping and was now on his way back. He even popped into a petrol station near the park and bought some sandwiches and a bottle of water, more so that he would have an obvious bag of shopping when he went back to the café than because he actually needed to eat or drink.

It was during his second stint in the café that he saw the policewoman emerge from the HQ.

She was alone, which helped. Carl had half expected her to be with the senior policeman — Lapslie — assuming he'd been released from hospital, but she seemed to be on her way somewhere. Carl watched as she walked quickly to her car — a red Audi with customised plates. Carl memorised the number quickly, but all the woman did was retrieve a coat from the back seat and then lock up the car again before walking off. For a second Carl thought she was going back inside the HQ, but instead she set off on foot towards the centre of Chelmsford.

Carl followed, hanging back so that he wouldn't be seen.

The woman seemed constitutionally unable to move at anything slower than a fast trot, and Carl got out of breath following. She led him past the entrance to a large Tesco's and then down a side street. Carl hung back at the corner, letting her get further ahead, not wanting to have her turn around and see Carl isolated in the middle of an otherwise empty street. When she turned into a larger road at the end, Carl rushed to catch up.

Coming into the larger road, which was lined with bars and places to eat, Carl saw her entering an Italian restaurant. He slowed down as he passed the window. Inside, she was approaching a table where a man was rising to greet her. He was tall, burly, with a leather jacket and a face that was hard-edged, grainy, looking like it had been carved into the bark of a tree. He wore a gold stud in his right earlobe. They hugged briefly, and he kissed her on the lips.

They sat, and Carl had to make a sudden decision. There was nowhere nearby where he could watch them from, except inside the restaurant. Should he keep on going, and risk losing track of his victim, or enter the restaurant despite the possibility that he might be idly noticed and then spotted again later, somewhere else?

Deciding quickly, he pushed open the door of the restaurant. Warm air laden with the sweet, smoky fumes of cooked garlic greeted him. Despite himself, he suddenly realised that he was hungry. He let a waitress guide him through the half-full room, where the tables were clustered tightly together, over to a small table partly hidden by a pillar. He sank gratefully into the chair.

'Would you like to order a drink?' the waitress asked, placing a menu on the table in front of him.

'Just a still mineral water, please.'

The waitress walked away and Carl made a big play of consulting the menu, whilst keeping an eye on his quarry over the top edge. The woman was talking to her brutal companion, resting her hand on top of his. He looked uncomfortable squeezed into the small chair, as if he was worried that it might come up with him, the arms trapped against his hips, when he stood up.

The man said something and she shook her head. His face was turned away from Carl; his voice was so deep that he couldn't hear the words and he couldn't see his mouth to lip-read. He said it again, more insistently. Reluctantly she took her BlackBerry phone out of her handbag and pressed the 'call' button. After a few seconds, she said, 'Hi, it's Emma Bradbury . . . '

Emma Bradbury! Exultant triumph water-falled through his body. That was who his next victim would be in five days! Emma Bradbury!

11

Lapslie woke abruptly from a blur of sensation where the colour green was smooth and glassy while blue yielded like marshmallow beneath his questing fingers, to find himself in bed, wearing a gown that didn't fit him properly. It took him a few moments to remember that he wasn't at home; he was in hospital.

He sat up, pulling his arms from where they had been left under the covers, and looked around the room. It was larger than the one he'd first been assigned in the station house when he was a constable, all those years ago. And it had an en suite bathroom, which his room in the station house hadn't. There was space for two beds, but although the medical paraphernalia remained the other bed seemed to have been removed. Perhaps the occupant was currently undergoing surgery.

He concentrated on the noises around him: the hushed conversations, the *beep* of monitoring equipment, the occasional *clang* of a dropped tray. Apart from a faint salty backwash in his mouth he couldn't taste any of it. Perhaps it was the tranquillisers, or perhaps his senses had been temporarily overloaded by events, but he felt like he remembered feeling when he was a child, before the synaesthesia had begun to creep up on him. Normal.

He leaned back against the pillows, letting the

memories of what had happened come floating back like fragments of flotsam pushed by the tide onto the empty beach of his consciousness. He tried to recall the faces of the journalists at the press conference but they had all blurred together, as they always did, into a pack of eager-eyed, open-mouthed, voracious carrion-eaters; predators who would cluster around witnesses or investigators and tear off bleeding chunks of the truth, fighting each other for the choicest morsels. He couldn't remember their features. All he could remember was himself, clutching at his head. Himself, falling unconscious to the floor.

He felt a metallic tang in the back of his throat, but this time it wasn't anything to do with what he was hearing. This was panic, raw and elemental.

His career was effectively over. Rouse's ploy had worked. There was no way he could think of that he could recover from this. His actions had brought the force into disrepute, not because he was taking drugs, accepting backhanders or seeing prostitutes but because he had shown weakness in front of the press. He could only imagine what the headlines were saying about him. What they were speculating. Rouse would have no option but to dismiss him on medical grounds. A lot of things could be hidden when you were a senior officer, many of them with the silent collaboration of your peers and superiors, but once they were out in the open there was nothing you could do. Your friends became strangely ambivalent, and those people who had previously been ambivalent were suddenly calling for your resignation.

He emerged from his dark depression to find Emma Bradbury sitting by the side of his bed.

'Hi,' she said, smiling wanly.

'They kept me in overnight,' he said, voice scratchy. He ran a hand over his chin and could feel stubble, like sandpaper beneath his fingers. 'For observation, they said, although I don't know what they were expecting to observe.'

'They probably didn't either,' Emma said quietly. 'Doctors are like policemen; if they haven't got a likely suspect then they wait for more evidence to come in. Still, at least you've got your own room. And I've had your suit and shirt cleaned. They're in the cupboard over there.' She paused. 'How are you feeling?'

'Embarrassed. And pleasantly tranquillised. They've got me on a mixed dose of sedatives and anti-stress medication; I can't remember what.'

'You told them about the synaesthesia?'

He nodded. 'Yeah, but I'm not sure it helped them much. They're treating it like a mixture of hallucination and panic attack. They've had me hooked up to a heart monitor to check for anomalies, and they've done an MRI scan to look for brain tumours, but they haven't found anything, which I guess is some kind of blessing.' He paused, listening to the background noise of the hospital. 'What happened?' he asked. 'Is it as bad as I think it is?'

Emma's smile was indistinguishable from a grimace. 'It could be better. You just fell down in front of everyone. It was chaos. Someone called

229

an ambulance, but the journalists just stood around taking photographs and filming the whole thing while we waited for it to turn up. You're on the front page of all the papers, and *Newsnight* had a piece about it as well.'

'And everyone's probably accusing me of being an alcoholic?'

'Not yet, but the rumour mill has started up. Someone told the press about what happened at Braintree Parkway as well. I think it was Dain Morritt; he seems to have friends in the media that he schmoozes on a regular basis. The chief has issued a statement giving you his full support — '

'God help me, I'm finished.'

' — But the media's split between using you as a clear example that all policemen are suffering from increasing levels of stress, and claiming that you're a drink-sodden relic from the 1980s who's unable to carry on with one high-profile investigation, let alone two.'

'Apart from ruining my reputation, did the press conference have any other effect? Anybody's mind loosened, any calls from witnesses who saw something we could use?'

Emma shook her head. 'The usual crank calls. There was one guy who swore blind that the bomb was planted by the Freemasons, but he apparently does this for all high-profile cases. He's convinced that Michael Todd — the Chief Constable who died in mysterious circumstances in the Lake District a few years back — was secretly assassinated by the Freemasons. Dr David Kelly, that Government scientist, as well.

Apparently the Freemasons are the root of all evil from Jack the Ripper onwards.'

'And when we have a witness who says they saw someone running away from the scene of the crime with their left trouser leg rolled up then I'll believe it. Anything else?'

'Nothing from the security cameras in the car park, and we've not been able to trace the explosive back to a seller either. Nobody's claimed responsibility, apart from the Scottish Liberation Front, but they claim responsibility for everything, just on the off-chance that someone might believe them. In any case, the lack of any credible claims of responsibility pretty much confirms the fact that it's not any terrorist organisation behind it. I'm more and more of the opinion that we're dealing with a one-off incident that wasn't aimed at anyone or anything in particular. A gratuitous act of vandalism writ large, if you like.'

'I don't like,' Lapslie growled. 'I don't like at all. People want there to be a reason for something like this. Rouse wants there to be a reason for something like this. What does it say about society if we accept that there are people just going around placing bombs at random for kicks?'

'As opposed to throwing a paving slab off a motorway bridge and causing a driver to swerve into a crash barrier, leading to a twenty car pile-up? We're already there, boss. Society is disintegrating around us.'

'Okay.' He sighed. 'Thanks for that cheery thought. We're pretty much at a dead end, then.'

'Pretty much.'

'Give me some better news. What's happening on the Catherine Charnaud murder case?'

'Ah.'

'Is that 'ah' as in 'we have a lead!' or 'ah' as in 'there's no progress in that case either'?'

'It's the latter. The forensic profiler, Eleanor Whittley, has been all through the evidence and the case files, and I believe she's seeing the body down at the mortuary today. I've passed on the statement given by the boyfriend, Darren Barlow, and she's going to give us an opinion on whether he meets her profile. Otherwise, we're at a standstill.'

'What about the boyfriend's alibi? Have you managed to break it yet?'

'Not yet.' Emma sighed. 'His teammates confirm that he was out drinking with them all night, but I think there's some laddishness going on there. They aren't going to grass him up.'

'What about that phone call from her mobile to the garage in Chingford?'

'Yeah; that's still an oddity. I had the car checked over and there's no damage that would require servicing. Some scratches to the paintwork, and the wheels needed realigning, but not the kind of thing you worry about at that time of night. I sent someone down to talk to the garage owner, but there's no sign he'd ever talked to Catherine Charnaud or ever had anything to do with her.'

'Do they have an answerphone? Did they record the message?'

'No. They switch it off at night, he said,

otherwise they'd get fifteen messages from drivers requiring urgent attention, which they couldn't do anything about, and half a dozen orders for an Indian takeaway.'

'Dead end then?' he said, feeling the medication turn what would otherwise have been a burning frustration into a mild irritation.

'Dead end,' Emma confirmed. She looked at him. 'Unless you know something I don't.'

'What do you mean?'

She was still scrutinising his expression. 'When I phoned Dr Catherall to make an appointment for Eleanor Whittley to go down to the mortuary, she asked how you were. When I told her what had happened, she strongly suggested that I ask you about your synaesthesia. Her exact question was: 'Ask Mark whether he thinks the murderer was at the press conference.' She wouldn't say anything else — said you'd have to tell me. Am I missing something? I thought you just had another attack, like you did at Braintree Parkway station.'

'Yes, but there's more to it than that.' He gazed back at her, evaluating her the way she had evaluated him. Things were bad enough already. If he told her the truth about what had happened, would he find it used against him one day?

Whatever. Nobody could really predict the outcome of even the simplest set of events. The only proper way to live your life was to stick to a simple set of rules, and one of his was: 'Tell the truth whenever you can.' Sometimes, when he was feeling particularly cynical, he would add: 'If for no other reason than it really confuses your enemies.' 'You remember in Catherine Charnaud's bedroom, when we were there with the body, I thought I heard drumming? Loud drumming?'

'Yeah.' She nodded. 'You thought there was a radio playing.'

'And again on the rooftop of the shopping mall in Braintree Parkway, where we think the bomber was positioned?'

'Yeah.' She was intrigued now, frowning. 'What's that got to do with the murders? I assumed it was your synaesthesia playing up again.'

'It was, but not the way you think. It was as if the synaesthesia kicked into reverse. Rather than a sound causing a taste, a taste — or rather, a smell — caused a sound. A drumming. And Jane Catherall believes that the smell was something to do with the murderer.' He opened his mouth to tell Emma that the murderer must also have been at the press conference, but he held himself back. That would have been an improbability too far.

Emma looked at him expressionlessly, waiting for him to continue.

'I know it sounds insane,' he said urgently, 'but stay with me. We know the murderer pissed on the rooftop of the shopping centre. What if they also used the toilet at Catherine Charnaud's house, and left some traces, some splashback? And what if there's some chemical in their urine that I can smell, something that only they give off?'

'I guess it's . . . possible,' Emma said judiciously. 'Whenever I eat asparagus, I can smell it within half an hour. Same with mushrooms. Goes right through my system like a dose of salts. But . . . ' She moved her hands as if trying to grasp something that was hanging just in front of her. 'But it beggars belief that these two cases are connected.' She saw the expression of hopelessness that he was trying to hide. 'Look, I'll make you a deal. I'll treat this theory as if it's real, and I'll go back and look for connections between the two cases. Your part of the bargain is to treat this theory as if it *isn't* real. As if you're hallucinating. Tell your doctor. Get him to refer you to a psychiatrist, or a neurologist, or something. While I'm investigating the cases, I want someone investigating you. Sorry if that sounds harsh, but that's the way it has to be.'

He thought for a moment. She was right — it *was* a reasonable request. The more he thought about it, the more convinced he was that Jane Catherall was right, but people who heard voices in their heads telling them to kill were just as convinced that those voices were real.

'It's a deal,' he said. 'First thing — get that toilet bowl in Catherine Charnaud's bathroom checked for traces of urine, and chase up the tests on the urine patch we found at the shopping mall.'

'I'll get right on it,' she said. 'And when I come back I want to hear that you've been talking to someone with credentials.'

After Emma left, Lapslie drifted for a while, suspended in the timeless routine of the hospital.

If it hadn't been for the way the light from the window pushed the shadows across the room he wouldn't even have been able to tell that time was passing. Breakfast arrived, and he ate listlessly. The food had no flavour, no texture, and he found that comforting. He was tired of tastes.

He must have fallen asleep again, because when he opened his eyes the shadows had moved again and a young doctor in a white coat was standing at the end of the bed holding a clipboard.

'Sorry,' he said. 'I was drifting.'

'Don't worry.' The doctor consulted the clipboard. 'I was just checking your vital signs.' Lapslie detected something tropical about his voice. Papaya, perhaps? Mango? The drugs had clearly worn off.

'When can I go back to work?' Lapslie asked, levering himself upright in the bed.

'Let's not rush things.' The doctor's face was open, pleasant. 'Everything in its own time. You're in the police force, aren't you?'

'That's right.'

'Stressful job, I imagine.'

Lapslie pursed his lips. 'Can be. Is that why I collapsed?'

'That depends. What cases are you working on at the moment?'

A small bud of suspicion began to unfurl in Lapslie's mind. 'I've got a couple of cases on the books.'

'What about that newsreader? Is that one anything to do with you?'

236

'I wanted to ask a question about my medication,' Lapslie said, changing the subject deliberately. 'What drugs am I being given?'

The doctor looked at the clipboard. 'Just the ones I'd expect, given your condition. Do you have any leads on the case?'

'What is my condition, exactly?'

'I understand the boyfriend, Darren Barlow, is still under suspicion. Is that true?'

'What dosage of medication am I on?' Lapslie snarled.

'Are you aware that he already has a criminal record for aggravated assault?'

'Are *you* aware,' Lapslie said with quiet menace, 'that it's an offence to impersonate a doctor?' He had no idea whether it was or not, but he was willing to take a chance on it being true.

The doctor smiled. 'You can't blame a man for trying. We'll offer £25,000 for an exclusive interview.'

'And I'll offer a broken nose if you don't get out of my sight now.'

'It's a good offer.' He raised his shoulders and spread his hands in an exaggerated gesture of fairness. 'Look, we can either interview you here, or we can just make it up and say you said it. Given how doped up you've been, you won't be able to prove otherwise. Be sensible — take the money. We'll pay cash, if that's a problem.'

'*Security!*' Lapslie shouted.

The doctor backed away, still shrugging. 'It's not like you've got a career left in the police,' he said. 'Give it a few days and you'll wish you had a nest egg.'

Two nurses ran into the room, but by that time the man had vanished. He explained what had happened, but he could tell from their faces that they were dubious. Rather than press the point, he asked if he could see someone from Psychiatry. He owed Emma that much.

Lapslie obsessed about the fake doctor's words for a while. So easy to earn a few months' wages — just give them some juicy quotes and let them do the work. And it wasn't as if his loyalty to the police force was going to be repaid. He was pretty sure that, after what had happened, he was going to be left to twist in the wind. Early retirement beckoned, and what was he going to do then? Live a silent life for the rest of his days? No noise, no taste, nothing but a flat, empty existence until he died?

''And we are here as on a darkling plain, Swept with confused alarms of struggle and flight, Where ignorant armies clash by night',' he murmured softly.

'Matthew Arnold?' Another man in a white coat was standing by the end of the bed. He was middle-aged, with an absurdly large grey moustache. His voice was rather like the taste of a rubber balloon. 'Not often we get anyone quoting twentieth-century poetry in here.'

'Sorry. It's a bad habit.' Lapslie squinted at the man. 'Who are you?'

'Dr Garland. From the Psychiatric Unit. Apparently you wanted to speak to someone.'

'Can you prove your identity?'

Garland laughed. 'It's usually me that asks patients that, although to be fair, that's after they've told me they're either Napoleon or the Deposed Secret Leader of the World.' He fished around in his pocket, and brought out a laminated pass with his photograph on it. 'Should do the trick. Doesn't get me a discount in the canteen, but I can park in the reserved spaces with it.'

Lapslie examined the pass. 'I realise this looks like paranoia, but I had a journalist here earlier pretending to be a doctor.'

'Ah. Heard about that.' Garland gazed at Lapslie. 'You're the policeman. Saw you on the news.' He hooked a chair over with his foot and sat down. 'Tell me everything.'

So Lapslie did. He explained about his synaesthesia, about the effects on his life and on his career. He explained about the two cases, about the drums and about his collapse. He even found himself talking about Jane Catherall, and the way he trusted her to get to the heart of any problem. He spoke for half an hour in a low, intense monotone and found himself close to tears on two occasions. Garland listened, nodding every now and then; maintaining eye contact and not taking any notes.

'So that's it,' Lapslie finished. He felt exhausted. 'If you *are* a journalist then I'm buggered, but frankly you deserve a scoop for listening patiently to all that guff. What do you think?'

'What do I think?' Garland stretched and glanced out of the window. 'I'm no expert on synaesthesia, although I know enough to know it's a neurological rather than a psychiatric problem. Don't think you're hallucinating. Think your colleague's theory is probably a good first assumption. Assume the cases are connected and see where that gets you.' He made eye contact with Lapslie again, and his gaze was disconcertingly warm and understanding. 'Think I can probably help you to integrate the synaesthesia and your work at the same time. There are some exercises I can take you through. Neuro-linguistic programming.'

'Sounds like brainwashing.'

'More like brain spring-cleaning. I'll drop you a line in the next week or so. Make an outpatients appointment.' He got up.

'So, can I go?' Lapslie asked.

Garland shrugged. 'Assuming there are no after-effects from the fall, I think you can be discharged. I'll talk to the nurses.'

He left. Lapslie pondered for a moment. He was feeling strangely upbeat.

When he looked up, Dain Morritt was standing beside the hospital bed.

'Dain.' Lapslie nodded, surprised and disconcerted. How much had Morritt heard?

'Sir,' Dain acknowledged briefly. As before, his voice had no taste.

'I'm surprised you're here,' Lapslie said. 'I would have expected you to be busy taking over the investigation, tracking down the bomber.'

'Chief Superintendent Rouse asked me to

accompany him. He's talking to one of your doctors now.'

'Ah.' Lapslie hoped to God it wasn't Garland. 'He's not expecting me to be able to continue with the investigation.'

'You collapsed in front of the assembled press. That doesn't make him look good.'

'It didn't do a lot for me either.'

Morritt continued as if he hadn't heard Lapslie interrupt. 'Rouse has to be seen to do something. You're a liability now. We need to make sure that the chain of command on this case is clear. We're risking evidence falling through the cracks if the troops don't know who to report to.'

'And that person is you?' Lapslie asked.

Morritt looked away. 'We both know that Rouse put you in charge of the case because he doesn't know what else to do with you. Your . . . disability . . . makes you difficult to place in normal police work.'

Disability. There was that word again.

'I'm not blind or deaf,' Lapslie said quietly. His head hurt, and he was tired, but he knew that this conversation was probably going to set the tone for the rest of his working life, and he needed to get it right. Somehow, the talk with Dr Garland had given him more confidence. 'I don't need special access into buildings. I can hold coherent conversations. Once I get out of here I'll be able to get right back to work, if Rouse lets me. And, just in case the thought had occurred to you, I'm not using disability legislation to force Chief

Superintendent Rouse to give me work.'

'Then why did you take over my case?' Morritt said bluntly.

'It was Rouse's call, but my guess is that before we knew the details of the bombing there was a strong chance that it was either linked to terrorism or gang-related activity. A bomber on a rooftop — think about it. That's not standard police business. It's like something you hear about in Basra or Islamabad. Chances were, when this started, that we'd immediately find ourselves working across constabulary boundaries, and possibly with SOCA as well. And separately from that, the press were bound to be all over it like ants on a picnic, looking for discrepancies, things to exploit in the headlines, signs of weakness. Everyone's watching us on this one. No reflection on you, but you've not had the experience of working at that level. If I had to make a guess, it'd be that Rouse wanted to ensure that he had someone at the top of the investigation with the clout to function at that level.'

'Not any more.' Dain's mouth didn't smile, but his eyes did, and it wasn't a friendly smile. 'I'm back in charge.'

'And yet . . . ' Lapslie felt along the fragile thread of thought that was unspooling in his mind. ' — And yet he's here. He didn't send you to tell me. He came himself.'

Morritt glanced out of the window, irritation on his face. 'I hate these places,' he muttered. 'Everyone thrown in together. No dignity.' Pulling his attention back to Lapslie, he continued, 'Rouse likes you. God knows why. As far as I'm concerned you're a dead weight dragging us back and you ought to be cut free and left to sink or swim, but Rouse seems to want to keep you around.' He smiled, with no humour. 'You used to work together, didn't you?'

Lapslie nodded. 'But I don't see him being overly sentimental about it.'

'Overly sentimental about what, Mark?' Chief Superintendent Rouse said, entering the room. He was in a suit, but he still made it look like he was wearing uniform. He was older than Lapslie, and bigger around the stomach, and the expression on his fleshy face made him look like a bulldog chewing a wasp.

Sitting in bed wearing a hospital gown, Lapslie felt suddenly vulnerable. 'DI Morritt was just giving me his opinion that you kept me around out of some misplaced sense of friendship, given that we used to go drinking together in Brixton. Or perhaps he thinks I've got some blackmail material on you from all those years ago. Naked photographs of you and some Polish waitress.'

Rouse snorted. 'I keep you around because you get results. You're one of the best investigating officers I've got. And I've already got enough photographs of me and that Polish waitress to keep me happy, thank you.'

Lapslie looked pointedly at Morritt. 'I think there's a pretender to the throne.'

Rouse sat heavily in the chair that Dr Garland had recently vacated and steepled his fingers. 'I'm aware,' he said carefully, 'that there is some tension within the team concerning who is in

243

command. It may be that my reasons for placing a Detective Chief Inspector in charge of a single murder inquiry weren't entirely transparent.'

'Actually, sir,' Morritt interrupted, 'DCI Lapslie has just given me his views on why a senior officer needed to be on the case.'

Rouse glanced at Lapslie. 'And they were . . . ?'

'The potential terrorism or gang connections, the possibility that liaisons with other organisations such as SOCA might be required, and the press angle,' Lapslie summarised.

'And, based on your inquiries so far, *is* this a potential terrorist incident or something connected with criminal gangs?'

Morritt shook his head. 'There's no evidence that it's anything more than an isolated incident, albeit one carried out in an unusual way.'

'By 'unusual', you are referring to the murder weapon?'

'Indeed,' Morritt continued. 'We're looking for someone with access to explosives and a reason to kill Alec Wildish: possibly a friend in the army or someone who just bought some Semtex off eBay. It's apparently not hard to find, if you know what you're doing.'

Rouse looked over at Lapslie. 'Mark — thoughts?'

'I agree that we're probably looking at an isolated incident,' Lapslie said judiciously. 'I disagree about the domestic aspect. Most incidents involving personal emotions — dumped boyfriends, love triangles and so on — take place at close range. The killer normally wants the victim to see how much the victim has hurt them, see what the victim has driven the murderer to. They're sending a very final message, and they want to know that the message has been received. This was dispassionate, long-range. The murderer didn't want to be near the victim. That suggests to me that the victim probably wasn't known personally to the murderer.'

'You're not suggesting that this was an assassination of some kind?' Morritt scoffed. 'The contract killing of shop manager? In Braintree?'

'All possibilities are being covered,' Lapslie said. 'But I don't think they'll lead to anything. Whoever the killer is, they're covering their tracks very carefully. We're not going to catch them out in a simple mistake. In my opinion — and the opinion of my team, by the way — this is an isolated incident of vandalism taken to an extreme.'

'So you do agree that this is not part of something larger? We don't need to bring in the Serious Organised Crime Agency just yet, or warn the local population to stay indoors?'

'Not yet,' Lapslie said. 'Not without more to go on. The question is, is the murderer satisfied with just the one body, or does he want more?'

Rouse glanced at Lapslie, and his eyes narrowed slightly. Lapslie had seen that look before. The two of them had known each other for many years, through various station houses and constabularies, and each had come to understand the other's body language and those transitory facial expressions that gave away what a person was thinking.

'Mark, is there something else?' Rouse asked mildly.

Lapslie grimaced involuntarily. Acutely aware of Emma Bradbury's advice — in fact, more or less instruction — that he didn't tell anyone else about his theory, he was aware that he was teetering on the edge of losing the case. For Christ's sake, he was sitting there in a gown while Morritt was in a decent pinstripe suit. Rouse was going to take it away from him unless he could pull a cat out of the bag, but the only cat he had was scrawny and undernourished. Even though he'd been reluctant to take the cases on at first, the thought of handing over his work was galling. He'd got caught up in the investigations, and he couldn't let them drop now. Not before he'd taken them as far as he could.

'There is one thing, sir, but I'm not sure . . . ' He let his voice trail off and glanced sideways at Morritt, hoping Rouse would get the message.

'Is it about the case?'

'It *involves* the case, sir. In a wider context.'

'Crack on, then.' Rouse nodded towards Morritt. 'If it involves the case then Dain ought to hear about it.'

Lapslie took a deep breath. This was going to be difficult. 'Sir, I know you're aware of my . . . medical history . . . but for DS Morritt's benefit I'll go over it quickly.'

'Mark, is your medical history really relevant to the bombing in Braintree?' Rouse interrupted.

'I believe it is, sir, yes. The way my brain is built, things that I hear can be translated into

246

tastes in my mouth, and occasionally the other way around. It's called synaesthesia. These things aren't hallucinations, they're a mix-up in the way that sensory input is treated within my brain.' He glanced briefly at Morritt. 'And as you know, sir, according to various medical experts it has no effect on my abilities as a detective.'

Rouse nodded. 'I've seen your medical file,' he confirmed, 'and I have full confidence in your abilities.'

'Thank you, sir. I would argue, in addition, that the synaesthesia *enhances* my abilities as a detective. I sometimes taste tropical fruit when someone is lying to me. That sounds like New Age witchcraft, but it's actually my brain picking up on the subtle signs of stress in someone's voice and bringing it to my attention via another route — '

Morritt breathed out through his nose, dismissively.

'I've recently become aware of another way in which my synaesthesia can help me in my job. You remember that I am dealing with the Catherine Charnaud murder?'

Rouse nodded briefly. 'The newsreader,' he murmured.

'While at the scene of the crime,' Lapslie continued, 'I had what I can only describe as an auditory experience. I heard a noise, a very particular noise, which I now believe was associated with a smell lingering at the scene — a smell associated not with the murder victim, but with the *murderer*.'

Rouse was now watching Lapslie with

247

considerably more interest than he had started with. Morritt was also watching Lapslie, but his expression was unreadable.

'While investigating the bombing at Braintree Parkway,' Lapslie went on, 'I also heard that noise. I believe it to be linked again to the killer — this time because they had urinated on a rooftop overlooking the station while they waited for their preferred victim to arrive.'

Rouse was leaning forward in his seat, eyes fixed on Lapslie's face. 'Are you suggesting that the two cases are *linked*?'

'There's more, sir.' Lapslie took a deep breath. This was going to be the really difficult one to swallow. 'I think the killer was at the press conference. That was why I collapsed. I was just . . . overwhelmed . . . by their presence.'

DI Morritt snorted. 'This is bollocks,' he said. 'Absolute bollocks.'

Rouse waved him down. 'Let's hear Mark out.'

'Thank you, sir. I believe there's a possibility that the killer in the Catherine Charnaud case used the toilet in her house. Even if they had flushed, there would be remnants of their urine on the upper reaches of the porcelain and perhaps splashes on the seat. I now think that's what I was picking up on.'

There was silence in the room for a few moments, broken only by Rouse drumming his fingers on the table.

'Two murders, each done in a different way, no connections between the victims that we can ascertain, and you're telling me that they're both done by the same person? And that person was at the press conference. It's hard to credit.'

'I second that,' Morritt said. 'Investigation throws up evidence which leads to theories. Resort to the sniffing out of criminals throws us back to the Dark Ages. Why not use phrenology as well? Why not profile the killer based on their likely star sign?'

Rouse gazed at Lapslie. 'I take your point, Dain,' he said slowly. 'Mark, assuming you're correct — and it's a stretch — then what kind of killer are we looking for?'

'Someone cautious,' Lapslie said. 'Someone who *needs* to kill, rather than someone who is doing it for fun or for gain. Someone who is making every effort to ensure that each murder is completely different from the last — different means of killing, different profile of victim, probably different lengths of time between the killings. Which means there will have been more deaths, in the past. Unsolved cases.' He paused, waiting for his thoughts to catch up, and a parallel occurred to him, one that Rouse would probably appreciate. 'The way I tend to think of it, sir, is it's like wine-tasting. If you're serious about it, there's two different ways you can do it. There's a vertical tasting, where you take different years of the same wine and taste them against one another, looking for the differences. That's the profile of most serial killers — they use the same method, and the only difference is the timing. Remember Madeline Poel, last year? She always used poison, always made the poison from some garden plant or other, always chose old ladies as her victims, and always mutilated their bodies in the same way. But there's also the horizontal tasting, where you choose wines all from the same year, but different grape varieties and different soil types, and look for the differences there. And that's what we have, I would submit — a horizontal set of murders, each one different from the others. The only common thread is the person who commits them.'

Rouse nodded slowly. 'You're presenting me with a difficult choice,' he said. 'Do I combine the investigations, based on your unproven and frankly implausible suggestion, or do I let them continue separately and risk missing some crucial evidence?'

'There's another option, sir,' Lapslie said. 'You could keep the investigations separate but assign me to sit above them all, looking for connections. If there are any.'

Rouse glanced at Dain Morritt. 'Dain — opinions?'

Dain Morritt pursed his lips. 'I don't believe that the investigations are connected, which means that I don't want the separate teams combined into some bloated superteam. On the other hand, if they are, then DCI Lapslie is effectively a busted flush. He's lost credibility in front of the press, and placed the police force in disrepute. I respectfully suggest that the investigations are taken away from him and given to . . . a qualified officer familiar with at least one of the cases.'

Rouse slapped his hand on the table decisively. He almost made it look as if he was making a

spur-of-the-moment decision, but Lapslie suspected that he'd been planning this moment for
a while. 'It's decided, then. Dain, you'll
co-ordinate across the two investigations, looking
for connections. Keep me informed. Mark, I
realise this is unwelcome news, but you need to
stay back from the investigations. If the press
find out about your medical history they'll have a
field day. I presume that you will be thinking of
taking early retirement on medical grounds, and
I can promise you that I will not query any
paperwork you care to submit. Are you okay with
this?'

Again, it sounded like a question but Lapslie
knew that it was more of an instruction. Bitterly,
he nodded. At the end of the hospital bed, DI
Morritt nodded as well. He was smiling.

12

Seething with repressed anger, Carl Whittley watched Emma Bradbury and her lunch companion until they had finished their meals and were sipping at their coffees. The woman kept leaning across and touching the hand of the man on a couple of occasions. Every time she did Carl had to punch his thigh with his clenched fist, asking himself why he had never been in a restaurant with a woman like that, touching his hand with the closeness of two people who cared for each other.

Because of his father, that's why. Because Carl had to spend most of his time at home, making sure his father was safe and well; cleaning the raw flesh of his stoma, where what was left of his intestine had been stitched to a hole in the abdomen; emptying the shit from his colostomy bag into the toilet, cleaning and disinfecting it, then reattaching it to the raw pink wound. What time did he ever get to be with women? What woman would ever want to spend her time with him?

It was painful watching them, but he forced himself to do it. He needed to know about them — about her. They were obviously close, although the man wasn't as physically demonstrative as Emma was.

He realised that he needed to go to the toilet, but he was worried that they might leave before he got back so he forced himself to wait. Patience, patience. The pressure on his bladder was making him uncomfortable, and the regular thudding of his fist on his leg was just making it worse, but he couldn't afford to make a move.

Finally, while they were having their coffees and before either of them could attract the waitress's attention to ask for the bill, Carl snagged her and got in first.

The man who was with Emma still bothered Carl. The way he carried himself — confident, watchful and not at all self-conscious — put Carl in mind of the men who had worked alongside the Essex Hunt — the dog handlers and farriers. Hard men. Self-reliant men. If he was present when Carl killed Emma then he might cause trouble. Carl would have to make sure he was out of the way. Or he would have to kill him as well.

Kill *both* of them? The thought took him aback. Until now, each of his murders had been single ones. Years of reading through his mother's textbooks, lecture notes and case files had taught him that the most common reason why serial killers got caught was that they repeated themselves. Not that he actually thought of himself in those terms, but Carl had fought hard to vary the characteristics of his victims and the manner of their deaths; close-up and personal, far away and impersonal, apparently accidental . . . But there was one common thread, he realised with a sense of shock. He had always killed one person at a time. Individuals. Even at Braintree Parkway station he could have killed five or six people together just by exploding the bomb five minutes before he actually did, but he had deliberately waited until there was only one person standing within the blast radius. If he was serious about the murders — and he was — then at some stage he needed to kill more than one person at once. A carload, perhaps. A busload. A trainload.

But not this time. He wanted that man out of the way when he killed the man's lover. He struck Carl as being dangerous.

Carl's bill arrived just as the man got up and walked towards the toilets. Watching him go reminded Carl again of just how badly he needed to empty his bladder. The man had obviously been in the restaurant before; he didn't hesitate or look around but headed straight for the dark corner where the toilets were located. As he went, Emma's phone rang.

'Hello?' she said, then, 'Dr Catherall? Is that you? Can you hear me?' A silence while she listened, screwing her face up as she tried to make out the reply. 'Hang on — I'll head outside to get a better signal.' She got up and moved rapidly towards the door.

Leaving her handbag hanging on the back of the chair.

This was his chance. Carl stood, placing a ten pound note on the table and picking his coat up from the back of his own chair. The money would cover his food, plus a tip that wasn't memorably large or memorably small. He moved towards the table where, moments before, Emma and her companion had been sitting. Carl glanced towards the toilets to see whether Emma's companion was returning, but he wasn't in sight. Carl moved in that direction, his path taking him directly past their table. His gaze scanned quickly across the restaurant, checking whether anyone was looking in his direction, but as far as he could tell he was unobserved. Emma was visible through the large front window; her back turned, talking into the phone. The only person who might have been scanning the room was the waitress, and she was busy scooping up the ten pound note with her back to him. Without deviating from his course, he let the hand holding the coat trail down, his fingers curled slightly beneath the cloth so that they caught on the strap of Emma's handbag. The bag slid off the back of the chair and the coat draped over it. Carl's hand took the weight without him having to shift his posture. He kept moving at the same speed, waiting for an outcry behind him, but there was nothing. He did his best to keep walking in a straight line and not dip or twist his shoulders. Odd movements like that tended to attract attention.

The man was just leaving the washroom as Carl entered. Carl kept his chin down, allowing his face to be shadowed. The handbag was clutched tightly beneath his coat.

Within moments he was in the toilet; a small room with a single porcelain toilet bowl, a sink and a hand dryer. He quickly locked the door behind him and rifled through the bag's contents, his hand still wrapped in the thin material of his jacket so that he would not leave any fingerprints. A chunky red leather purse caught his attention, and he hooked it out. He flipped it open: Emma's driving licence was obvious inside. That would be enough to give Carl her address, but he had to make it look like a robbery rather than a fishing expedition for information. The woman was a police officer, after all. Slipping the purse into a pocket of his jacket he thrust the handbag behind the toilet bowl and then, unzipping his flies, emptied his bladder into the toilet bowl with a deep sigh of relief. The urine was purple against the white of the bowl, swirling like blood into the drain, but he thought it wasn't as dark as it had been. The haematin tablets were kicking in.

Emma was still outside the restaurant, talking into her phone when he emerged. Her companion had returned to the table and was waiting for her. His gaze — grey and emotionless — swept across Carl, evaluating him for a heart-stopping moment, and then moved away to look at something else once he had dismissed Carl as a threat. He hadn't noticed yet that the handbag was missing. Heart pounding, Carl kept on walking; past him, past the waiter, past his table and out through the door into the street, making sure that he turned immediately away from Emma so that all the woman would see of him was his back.

He stopped fifty yards or so down the street, looking in the window of a charity shop. A faint mist of rain coated the shop window from the outside while humidity steamed it up from the inside, rendering the candlesticks, flowery

256

blouses and porcelain horses inside into objects of mystery rather than assorted knick-knacks that would only swell the charity's coffers by another pound or so if they sold. Back along the street Emma finished her phone call and re-entered the restaurant. Nobody came running out looking for Carl. He imagined the confusion, and then the panic inside as Emma realised that her handbag was gone; the fruitless searching under the table, the questioning of the waitress and anyone sitting nearby. Someone appeared in the doorway; he couldn't tell whether it was Emma, her companion or the waitress, but whoever it was looked around and then went back inside.

Carl wanted to walk back past the restaurant again, partly to see what was happening inside and partly to establish himself as a harmless patron who was ambling up and down the street rather than a handbag-snatching thief, but he decided against it. There was no point in tempting fate, and he had what he needed. Instead he walked away from the restaurant, slowly so as not to attract any attention, stopping every now and then to check other shop windows. Just another shopper, idling the hours away.

Back at his car, he checked the contents of the purse. Fifty pounds in notes plus a small amount of change; twenty euros in small bills; three different credit and debit cards in the name of Emma Bradbury, several receipts, an old raffle ticket; three first-class stamps in a cardboard folder; a plastic bubble pack of aspirin; a

Starbucks loyalty card; a condom in a creased foil wrapper; and a handful of business cards. No warrant card; she probably kept that in her jacket. And there, at the front, was the driving licence: a lilac plastic card with Emma's photograph on it alongside a tiny facsimile of her signature and, in print so small it was almost unreadable, her address.

Carl breathed a silent sigh of relief. He had been worried that the woman was living in a police section house somewhere in the region, which would have made a long-range shot tricky if not impossible, but the address appeared to be a block of flats in Brentford. *BRENTWOOD*

He drove back home carefully, not attracting any attention. He would have to spend some time in Brentford, he decided. Scope out the flats and any possible vantage points and lines of sight; establish escape routes; understand Emma's pattern of life — what time she got up, what time she left for work, what time she got back, what she did at weekends. He would have to work it around his father, popping back at regular intervals to check on him, but Carl was willing to make the sacrifice if it guaranteed him a clean shot.

It was what he had done with Catherine Charnaud. He needed to know everything about her and the way she lived if he was going to successfully kill her. Not, he reminded himself, that killing her was the aim. It was a means. The aim was to get his family back together, and everything was subordinate to that. It was like hunting and killing animals; doing it for a reason, like because you needed food, or pelts for clothing, was okay. It was when you did it for fun that it became difficult to defend. That was why he'd eventually stopped following the Essex Hunt. He was just too uncomfortable about the pleasure the hunters took from the chase and the kill. When he killed, there was always a reason.

Twenty minutes from home he realised that his mother's place was only a short detour away. He made a quick mental judgement; his father was probably going to be okay for another half hour, and he would really like to know what was happening to the case she was working on. And he could do with using the toilet again. Damn this stupid illness!

He parked outside her house. Her car was there, so she was in. Probably working.

She seemed surprised to see him when she opened the door. She was wearing a long dress that clung to her figure, and her hair was loose across her shoulders and down her back. He got the impression she was waiting for someone else. The house smelled of tomatoes and garlic. Was she cooking for someone?

'Sorry to barge in,' he hurried, bladder suddenly feeling so full that it overrode all other concerns. 'Can I use your toilet?'

'Of course,' she said, puzzled. As he pounded up the stairs, she called after him: 'Carl! Is this another attack? Have you seen a doctor? You know you ought to be on medication if you're having another attack.'

'*I'm on medication!*' he called down the stairs. The pressure in his groin was so heavy now that he could feel shooting pains along his forearms. He'd only been to the toilet half an hour before! How could he need to go again?

He slammed the bathroom door shut and yanked his trousers down, then pissed a long torrent of dark liquid into the toilet bowl. The sudden relief was almost more painful than the pressure had been.

Washing his hands after he had finished, he noticed that there were two toothbrushes by the sink. One red; one green. What was the deal? Was there someone else living in the house? He felt another pressure building, this time in his chest. In his heart. How could she just move someone else in like that to replace his father? His fingers clenched on the cold enamel of the sink's rim. He had to move quickly. He had to overload her with cases she couldn't solve.

'What are you taking?' she inquired as he came down the stairs and entered the kitchen. She was chopping onions. A pan of pasta was bubbling on the cooker, and a glass of some clear liquid was sitting on the table beside her.

'Haematin,' he said. 'Just started.'

'Intravenous?'

'Tablets. New form, apparently.'

'Okay.' She wouldn't meet his gaze. 'You can't stay. I'm expecting company.'

'I wasn't going to. I have to get back. To Dad.' No reaction. 'How's the case coming along?' he asked.

Eleanor dismissed the question with a shake of her head. 'I can't talk about it; you know that. All of the details are confidential.'

'I don't want to know the details,' he pressed. 'They're all over the news. I just wanted to know whether you were making any progress. I'm . . . ' He paused, artfully. 'I'm interested in your work. I always have been.'

Her expression softened. She reached out to ruffle his hair. 'It's odd, but I keep forgetting how much you wanted to know what I was doing when you were young. I used to find you in your bedroom or down in the lounge, reading my textbooks, looking at my photographs. I did worry for a while that they would affect you, but you've grown up into a good boy. I'm proud of you, and of what you're doing to look after your father. I know how much of a sacrifice you're making.'

'I miss you,' he said simply. 'I wish you'd come home.'

Eleanor shook her head. 'It's not going to happen, Carl; you know that. Your father and I . . . we've moved too far apart now. I know this sounds harsh, but he is not a husband any more. He's an invalid. There is nothing left for us to share — no conversations left to have, no new memories to build on. I have moved on, and he never will. He's trapped by the accident, and by his illness.' She sighed. 'In many ways, we've all three of us switched roles. Nicholas was always a very traditional man. He wanted to be the breadwinner, while I was meant to be the one who looked after the family and you were the child who had to be cared for. Now I'm the breadwinner, you're doing the caring and he's the child. It's not what he would have wanted.'

But it's what you love, Carl thought, and immediately tried to call back the thought. But it was out there now, and he couldn't help but think about it. His mother was successful and independent. She was in her element.

'You never ask how he is,' he blurted.

She winced. 'Carl, I know how he is. He's crippled, in mind and body, and he's going to require constant care until he dies.'

He realised that he could use her discomfort at the direction the conversation had taken to manoeuvre her back to the subject he really wanted to talk about. He decided to come at it sideways. Looking across the kitchen, he noticed a business card on top of his mother's handbag, which was sitting on the kitchen counter, beside the microwave oven. 'I saw that policemen you met. Is that his card? He was on the news. It looked like he'd had an attack of some kind.'

His mother shook her head in irritation. 'I don't know what was happening there,' she said. 'One minute he was talking to me about the Catherine Charnaud case and the next he's popping up on the news holding a press conference about a bombing. Is it too much to ask that he dedicates himself to one case at a time? And then he collapses. I was watching from an office on the second floor. I've not heard from him since, and where does that leave me?'

'The two cases,' Carl said carefully. 'They're not connected, are they?'

Eleanor frowned. 'Why should they be?'

He wasn't sure whether to be pleased or annoyed that his two most recent murders

262

hadn't been brought together. Still, there was plenty of time. 'I just thought, if the same detective was in charge . . . '

'That's more to do with short staffing in the police force, I suspect.'

'But even so,' he pressed, 'that must make it difficult for him to do a good job.'

'That's obviously why he needs a forensic clinical psychologist,' Eleanor said. 'To help out. And, given the nature of the killing, I think he is out of his depth. But I really can't discuss it any more.'

'I understand. I'd better get going, anyway,' he said, turning to leave. 'Dad will be worried.'

'Of course. Thank you for popping around. Oh, can you just do me a favour before you go?'

He turned back, surprised. 'Yes, of course.'

Eleanor walked across the kitchen and retrieved something from on top of the fridge. While her back was turned, Carl reached out and took the business card from on top of her handbag. He wasn't sure why, but he thought it might come in useful, and at the very least it might make it more difficult for his mother to communicate with the policeman.

When she turned back she seemed almost girlish, and wouldn't meet his eyes. 'Could you help me put this necklace on? I haven't worn it for a long time, and I can never manage the catch properly.'

She placed the necklace in his hand and turned around, running her hands beneath her abundant grey hair and leaning forward, exposing her smooth neck.

Carl gazed at the necklace. It consisted of numerous small glass beads in an iridescent, peacock's tail colour, all strung together. Rather than the kind of sprung hook-and-eye clasp that he was used to, this one had a kind of double-cylinder screw arrangement that he'd never come across before.

He looped it around his mother's neck and held the two ends for a moment, trying to figure out how they fitted together. The position suddenly reminded him of something, and it took him a moment to work out what it was.

Oh yes. The taxi driver.

'Carl?'

'Sorry.' He fastened the catch and then stood awkwardly, hands gently resting on her shoulders, remembering.

He'd taken the train to Gants Hill and then called a local taxi company at just past midnight from a prepaid mobile phone bought especially for the purpose. He was standing in front of the randomly-chosen address that he had given in the call when the taxi turned up. He had got in the back and then said: 'Can you take me to Barking Station?' From there he could get the train home again.

He had felt in his pocket for the 0.35mm, 20lb breaking-strain monofilament fishing line that he had slipped into his pocket that morning. It was camouflaged; coloured in random green, brown and black sections so that the fish couldn't see it in the water. Carl had used it many times, fishing in the creeks of the salt marshes. The fishing line was held on a spool, and he had pulled a metre or so off, wrapping it around each hand while holding them low so that the driver couldn't see what he was doing. There were ten metres on the roll, giving him plenty of spare if he needed it.

The car had sped through the streets of east London, past all-night kebab shops and Chinese restaurants, past pubs that looked like they had been there since the 1700s and pubs that looked like they had been converted from flat-roofed 1950s bungalows, past night-clubs and rows of terraced houses — often side by side. Carl had tested the fishing line in his hands as they drove, pulling it tight and checking for any give or slack in it.

As they entered Barking, the taxi had taken a curved route through the one-way system. Carl had waited until they were heading up the rise which marked the progress of the Underground system, and said, 'Take a left just past the station. My place is halfway down.'

The side street had been dark; most of the street lights had been broken at some time in the past and never replaced. The driver had tucked the car into a space between a BMW and a Volkswagen, keeping the engine running.

'Eight quid, mate,' he had said, gazing casually out of the window.

In response, Carl had leaned forward and looped the fishing line over his head, pulling it tight as hard and as quickly as he could. The driver had jerked, spasmed, hands clawing at his throat. The line had sunk deeply into his flesh. His body had bucked and jerked violently but Carl had kept the line taut, imagining the blood thumping in the driver's temples and the encroaching darkness.

The driver's body had slumped slowly into immobility. Carl had kept up the tension for another minute, just in case he was faking, but he wasn't clever enough for that. The car had filled with the stench of faeces and urine as the man's sphincters relaxed in death.

And when he had finished moving, when his hands had fallen to his sides and his body had slumped into ungracious limpness, Carl had left him, lying there in his car with the engine still running, and he had walked away. Almost a year ago now. That was his organised, premeditated, one.

'What are you smiling at?' his mother said, glancing over her shoulder.

'Nothing,' he said. 'Just memories.'

She patted his hand. 'Good memories, I hope.'

'The best,' he said. 'The best.'

13

By late morning Lapslie was fully dressed and ready to leave the hospital. No concussion, no lasting damage, no issues with blood pressure. The nurse confirmed that there was a note on his file from Dr Garland specifying a follow-up appointment with the Psychiatric Department. Seeing it written down made him feel slightly scared. *He* knew he wasn't mentally ill; Dr *Garland* said he didn't think Lapslie was mentally ill; and yet the words 'Psychiatric Department' were there, on his medical notes, for everyone to see.

He felt low, empty, but that wasn't something that the doctors could do anything about. His career was effectively over. The arid plain of his life stretched before him up to the horizon of his death: no landmarks, nothing interesting or unknown to look forward to, just a flat and featureless stretch of ground that could only be trudged across, step by step, until the end.

He was off the case. Off the cases. Off *all* cases, as far as he could see. He still had to work out what that really meant as far as his life was concerned. He had to talk to Emma Bradbury and Jane Catherall to see whether there was any way he could still get a window on what was going on without Dain Morritt knowing about it.

But first he had a lunch to go to.

He got lost on his way out of the hospital. He

followed the signs for the exit and ended up walking through a large hall that was a combination of a café, a travel office for those patients who needed assistance getting home and the Phlebotomy Department.

As he pushed through the three different queues that snaked across the room, looking for the way out, he suddenly heard a distant drumming. His head jerked around, eyes darting left and right, looking for anyone watching, anyone familiar from the press conference. Panicking, he wondered if he was about to pass out again. It took a few seconds for his mind to catch up with his senses; the drumming was dissimilar to the one he'd heard before, lighter, with a different beat. It grew fainter, and he stopped; turned around. The drumming got louder again. He pushed his way through the crowd; crossing and criss-crossing the queues, ignoring the complaints and the glares that followed in his wake, always seeking to make the drumming louder and louder, until he was outside the hall and in a lobby lined with large lift doors. One of the doors was open, and a bed was being wheeled inside by a porter in blue medical shirt and trousers. In the bed was a woman. She was obviously ill; head slumped to one side and barely conscious. For a moment he thought that the fingernails clutching onto the bed sheet were painted, but then he realised that the blotchy redness was something natural, not applied. She turned her head to glance incuriously at him, and he recoiled slightly at the fierce redness of her eyes. She turned away again and gazed at the floor.

A young doctor was standing behind the bed. Her hair was dark, tied back with a band, and she looked thin and intense. 'Family?' she asked. 'Or just lost?' Appropriately for a hospital, her voice was strongly tinged with menthol.

'Police,' he replied, stepping into the lift and showing her his warrant card. 'Can you tell me what's wrong with this lady?'

'No, I can't.' Her stare was challenging.

'Sorry,' he said as the doors closed and the lift set off slowly upwards. 'I don't mean to be rude.'

The doctor's gaze didn't soften. 'If she's a suspect in some investigation, I have to tell you that she's been here for two weeks now, and she's not capable of moving out of the bed. We're just transferring her to another ward. Any more than that and you'll need a warrant.'

He raised his hands placatingly. 'It's okay. She's not in any trouble, and neither is the hospital. It's just . . . ' His brain raced, looking for some explanation saner than 'I think I recognise the sound of her smell', and he noticed again her eyes and her fingernails. That would do. 'It's just there's something about that reddish coloration that I've seen before. It might help me with a case I'm working on. Is it some kind of infection?'

'If you're not family and she's not under arrest then she has a right to privacy. If she doesn't want to tell you what's wrong with her, then I'm not about to violate that right.'

Lapslie looked down at the woman. She was staring at the light in the lift's roof with no change of expression on her face. 'She's not actually refusing,' he said carefully.

'Nice try. No deal. Come back with a warrant.'

He shook his head. 'I hate it when people say that. There's too much crime drama on TV these days. One more question, if I may?'

'Is it about the patient?' the doctor challenged.

He shook his head. 'No — I just want to know how to get out of this hospital.'

With the doctor's help he finally found the exit. The Café Rouge wasn't far from the hospital. Rather than get a taxi back to the police HQ where he'd left his car, Lapslie decided to walk. The overcast cloud from earlier had burned away, and now the sky was a pale eggshell blue marked by stipples of cloud. He slipped his jacket off and slung it over his shoulder as he left, taking in the surroundings that he usually only glimpsed through his car windscreen.

Chelmsford was an ancient town, dating back over eight hundred years, and indeed there were signs everywhere of its history. As he cut through the town's central park he noticed, through the trees, an eighteen-arch red-brick viaduct crossing over a river, carrying trains to and from the central station as it presumably had for a hundred years or more. Nearby, a single lane flyover delivered the A12 into the centre of the town, although bizarrely it didn't seem to take it out again. Maybe they just reversed the priorities on the lane at some point during the day. Everywhere, modern glass shopfronts jostled shoulder-to-shoulder with wooden beams and whitewashed exteriors, while in the town's centre a small cathedral, barely larger than a church, sat surrounded by office blocks, crouched like a nervous cat.

Somewhere, probably while researching the Essex Police, Lapslie had come across the information that Chelmsford had, for a short while, been declared the capital city of England during the Peasants Revolt of 1381. That, he mused, was a time well before any formalised system of policing in the country. In those days, the lords of the manor had effectively policed their areas themselves. Was that why policemen, especially in London, still referred to the area covered by the local police station as their 'manor'?

He found the Café Rouge set off to the side of the main shopping area. Seeing it, he paused, feeling a sudden breathlessness. When was the last time he had seen Sonia? Probably a month before, when he had attended a parents' evening at the school where the kids were based. Sonia had been very good at not insisting that he take the kids every second weekend or whatever. Given his medical condition, that would have pretty much negated the whole point of them separating in the first place: to give him a quiet space in which to live his life. The *quid pro quo* was that he paid as much as he could to her to keep them going, which he did gladly, and that he still tried to be a part of the kids' lives. Which, again, he did gladly.

The frontage of the café was a large sheet of plate glass, stencilled with its name in ornate, almost art-deco script. Through it he could see small tables dotted around the floor space. It was reasonably crowded, given that it was lunchtime, but he had no problem picking Sonia out of the crowd. Her red hair cascaded across her shoulders, and her rather sharp features were pinched in an irritated expression. She checked her watch; a quick, reflex movement that probably didn't even register the time in her mind for more than half a second before it slipped away.

And Lapslie knew that even if she was facing the other way, with her back to him, even if she had been wearing a hat or a scarf to cover her hair, he would have felt the same catch in his breath, the same faltering in his heartbeat, as his gaze had swept over her. Staring into his wife's face, he felt the sacrifices that he had been forced to make weighing him down. Even before his career had been shattered, his life had been ruined. He'd just refused to admit it.

Sonia looked up at him with a smile on her face and trepidation in her eyes.

'Hi, Mark,' she said. 'You're looking well.'

He forced a smile that felt too tight on his face. 'I'm feeling well. I'm back at work full time.'

'I know.' She looked him up and down. 'You need a new suit. I remember that one from . . . before.'

Before we split up. Self-consciously he ran a hand down the lapel of his jacket: the same one he'd been wearing yesterday. He remembered the PR girl — what was her name? Seiju? — being vaguely critical about it. Lapslie tended

272

to wear suits until they gave out on him and then buy a replacement. DI Morritt probably bought a batch of three suits every year, just to keep current: two for use on alternate days during the week and one spare for press conferences, if he ever had to give one.

'I think you look very professional,' Sonia added. 'What case are you working on?'

She hadn't seen the news or watched *Newsnight*. Lapslie felt his heart loosen a little. At least they wouldn't spend the meal talking about his condition, and whether he was okay. She'd hear about it eventually, but not now. Not from him, at least.

'It's the newsreader murder. Alan Rouse put me on it. In fact, he's put me on two cases. You remember Alan?'

She nodded. 'You were at Brixton together, back in the eighties, weren't you? I think we had dinner at his house, once. His wife got drunk and made a pass at you.'

'And you,' Lapslie countered, smiling. 'She ended up making a pass at Rouse as well, forgetting that she was married to him.'

Sonia caught herself. 'Sorry — please, sit down. Did you want something to drink? I ordered water already.'

'Water's fine. Have you ordered food?'

'I thought I'd wait until you arrived.' She offered him a menu, then took one herself. 'How's the cottage?'

'Quiet,' he said. 'Thank God.'

'And the . . . the tastes?'

'The synaesthesia?' he shrugged. 'It's there, all

the time, in the background. Some people get a constant ringing in their ears, some get a constantly irritable bowel. I get tastes. It could be a lot worse. At least some of them are pleasant.' He glanced at the menu. It was full of things he seemed to spend most of every day tasting anyway. What was the point of paying money for it?

A waitress arrived with a tall blue bottle of water, and then hovered with her notebook ready.

'Salmon linguine, please,' Sonia said.

Lapslie eventually selected the most tasteless thing he could find. 'I'll just have the chicken and mozzarella salad,' he said, closing the menu and putting it back in the centre of the table. The girl collected the menus and left, with a smile.

'How about you?' Lapslie asked. 'How's the holistic therapy business?'

'You can always tell when you're in an economic slump. Aromatherapy massages are the first to go.'

'Business bad?'

She nodded. 'Across the board. The whole therapy centre is feeling the pinch.'

He took a deep breath. 'Do you need some more money?' he asked tentatively.

Sonia shook her head, a pained expression on her face. 'No, we're managing okay. That's not why I wanted to meet.'

Then why?

'Kids okay?' He twisted the cap off the bottle of water and poured two glasses.

'Yes. Robbie's had a cold over the summer

which never quite seemed to go away, but I think he's just about rid of it now. Jamie's been going through one of those testosterone surges that kids seem to get. He's suddenly grown out of every single pair of trousers and pair of shoes he has, and everything I ask him to do provokes a massive strop.' She smiled. 'It's almost funny. His favourite phrase at the moment is, "This is the worst day of my *life!*" I've heard him say it five days in a row.'

'You've got to remember that at their age, everything is exaggerated,' Lapslie said. 'It probably feels like the worst day of his life, given that he hasn't got anything much to compare it with. Not the way that we do.'

She winced, and looked away. 'No,' she said eventually. 'I suppose you're right.'

'Did you look after them all summer?'

'No — I booked them into one of those kids' play places. They did swimming, archery, games, crafts . . . all kinds of things. Why didn't they have places like that when we were growing up? All I remember is a chess club at the local library during the summer holidays.'

'Aye,' Lapslie said in a fake Yorkshire accent. 'We had to make our own entertainment in them days.'

She laughed, genuinely, then caught herself. 'They seem to enjoy it,' she said, almost apologetically. 'And it gives me time to see whatever clients I still have left.'

The waitress returned with her salmon and his chicken salad. For a few moments neither spoke as they each took a forkful of food.

275

'Mark . . . ' she said, breaking the silence.

'Yes.' He noticed she kept her gaze fixed on her plate as if there was something intrinsically fascinating about the way the salmon was flaking into the buttery coils of pasta.

'I know we never really talked about the long term, when the kids and I moved out. We never said that it was permanent, but we never said that it was temporary, either. We just ducked the issue.'

His heart felt as if it had just doubled in weight. He could feel it dragging downwards within his chest, a hard lump that was pumping harder and harder to keep his sluggish blood flowing. 'I think we were hoping that the synaesthesia would go away, or that there would be some kind of treatment . . . '

'But it didn't. And there wasn't. Mark, we have to make some kind of decision about the future. We can't — *I* can't — keep going on in this state of uncertainty.'

Which was the point at which Mark Lapslie found himself saying the words that he thought he'd never have to say, the words that he knew too many of his colleagues had used over the years, the words that occurred more often than he could count in witness statements from domestic disputes that he'd been called out to.

'There's someone else, isn't there?'

Her fork, which was half way to her mouth, was lowered, as if there was something suddenly distasteful about the food. 'It's not . . . serious. Not yet. But I need to know whether I can . . . move on. Or not.'

'Do you feel like you need my permission?'

There was something so endlessly fascinating about her forkful of salmon which meant that Sonia couldn't tear her gaze away from it. 'You and I were together a long time,' she said eventually.

'Were?'

'Mark, we're neither one thing nor the other at the moment. Not a couple and not individuals. We're in a halfway house, and we need to choose which way we go.'

'And do we make that choice together?'

This time she did look up at him. 'We have to,' she said simply. 'We can't have one of us thinking the marriage is still staggering on and the other thinking it's dead. It has to be a mutual decision.'

Lapslie found his gaze attracted away, towards the window and the sunlit world outside. Two teenagers walked past. Despite the cold wind the boy was wearing a T-shirt and cargo pants; the girl had on baggy shorts and a strappy yellow top. They were holding hands as if it was the most natural thing in the world. The whole of their lives stretched in front of them — the pain, the misery and the grief — and they were blithely indifferent. Which was as it should be, he reflected. If kids knew what was to come they would just give up now. Evolution knew what it was doing when it gave them a short attention span and a complete inability to learn anything from what their parents said or did.

'I remember,' he said, surprising himself with how harsh the words sounded in the bright surroundings of the café, 'when we used to make love, the sounds you used to make — '

'Mark. Don't.'

'I could *taste* your cries, and it was the most perfect taste in the world. There's nothing I could ever compare it to: no taste in the real world that was anything like it. People would die for that taste.'

'*Please.*' She sounded like she could only get one or two syllables out before the tears would start to come.

'I guess that's the definition of getting old,' he said. 'When you suddenly realise that you've already made love for the last time in your life.'

'You're not that old. There'll be other . . . there'll be others in your life.'

He had to bite back on his automatic response: *I don't want any others: I want you.* Instead, he asked: 'Who is he?'

'Someone from the holistic centre. He lives in Ipswich.'

'What's his name?'

'Why? Are you going to have him checked out?' She raised a hand to her lips. 'I'm sorry. That was uncalled for.'

'Have the kids met him? What do they think?'

'I haven't brought him home yet. I haven't even been *out* with him yet. I just want to know what to say when he asks me. *If* he asks me.'

'Say yes.' The words were the right ones, for her and for him, but they felt like ashes in his mouth. 'Say yes,' he said again, just to see whether he could. Whether the decision would stick.

'Are you sure?'

'Let's think about this logically,' he said.

'Oh yes,' she murmured. 'Let's.'

'The synaesthesia isn't going to get any better. Actually, I think it's getting worse. And it's already at a level where I can't stand to be around people for very long. I need absolute quiet in my life somewhere, and if I can't get it at work then it has to be at home. I wish that didn't exclude you and Jamie and Robbie, but it does. And it's unfair on you for me to expect you to be there as a kind of long-distance partner.'

'I'll always be your partner,' she said, eyes wet. 'If not for the memory of what we had then for the kids at least. I just won't be your wife any more.'

'Are we talking about a separation or a divorce?'

'I've always assumed that they were two stages on the same journey,' she said. 'And we're already separated.'

He sighed. 'I'll contact a solicitor. It should be easy enough as it's uncontested, and we've been living apart for long enough. Irreconcilable differences?'

'Yes.' Sonia pushed her plate away. 'I don't think I can . . . ' She suddenly stood up. 'I'll be back,' she said, and headed off towards the back of the café.

Lapslie pushed the remnants of the chicken salad around his plate, trying to analyse his reactions and finding only a mixture which, although it contained bright elements of several emotions, had ended up as a dull mish-mash of

279

feelings, just like bright paints when mixed together just produce a brown mess, or strong flavours made something muddled and unpleasant.

By the time Sonia returned he had signalled to the waitress for the bill, and paid it.

Sonia didn't even sit down. She hovered behind her chair, cheeks pale and hair still slightly damp where she had washed her face. Even now, he couldn't help analysing evidence and drawing conclusions. He supposed it was what he fell back on when all else failed.

'I need to go,' he said, making it easier for her. 'I've already paid.'

She moved a hand towards her handbag. 'Do you want me to . . . ?'

'No. Thanks, but no. I'll be in touch.' He caught her eye. 'Good luck. And don't be a stranger.'

'Don't become a recluse,' she said. 'I know how easy it would be for you to just curl up in your cottage. Make sure you have a life.'

She walked around the table and reached up to kiss him. He kissed back, savouring the taste of her lips for that brief moment. 'Goodbye,' she said. 'And thank you.'

Lapslie watched her leave: that body that he knew so well, hidden and yet emphasised by her clothes, now separated from him for ever.

He sat there for a while, nursing a glass of water. The waitress progressively cleared the remains of the two meals and hovered in case he ordered something else, but the café wasn't busy enough for them to want him to leave. As customers and staff ebbed and flowed around him he felt himself slipping into an isolated bubble where time did not pass and emotions did not register; where his synaesthesia had somehow become passive, so that sounds were for a while just sounds and not tastes, where he could flit back and forth over memories and take elements of them, recreating for himself a perfect summer's day with a perfect wife and perfect children. A perfect day that had never happened, but which symbolised for him all that he had lost.

He surfaced from the half-dream to find that somehow he had finished the water and that two hours had passed. His mobile, which sat on the table in front of him, had received a text message at some stage; a message that he had neither heard nor tasted. It said: *Developments in Charnaud/Wildish cases — please phone Sean Burrows.* Instead, wanting to delay the moment that he had to return to his desk, Lapslie walked back to the police HQ and retrieved his Saab from the car park. Whatever Sean Burrows wanted to tell him, he wanted to hear it first hand, and not over the phone.

Thoughts of Sonia and the kids occupied his mind fruitlessly until he arrived at the forensic laboratory. As before, he had to leave his car in a car park outside the wire fence and book in at the security portacabin, where he was issued with a pass with his photograph grainily printed on it on a green lanyard, which he had to hang around his neck.

Eventually, someone came down to escort him

up the slope to the 1950s red-brick building that housed Burrows's laboratory. A cold wind tugged dry leaves across the road as they walked. Piles of leaves were building up against the wire fence that surrounded the site.

Lapslie found Burrows perched on a corner of a bench in his starkly white lab. A large computer screen had been placed on the bench behind him. Disconcertingly, Jane Catherall was sitting on a lab stool next to him, her short legs crossed demurely a foot or so above the tiled floor, and Emma Bradbury stood, arms crossed, behind her. Emma nodded at him. 'Boss,' she murmured, face grim.

'What's the matter?' he asked. 'You've got a face like a bulldog licking piss off a thistle.'

She scowled. 'Some fuckwit stole my handbag in a restaurant. They took the purse but abandoned the handbag in the gents' toilet. Why are gents' toilets so smelly, by the way? Women's ones don't get that bad.'

Lapslie shook his head. 'It's like dogs,' he said. 'Pheromones in the urine. We have to mark our territory. Did the thief get anything?'

'Just some cash and my credit cards. Fortunately my warrant card was in my jacket. Mr Burrows here has kindly offered to have the handbag checked for fingerprints. It's a long shot, but it'll make me feel like something's being done.'

'Make sure you cancel the cards.' He turned to Jane. 'And Dr Catherall, I didn't expect to find you here.'

'I realise that I do appear to be something of a

282

cross between a hermit crab and Dr Franken-
stein,' she replied, her voice as smooth and as
tingly on Lapslie's tongue as aged brandy, 'never
leaving the mortuary except to collect fresh
cadavers, but I do occasionally get out for other
reasons. Sean and I often chat about the cases
that we are working on, and there was something
about the confluence of these two cases that
caused us to start thinking.'

'Jane mentioned your reaction at both crime
scenes,' Sean Burrows said, his Irish brogue
reminding Lapslie, as always, of wild fruit and
strong gin. 'And she also mentioned your
medical condition. Synaesthesia, is it? A
fascinating and little-researched condition.'

'I hope I was not breaking a confidence . . . '
Jane ventured, a cloud crossing her face.

'Don't worry,' Lapslie said wryly. 'Everyone
else seems to know.'

'Jane mentioned that there was something to
do with both murders that triggered the same
synaesthetic response in your brain,' Burrows
continued. 'Something to do with the crime
scenes.' He nodded over at Emma. 'When your
sergeant pitched up and asked me to put a rush
on the urine sample from Braintree Parkway, and
to take more samples from the toilet at the
Charnaud house, I put two and two together. So
I ran them through a gas chromatograph.'

'What's that when it's at home?' Emma asked.

'It's a piece of equipment that takes a vapour
sample, heats it up and then pushes it into a
column packed with capillary columns made of
fused silica with a polyimide outer coating. The

molecules are absorbed or deposited on the capillaries at different rates, because they all have different weights and sizes. We monitor the time it takes them to emerge — '

'The proper word is 'elute',' Jane murmured.

' — And then identify them by their position.'

'I'll take your word for it,' Lapslie said. 'What's the result?'

Instead of answering, Burrows used the computer mouse to click on a couple of buttons on the computer screen. A picture appeared: two graphs, stacked on top of each other. Each graph displayed a jagged line that was flat in places and spiked in others, like a representation of the value of the pound against three currencies over a ten-year period.

'These are the spectra of the two traces,' Burrows murmured, still fiddling with the mouse. 'As you can see, there are several common elements in each of the spectra — chemical compounds that occur in both samples.'

And Lapslie *could* see it. The two traces had several peaks in common, albeit at different heights.

'Would we not expect that?' he mused, almost to himself. 'After all, one trace is from a pool of urine and one from a toilet bowl. Both areas would have traces of urine, surely?'

'Yes, but we know the chemical signature of the various components of urine,' Burrows said. 'We can factor them out. And that still leaves us with one peak that's common to the two samples.' He used the mouse to draw a straight line down the screen, highlighting a peak that appeared in the same place on both graphs. 'This molecule does not occur naturally in urine, but is present in both samples.'

'Which means it is probably the molecule you smelled at both crime scenes,' Jane said. 'Not smelled, perhaps, but *heard*.'

'So what is it?' Lapslie asked.

'Difficult to be sure,' Burrows relied. 'It's a high molecular mass, long-chain, aromatic compound of some kind. The trouble is that I've not got enough of a sample from either crime scene to be able to run chemical tests. I know something's there, but I can't work out what it is without destroying the samples, and even then there's no guarantee. And you've also lost your evidence.'

Lapslie sighed, and looked away from the three faces that were turned towards him. He supposed he had to tell them some time. 'Look, grateful as I am for all this, it's DI Morritt you need to be talking to, not me. I'm off the case. Chief Superintendent Rouse has removed me.'

'Nobody's told me yet,' Emma said. 'As far as I'm concerned, officially you're still in charge.'

'Your mobile's rung five times since you arrived,' Sean Burrows pointed out softly. 'And I can see three unread messages from here.'

'Bugger the man,' Jane snapped. 'He's barely making progress on one case, as far as I can see, whereas you've linked up two cases. And possibly more.'

'More?' Lapslie frowned.

'We've got to locate some more evidence, yes?

I want you to come back with me to the mortuary. In fact, I want you to give me a *lift* back to the mortuary, given that I got a taxi here at police expense. I've got an entire room full of cold cases waiting for me, and this time I want *your* expert opinion on them.'

Lapslie shrugged. 'Okay,' he said. 'It's not like I have anything else to do at the moment. And the longer I stay out of Rouse's way, the better. Emma, you follow us. Mr Burrows — keep up the good work.'

The drive back to Braintree took half an hour. Lapslie spent the time in a daze. In the space of a few hours he'd gone from the depths of despair to the heights of excitement. He wasn't mad! The cases *were* connected!

Lapslie's car got to the mortuary before Emma's, surprisingly. His phone rang as he pushed the car door shut. Probably Rouse, knowing his luck. He switched it off, unanswered. Rather than wait for Emma, he and Jane went straight in. She led him into a room that Lapslie had been in before, the one where she had shown him the stun gun marks on Catherine Charnaud's shoulder. His breath gusted in front of his face in the chill. The far wall of the room consisted almost entirely of drawers, each one containing a body.

'Now, pull this drawer out.' She indicated the extreme left hand body drawer on the lowest level. 'Come on, man; strike while the iron is hot!'

Moving to the door that she had indicated, Lapslie pulled it out. The body inside was that of an elderly man; bald, with a massive and bloodless injury to the side of his head.

'Stop gawping. Can you hear anything?' Jane asked impatiently.

'Nothing more than I did before. I can smell plenty, though.'

'Stop complaining. Push that drawer in and pull the next one out.'

Lapslie returned the old man to his place of rest and tugged the next drawer out. The body inside was that of a middle-aged woman with dyed brown hair. There were no marks of violence or injury on her.

'Anything?'

'Nothing.'

'Next one.'

The next body was a child, badly burned. The one after that was a girl slightly older than Catherine Charnaud. The next two drawers were empty. The seventh drawer contained a body whose badly bruised and battered head was missing its entire left side. It looked like the flesh and the bone had been rubbed off with sandpaper.

'Sorry,' Jane said. 'Car crash. The poor chap was leaning out of the window when the car tipped over. Any drumming?'

'No,' Lapslie said, choking back his nausea.

She shrugged. 'On with the motley.'

In the end it was the third drawer along on the second level, ironically the one next to the drawer containing Catherine Charnaud's body, that caused the level of the drumming in his mind to suddenly escalate to a level where it competed with Jane's voice for attention. 'There,' he said, trying not to shout over the sound. 'It's there.'

The body inside was that of a man in his seventies. The body was far from fresh, but Lapslie could see purple ligature marks around the neck.

'Strangling,' Jane said from behind him. 'The poor man was found in an isolated farmhouse. He had hanged himself of his own volition or been forced to do it. It's an unsolved case.'

The drumming was so loud that Lapslie almost expected the room to be shaking.

He gazed down at the body. His heart was pounding at the same rate as the drumming in his ears. 'And then there were three,' he said.

The door to the room opened and Emma burst in. She was holding her BlackBerry out. 'Boss, you need to hear this.'

'If it's Rouse,' he hissed, 'I really *don't* want him to know I'm still working the case!'

'It's not a phone call; it's the radio,' she said. 'I heard it in the car. That's why I got delayed — I was trying to work out how to record the thing using the BlackBerry. Listen!' She pressed a key, and a voice underpinned by static filled the room, covering Lapslie's tongue with the tingling flavour of chorizo sausage.

' . . . Can somehow *smell* a murderer. Detective Chief Inspector Lapslie was discharged from hospital this morning, and is unavailable for comment, but his superior, Chief Superintendent Alan Rouse, released a statement saying that DCI Lapslie was no longer heading up any investigations within Essex Constabulary and was currently on sick leave. Lapslie was, crucially, heading up the investigations into the murder of TV presenter Catherine Charnaud and the bombing of Braintree Parkway station, and it is unclear where his removal leaves these investigations . . . '

Lapslie felt like someone had doused him in freezing water. That was exactly the conversation he'd had with Rouse. But only he and Rouse knew about it.

He, Rouse and Inspector Dain Morritt.

'Bloody Dain Morritt,' he growled. 'Not content with grabbing the Wildish case back from me, he's also doing everything he can to undermine me. I'll bloody have him for this! He doesn't want to share the investigation with anyone, so he's spreading rumours about my mental state in order to discredit me. I'll tell him to wind his neck in. If he doesn't, I'll wind it in for him.'

'And prove that you're unstable?' Jane rested a hand on his arm. 'Mark, you'll lose your job, your pension and your self-respect. And if that's not enough, the murderer will go free. Don't you realise — you're the only person with the capability to catch him!'

'And the last person in the world with the resources,' Lapslie growled.

14

There had been a time when Carl Whittley would have spent hours poring over an Ordnance Survey map of a section of English countryside, painstakingly translating the contour lines into a three-dimensional picture in his mind. Which was the best route to walk? Which way was uphill and which way was flat? Was that slope too steep to climb? Where was the best place to position himself in order to see a badger's sett or a bevy of roe deer? Now, sitting in the outbuilding in the back garden where he kept his computer, all he had to do was to type the name of the place he wanted to look at into Google Earth and within seconds he was looking at a photograph — not a map, not a representation, but an actual *photograph* — of the place he was interested in. Actually, not a single photograph but a mosaic, a jigsaw of tens, hundreds, thousands of images from satellites in orbit around the Earth, all painstakingly pieced together into an image of the entire world's surface in perpetual daylight. Two clicks of his mouse and the image would zoom in to a point where he could make out cars on roads. Another click on a particular box on the screen and the image would tilt sideways until he was looking *across* the landscape rather than down onto it, and thanks to the miracle of cheap personal computing the photographs that made up the image would be distorted to account for the shape of the underlying terrain, so that if there was a hill or a mountainside present the photographs would bend up and then down again. It wasn't perfect, but the images were getting better all the time and it was good enough that he could get an impression of any place he might be going.

What with Google Earth and the MultiMap site, which could pinpoint a particular street or postcode anywhere in the UK for him, he located Emma Bradbury's flat in less than ten minutes. It was part of a block in Shenfield, on the outskirts of Brentford in Essex — a convenient driving distance away from the police HQ in Chelmsford. A quick trawl around Brentford estate agents' internet sites threw up three who were selling flats in that block. That got Carl a set of photographs of different elevations of the block, allowing him to pinpoint Emma's living room, bathroom and bedroom windows with a fair degree of accuracy. Even better, he found another, taller block within a few hundred metres of the block containing Emma's flat. It was the same height, but the roof looked down onto the side of Emma's block, and her flat was about halfway up. From that roof, or from an empty flat on the top floor if he could locate one and break in, Carl would be able to take his time in lining up the shot.

He could even work out what time of day he wanted to do it. The line from the roof of the block he would be firing from to Emma's bedroom window was roughly east. That meant in the morning the sun would be shining into Carl's eyes, and Emma's side of the block would be in shadow. Not ideal. Evening would be better, with the sun behind Carl and with Emma's flat illuminated by orange light, but there was always the chance of the sun's glare reflecting off windows and into his eyes and perspective could be thrown off by that particular kind of sunlight. That meant midday and night were the best options. At midday the sun would be shining directly down onto the roof from which he would be firing, if he couldn't find a flat on the top floor to break into, leaving him potentially vulnerable to being seen, and he would be restricted to weekends, when Emma was not at work, which would mean more people would be about. That might increase the likelihood that he would be seen when he left the area. And with the sun in that position there was likely to be significant shadowing of the block's elevation from balconies and ledges. At night, however, Emma's flat would be illuminated, at least while she was cooking, or watching TV, or preparing for bed, guaranteeing a good shot. So, evening it would be.

He would have to come up with some explanation for his dad. Perhaps he could say that he'd met a girl and was taking her out for dinner. His dad would be pleased for him. So long as he left a meal on a tray and made sure Nicholas had access to a phone, he should be all right.

His eye was caught by the latest glass-fronted wooden box on the shelves. This one was a scrawny cat that he'd trapped inside a plastic box and then gassed with fumes from the exhaust of his car. The carbon monoxide had turned the skin of its paws and nose bright pink, but Carl had used a blowtorch to burn and scorch the cat's face back to the skull, and he'd pinned the paws to the wood so that the cat's body was lying backwards with its ruined face staring upwards, just like the commuter on Braintree Parkway Station. He'd spent hours on it the night before, after he'd got back from Chelmsford. Placing it on the shelf, at the end of a long line of his trophies, gave him a thrill of accomplishment and the sense of a job that was, if not well done, then going well.

Carl knew he would have to leave rapidly after he had fired the shot. Even if he had managed to break into a flat on the top floor of his preferred location, it wouldn't take the police long to work out where the shot had come from — once they had got over the initial disbelief that someone had shot one of their own people in the first place. Carl estimated that he probably had twenty minutes after the shot had been fired before the police identified the ten or so windows it could have come from. That was, of course, assuming that the shot was heard and reported, but the rifle Carl had wouldn't take a silencer, and he wouldn't know where to get one from even if it would. He had to assume that someone would call the police. After all, the locals couldn't be used to *that* much gunfire. Not even in Brentford.

Using the estate agents' sites again, Carl

located a flat on the top floor of his preferred firing location that was currently for sale. It might be empty; it might not: he would probably have to conduct a reconnaissance in person to find out. If it was empty, and assuming it wasn't under offer and didn't sell between now and the fifth day, then it would make a good location. He wouldn't make the mistake of approaching the estate agents for a viewing and then somehow copying the keys — he would be remembered, and the last thing he wanted to do was leave a trail. No, as long as the flat wasn't actually boarded up then he would be able to break in.

He printed out the various maps and images, just to be sure, and then bookmarked the sites so that he could revisit them later. He'd paid someone to install security software on the computer. It wasn't just password protected, but if anyone tried to bypass the password control then the software would activate and wipe the hard disc. The person who fitted it for him had obviously assumed that he wanted to download hard-core porn from the internet without his parents finding out. He'd done that as well, but with his mother moved out of the house he felt he was pretty safe. His father used to be an architect. He had no idea how to get into computers.

Closing the system down, Carl leaned back in the chair and closed his eyes. He could feel the muscles in his back protesting at the strain they had been under. He needed a bath. No; he needed a cup of tea and *then* a bath.

Carl left the computer room and headed up

the garden path to the kitchen. The house had a faint musty smell that he only ever noticed when he returned after a while away. He knew what it meant; it was the sign of a house built on marshy, waterlogged ground where dampness had seeped into the foundations and up through the walls. It was the smell of a house where rot was almost inevitable in brick or wood or plaster or anything that wasn't solid stone.

His father was sitting in the lounge, reading.

'Carl!' he said, looking up eagerly. 'I thought you'd gone out again.'

'I was down in the shed. Just doing some work.'

'Oh.' He paused. 'I thought I'd spend some time downstairs. Is that okay?'

Carl forced a smile. 'That's fine. Of course that's fine. I was just about to put the kettle on. Do you fancy a cuppa?'

'Please.'

Carl switched on the radio while the kettle boiled. BBC Essex would occasionally run a news item or a feature on the Catherine Charnaud murder or the bombing at Braintree Parkway, just as they had on Carl's previous murders, and he liked to keep abreast of what was going on. It wasn't anything vainglorious, like craving the excitement and attention that being referred to, even in passing, on TV or radio could create. It was more that he wanted to check on whether his mother was having any impact on the case, or whether she'd been brought in to consult on any others.

'Actually, dad . . . ' he called out.

'What?'

'I was wondering . . . You've been so much better recently. Would it be okay if . . . if I went out for an evening?'

A longer pause this time. 'That's fine. You go ahead. I'll be fine.'

'If it's a problem then I can put it off.'

'No.' Warmer. 'You're a good boy, Carl, looking after me. I know how much hanging around the house winds you up. You always preferred to be out in the countryside, watching the birds and the animals, to being stuck inside. It's been difficult for you since Eleanor left. You deserve some time to yourself. Go and have fun.'

'It's just . . . '

'It's a girl, isn't it?'

'Yes.' Carl tried to inject a little awkwardness into his voice. 'We met . . . at the supermarket. I said I'd take her to a film. We haven't arranged a date yet.'

'I'm glad. You go and enjoy yourself.'

The local news came on just as Carl was pouring out his dad's cup of tea. The lead story was still the Braintree bomb, but this time there was a twist, a new piece of the puzzle. Carl concentrated, turning the volume up so that he could hear more clearly through the static.

' . . . While Essex Police have stated that Detective Chief Inspector Mark Lapslie, the man who had until now been leading the investigation, has been removed from the case. Anonymous sources within the police have told the BBC that DCI Lapslie was removed because he apparently believes he can literally *sniff out* a criminal by the odour they leave behind at a crime scene. Essex Police have declined to comment on these claims, or on the suggestion that a serial killer is at work . . . '

Carl dropped the cup. It seemed to fall for ever, liquid glinting as it turned before smashing on the kitchen floor, sending the tea spilling in a steaming brown wave across the tiles. Hot water spattered against his legs, but he barely noticed. He felt sick.

'Carl? What happened?'

'Sorry. The cup was hotter than I thought. I'll . . . I'll clear it up and pour another one.'

Lapslie. Mark Lapslie. The police officer he had seen conducting the press conference about the bombing. Emma Bradbury's boss. Despite the barely veiled scorn of the newsreader, and the suggestion that Lapslie had been removed from the case because he was delusional, he somehow *knew* that the two deaths were connected. Either he had worked it out, or he actually *could* smell Carl's involvement.

Carl thought, feverishly, as he mopped up the spilled tea. He had spent long enough working on Catherine Charnaud, stripping the flesh relentlessly from her bones, that his perspiration had almost certainly fallen onto the girl's skin. He'd also used the toilet in the house. Could Lapslie have smelled that? The bombing confused him for a moment — he had been hundreds of yards away from the site of the explosion — but then he remembered urinating on the roof of the shopping centre, squatting out of sight and relieving himself after several hours of waiting for the right moment to arrive. Had he left a scent there, a spoor that Lapslie had somehow been able to pick up?

Carl picked up the shards of pottery and put them in the bin. The thought was insane, but it kept on circling around his mind like a bloated fly lazily circling a light bulb as he continued clearing the smashed mug and the spilled tea away. Animals had incredibly acute senses, he knew. Dogs could apparently detect early-stage breast and lung cancer with amazing accuracy just by sniffing the breath of someone who has that diagnosis. People could sometimes develop their own senses to match. He'd once heard in hushed tones about a hunter up in the wilds of Scotland whose night vision was better than a cat's. He lived in the dark; sleeping during the day in a bedroom lined with thick black cloth to keep out the light. Nobody was allowed to smoke near him because the glow of their cigarette would disrupt his finely honed vision. To him, a starlit sky was like the noonday sun, and on a cloudy, moonless night he could see for miles when everyone else around him couldn't see their own hand in front of their face. No, Carl believed that people could sense things, if they put their mind to it, especially if they were compensating for something else. How else could blind people read the Braille signs inside lifts, which felt no more distinct than raised scar tissue to Carl? Their fingertips must be incredibly sensitive.

Pouring out another cup of tea, the logical corollary to Detective Chief Inspector Mark

Lapslie's preternatural abilities struck him with the force of a fist in his gut; if Lapslie *could* smell Carl, then there was something about Carl that he could smell, something that was different to everyone else. Perhaps the porphyria meant that he was secreting some chemical in his perspiration, something that the policeman could detect. Carl bent his head and sniffed his armpit as best he could. Nothing. He ran a finger across his forehead and smelled it. Still nothing. But then, people got used to smells, didn't they? If you lived with a smell, like damp and mould, for enough time then you stopped smelling it; just as your mind automatically filtered out the sounds of traffic if you lived near a road. *Did* he smell of something, but just couldn't detect it himself?

The haematin tablets he was on — would they help mask the smell or just add to it? Either was possible, but he just didn't know enough about biochemistry to be able to tell, and it wasn't like he could go and ask the doctor.

Carl cast his mind back. Nobody had ever mentioned that he smelled. His mother or father had never said anything. No doctor had ever raised it as a symptom. Nobody had ever bought him a deodorant as a way of telling him that he stank. Some of the men that he'd met in the Essex Hunt had smelled like polecats, and were taunted about it on a daily basis. There was certainly no holding back of opinions in the countryside. No animal that he'd watched, or stalked, had ever become spooked and run off because they had smelled him in the area. No, if there was something about him that Mark

Lapslie was picking up on, then it was something subtle. Something that nobody else could sense, or scent. Only him.

Which meant that Lapslie, not Emma Bradbury, should be his next victim.

Carl's main safety net at the moment was the fact that each of his murders was completely separate from the others. He needed to get to Lapslie before he convinced anyone senior in the police that he was right, that the murders were connected. He still had to humiliate his mother; ensure that she was never approached by the police again and had to come back to the house, complete the family again. But if the news report could be believed then Lapslie had been marginalised within the force. Removed. Side-lined.

As he leaned against the kitchen counter, thinking his way through the maze of logic and speculation, something else occurred to him. The story on the BBC hadn't been based on a press release or anything formal. It had been an anonymous accusation; something only slightly more than gossip. It indicated that there was some tension within the police; that Lapslie had enemies who were trying to blacken his name, discredit him in the eyes of the public and thus in the eyes of his superiors. And that meant there was an inbuilt desire within the police to not believe him. If he was out of the way, if he could not fight his own corner, then his beliefs would be rubbished by whoever it was that had released the anonymous statement. And Carl would be safe to keep killing until his mother came back.

That meant his plan to use the rifle to shoot Emma Bradbury couldn't be transferred across to Mark Lapslie. Shooting her would have looked like a bizarre, apparently motiveless crime; shooting *him* would vindicate his theory about the murders being connected. He would have to make his death look accidental. His mind raced. A car accident, perhaps — a hit-and-run where he ran him over in some country lane or forced his car off the road and into a crash barrier. Tricky to arrange, and fraught with the risk that he might be seen, followed, caught. A fire at his house: Carl could break in and fray an electric cable to the point where it would catch light, or remove the screws that retained the bare wires inside an electrical plug and then pull the cable so that the wires touched and would spark when the socket was switched on. He could do it. Or perhaps just the simplest thing possible — a mugging, crushing his skull from behind with a crowbar and then taking his wallet. It happened all the time to people. Especially in Essex.

Carl thought for a moment. If there *was* something about his biology that this policeman was able to home in on then he needed to do something about it in a hurry. He couldn't take the risk that there might be some small scrap of evidence linking him to one of the murders that could result in him being questioned by the police, if only as a potential witness, and if that happened and the man questioning him was Mark Lapslie then he might suddenly find himself in the frame for all the murders that the police knew about, and more besides. Or worse; if Carl was following Lapslie, waiting for an opportune moment to push him under a train or smash his head in, then Lapslie might be able to tell that he was in the vicinity, and stop him.

The first thing he needed to do was take a shower. A long shower. He looked around the kitchen for something that might help deodorise him. He remembered that he had half a lemon in the fridge, kept for squeezing over chips instead of vinegar, which always caused his father's digestion problems since the operation. He could rub it all over himself, couldn't he? Cleaning products often advertised themselves as having lemon in them. 'Nature's cleaning agent', they called it. The citric acid should cut through grease and dirt, and hopefully whatever substance it was that Mark Lapslie was able to detect. Or at least cover it up with a stronger smell.

He felt soiled. Dirty. And the worst thing was that he couldn't even tell what was wrong. He felt like a dog that had been told it was a bad boy but didn't understand why. He wanted someone to take him to one side and explain it to him, but there wasn't anyone. He was on his own.

He grabbed the lemon and slipped it into his pocket, then carried his father's cup of tea through to the living room.

'Everything all right?'

'Fine,' he lied. 'I'm just . . . tired. I'm heading up for a shower. I'll do some lunch when I come down.'

He went up to the bathroom and turned the

shower on as hard and as hot as he could stand, then undressed. Steam wreathed the bathroom and his naked body. Gingerly, he climbed in. The water was like scalding needles impacting all over his chest and neck. His skin turned instantly scarlet and blotchy. Bracing himself, Carl turned around, letting the water scour every square inch of his body, raising his arms so that his armpits were washed clean and then, taking a deep breath of the tropical air, he shoved his head under the streaming water. It burned. Jesus *Christ*, it burned. He cried out, despite himself, feeling blisters rising all across his scalp but knowing that the water wasn't quite that hot. He stuck it out for as long as he could, then jerked his head back, gasping. The relatively cooler air on his skin stung even worse for a moment. He felt dizzy, and had to grab hold of the edge of the shower to stop himself falling.

He turned the shower off and stood there for a moment, feeling the water running off his skin. Cool air infiltrated its way across his body, making him shiver suddenly. He felt like crying. Before his resolve crumbled he grabbed the lemon half from where he had left it in the soap dish and rubbed it over his chest, his shoulders, his arms, his scalp, his buttocks and legs, and then between his legs, around his scrotum, squeezing the lemon harder and harder as he went. The shower filled with the sharp, aromatic smell of lemon oil. His skin stung where the oil penetrated the pores opened by the steaming water or the small cuts that he had on his hands from building the explosive devices for the bombing.

Wincing, he kept going, scrubbing his hands, his scalp and the soles of his feet. The steam from the shower combined with the lemony odour to form a fragrant cloud that he could feel deep down in his lungs.

He put the lemon back on the soap dish and picked up the soap that sat beside it. Coal Tar soap, coloured a deep waxy yellow, like the skin of the lemon, but smelling of woodsmoke and tar. He quickly rubbed it all over his body, following the path of the lemon. The soap suds combined with the remnants of the lemon juice to form a scummy mess, but he kept going, rubbing it obsessively into his skin until he was covered from head to toe in dirty grey curds. And then he turned the shower on again, full blast, took the shower head down from its hook and blasted it across his body again, washing everything off with scalding water. Finally, taking a deep breath, he directed the shower head between his legs, gasping at the pain but keeping the jet of water pointed straight up, then prised the cheeks of his buttocks apart with his thumb and forefinger and sluiced himself out. This time he nearly screamed at the pain.

To finish he put the shower back onto its hook and turned it onto its coldest setting. The water went from boiling to frozen within a few seconds. Carl gasped again as his skin seemed to flinch all over, forming goose-pimples from the top of his head down to his toes. The shock of the cold made him feel as if he had lost two inches off his waist and his height in as many seconds. He felt his scrotum shrivel and his testicles retreat back into the warmth of his body. He hung his head, letting the water course down over him, sheathing his body, closing the pores and washing the last remnants of the lemon juice and the soap suds away.

Carl turned the water off and stood there for a few minutes, feeling it all trickling away, letting his muscles relax. He sniffed cautiously, but he didn't smell any different from the way he did after any shower or any bath, apart from the lingering scent of lemon. He didn't know whether it had worked or not. He could only hope.

Stepping from the shower and towelling himself dry, Carl took a container of his father's chlorhexidine antiseptic talc from the bathroom cabinet and shook it all over his body. He kept shaking until his body was white, like an alabaster statue, and surrounded by a cloud of floating dust. The sharp, medicinal smell got up his nostrils and he coughed, convulsively, but he couldn't stop.

He saw a can of antiperspirant/deodorant on top of the cabinet, and reached for it, then pulled back. This was stupid. Where would it stop? Where would it all stop?

15

The drive to the farmhouse had taken Lapslie, Emma and Eleanor Whittley down a winding dirt track which seemed to peter out and restart several times and eventually ended in a patch of churned-up ground where they left their cars. They pushed through a gap in a hedge that looked natural rather than forced and across a bare patch of waterlogged ground. The forensic clinical psychologist hadn't been too happy at the walk: she hadn't said anything but she had a downward twist to her lips and she kept casting dark side-glances at Lapslie. Her high heels were unsuitable to the terrain. Lapslie's leather shoes were hardly any better, but he wasn't going to give her the satisfaction of knowing that.

Now the three of them stood in the shelter of a half-demolished barn, gazing at the farmhouse. The rain soaked into Lapslie's hair and trickled down his cheeks, but he didn't react to it. He had endured worse, in his time. Inside his waterproof jacket he was uncomfortably warm, sweat prickling his skin despite the coldness outside, but again he hardly even noticed.

The farmhouse was a ramshackle affair of mismatched bricks and old wood, apparently built in fits and starts over several generations. There was nothing about it that stood out against the marshy ground and the trees surrounding it. It was almost organic in its decrepitude: like some monstrous fungus that had grown gradually, incrementally, over time. Another few years and Lapslie felt that it might just fade away, still part of the local topography but somehow separate from it, removed, abstracted.

'Do we know who owns this place now?' he asked Emma.

'Apparently it's in something of a legal limbo,' she replied. 'The only person with a claim to it is the old man lying dead in Dr Catherall's mortuary — one Jeffrey Hawkins — but he's in no position to do anything about it. He's a widower with one daughter, apparently, but nobody could locate her during the investigation of the father's death. The police wanted to track her down, partly to actually tell her that her father had been strangled and partly in case she was responsible, but she fell off the radar ten years ago and hasn't been seen since. Drug problems, apparently, and a diagnosed schizophrenic. Her father always told the neighbours that he thought she was living rough in London.'

Lapslie looked at the desolation around the farmhouse. 'Neighbours?'

'About a mile down the track,' Emma confirmed. 'It was them who found the body. They used to check on him every few days; when he didn't open the door they went in. He was in the front room, dead. The council will repossess it at some stage and then auction it, but for the moment we still have the key.'

Eleanor Whittley snorted. 'Really, I don't know why I am here. The two crimes are patently completely divergent. The Catherine Charnaud case is clearly the work of a sexual sadist with a deep-seated hatred of women, whereas this may well not be a murder at all but simple suicide. There's no sexual element here, no torture, nothing that relates to the Charnaud case.'

'Trust me,' Lapslie ground out, 'it's the same killer.'

She shook her head. 'Why consult me if you're not going to accept what I say?'

'Consultancy is like a birthday present,' Lapslie replied. 'It should be accepted with good grace, but you're not obliged to actually make use of it.' He nodded towards Emma. 'Come on; let's go in.'

Emma slid the key into the lock. The key *snicked* into the mechanism and she pushed the door open.

Lapslie waited in the doorway for a moment, sniffing in the stale air of the house. Nothing . . . nothing . . . and there it was, faintly, as if someone were playing bongos in the far distance. The murderer had been there.

'Spread out,' he instructed. 'Emma, take upstairs. I'll take downstairs. Mrs Whittley — stay in the front room. You've got a copy of the case file. See if you can pick anything up that we miss.'

'Yeah, on that subject, boss — what is it that we're actually looking for? This place was searched when the body was discovered. There was nothing.'

'At the time they didn't know this was part of

a series of deaths. Sean Burrows has confirmed that the same long-chain molecule was found on the body, but he's not got enough of a sample to do a chemical analysis. We need more.' He met her sceptical glance. 'Look, if I knew where to find it, I'd tell you.'

They went off in different directions. Lapslie's search of the upper floor only took ten minutes or so, and was underpinned all the time with drumming, like a rapid fluttering pulse. The place was cluttered with clothes and cardboard boxes, but there wasn't any evidence of a murder, let alone a murderer. He'd reserved his best hopes for the bathroom, but when he saw the state of it — the mould in the corners, the stained tub, the toilet bowl so encrusted with limescale and dried clumps of stuff he didn't even want to think about that it was probably near-as-dammit blocked — he gave up. This was a stupid idea to begin with. He wasn't even on the case, and he was grasping at straws so thin they were just fading away in his hand.

He walked heavily down the creaking wooden stairs. Eleanor Whittley was standing in the centre of the living room — more clutter, along with a sofa whose stuffing was emerging from several holes and a TV so old that it had a tuning dial rather than a remote — looking completely lost. She glanced at him darkly. 'You realise I charge by the hour,' she snapped. 'I'm costing you money just standing here doing nothing.'

'Not my money,' he murmured.

Emma came into the living room. She had an odd expression on her face.

'Got something?' Lapslie asked, momentarily excited. 'The kitchen?'

'No — the chemical toilet.'

'What?'

'There's a chemical toilet in what was probably a pantry. It looks in pretty good nick.'

Lapslie followed her out while she was still talking. 'The toilet upstairs is nearly unusable,' he said. 'He probably bought a chemical toilet in order to — '

'Yea, I get the picture.'

'Or someone bought it for him. A neighbour, perhaps.'

'If you haven't found anything upstairs . . . ?'

'Which I haven't.'

'And if we still think that the murderer has some kind of bladder problem . . . ?'

'Which we do.'

'Then there's a chance that they took a slash in the chemical toilet before they left.' She led him through the kitchen — piled with unwashed pans and plates — to a side door. In the small room beyond there was a plastic pedestal toilet with a large base standing isolated in the centre. It looked absurdly modern in the clutter and mess of the rest of the house.

'And there's a chance that there might still be traces of the sample we need still inside. Good work.'

She nodded. 'You want me to get Sean Burrows out to take samples?'

'No, I want you to dismantle this toilet and take the reservoir directly to Burrows.'

'But — '

'No arguments. We're up against a time constraint here.'

'What time constraint?'

He gazed levelly at her. 'We've got until Rouse finds out I'm still working the case, and then everything stops. Do you think Dain Morritt will have any time at all for this theory?'

Emma gazed at the chemical toilet. 'I'll need a screwdriver and a pair of gloves,' she muttered. 'What about you? Where are you going?'

'Hospital,' he snapped. 'Get a squad car out here to drive Mrs Whittley home.'

The journey to Chelmsford Hospital took forty-five minutes. He turned his phone back on and as every minute went past he expected it to ring, with Chief Superintendent Rouse on the other end, but it stayed resolutely silent.

He strode into the hospital and through the corridors and wards, looking for the doctor that he'd seen before. If she was off duty then he was out of luck, but he found her eventually talking to a nurse in a rest area.

'I need to ask you a question about that woman,' he snapped.

'What woman?' Her voice was still menthol, but sweeter than he remembered. More like toothpaste. She stared at his face. 'You were in the lift. You're a policeman.'

'That's right. It's very important that I know what was wrong with the woman in the bed, the one you were moving. You said she was ill. I need to know what that illness was. If necessary, I can get a warrant, but I'm appealing to you as someone who can stop a murderer from committing any more crimes.'

'I'll tell you.'

Lapslie was taken aback. 'What?'

'She died. Heart attack — not directly caused by the illness, but linked to it. Whatever human rights she had have been revoked now.'

He breathed out, trying to calm his racing heart. 'I'm genuinely sorry to hear that, but I'd be grateful if you can explain what was wrong with her in the first place.'

The doctor thawed slightly. 'The patient wasn't suffering from a disease caused by bacteria or viruses; she had a hereditary malfunction in the way her body actually worked. Erythropoietic protoporphyria it's called — or just porphyria.'

'What are the symptoms?'

'Take your pick. Hallucinations, depression, anxiety and paranoia. Cardiac arrhythmias and tachycardia. Severe acute and chronic pain. Constipation is frequently present.' She closed her eyes, as if recalling notes memorised some time ago. 'Excessive urination, sometimes of a dark colour due to the chemicals being excreted. Photodermatitis, blisters, necrosis of the skin and gums, itching, and swelling, and increased hair growth. Basically, anywhere that has nerves can see an effect.'

'What's the treatment?'

'Haem or haematin, taken intravenously or in tablet form, can both reduce the symptoms. If that doesn't work then direct blood transfusions can help. Painkillers, antidepressants — basically, we treat the symptoms while we replace the material that the body can't make properly.'

'And is it . . . always fatal?'

The doctor glanced down at the floor. 'Not directly,' she said, voice quieter, 'but if left untreated, it can lead to other conditions such as liver failure or hepatocellular carcinomas. But the extreme pain and the mental confusion can also lead to suicidal behaviour.' She smiled. 'I should charge a tutoring fee. Have I helped?'

Lapslie nodded. 'More than you know. What can I do to thank you?'

She glanced up into his face quizzically. 'Buy me dinner, if you can find a time when your schedule and mine coincide. I'm intrigued to know what porphyria has to do with murder, but you look like a man in a hurry.'

'Matching schedules might be easier in my case than you might expect. Thank you.' She moved away, smiling, but he reached out to hold the doctor back. 'Two more questions, if I may.'

The doctor glanced up at him. 'Be quick.'

'Could the chemicals building up in the body be released in sweat as well as urine?'

'Easily. Perspiration, like urination, is one of the mechanisms by which the body rids itself of toxins.'

'And how do I get out of this place again?'

'I can't help you there,' she said as she turned away. 'I already feel like I spend my entire life in here.'

Lapslie returned to the ground floor, thinking furiously. Porphyria. He'd heard of it before. 'The vampire disease', they called it, due to the way it sometimes coloured the eyes and the fingernails red. George III was supposed to have suffered from it. Was it possible that the murderer of Catherine Charnaud and Alec Wildish suffered from porphyria? Was *that* why Lapslie could smell them?

He drove furiously back to Sean Burrows's laboratory, on the assumption that at least some of the answers could be found there. In fact, Emma Bradbury and Jane Catherall were already waiting in Burrow's lab. Burrows himself entered just after Lapslie, holding a transparent plastic bag with what looked like Emma's handbag inside. It was dusty with fingerprint powder.

'Here,' he said, passing the bag to her. She put it beside her on a bench, grimacing. 'There's several sets of prints on it, but until we've got something to compare it to we're at a bit of a loss. Sorry.'

'Forget the bag,' Lapslie barked. 'What about that chemical toilet from the cottage?'

'That *was* a messy job,' Burrows said, 'but I've got something. I've not only managed to detect the same chemical in that toilet as at the two previous crime scenes, but I've also isolated enough of a sample so that I could determine what it was.'

'Try protoporphyrin.' Lapslie took some pleasure in the look of surprise on Burrow's face.

'Protoporphyrin . . . ' Jane murmured, looking away into the corner of the room, still perched on the lab stool like a garden gnome. Part of Lapslie's mind registered the soft cadence of her voice, while another part told him that it tasted of warm brandy. 'Precursor to haem, which is a

314

precursor to haemoglobin. You think the murderer has porphyria, then?'

'I'm almost certain of it. I found someone in hospital who suffered from the disease, and who triggered very nearly the same reaction in me.'

'You're sure they're not the killer?' Emma asked dubiously.

'She was in her seventies, and she's dead now. I'm pretty sure it's not her.'

'What's porphyria?' Emma asked. 'I've never heard of it before.'

Jane shifted on her stool. 'It's caused by a deficiency of an enzyme called ferrochelatase which leads to an accumulation of protoporphyrin in the bone marrow, red blood cells, blood plasma, skin, and liver.' Seeing Lapslie's incomprehension, she smiled. 'I spent years at medical school memorising this kind of thing. It's nice to be able to regurgitate it all again. Those chemicals are both what we call 'precursors' in the production of haem. It's a substance which is important for the production of haemoglobin in the blood — hence the name. The disorder can be inherited due to a single abnormal gene from one parent, but in these cases the normal gene from the other parent keeps the deficient enzyme at half-normal levels, which is sufficient to stop any symptoms from occurring. Very rarely, the disease is inherited from both parents, and in this case symptoms may then appear in childhood and include developmental abnormalities.'

Emma sighed. 'This is really doing my head in,' she said. 'The idea that you can actually smell somebody's illness, and the smell persists for months after they've gone. That's just . . . just so *Harry Potter*.'

'You know, I have come across several people in my career who have a distinctive odour,' Jane said. 'One of them showered night and morning, but he still smelled like a rotting fish. His body excreted a chemical called methylmercaptopurine because he was deficient in the enzymes necessary to break down certain ingredients of normal food. Without these enzymes this chemical accumulated in his body and was then excreted through the glands in his skin.'

'And it's pretty well established that diseases *can* cause changes in body odour,' Burrows added in his blackberry-wine voice. 'Hippocrates, the Greek physician who is generally regarded as the father of modern medicine, recommended sniffing patients' body odour as an effective means of identifying their ailments.'

'The average human can distinguish between thousands of different scents,' Jane continued, undeterred. 'Women generally score better than men, by the way, and the differences there can be quite remarkable. Female sensitivity to smell alters dramatically during the menstrual cycle, for instance. Tests have shown that female sensitivity to male pheromones is approximately 10,000 times stronger during ovulation than during menstruation.'

'How do you know all this stuff?' Lapslie asked, astounded.

'I read a lot,' she replied.

Lapslie shook his head. 'But we're not talking

about the general sensitivity of the human race to smells; we're talking about me being able to distinguish a scent that apparently nobody else is able to. How can that be possible?'

Sean Burrows said: 'One possibility is that your synaesthesia has somehow resulted in the part of your brain that deals with taste becoming more developed, more sensitive, and that has had a knock-on effect on your sense of smell. Taste and smell are linked quite closely in neurological terms.'

'Okay.' Lapslie closed his eyes and pinched the top of his nose, trying to think his way through this morass of scientific speculation. 'Let's accept, for the sake of argument, that I can detect certain smells that other people cannot, and that they trigger my synaesthesia in reverse, as it were. Let's also accept that the killer produces a distinctive smell in their urine, due to the fact that they are ill. How does this help us? It's going to be hard to convince Rouse to let me back onto the case, let alone convince a jury if it ever comes to trial. And while I can just about accept being able to detect the smell of the murderer in the cases of Catherine Charnaud and Alec Wildish, the old man had been dead for nearly a year. How could a smell persist for so long?'

'The only thing I can suggest,' Jane said, 'is that because the body was held at a very low temperature for all of that time, low enough to prevent any decomposition, the chemical basis of the smell was preserved on the body. Somehow — and I have trouble working out how — you are able to detect trace amounts of that smell.'

'Okay, I reiterate,' Lapslie said with more force. *'How does this help us catch the murderer?* I have no intention of sniffing every person in Essex just on the off chance.'

There was, uncharacteristically, a silence in the laboratory. Both Jane and Sean Burrows looked pensive.

'Assuming there's a treatment for porphyria,' Emma mused, 'check with pharmacists to see how many prescriptions they fill.'

'There is a treatment. Do it,' Lapslie snapped. 'Anything else?'

'The best alternative I can offer is that if you have a suspect then you can see how they smell,' Jane ventured timidly. 'It may be an unconventional investigative technique, but it may be all you have in the end.'

'Thanks,' was all that Lapslie could think of to say. 'That brings us back to the crimes themselves, and looking for connections.' He pinched the bridge of his nose again. 'The only common element in these crimes is the fact that there is no common element,' he said quietly.

'Sorry?'

'What is it that gets a murderer caught, in the end? I mean someone who kills several times. A serial killer.'

Emma mused for a moment. 'It's usually either an accident, or they set up a pattern which gets spotted. David Berkowitz, the so-called 'Son of Sam' in New York in the nineteen seventies killed his victims either just before or just after a full moon. Doctor Harold Shipman killed probably two hundred and fifty of his patients over the years, the vast majority of whom were elderly, in poor health and female. Dennis Rader, in the US, blinded, tortured and killed at least ten people, leading to him being referred to as the BTK killer before he was caught. Dennis Nilsen picked up young men for sex in bars and on streets and then either strangled or drowned them, then kept their bodies around his flat for months at a time as company before disposing of them. There's always a pattern, always something obsessive they do every time. A signature. A statement of some kind.'

'Okay,' he said. 'You're scaring me now. How come you know so much about serial killers?'

She looked away. 'I'm working on a Masters Degree in Criminology, okay? My dissertation is on psychological profiling of serial killers. It's not a crime. Well, technically it is, but you know what I mean.'

'The point is,' Lapslie said, 'that most killers are obsessive, and that means they obsessively repeat the same thing again and again. They can't help themselves. But what if we have a serial killer here whose obsession is never to repeat themselves? What if their signature is that they have no signature?'

'Boss, that's . . . ' She paused. 'It's either mad or it's genius. You're suggesting that there's a killer out there who makes a point of never doing the same thing twice. No two means of death the same. No two victims the same. No two scenes of crime the same. That's . . . ' She paused,

319

stunned. 'Almost perfect. How could we investigate that?'

'We look for the pattern outside the pattern,' Lapslie said, gazing into the depths of the whiteboard. 'Whoever the killer is, they have to choose their victims somehow. They can't just pick them at random — they have to actually go out and make sure they're not repeating themselves. That means they are actively making choices, *avoiding* things rather than choosing things, and that's what will trip them up in the end. They are running out of options.'

Emma looked dubious. 'If you're suggesting we make a list of all the places they haven't killed in yet, or all the ways they haven't killed, then we could be here for some time. Nobody's been stabbed with a swordfish yet, as far as I know.'

Lapslie laughed. 'Fair point, but let's work with what we've got.'

'There's an alternative approach,' Emma said seriously.

'What's that?'

'How does the killer come to know so much about the investigative process?'

Lapslie frowned. 'What do you mean?'

'They're deliberately avoiding the kinds of things that we would latch onto in order to catch them. Doesn't that indicate some knowledge of forensic techniques and profiling?'

'What — more than they might pick up from watching *Law and Order* or *CSI*?'

'It's just a theory,' Emma said defensively. 'If there was a series of murders in swimming pools, we'd be profiling lifeguards. If there were a series

320

of murders in army barracks we'd be profiling soldiers. We've got a series of murders that don't fit any pattern we can see. Maybe that means we ought to be looking for a profiler . . . '

Lapslie laughed, thinking she was joking, then choked back on the laughter. 'Are you seriously suggesting that *Eleanor Whittley* might be the killer?'

Emma shrugged. 'She's not come up with anything useful so far.'

'What possible motive could she have?'

'Maybe she's setting up murders so that she can be brought in as a consultant and charge us for the privilege. Greed is a powerful motive.' She shook her head. 'Sorry, this is stupid. I have no reason for thinking that Eleanor Whittley might be a killer apart from the fact that I don't like her very much, and she's taking our money without giving very much back. Forget I said anything.'

Lapslie thought for a moment. 'Let's say you might be correct,' he said. 'The first time I met her was at Catherine Charnaud's house, where I had already suffered an attack and where I heard drums again. When we left, we went to Chelmsford police station, where I suffered another attack — the worst one so far. Then we went to the house where Jeffrey Hawkins had lived, where I heard drums again, although very quietly. She was there every time.' He rubbed his chin, thinking. 'Although I would expect the attacks to be louder the closer she got, but that's not the way it worked.'

'Perhaps she's been trying to cover the smell

up with perfume, or deodorant,' Emma mused, 'and you've been registering it very dimly, in the background. Perhaps the worst attack happened when she got stressed, and the smell, whatever it is, overwhelmed whatever she was using to mask it. Not that *I* can smell anything, of course.'

They looked at each other for a long moment.

'Stupid though this is,' Lapslie continued, 'and it *is* stupid, check into her history. Find out where she lives and what she does in her spare time. Talk to people who've used her before as a consultant. Talk to her family. If she finds out, tell her we're running background checks. Standard procedure.' He shook his head. 'Jesus, we'll be investigating the chief next. Let me know if anything comes up on the prescriptions, by the way.'

'Where will you be?'

'Holding Dain Morritt's head down a toilet bowl in the gents' loos.'

'Hang on — I'll head out with you.' She retrieved her handbag from the bench, taking it out of the plastic evidence bag as she crossed back towards Lapslie. He became aware of a distant noise when the evidence seal was broken, a pulse, a drumbeat that got suddenly louder as she pulled the bag free. And this time he recognised it; the sound was, bizarrely, identical to the first few bars of a Paul Simon song he had on CD back at his cottage.

'Can you hear it?'

'What, sir?'

'The drums again. Where . . . ?' Lapslie paused, trying to work out why the drums had suddenly started. Then he looked at Emma with her handbag in one hand, the evidence bag in the other. 'Put that handbag down,' he snapped. 'Burrows — get your team up here. I want that handbag checked from top to bottom! And get those fingerprint records here now!'

Emma's face was a mask of puzzlement. 'Boss — why?'

'I think the smell is on your handbag. Which means the killer stole it; he must have been watching you.'

Understanding suddenly hit Emma and her face went pale. 'Oh, God!'

'You could be the killer's next victim!'

16

Slamming the car door behind him, Carl Whittley took a deep breath through his nose. The familiar smells of the car assailed his nostrils: the comforting undertone of leather upholstery, the slight stuffiness, the sharp trace of petrol vapour, the dampness of the Essex wetlands outside drifting in through the ventilation system. And overlaid on that was the citrus scent of lemons rising from his pores as the heat of his body evaporated the essential oils, the tarry smell of the soap with which he had scrubbed himself and the medicinal tang of the antiseptic powder. Nothing else. He sniffed again. No body odour, nothing. Jesus, he had been out in the salt marshes stalking animals, and *they* hadn't smelled him. The polecat he had blown up with the bomb hadn't taken fright and run. Neither had the fox that he had shot with the rifle. They were *animals*, for God's sake. If they couldn't detect him, how could a person?

It had to be a confidence trick of some kind. The police were trying to spook him; force him to make a mistake. Rattle his cage. It was the only answer.

His thoughts were spinning in circles. He felt a tightness across his chest. Despite the haematin tablets he was taking, which had cleared up the skin rash, he was feeling more panicky than he ever had before. Was this the porphyria making him paranoid, or was he just losing it? Going to pieces?

He started the car, and the ventilation system blew hot air into his face. He passed a hand across his forehead. What was he going to do? What *was* he going to do?

He'd have to change his diet as well. The sudden thought made him flinch, as if a bucket of water had been thrown at his chest. Perhaps something in his diet was leaking through into his perspiration, like garlic was supposed to do. He should start eating bland food, like cauliflower and rice. Nothing with any taste, just in case.

No, get a grip, he thought. It's just one man; some kind of freak. Take him out, erase him, and you'll be safe.

But killing the policeman, Lapslie, only made sense if Lapslie could somehow track Carl. If the story about the man being able to sniff him out was true then he was the weak link; the wild card that the enemy had on their side. It was a risk — by killing him unplanned, by improvising in order to get him out of the way, he would be exposing himself — but it would be worth it if he could walk away from it with the certainty that he was back in control again. That they had no handle on him any more. And surely that would bring his mother even closer to the investigation, if the man who was employing her was killed. How helpless would she feel then? How much longer would her career last if she couldn't even track down the killer of the detective who had hired her? She would have to come back to the family home, tail between her legs, beaten and humiliated.

Thoughts of his mother triggered a memory of the last time he'd seen her, in her kitchen, when she was preparing dinner for a guest. A boyfriend. A lover. Alongside the impotent rage that welled up within him was something else — a rogue memory, clamouring for his attention.

The card. The business card he'd slipped off her kitchen table and into his pocket.

He'd left it on the passenger seat of the car. He turned to look. It was still there; a little rectangle of cardboard. Picking it up, hardly breathing, he examined it. *Detective Chief Inspector Mark Lapslie* it said, followed by the words *Essex Constabulary* and a phone number and email address.

And, scrawled on the back in an untidy hand, was an address. *Thyme Cottage, Moss Lane, Saffron Walden, CB10 4ZT*, along with a mobile phone number.

Lapslie's address. Lapslie's home address.

The sun was setting outside, casting long shadows along the road. Street lights were glowing dimly. A cat curled its way around a gateway and into the driveway of Kev Dabinett, next door. Carl clenched his fist and banged it against his thigh. This was his chance. If he wanted to get the policeman out of the way quickly, he could just drive over there now, take the man by surprise and slice him up. Nothing clever, nothing sophisticated — just get in there, kill him and get out again.

Tearing his gaze away from the house, Carl drove away.

It took him nearly forty-five minutes to get there. It was dark when he arrived, and the moon was rising above the trees. Lapslie's house was actually a cottage out on the edge of Saffron Walden, away from other houses and set back from the road, behind a screen of trees. Carl parked half a mile away and then, having checked there was nobody around, sprayed himself with an odour neutraliser that he'd bought from the supermarket on the way. According to the blurb on the side of the tin it neutralised smells on bins, around toilets and in areas used by dogs and cats and other animals. Having showered until his skin was red and raw, it was the only other thing he could think of to mask his smell. And then, having done that, he walked along the edge of the road to a position where he could see the entrance to Lapslie's driveway, then cut through the trees until he could see the front door. There was no car around. Wherever Lapslie was, he wasn't at home.

Carl settled down to wait, lying in a pile of dead leaves behind a bush. He chose a position where what little wind there was blew from the cottage towards him, rather than the other way around. Even if Lapslie *could* smell him, the scent would be carried away from where Lapslie would be standing.

The rising moon cast a silvery light over the cottage and the surrounding ground.

His heart was pounding, and he was having

difficulty catching his breath, even though he was lying still. Despite the cold nip in the air there was a warm dampness across his forehead and across his shoulder blades. He could feel sweat trickle down his ribs, down his cheeks, down his spine, and the thought of the sweat made him panic again about Lapslie being able to smell him, which made him sweat even more. He imagined the smell as being like a cloud of green vapour emerging in spirals and gusts from his collar. He imagined it trailing above him like greasy smoke from a burning tyre before evaporating away into the atmosphere.

No, this was stupid. Stupid! He had to get a grip! Nobody could smell him, apart possibly from Mark Lapslie, and Lapslie wasn't here.

Events were spinning out of his control. Carl was used to having a plan, knowing what he was doing and why. Now he was trailing someone with no clear aim; just an overwhelming desire to kill him quickly.

He slipped his hand in his pocket, where he kept a knife. It was a Sheffield steel rabbiter's knife with a five-inch blade and a rosewood handle. It was the same knife he used to prepare his dioramas: cutting the wire that held the animals in their positions and slicing through their flesh where he needed to sculpt them into particular shapes to match the killings he had committed. Carl's thumb and fingers caressed its surface, imagining how easily it would slide between Mark Lapslie's ribs, cutting through the muscle and the fat, slicing through gristle, tendons and ligaments, plunging through the walls of the heart and letting his blood spill out so that it filled his abdomen, coating the other organs with its warm stickiness. It wasn't the same knife he had used to strip the flesh from Catherine Charnaud's forearm — that knife he had deliberately taken from her kitchen, knowing that his mother, if she was ever called in to help with the murder, would make a big thing of all the implements having been found in the house rather than brought with the murderer. The gleam of moonlight on the blade, however, reminded Carl of how Catherine's eyes had widened until Carl thought they might explode with the strain as Carl had cut deeply through the skin, firstly around the elbow joint, then down the arm following the line of the bone, and then around the wrist, and how the ball that Carl had shoved in the girl's mouth had bulged against her teeth as she tried to scream while Carl had taken hold of the blood-slicked flesh with his left hand and gradually prised it off, using the knife in his right hand to ease it away from her bones. Carl shivered as he recalled scraping the last remnants of flesh from Catherine's elbow joint with the flat knife blade, and using the knife point to score gristle from in between the bones of the wrist, while the girl's body writhed and spasmed on the bed. It was the murder that had taken him the longest but, like a good workman, he was proud of the final result.

Headlights spilled light across the ground as a car swept around the curve of the drive and up to the front door of the cottage. Carl watched, breathless, as the driver cut the engine, opened the door and stepped out.

It was Lapslie.

He locked the car door behind him and walked towards his front door, then turned and looked around, his gaze flashing across the bushes and trees like a searchlight. Carl was struck by the way he held himself; like a man who was bracing his body against a continuous battering. He seemed to raise his head slightly, sniffing. Carl held his breath. Had Lapslie *smelled* him, even at this range, even with the wind blowing in his direction and carrying whatever scent he had away from Lapslie? The world seemed to spin around him. It was like being trapped in an earthquake. His feet felt like they were wrapped in cloth; unable to feel the ground properly. His hands began to shake, and saliva flooded his mouth. He could feel the burning of vomit at the back of his throat, and the surge of muscles in his abdomen trying to expel the lunch he had eaten. Despair washed over him, making his muscles weak and his joints ache. How could he fight against this witchcraft?

After an eternity of waiting, Lapslie turned back to his cottage and let himself in.

Carl waited for hours, while Lapslie — occasionally visible through one or other of the windows in his cottage — made a couple of phone calls and then cooked himself some dinner and ate it, alone, in silence. He waited while Lapslie turned the lights off downstairs and while he apparently had a shower, judging by the steam that drifted out of the open bathroom window. He waited until all of the lights were turned off, and then waited while Lapslie drifted off to sleep. The moon rose higher and higher over the cottage, illuminating it with a flat light, like a stage set. Small animals scurried through the leaves and across Carl's prone body, but he didn't mind. They didn't mean him any harm.

Eventually, when he was sure that Lapslie had to be asleep, Carl unfolded himself from the pile of dead leaves and stretched to get the kinks out of his muscles.

Carefully he edged around to the back of the cottage, keeping himself in the shadows of the trees. The back garden seemed to have been laid out as a herb garden, but the sage and lavender bushes were overgrown and had gone to seed, while the chives were patchy and stunted. The cottage was obviously pretty old, and the window frames and doors were made of wood. The back door from the kitchen into the garden was locked, but Carl knew how to deal with that. He took the rabbiter's knife from his belt and slipped it between the door and the frame, just above the tongue of the lock. He threw the whole weight of his body behind the knife's handle, exerting as much pressure as he could. The frame audibly creaked as the wood bent. The tongue popped out of the lock and the door opened.

There was no cat flap in the door, and no dog came to investigate the noise. No pets to raise the alarm. Things were looking good.

He waited for ten minutes, silent and motionless, until he was sure that Lapslie hadn't heard him breaking in.

Keeping the door open, he moved cautiously into the kitchen. Moonlight poured through the window, illuminating a neatness that belied the way the garden had been left alone. Everything was washed, everything had been put away.

Carl glanced around the corners of the room. No obvious motion detectors. He kept the door open anyway, just in case he had to make a rapid escape.

He moved silently from the kitchen into the hall. The living room was off to his right; dark and still.

Carl slipped to the foot of the stairs, and listened. Nothing. He was so used to the sound of his father constantly tossing and turning, snoring and sighing, that he'd almost forgotten that some people could sleep without making a noise.

He put his weight gradually onto the first step. It didn't creak. Steadily he made his way up the stairs, always putting his weight on the sides rather than the centre to minimise the chance of any noise. He kept the knife clutched in his hand, ready for action.

He paused again on the upstairs landing, orienting himself. The bathroom was at the front of the cottage; he could feel the humidity of Lapslie's recent shower still radiating from the half-open door. There was a front room and a back room. Which one would Lapslie be sleeping in?

The door to the back bedroom had stickers on it: kids' stickers — a mixture of dinosaurs and superheroes; Batman and Superman and a couple that Carl didn't recognise. For a second he almost freaked, thinking that there were kids in the cottage, but he calmed himself down. If there were kids in the cottage then there would have been signs in the kitchen, and a lot more mess than there actually was. There had been kids, but they weren't there any more.

He moved towards the front room and edged his head around the door.

Moonlight flowed across the duvet and onto the floor, revealing a long lump on the bed where Lapslie had to be lying. His face was turned away from the door. Carl could just make out a slow susurration as Lapslie breathed.

Someone was standing over by the wardrobe. Carl spun around, knife held high and ready, but the figure didn't move. Carl took an unsteady breath. Now that he was looking directly at it, he realised the figure was just Lapslie's suit, carefully hung up in front of the wardrobe, along with a fresh shirt and tie.

He turned back to the bed. A quick slash across the throat and then a step back, watching as Lapslie woke up to find his life waterfalling out of him.

He stepped forward, knife raised.

'Drums . . . ' murmured the man in the bed, and turned over, eyes open, staring at Carl.

For a suspended moment the two men locked gazes. Carl jabbed the knife forward but Lapslie's feet crashed out under the duvet, knocking Carl backwards. The element of surprise was lost. Lapslie would fight like a cornered animal to survive, and he was bigger than Carl. Bigger and stronger.

Carl turned and ran out of the bedroom. He heard Lapslie blundering out of the duvet and across the floor behind him. Carl thundered down the stairs, two at a time, skidding on some loose carpet at the bottom and almost losing his footing but turning and heading back towards the kitchen. For a split second he had thought about heading directly for the front door and getting out that way, but the door might be locked, barred, bolted, and while he struggled with it Lapslie would be heading down the stairs towards him. Instead he pounded through the hall and out into the kitchen, heart thudding within his chest.

He raced through the kitchen and out into the cold night air, pulling the door closed behind him. He was running but he didn't know where he was running to. Panic burned corrosively through his veins. Not only did Lapslie apparently know how he smelled, now he knew what he looked like!

Time seemed to catch up with him, and he suddenly realised that it was all true. The way Lapslie had turned to see him, head tilted and a puzzled look on his face. Somehow he had known Carl was there. He had sensed his presence.

Carl didn't know what to do. For the first time in years his plans had unravelled. There was nothing ahead of him but blankness.

He bolted around the cottage to the front, past Lapslie's car.

Behind him the front door was wrenched open and Lapslie burst out, dressed only in boxer shorts. His hair and his eyes were wild, but he caught sight of Carl and let out a roar.

Carl accelerated as fast as he could down the driveway, hearing the pounding of Lapslie's footsteps behind him. He twisted, expecting a hand to come down on his shoulder any second, but bright headlights suddenly blinded him from the road as a car pulled in. He jerked to one side, heading for a gap in the trees. Risking a glance over his shoulder he saw Lapslie with a hand raised to his face, shielding his eyes from the light as the car skidded to a halt just in front of him. And then the trees were covering the scene and Carl was away, racing through the darkness, avoiding holes and fallen tree trunks more through luck than instinct but still feeling thin branches whipping across his face as he ran.

He had taken a roundabout route back to his car, checking all the time for signs that he was being followed, or that somehow Lapslie had got ahead of him and was staking the car out, but it was safe and alone when he got there. He could feel the tension draining away from his muscles, leaving them weak and trembly. He'd screwed up. He'd screwed up *really* badly. The only saving grace was that Lapslie didn't know who he was, so as long as he stayed out of the detective's way he might be safe. He didn't stop until he got back to his car. His breath was volcanic in his lungs, and he didn't seem to be able to suck in enough air. He was sure he was going to suffocate. Eventually, however, his chest stopped burning and the pounding in his neck, his temples and behind his eyes subsided.

He'd escaped.

Perhaps he should stop murdering for a while.

But things were just coming to a head with his mother. She was investigating one of his crimes, and if he was lucky she would get sucked into at least one of the others. He just needed her to admit that she was defeated, and he could stop. She just needed to come home.

Lapslie would be on the lookout for Carl now. He should go back to his original idea — killing Lapslie's sidekick, Emma Bradbury. His mother would almost certainly still get involved.

He drove home slowly, through darkened streets, calmer now than he had been. Things could still work out all right.

He parked the car outside the house, and glanced up at the bedroom where his father slept. The light was off. He'd probably put himself to bed.

Carl went inside.

The lights were on downstairs, which was strange, and Carl could feel a breeze through the house. Had he left the back door open? He paused for a second, glancing back and forth between the stairs and the doorway into the kitchen. Should he check on Dad, or shut the door? He decided to shut the door first. If his dad was in trouble, or if his colostomy bag needed changing, then Carl might be up there for some time, and a cat or a fox could get into the house.

He walked through into the kitchen and was

just about to shut the back door when he noticed a light down at the bottom of the garden.

The light in his outbuilding.

A chill flushed across his chest and back, bringing out goosepimples. He knew — *knew* — that he had turned the light off before he had left the house. He always did.

But had he locked the door?

He moved rapidly down the garden path towards the outbuilding, stepping across the green curls of the hosepipe.

The door was ajar. Softly, he pushed it open.

Nicholas Whittley was standing beside the table in the middle of the room, leaning on a cane. He turned as Carl entered the building.

'Dad?'

Nicholas turned. His face was . . . what? Thunderous, certainly, in a way that Carl hadn't seen since the accident, but also sad.

'I knew this would happen,' Nicholas sighed.

'Knew what?'

'Your mother's books. Her files. Her photographs. I told her that letting you see them was going to have an effect on you, but she wouldn't listen. She said you were stronger than that.' He shook his head. 'I should have insisted.'

'Dad, you're not making any sense. You should be in bed by now.'

'I wanted to talk to you about the girl you mentioned, about getting some time to yourself, so I came down here to see whether you were still awake. You weren't here, but the door was open, and I found . . . ' He waved the cane vaguely around at the shelves, and the dioramas of the rotting, unpreserved bodies of gulls and voles and badgers that lined them. 'This — this *sickness*. What on earth have you been up to, Carl? And then I went into the other room, and . . . ' Words suddenly failed him.

The other dioramas. The *special* ones. The ones Carl had constructed to commemorate his killings. Nicholas had found them.

'I can only think,' Nicholas choked, 'that you were reconstructing something you'd seen in your mother's work, but it's *wrong*, Carl. You have to *stop*.'

'I can't stop,' Carl found himself replying.

'What woman is going to want you if she finds out that you're obsessed with . . . with building these grotesque versions of murder scenes?'

'The only one that matters,' Carl said softly. He turned and walked out of the building.

'Carl! Come back here! I'm not finished!'

'Yes, you are,' Carl whispered, picking up the hosepipe from where it lay on the garden path and reaching out to turn the outside tap on. Water began to spill from the nozzle; hesitant at first, then gushing with more force.

His father knew. Not about the murders, but about the models of the murders, and it wouldn't be long before he worked the rest of it out. Nicholas was an intelligent man. He would work out that Carl was recreating current crimes rather than old ones, and then it was only a matter of time before it occurred to him that Carl was creating, rather than just *recreating*.

Carl had to stop him. He could still get his mother back, but his father had to go.

He walked back inside the outbuilding, still holding the hosepipe. Water began to splatter across the walls and ceiling and table, the shelves and the glass-fronted boxes.

'What on earth do you think you're doing? Carl, you need help!'

'It's okay,' Carl said, crossing the room to his father, 'I've never needed any help.'

He knocked the cane from his father's hand and pushed him backwards. Nicholas stumbled to his knees. Carl bent and tugged his father's shirt out from the waistband of his trousers, revealing the colostomy bag adhering to his father's side. With one savage movement he tore it off. His father cried out. The revealed stoma, a hole of raw pink flesh, gaped in amazement like a tiny mouth.

Carl thrust the gushing hosepipe into the wound and held it there while his father thrashed and screamed, watching as the water that backspilled out of the hole turned a muddy brown with the half-digested residue of Nicholas's last meal, and then a foamy red as something inside his father ruptured, sending his lifeblood pulsing into and out of his twisting, writhing body.

17

The sound of drumming still blanked out all other sounds, including the ragged rasp of Lapslie's own breathing. Blinded by the headlights of the car in front of him, he sat on the ground, grass cold and damp beneath his boxer shorts, waiting for the sharp pain that started just under his ribs and radiated through his entire body, and which flared up when he breathed, to subside. He was terrified that he might have to spend the rest of his life doubled over.

The murderer had been in his house. In his *bedroom!* There was no doubt in his mind. He would never be able to convince a court of law of the fact, but the drumming noise in his head had woken him up, and when he turned over there was a hooded figure with a knife standing there. If he hadn't lashed out with his feet then he would be dead. Whoever it was obviously wanted it to look like a burglary gone wrong, but it was clear to Lapslie that they wanted him out of the way. They must have been listening to the radio reports that he could smell the killer out, the one leaked by Dain Morritt, and decided to act.

The ache was receding now, more the memory of agony than the agony itself.

The slam of a car door made him look up, into the dazzling lights. Another door slammed. A bulky figure obscured the driver's side headlamp,

340

walking towards him.

'Well fuck me backwards,' a voice boomed, dripping with vinegar and mustard seeds, 'if it isn't Mark Lapslie in his underwear. Very fetching kecks you have there.'

'McGinley?' Lapslie was stunned. *'Dom* McGinley? What the *hell* are you doing here?'

'Someone told me you were dead,' the voice said. 'Or dying. Can't remember which one it was. Thought I'd come and check, for a laugh.'

A smaller figure cut into the bright splash of the passenger side headlights. 'Boss? Are you okay?' Mandarin and lemon and lime. 'Who was that running away?'

Lapslie felt as if his world had received a tremendous clout around the ear. What the hell was happening to him? Was he actually dreaming all this? 'Emma? Is that you?'

She came closer, crouching down so that her face was on a level with his. McGinley loomed above them both, hands in the pockets of his leather jacket, breath pluming in front of him like cigar smoke, haloed by the light.

'I saw a knife. Are you injured? Shall I call for an ambulance?'

'I'm okay. I think you scared him off.'

'Him?'

'I'm pretty sure it was a bloke. And young with it, judging by the way he ran off.'

'Not Eleanor Whittley, then?'

'No. And not Catherine Charnaud's boy-friend, either. Not tall enough or muscular enough. We were wrong about him, too.' He squinted into her face. 'What in the name of all that's holy are you doing in a car with Dom McGinley? The man's a certified villain.'

'And he's my boyfriend, boss.'

Lapslie's world reeled from another clout to the side of the head. 'Boyfriend? McGinley? Since when?'

'Since about two years ago,' McGinley said from above them. 'Met at a wedding, of all things. Hit it off, and moved in together a few months later.'

'Emma,' Lapslie said urgently, 'this man has more blood on his hands than a halal butcher. You're risking your career just breathing the same air as him. Ask him about Dave Finnistaire.'

'Your hands aren't exactly clean, sunshine,' McGinley countered. 'There's more than a few guys still have problems hearing or seeing because of you. And there's at least one whose missus left him because he couldn't have kids any more after you 'questioned' him in the interview room. 'Let he who is without sin cast the first stone', eh?'

Lapslie sighed. 'We'll talk about this, Emma, but not right now. What I want to do right now is have a shower and get some clothes on, and then I want you two to tell me exactly what you're doing here.'

'Boss — you can't have a shower. Evidence!'

He shook his head tiredly. 'One, I don't care. Two, I only touched him once, and the duvet was between me and him. By all means let Burrows try his DNA tricks on my duvet. There won't be much else to contaminate any samples, believe me.'

He led the way back to the cottage and, while Emma put the kettle on downstairs, he went upstairs and had a long shower, letting the hot water sluice the dirt and the sweat and the tension from his body. After he'd finished, he dressed in the clothes he'd left hanging up in his bedroom. When he came down again Emma was sitting at the breakfast bar staring into her cup of tea and McGinley was prowling round the room looking at Lapslie's photographs. His hair was greyer than Lapslie remembered, but his face still looked like a canvas bag full of rocks.

'Where's the little lady, Lapslie? She and the nippers are in all the pictures, but there's no sign of them in the house.'

Lapslie ignored him. 'Talk,' he said to Emma.

'I got worried about you,' she said, still not looking up from her cup of tea. 'Dom and I were talking, and he said that if he was the killer, and he thought that you had a way of tracking him, he'd get you out of the way.'

'Better safe than sorry, eh?' McGinley interjected. 'Doesn't matter how Dagenham it all sounds — it's worth getting you out of the way, just in case.'

'Dagenham?' Emma queried, looking up at McGinley.

'Several stops past Barking,' Lapslie explained tiredly. 'You've been discussing the case with him? Jesus, this just gets better and better. They may have to invent an entirely new set of disciplinary offences just to cover it.'

The adrenalin was only now fading out of his system, leaving behind it a sick realisation that he might have died, less than an hour ago, with only him and his killer knowing what had happened. He might have become just another of the killer's 'horizontal murders'; a stabbing in a bedroom, following on from a bombing on a station, a torture in a bedroom, a strangling in a farmhouse and God alone knew what else before. He didn't know whether he had been saved by luck or by design, but he knew for sure that he couldn't just sit there.

The taste. He kept tasting the sound of the knife as it hissed through the air in front of him. It was the coldest taste in the world.

Emma's mobile rang. While she took the call his eyes settled on the back door. The lock had been jimmied open, but it didn't look too damaged.

'Boss,' she said, closing the phone up, 'that was the local police in the Dengie Hundreds area. They were called to a disturbance a few minutes ago and found a dead body.'

'Another one,' Lapslie murmured. 'Just what we need.'

'But this one is Eleanor Whittley's husband. Someone in the incident room made the connection and notified me.'

Lapslie nodded. He felt no emotion: no shock, no surprise. Nothing could surprise him tonight. 'Here we go again. We'll go in your car. You've got the directions.' He glared at McGinley. 'And I'm sitting in the front.'

'You trust me sitting behind you?' McGinley

waggled his huge, sausage-like fingers at Lapslie. 'Remember Toby Rumford?'

They walked out towards the car, Lapslie locking the cottage behind him. 'Christ knows why I'm doing this,' he muttered. 'The back door's wide open. I'll get it fixed tomorrow, I suppose.'

'Should we tell DI Morritt about the attack on you? After all, it is his case.'

'Let's not,' Lapslie said grimly. 'After all, let's not jump to conclusions too early. Let's wait for the results of the forensic examination before we say anything.'

Emma smiled. 'I understand. After all, there *is* a process we have to go through, isn't there?'

During the drive, Lapslie found himself obsessing about Dom McGinley and Emma Bradbury, and why he hadn't seen it coming. But what the hell did Emma see in the man? He was a London villain, as old-time East End as pie, mash and parsley liquor, or jellied eels in waxed cardboard cartons. Not that the East End was like that any more, apart from the odd, self-conscious, 'Authentic Pie & Mash' shop. Dom McGinley had started off as a runner for an East End gang that mainly dealt in protection rackets amongst small shopkeepers ranging from Canning Town, Plaistow and Stratford out to Ilford, Barking and Romford, extending into prostitution and drugs as time went on. He had beaten and killed his way up through the ranks until, when Lapslie and Rouse had been at Brixton, he had been in charge of all crime from the edge of the City of London out to the Essex

345

borders. In those days the police spent more time preventing, or tidying up after, the internecine gang-warfare that erupted between the resident villains — who, incidentally, had no creed or colour bars — and the various immigrant gangs who tried to muscle in on their territories. Then it was the Yardies that were trying to wrest control away from them; somewhere in the middle it had been the Turkish and Cypriot gangs and now it was the Russian Mafia. In ten years time — who could tell?

The last time Lapslie had seen Dom McGinley had been about a year before, when McGinley had given him some information about a secretive Home Office organisation that rehomed notorious murderers whose sentences were up but who would have attracted physical attacks and arson if they had moved into an area under their own names. Since then, the two men had not been in contact. And now McGinley turned up outside Lapslie's cottage at some unearthly time in the morning, apparently shacked up with Lapslie's sergeant. What kind of world was it where things like that were allowed to happen?

They drove out of Saffron Walden and along the A roads leading towards Thorpe-le-Soken, then looped up above the seaside town and headed out through crooked roads and past small villages and fields bordered by raised banks in the direction of the ancient Essex district of the Dengie Hundreds. Sand began to appear on the edges of the roads where it had been blown in by the wind and then trapped in corners by

346

grass and mud. The sky took on a translucency that spoke of a nearby sea, just over the horizon. The roads were lined with industrial estates surrounded by high chain-link fences and they were so narrow that two cars couldn't pass each other unless one steered off the road and onto the grass verges that dropped away towards the fields and the stretches of marshy earth. Every now and then a road came to a dead end and a sign that warned of private property, and they had to backtrack to the nearest junction. Once or twice as they drove, Lapslie caught sight of a questing finger of water that had pushed inland from the North Sea, with small tarpaulined boats bobbing on the surface, tied to a block or a pole on the bank. They might have been there for years, abandoned to the elements. They missed the turn-off to Creeksea the first time they passed it, and ended up in Burnham-on-Crouch, which seemed, with its coffee shops and delicatessens, like the last outpost of civilisation before the world ended. It even had a marina of jaunty sailing boats, sails furled, masts like a forest stripped of leaves and branches, although Lapslie found himself wondering where there was to sail to. Off the edge and into the abyss, perhaps?

Backtracking, Emma stopped the car on a stretch of road that separated a rutted field from a deserted railway station and a new housing estate, all orange brick and UPVC window frames. Emma and Lapslie got out of the car. McGinley stayed where he was, probably

347

guessing that Lapslie would have told him to do that anyway.

The air had a tang of salt in it, and the crying of the seagulls was bitter, like herbs, on Lapslie's tongue. He breathed in slowly.

Several police cars and a forensics van were drawn up in front of one house in particular, their flashing blue lights illuminating the street like a cheap mobile disco. Bedroom lights were on all down the street, and Lapslie could see figures silhouetted in the windows, watching them with fervid curiosity.

Emma led him through a side gate and round the back of the house, to a wooden outbuilding in the back garden. A green hosepipe led from a tap on the wall of the house to inside the outbuilding. More police were clustered there, along with several white-suited crime scene investigators. Sean Burrows was just emerging from the outbuilding. His face was set in stone.

'Nasty,' he said, seeing Lapslie and shaking his head. 'Very nasty.'

Emma stepped to one side and allowed Lapslie to go in.

The body of an elderly man lay on the floor in a foul-smelling pool of watery blood that spread from one wall to the others. His abdomen was bloated, and his face was contorted in a rictus of agony. His clothes were in disarray, and it took Lapslie a few moments to realise that he wasn't lying *on* the hosepipe, but was somehow connected *to* it.

The sound of tribal drumming was stronger there than Lapslie had ever heard it before. It seemed to be imbued into the very walls, the air itself.

On the other side of the room, a doorway led off into darkness. The walls were lined with shelves containing what Lapslie thought at first were stuffed animals in various poses, until he realised that they weren't stuffed but were dry, desiccated corpses with dowdy feathers or dull fur.

Jane Catherall was bending over the body. She was wearing wellington boots.

'What can you tell me?' Lapslie asked.

'You are looking at Nicholas Whittley,' she said without looking up. She appeared to be examining the wound where the hosepipe had been shoved into the body. 'My initial diagnosis is massive internal trauma to multiple organs following the insertion of a high-pressure jet of water into a pre-existing colostomy stoma. At first glance the pressure of the water has burst his intestines. Suffice it to say that in all my years of pathology I have never seen anything as sick and as twisted as this. Never.'

Lapslie shook his head and glanced back at Emma. 'Has anybody notified Eleanor Whittley?'

'Uniform's over at her place now. Apparently she's in shock. She was asking after her son, Carl. He's meant to be here, but we can't locate him.'

'Young?' Lapslie asked. 'Stocky? Relatively small in stature?' His pulse started racing in time with the pounding of the drums that only he could hear. 'Check his bedroom and the medicine cabinet for any drugs that might be

349

used to treat porphyria!'

'Right, boss.' She vanished out of the doorway. 'Oh, you might want to check the back room,' she called from the darkness.

Stepping cautiously through the diluted blood covering the floor, Lapslie entered the second room. It took his eyes a few seconds to adjust to the darkness, but when they had he noticed a large central table with a computer and printer on it. Apart from that the walls, like those of the first room, were lined with shelves, and on the shelves were cases with dead birds and animals in. Lapslie was about to dismiss them from his mind as being the same as the ones in the first room, but something made him look again.

They were not the same.

These scenes were posed as if the animals were human, their limbs and heads wired into poses of horror, terror and despair. Some of them had been stabbed repeatedly; others had wire biting into their necks.

One was lying on a fake bed, with the flesh of its left arm stripped away.

Another was lying on a patch of what looked like tarmac with its head and chest burned away.

'Jesus Christ,' Lapslie whispered. 'It's a catalogue of all the crimes that the killer has committed. A museum of murders.'

Emma came rushing in, her feet splashing in the red-tinged water. She was holding a plastic evidence bag containing a plastic pill bottle. 'Haematin,' she said breathlessly. 'Treatment for porphyria. In the son's bedroom.'

'Find him,' Lapslie snapped, turning to go. 'I

want teams with dogs all around the area.'

'Car's still outside,' Emma pointed out. 'He may be on foot.'

'This estate backs onto the salt marshes,' Lapslie mused. 'If these abortions are any indication, the sick fuck has a thing about wildlife. He may have gone to ground out there.' He rubbed his forehead. 'I need to get out of here. The noise is too much.'

He and Emma walked out, past Jane Catherall and Sean Burrows, to a position outside the front door of the house. Lapslie noticed that Dom McGinley had left the car and was talking to one of the uniformed constables.

'We have to tell Rouse about this,' Lapslie said to Emma, thinking as he spoke. 'We've no choice. He'll pull me off and put Dain on, but there's no way we can keep this to ourselves while we look for the kid, Carl.'

Dom McGinley caught sight of Emma and started to make his way up the garden path towards the two of them.

'We should go and talk to Eleanor Whittley. I want to know how she can claim to be profiling the murderer when it's actually her own son. How much did she know?'

McGinley reached the door, and opened his mouth to say something.

The first shot splintered the wood of the front door, spraying Lapslie with splinters that stung like sparks against his skin. He closed his eyes involuntarily and stepped back, catching his calves against a low fence that ran along the side of the garden path. He fell backwards. The second shot hit one of the stones of the house, beside the door, and ricocheted away with a scream of mindless frustration, sending stone scabs flying in all directions. The sound of the shots caught up with their actions, and to Lapslie they were like biting into red hot chilli peppers. He rolled away across the dirt of the garden, careless of his suit.

The third shot hit Dom McGinley in the chest, lifting him off his feet and knocking him back into the door, splashing blood across the white of his shirt. Emma cried out in shock.

Lapslie climbed to his knees and scanned the area. Policemen were either standing around in confusion or diving for cover. There weren't many places where the shots could have been coming from. Narrowing the possibilities down, he concentrated on the end of the road, where the estate gave way to the Essex wetlands, the salt marshes that had been reclaimed for housing and farmland and industrial areas. He knew from the maps that part of the area out there extended into the sea, but the rest of it covered several villages and small outcrops of buildings, plus a great deal of marshy ground intersected by rivers and tributaries. It wasn't going to be easy, searching.

A flicker of motion caught his eye. A figure, darting through a hole in the fence that surrounded the estate. Heading into the wetlands.

Without thinking, Lapslie gave chase, feet pounding across the tarmac, pushing through the crumbling wood and suddenly finding himself in the open, in darkness, with all the streetlights behind him and only the moon for illumination. The back of the estate faced onto a field that stretched out towards a distant raised bank, part of the ancient defences that held the sea back from the land. The field was muddy and rutted with parallel grooves. There was no sign of Carl Whittley. Had he made it to the bank? It seemed like the only possibility.

Lapslie ran in the direction he assumed Carl must have taken. The mud stuck to his shoes, clumping onto the soles and making his feet heavy and difficult to move. He had to raise them up higher than normal to get them over the ruts, and he could feel his energy flagging as he ran. It was like some deadly form of circuit training.

He looked behind, at the estate. There was no sign of Carl Whittley. No sign of anyone.

Weeds and grasses caught at his feet as he laboriously ran. Once he miscalculated and caught the top of one of the ruts with his right foot, and went sprawling into the mud. He pushed himself back up, one hand in a pothole full of cold, brackish water, and kept going.

His breath wheezed in his chest. Black spots were swimming in front of his eyes. He glanced back over his shoulder, but his eyes were watering in the cold and he couldn't see for sure whether Carl was coming for him or he was coming for Carl.

And then there was suddenly no ground beneath his feet. He fell, landing in a stream that meandered across the field and which had been hidden from him by the roughness of the rutted surface. It was only a few feet across, and less than a foot deep, but it was cold and the salty water made his eyes sting.

Lapslie crouched there for a few moments, catching his breath. The air burned in his lungs, and he couldn't suck enough in. Desperately he glanced along the stream. On his left it was straight for a hundred yards or so, then curved towards where he imagined the sea to be. On his right it curved back towards the estate.

And that gave him an idea.

Staying crouched, he splashed his way along the stream. He had to navigate based on what he could remember of the layout of the field. As far as he could tell the stream was bringing him around to the back of the bank. If it went all the way, if there was a break, or a culvert of some kind, then he could possibly get behind Carl.

The stream suddenly hooked right along the edge of a bank. Lapslie couldn't tell whether it was the one that had been ahead of him, or another one that was edging the field. He risked raising his head up and looked around, hoping that he would be disguised against the grass and the earth of the bank. Somehow he appeared to have doubled back on himself; the estate was closer than he had thought, and he was looking sideways at a corner where the fence suddenly turned ninety degrees around someone's garden.

And there Carl was, standing in front of the fence and staring towards Lapslie, an old Lee Enfield rifle held in his hands, ready to fire. He was still dressed in the hooded top and dark trousers that he had been wearing when he had tried to stab Lapslie, but he had thrown an anorak over the top. There was no expression on his face.

He moved slowly around the corner of the fence.

Lapslie scrambled up out of the stream and ran along the side of the bank, air whistling in and out of his lungs, muscles burning with fatigue.

He reached the corner of the fence and stopped there, then eased his head around the edge.

The fields and banks fell away in the distance, to where a dilapidated warehouse sat.

There was no sign of Carl Whittley. No sign at all.

18

It was all falling apart in his hands.

Despite all the planning, and every iota of care he'd put into his preparations and execution, Carl could feel it all sliding away and out of control. All because of one moment of stupid anger.

As he moved quietly through the darkness of the salt marshes, rifle clamped in his shaking hand, making sure that he kept low so that his body was never silhouetted against the horizon and trying to ensure that whatever breeze there was blew away from him and out towards the amorphous area where the salt marsh turned to coast, he knew with bitter certainty that he would never get his family back together now. It didn't matter whether his mother was humiliated or not; Carl had just blown it all apart with one ill-advised action.

But what else could he have done? His father had discovered his lair. It was all out in the open. The very least Nicholas would have done would be to get psychiatric help for Carl, and then his mother would have got involved because Nicholas could never have managed it by himself, and then everything would have spilled out like guts from a skinned animal.

And now he didn't know what to do. He had no plan, no vision, no goal. Nothing apart from survival; the most basic drive of all.

He was scurrying along one of the streams that criss-crossed the fields, carving out their own marshy grooves in the landscape regardless of what the farmers wanted to do with them. He was keeping low, with no aim in mind other than evading capture by that policeman and trying to keep his feet to either side of the water, rather than splashing in it. Small animals scurried away from him as he moved. Something surfaced in the stream, splashed at him, then vanished again. The smell of damp vegetation and rot was even more overwhelming in the darkness than in the daylight.

What had possessed him to take a shot at the man? Panic, that's what; panic and a sense of frustration that he hadn't been able to get Lapslie earlier, in his bedroom. If he hadn't fired, he might have been able to sneak away in the darkness, but seeing the man there, standing by Carl's front door as if he owned the place, Carl hadn't been able to stop himself. He'd raised the rifle without thinking, from where he stood in the shadow of a Toyota 4×4 parked at the end of the street, and loosed three shots.

None of which had hit the man, although the other one, the one who had been at the restaurant with Emma Bradbury, had been hit in the chest when he crossed in front of Lapslie.

This was just a fucking disaster.

Carl stopped and sank down on his haunches with his head in his hands, regardless of the dampness of the ground. He could run, but where would he go? What could he do?

He risked a glance over the top of the banks

which lined the stream. He could see the streetlights of the estate glowing above the dark line of the boundary fence, and against the lights he thought he could make out the shape of Mark Lapslie, standing like a statue, looking for Carl. Or *sniffing* for him, for God's sake. He could take a shot now, blow the man's throat apart and then run, run as far and as fast as he could. He brought the rifle up, sighting through the groove at the back and along the barrel to the projecting triangle of metal at the far end, but by the time he'd lined it up the man had gone, vanished from Carl's field of view.

Damn.

With Lapslie following so closely, Carl wouldn't get far. Now that the policeman had been separated from the flock, Carl would have to switch the chase around, become the hunter rather than the hunted, and take Lapslie out of the equation. Then he could think of his next step.

Without his father. Without his mother.

It was her who had provoked all this. Leaving them. Abandoning them. And with Carl's father dead, there was no way Carl could ever get the family back together again.

A crushing wave of grief swept over him for all the things he had lost along the way; a chance at a normal life, a family, a father, and now his entire future. He wanted to open his mouth and scream at the skies, but he was too paralysed by the weight of what had happened. The only thing that snapped him out of it was the gleam of absolute truth in the slurry of horror that he swam in.

Eleanor had to die as well.

It made perfect sense. If Carl couldn't have the perfect family then he wouldn't have *any* family. He'd killed Nicholas in a fit of rage, but he could kill Eleanor calmly and simply. And then he could move on.

Maybe find another family.

Maybe *start* a family.

The North Sea was somewhere over the horizon; fresh and nostril-tingling. Clouds were massing there in the darkness, blocking out the stars. In the moonlight they looked like shallow grey mountains. Part of him wanted just to make a break for it; keep going until he hit the waves and then just keep walking out into nowhere, but he had a job to do.

He scrambled one-handed up to the top of the dip and rolled across the lip, ignoring the cloying mud. He crouched, looking around. There was no sign of Lapslie. He could see the dark bulk of the estate looming low on the horizon. If the policeman had any sense then he would head back to his friends, and if Carl moved fast enough then he could intercept him.

Keeping low, he moved across the field, keeping to the furrows where he could but crossing them diagonally when they led him away from the estate. The mud clung to his boots, slowing him down. He could hear the sucking sound as he walked, and hoped it didn't carry. He tried to keep the barrel of the rifle from touching the ground in case it scooped up mud and became blocked. Then it would be useless.

He was coming up to the corner of the estate now. He didn't dare look over his shoulder, but he had a sense that Lapslie was behind him, following him. It was like knowing that there was a bird of prey hovering above him, a hawk or a kestrel, sharp gaze fixed on the back of his neck. He slipped around the corner, letting his free hand trail against the wood of the fence. Splinters dug at the pads of his fingers.

It began to rain; fat splashes of water against his forehead and neck, trickling through his hair and tickling his scalp.

Once he was out of sight he sprinted along the fence and then slipped through a gap that he knew about — one of the ways he slipped out of the estate and into the wetlands and back again. He was in the back garden of one of his neighbours; a retired couple. He jumped the fence into the alley that ran between their house and the next and ran to the street. Glancing both ways, he couldn't see anyone. All attention was focused on events around the corner, where his house was located. He raced in the opposite direction, back to where the access road ran into the estate, and doubled back around the end of the fence. The salt marshes spread out in front of him, gilded with silver by the moon. One of the banks that divided the fields from the salt marshes ran parallel to the fence, about a hundred yards away. He quickly ran across the fields, jumping from furrow to furrow, to get to it, using the weight of the rifle for balance. His head swung from side to side looking for Lapslie or some other watcher, but there was nobody. He might have been the only person in the world.

When he got to the bank he scrambled up to the top. He kept himself hunched down, just another lump on an already lumpy bulwark of earth that extended to the horizon on either side. His gaze scanned the fields, the raised road and the various buildings on the far side of the bank heading out to the sea a few miles away, and then back towards the estate. There was no sign of Lapslie.

He waited, rifle laid out on the ground. Either the policeman had gone back to the estate or he was still out there, searching for Carl, but Carl had seen his eyes, outside Catherine Charnaud's house, and again at the press conference, and then again in his bedroom when Carl had tried to kill him. He was a hunter too. He wouldn't give up.

A gust of wind blew across the bank, bringing with it the smell of the sea and the sound of a distant horn from the Wallasea Island ferry terminal. Carrying with it, perhaps, Carl's own particular spoor, but it was too late to worry about that now. Carl waited. The lights of a car swept along the raised road, illuminating bushes in bursts of green. Something splashed into a stream, too small to be a man. Raised voices drifted across from the estate. A moth fluttered close by his head. Somewhere above his head an owl swooped over like a kite, silent wings outstretched, feathers reaching for the air.

Below him, a figure emerged from a culvert and stood up on the far side of the bank from the estate. Its trousers were stained with mud and water and its hair was dishevelled. It straightened up and gazed across the flat terrain towards the buildings that broke the horizon, hand raised to shield its eyes from the moonlight. It was Lapslie.

Carl reached down silently and picked the rifle up from the ground. He'd fired three shots already, which meant he had seven left. He raised the rifle to his shoulder and sighted along the barrel, towards Lapslie's head. Everything else faded away into darkness; his vision was just a tunnel with his eye at one end and Lapslie's face at the other. The policeman turned slowly, scanning the horizon. Carl could see him in profile now. When he pulled the trigger the bullet would speed directly towards Lapslie's right temple, transit through his right frontal lobe and sinuses and exit somewhere around his left cheek.

His right index finger curled around the trigger. Just a small amount of pressure; that's all it would take.

He tightened his grip slightly.

Lapslie vanished from his narrowed field of vision. Too late, the rifle jerked in his hand. He saw a divot of earth fly up as the bullet ploughed uselessly into the ground. Raising his head from the sights, he tried to locate the policeman. He seemed to have fallen, foot caught in a pothole. He'd been trying to lever himself up but the shot had startled him. He was rolling over the ground now towards one of the streams that meandered across the field. Before Carl could bring the rifle up again, Lapslie had rolled over the edge and into the stream.

Carl cursed. He'd missed his chance, and the policeman knew he was being tracked now. He glanced back over his shoulder, towards the estate. Was it his imagination, or had things gone quiet there, shocked by the gunfire? Desperately he tried to trace the direction of the stream across the field. It headed towards the buildings on the horizon. Lapslie would be making his way along the stream towards them, looking for shelter; the hunter become the prey.

Carl set out in pursuit.

He headed directly across the corrugated field towards the buildings, but in the darkness he kept catching his feet on the tops of the furrows and stumbling, taking his eyes off the stream so he might miss the moment when Lapslie left its safety. After a few minutes he changed tack and ran along the furrows, towards the raised road. He reached it next to an industrial estate storing what looked like piles of sleepers for railway tracks. He knew, from having lived in the area for so long, and from his long walks out in the wetlands, that the road wasn't a thoroughfare, just a hangover from the time when there had been more of a community there, a village that hadn't really died but just faded away to invisibility. He sprinted along the road to where he estimated that the stream passed under it, passing a couple of dilapidated bungalows and a small church built out of dark grey stone which squatted in a small churchyard complete with leaning headstones. It looked almost medieval. It probably was; Carl had never been inside. A sign by the wooden lychgate said that the church was only open on Tuesdays and every fourth Sunday. In this area of Essex the grace of God was in short supply.

A few yards away was a barn-like structure of corrugated sheet metal. The doors were gaping open, and there was nothing inside but scatterings of hay and some rusty farm machinery which was painted in greens and reds, like fairground equipment. Carl jumped down off the road and into the field, straddling the stream at the point where it narrowed down to enter the culvert that would take it beneath the road.

No sign of Lapslie.

Somewhere in the distance he could hear the buzzing of a helicopter. Had the police called one out to look for him? It wouldn't do them any good; he knew a thousand places to hide between there and the sea. He could outlast them, once he had got Lapslie out of the way, and then, when the hunt had died down, he could come back for his mother.

He gazed wildly around. There was nowhere else that Lapslie could have gone. Nowhere . . . except the barn. The policeman must have climbed up the side of the road while Carl's attention was distracted.

He approached the barn slowly, cautiously. The moonlight pushed a few forlorn yards inside the doors and then petered out into cobwebby darkness, broken only by myriad rays of moonlight penetrating through rust holes and cracks in the corrugated metal structure. Dust motes and small insects, gnats or mosquitoes, circled in the silvery spotlights. He could smell mould, and beneath that a faint, unpleasantly rotten trace of old diesel.

He'd intended to call out something like 'Make this easy on yourself!', or 'Come out where I can see you!' but instead he heard the words 'Is it true? Can you really smell where I've been?' coming from his lips. They hung in the air, disturbing the paths of the insects and the dust, mocking him with their banality, their stupidity.

'Yes,' a voice called back. Carl couldn't tell which direction it came from. The only thing he knew was that Lapslie was definitely inside the barn.

'But *how?*' he yelled. 'How is that possible?'

'Don't ask me,' Lapslie called back tiredly. 'I just live here.' A pause, then, 'Your dad's dead, you know?'

'I had to kill him. He'd found . . . '

'Found what? Your sick little menagerie? Your collection of trophy cases?'

'He would have told — '

'Told who?' Lapslie interrupted. 'Your mother? And what would she have done? Realised how many murders you were responsible for?'

Carl edged forward into the barn, the rifle swinging from side to side, covering all the areas where Lapslie might rush at him. 'It was all for her,' he said, hearing with contempt the pleading

365

note in his voice, as if he was standing outside himself and listening to what he was saying without being able to influence it.

'Ah, 'Mummy *made* me do it.' The next best excuse to 'I was only following orders.''

'She did! She hurt my dad, left him crippled, and then she left us so she could concentrate on her career! If I could prove to her that she couldn't manage, that she *wasn't* the best forensic psychologist around, like she thought she was, then she would have to come back to us!'

'Well that's not going to happen now, is it?' Lapslie taunted. 'Your cosy little family has been destroyed. You've killed Daddy, and Mummy's never going to speak to you ever again. Yes, you *have* destroyed her career, but it's not going to do you any good. The best thing you can hope for is that she writes a book about you. *My Son, the Psycho-Killer.*'

'I'm not mad,' Carl warned. 'I'm ill, and that makes me slightly paranoid, but I'm being treated for that.'

'Ah,' the voice came at him out of the darkness, barbed and harsh, ''I'm ill, *that*'s why I did it.' Even better than blaming Mummy.'

'It's true!' he screamed. '*I'm not mad! I just want my family back!*'

'I've seen your little models, remember? If you're not mad, then explain *them*.'

Carl shook his head violently, feeling water spraying from his hair; either sweat or rain, he couldn't tell. 'You don't know what it's like, inside my head,' he whispered. 'I saw the photos from my mum's work when I was *eight*. I can't get those pictures out of my mind. Rape, torture, sexual perversion ... I saw the insides of people's heads and the inside of their bodies, and the things they do to each other. How do I get that out of me? How do I clean my mind of what I saw?'

'You don't,' Lapslie said, and he sounded strangely sad to the part of Carl that was watching and listening from outside his own body. 'You were screwed over by your mother a long time before you started returning the favour. But that doesn't make it right. It only makes it understandable.'

'Animals don't torture each other. They just fight and eat and die. Not like people.'

Lapslie laughed. 'Ever seen a cat throw a bird up in the air and catch it in its mouth, or bat a mouse around with its claws? Don't tell me that animals are any more pure than humans. We're all in the cesspool together, son.'

Carl took another step into the barn. Neither the 'he' who was holding the gun or the 'he' who was standing back and watching the whole drama unfurl could tell yet where Lapslie was hiding.

Outside the barn, the clouds building from the east, over the North Sea, covered the moon. The thin wands of light that penetrated the holes in the corrugated metal like so many parallel flying buttresses abruptly vanished. The barn fell into darkness.

And Carl heard behind him the sound of the barn doors being pushed closed.

He whirled, firing at where he guessed Lapslie had to be, behind the door. His bullet tore a long, silver scratch in one of the painted farm implements, and then the door closed fully and the barn was completely and utterly black.

Carl whipped to one side, so that he wasn't where Lapslie remembered. He laid the rifle down, then crouched on all fours and scurried across the hay-covered barn floor, stopping just before where he thought the wall was. Slipping his hand in his pocket, he retrieved the rabbiter's knife and slipped it from its scabbard. He tried to still his breathing. Lapslie would make a move eventually. Carl could wait. He could wait for ever. He'd lain in the cold and wet for hours, just to get a glimpse of a badger and its cubs. He could do this. All he had to do was to be patient. Lapslie didn't know where he was.

An arm encircled his neck, crushing his windpipe. He tried to slash backwards with the knife, but another hand caught his wrist and twisted it savagely, forcing him to drop it.

'You forgot,' Lapslie hissed in his ear. 'I can smell where you are, even in the dark.'

19

'She still hasn't been in to see him?' Emma asked. 'I know she's as cold as a witch's tit, but that's just . . . wrong.' She moved closer to the mirrored glass between the interrogation room where Carl Whittley sat and the observation room from which she and Lapslie were watching. 'How can she treat her own son like that?'

'Eleanor?' Lapslie glanced at Carl through the window. He was alone in the room, apart from a uniformed constable who was standing by the door and avoiding eye contact. 'She hasn't even asked after him. I'm beginning to think he was right. All his problems started and finished with her.'

'And yet he's the one we have to punish.' She shivered. 'Was he right when he told you that she'd been responsible for his dad's condition?'

Lapslie shrugged. 'I asked Jane Catherall to check into it for me. This is just rumour, mind you, but the story goes that she used to act out some of her cases using her husband. He was an architect or something. If she had a situation where someone had been tied to a bed or gagged in a particular way then she used to do it to him so that she could actually see what it was like, feel what the killer felt.'

'And he went along with it?'

'Apparently. Maybe he got a kinky thrill from it. Anyway, it all went wrong on one occasion.

She was consulting on a case in Norfolk where the killer used to kidnap women, tie them up and then pour wax into their mouths, suffocating them. She had a theory that it had to do with breast feeding, and the killer being nearly stifled by his own mother when he was a baby.'

'How very Freudian,' Emma said. She glanced again at Carl, staring at his hands in the interrogation room.

Lapslie snorted. 'That's what Jane Catherall said. Apparently Eleanor was known as a bit of a drinker, and she'd been knocking back the gin and tonics. More gins than tonics, by all accounts. She'd just poured the wax into his throat, but she left it too long to untie him and help him lean forward to spit it out. He swallowed some, and choked. By the time she called an ambulance he'd suffered brain damage due to lack of oxygen, and some of the wax had solidified in his throat and stomach and intestines. Impacted bowel, they call it. They had to operate to get it out, but there was damage: perforations, and obstructions. In the end they had to perform a colostomy, and attach what was left of his bowel to a hole in his stomach. Jane's theory is that Eleanor felt so guilty, confronted every day with the evidence of what she had done, that she had to get out, leaving Carl holding the baby, caring for his crippled father.'

'And sowing the seeds for what happened later.' Emma's voice was grim.

Lapslie shook his head, remembering the despair in Carl's voice back in the barn when he had talked about seeing the things his mother was working on. 'I think the damage was done earlier than that. *I* don't particularly like seeing autopsies myself. Think what it would do to an eight-year-old, even just seeing the photographs. He was warped for life, and it was her fault. She destroyed the family; more through carelessness than deliberate action, but it's still her fault.'

'I'm having a hard enough time helping Dom change his dressings,' Emma confided. 'Blood and stuff like that just doesn't appeal to me.'

The ghost of his old life brushed across the back of Lapslie's neck, but he pushed it away. 'We still need to have that chat,' he said, 'but not now. Not here.'

'Oh,' Emma said suddenly. 'Jane Catherall called while you were taking the kid's statement.'

'If it's more evidence, she can keep it. I think we've got enough to convict him many times over. He's admitted everything.'

Emma grimaced. 'Did he mention what he did with the flesh from Catherine Charnaud's arm?'

Lapslie frowned, remembering. 'I didn't ask,' he said. 'It seemed . . . incidental . . . to the fact that he killed her. He said that he didn't *want* to torture her; it was just another tick in the box, another thing to distinguish it from his previous murders. And, I suspect, to attract his mother's attention. I presumed he'd just disposed of it somewhere.'

'In a sense,' Emma said. 'Dr Catherall found traces of food in Nicholas Whittley's stomach, and in the discarded colostomy bag. Something about it bothered her, so she ran some tests. She says it's human flesh — cooked. Carl Whittley fed Catherine Charnaud's arm to his father.'

'And presumably ate it himself,' Lapslie said. 'It's one way to dispose of the evidence, I suppose.' He felt as if the world was bearing down on his shoulders. He should feel triumphant, having solved two current cases and so many old ones, but he just felt tired and old. He wanted to go home and never come back. Somehow, spending the rest of his life in stillness and silence seemed appealing now. In that sense, perhaps Alan Rouse had won after all.

'And what about you?' Emma asked, somehow picking up on his thoughts. 'How's things with the Chief Super?'

'I don't know,' Lapslie confided. 'I keep making appointments and he keeps cancelling. I may have to pretend to be Dain Morritt to get in through the door. If I can be bothered any more.'

He glanced again at the one-way mirror that showed them what was going on in the interrogation room. Carl Whittley looked to him like an animal in a glass-fronted box; part of a tableau that would never change apart from the gradual ageing of its motionless central character. Tortured by his memories of straight horizons and blue skies which he would never, ever see again.

His voice had tasted of grass. Grass and salt water.

Without saying goodbye, Lapslie left the interrogation suite and walked out of the police station. Gulls wheeled in the air above him. He started walking, not caring where he went, and was surprised to find himself eventually outside the hospital where he had been taken after his fit, and where he had returned to try and find the old lady with porphyria.

He walked up to the reception desk. The receptionist turned a professionally blank face towards him. 'Can I help you?' she asked.

'I'm trying to find one of your doctors,' he said, the words surprising him as he said them, 'but I don't actually know her name.'

'Can I ask what this is concerning?'

He smiled, for what felt like the first time in a long while. 'I was hoping to ask her out to dinner,' he said.

Acknowledgements

With grateful thanks to: Steve Gallagher, David Morrell, Jack Curtis and the late Kenneth Royce and Geoffrey Household, excellent thriller writers all, and the ones who I keep going back to, time and time again. Thanks also to: Andrew Lane, for editorial assistance; Nic Cheetham and Gillian Holmes for detailed comments and lots of patience; John Catherall, for allowing me again to use him as a template; and Dain Morritt, Katherine Charnaud, Alex Wildish, Sancha Starkey, Toby Rumford and Seiju Desai for use of their wonderful names (but not, of course, their wonderful characters . . .)

Acknowledgements also to the Social Issues Research Centre for their fascinating smell report (http://www.sirc.org/publik/smell–human.html) and to Ronald Blackburn for his instructive *The Psychology of Criminal Conduct* (Wiley, 1993)

We do hope that you have enjoyed reading this large print book.

Did you know that all of our titles are available for purchase?

We publish a wide range of high quality large print books including:
Romances, Mysteries, Classics
General Fiction
Non Fiction and Westerns

Special interest titles available in large print are:
The Little Oxford Dictionary
Music Book
Song Book
Hymn Book
Service Book

Also available from us courtesy of Oxford University Press:
Young Readers' Dictionary
(large print edition)
Young Readers' Thesaurus
(large print edition)

For further information or a free brochure, please contact us at:
Ulverscroft Large Print Books Ltd.,
The Green, Bradgate Road, Anstey,
Leicester, LE7 7FU, England.
Tel: (00 44) 0116 236 4325
Fax: (00 44) 0116 234 0205

DCI Mark Lapslie suffers from synaesthesia — a rare neurological condition that has cross-wired his senses. The sickening clamour of sounds he can taste has smothered his marriage and stifled his career. At the scene of a fatal traffic accident, Lapslie's interest is in the desiccated corpse found lying next to the recently deceased driver. He has a fleeting recollection, only for him, it's something he can almost taste . . . Memories haunt Violet Chambers too. She does what she can to stay ahead of them. Taking tea with her elderly friend Daisy, she knows it's time to move on again. As Daisy falls to the floor, skin burning, eyes streaming, Violet calmly waits. Black hellebore is remarkably potent poison. It won't be long now . . .